Overh… man … The … Tanaka slid back inside, sealing the hatch with a …

"Too many up there, man," Tanaka said, his voice shaking.

"Then let's take some down!" Fitz shouted.

"What if this is the start of a bigger attack?" Rico said. "What if there are more on the way?"

Fitz knew the answer, but he kept his mouth shut. If the Reavers were just the advance party, then the Twenty-Fourth MEU was screwed.

"Suck it up, Team Ghost!" Fitz pulled up the joker bandanna around his mouth, rolled down his window, and jammed his rifle between the metal bars while Dohi pulled back onto the road.

A squeeze of the trigger sent a round into the spine of a Reaver making a run for the southern side of the camp. It shrieked in pain, reaching back with a winged arm before flopping to the ground.

One down. A hundred to go.

Apollo jumped into the front seat with Fitz, snarling. A wave of fur trembled across his body, not from fear but from anger. The dog wanted back into the action.

Me too, boy.

By Nicholas Sansbury Smith

THE EXTINCTION CYCLE SERIES

Extinction Horizon
Extinction Edge
Extinction Age
Extinction Evolution
Extinction End
Extinction Aftermath
"Extinction Lost" (A Team Ghost short story)
Extinction War

TRACKERS: A POST-APOCALYPTIC EMP SERIES

Trackers 1
Trackers 2: The Hunted
Trackers 3: The Storm
Trackers 4: The Damned (Coming 2018)

THE HELL DIVERS TRILOGY

Hell Divers 1
Hell Divers 2: Ghosts
Hell Divers 3: Deliverance (Summer 2018)

THE ORBS SERIES

"Solar Storms" (An Orbs Prequel)
"White Sands" (An Orbs Prequel)
"Red Sands" (An Orbs Prequel)
Orbs
Orbs II: Stranded
Orbs III: Redemption
Orbs IV: Exodus (Coming 2018)

EXTINCTION

WAR

The Extinction Cycle
Book Seven

NICHOLAS SANSBURY SMITH

orbit

www.orbitbooks.net

Orbit
Hachette Book Group
1290 Avenue of the Americas
New York, NY 10104
orbitbooks.net

First Edition: November 2017

Orbit is an imprint of Hachette Book Group.
The Orbit name and logo are trademarks of Little, Brown Book Group Limited.

The publisher is not responsible for websites (or their content) that are not owned by the publisher.

The Hachette Speakers Bureau provides a wide range of authors for speaking events. To find out more, go to www.hachettespeakersbureau.com or call (866) 376-6591.

ISBNs: 978-0-316-55821-1 (mass market), 978-0-316-55823-5 (ebook)

Printed in the United States of America

OPM

10 9 8 7 6 5 4 3 2 1

This book is dedicated to all of the Extinction Cycle readers. Thank you for your support over the years and for coming along on the journey with me and Team Ghost. I hope you enjoy Extinction War!

The soldier above all others prays for peace, for it is the soldier who must suffer and bear the deepest wounds and scars of war.

—*Douglas MacArthur*

Prologue

They were fucked.

It wasn't a question of whether the monsters would find Captain Reed Beckham and Lieutenant Jim "Ten Lives" Flathman but a matter of how long. After being tossed out of a Black Hawk into a city overrun with monsters, Beckham was back in action and on a path straight through hell.

He squirmed across the rooftop toward Flathman. The glow of the half-moon illuminated Beckham's ruined body and the twisted metal of his prosthetic leg. He'd lost his prosthetic hand, leaving only the stump where Big Horn had hacked it off with Meg's hatchet to save his life. Dozens of cuts and scars adorned his exposed flesh like tattoos.

At the edge of the rooftop, Beckham pushed himself up to sneak a glimpse over the side. His eyes were swollen and bruised, but he could still see the destroyed metropolis in the moonlight.

Empty skyscrapers, blown to pieces during Operation Liberty, staggered across the skyline. As a result of the firebombing, raging fires had consumed entire city blocks, leaving a darkened landscape behind. Skirts of debris dressed the shops and businesses like scree around the base of a mountain.

Every road out of the destruction led through Variant territory. Despite multiple efforts to take it back, the monsters still owned Chicago. A small number of Alphas and Variants had gone underground during the deployment of VX9H9. Beckham hadn't seen many of them, and he wasn't sure how many were out there, but Flathman had warned him the beasts were lurking in the shadows much like the two men. There was also a small percentage of the powerful Variant juveniles that had survived Kryptonite.

But the old monsters weren't the only threat. The streets below were filled with the newly infected people from safe-zone territory 15—people like President Jan Ringgold's cousin, Emilia.

Beckham could see their pallid flesh as they prowled for prey, their infected yellow eyes flitting, blood dripping from multiple orifices. It was like the first days of the outbreak all over again.

Lieutenant Andrew Wood and his army, the Resistance of Tyranny soldiers, had restarted the epidemic by infecting several of the SZTs, including this one. The ROT army, whose goal was to consolidate power under its own flag, used terror as its main weapon and the hemorrhage virus as the vehicle to deliver that weapon. Wood threatened to ruin everything Beckham and the military had fought for since the raid on Building 8 on San Nicolas Island seven months ago.

The newly infected were closing in—and so were the ghosts of the men and women who had died to stop the end of the world. Beckham could visualize several of his friends standing on the rooftop. Meg Pratt, Sheila Horn, Staff Sergeant Alex "The Kid" Riley, Lieutenant Colonel Ray Jensen, and a handful of others stood there glaring down at him as he hid from the beasts.

Under the cover of darkness, he brought the advanced combat optical gunsight of his M4 to his swollen eye and zoomed in, searching for a vehicle that would help them escape. Motion flickered in the limbs of an ancient oak tree next to the building. Hundreds of black birds nested on the spiny branches, their weight causing the tree limbs to creak, a sound that reminded him of the cracking of Variant joints.

They had selected the rooftop for that reason: If an infected got too close, the birds would take to the skies. Most of the time the Variants stuck to bigger prey, which explained the lack of animals and humans in Chicago, but the mindless beasts would likely be forced to turn to birds, rats, and perhaps even insects if they got hungry enough.

Beckham moved the ACOG's sights to the street, where the infected beasts were hunting. One of the creatures, a sinewy female still dressed in blue jeans and a shredded Chicago Bears sweatshirt, scrambled over to the trunk of the tree. Beckham backed away from the ledge, keeping to the shadows, out of view.

The monster glanced up at the birds with yellow eyes, blood dripping from a sharp nose as it sniffed the chilly air. Beckham's muscles froze. He didn't dare move an inch. The beast couldn't see him, but that didn't mean it couldn't smell his body odor or the pus oozing from his wounds.

The sound of joints popping echoed through the city as the abomination bolted back into the road on all fours, uninterested in the birds and oblivious to Beckham.

Beckham slowly moved so he could see the buildings down the block. An armored bank truck sat on the curb at an intersection. He used the ACOG to zoom in on the vehicle but then pulled the scope away when he saw a pack of infected clambering over the exterior of the old warehouse behind the truck. From the height of the roof they looked like an army of albino ants.

There was no telling how many monsters were out tonight.

Beckham flashed a hand signal to Flathman, who looked over the ledge and followed Beckham's finger toward the armored truck. He nodded and then flashed his own signal.

They retreated from the stone roof ledge and sought refuge in the shadow of the wall. Keeping low to the ground, Beckham followed the lieutenant to a cluster of air-conditioning units.

Beckham crawled across the roof, trying to minimize the noise his prosthetic blade made. When he got to the units, he rested his aching back against one of them and kept his gaze on the south and west sides of the roof while Flathman watched the north and east.

After a few moments of silence, Flathman pulled out a flask of whiskey and took a slug, then offered it to Beckham. It was the tenth time Flathman had reached for his flask that evening, and Beckham finally decided to take the edge off with a drink. The smooth liquor slid down his throat and burned his empty gut. He welcomed that burn, savoring it with closed eyes for a fleeting moment. The burn passed, and Beckham wiped his mouth with the tattered sleeve covering his stump. He reached into his vest pocket, where he used to keep a picture of his mother.

That picture hadn't survived, but it was carved in his memory like the scars on his body. Instead, he pulled out a handkerchief that he had soaked with antibiotics and then dabbed the cloth against his forehead. The fluid stung the patchwork of cuts and bruises.

Pain raced down what was left of his right arm and prickled where his hand should have been. He gritted his teeth but made himself stop when he heard their grinding. If he could hear the sound, so could the monsters.

The ache in his missing arm was getting worse, something Master Sergeant Joe Fitzpatrick had warned him about. Phantom limb syndrome: It was a condition many soldiers dealt with after losing an arm or a leg.

Beckham gestured for the flask again.

"Easy there, Captain," Flathman whispered with a smug grin. He handed it over, and Beckham took another gulp, hoping for some relief—not just from the physical pain but also from the mental anguish.

He'd watched helplessly as Doctor Pat Ellis had been executed on Plum Island. The memory flashed across his mind, his fatigued muscles tensing at the remembered crack of the gunshot.

Beckham still didn't know the fate of the rest of Plum Island's inhabitants and wouldn't have been able to help them even if he did. For all he knew, Kate was already dead and he'd never get the chance to meet their son. Images of his best friend, Big Horn, torn to pieces and of President Ringgold, lying dead in a pool of her own blood, swarmed his mind. He couldn't bear to think of Kate that way...

The grief and uncertainty were tearing him apart inside. He was trapped here in the wildlife preserve that was Chicago, surrounded by infected monsters. Now he could see why Flathman had turned to drinking.

The world was a dark, horrifying place.

He shifted for a better view of the rooftop to the south. The skeletal branches of the trees below scraped the exterior of the building, creaking and groaning in the wind. A crow cawed, the sound reverberating through the night.

The wave of alcohol-induced calm had just begun to settle over Beckham when the sound of clicking joints set his heart slamming against his ribs.

Flathman pushed up the bill of his Chicago Cubs hat for a better view of the roof. He rose to a crouch and directed his gun's muzzle to the north, using his other hand to signal.

One finger.

Two fingers.

Three fingers, indicating the number of Variants clambering across the gray brick surface of the building adjacent to their location. Beckham couldn't see the beasts from his vantage, but he trusted Flathman's report. Even tipsy, the man was sharp.

Beckham slowly raised his M4, a round already chambered. He flicked the selector to the happy switch, a three-round burst, wincing at the click. The faint rustling in the oak tree had stopped.

If the monsters found him and Flathman up here, they would call in reinforcements and overwhelm them. They had come here to seek refuge, but inadvertently they might have also sealed their fate. This time there would be no Black Hawk descending like an armored angel to evacuate Team Ghost off the roof.

There wasn't even a Team Ghost to speak of in the United States—just Beckham and the alcoholic lieutenant who had survived by running his ass off and fighting like a madman.

I'm not dying on some shitty rooftop. I will get back to my family.

Beckham repeated the words in his mind until it was a mantra. He pointed his stump at the steel door leading back into the building. Flathman shook his head and brought a finger to his lips. It wasn't the first time they had butted heads on strategy over the past few hours. It had been Flathman's idea to come up here in the first place. He had survived on his own for a long time, but that didn't mean he was always right.

Beckham got to his feet and crouch-walked around the air-conditioning units. They had to move, and they had to move now.

Flathman remained on one knee. He shook his head in defiance. *No*, he mouthed, and then pointed firmly at the ground.

Beckham jerked his chin toward the door.

An eerie silence fell. Even the wind had stopped. Beckham held his position, frozen like a statue and feeling naked in the rays of moonlight.

The fluttering of wings snapped him alert. He slowly twisted to survey the south side of the rooftop. The noise started off as a faint whipping of the air, and then there was the creak of a limb as a single black bird tore off into the night sky. Then, all at once, a flickering wall of birds erupted. Hundreds of the creatures took to the sky in a dense column formation and blocked out the stars like a strip of painter's tape.

Beckham pushed his stump under the barrel of his suppressed M4 and steadied the carbine while moving his finger toward the trigger. Sweat trickled down his face, salt stinging his cuts. He closed his swollen left eyelid and looked through the scope with his right.

A naked, meaty figure leaped over the side of the building and landed on the roof. The infected beast held a crushed bird and was using its hands to rip the bird in half. It stuffed the head and wings into its maw, crunching loudly.

Beckham had been wrong before; the monsters did eat birds.

He gave it something else to chew on with a round through its wormy sucker lips. Two more of the monsters skittered over the stone ledge as the first beast slumped to the ground.

Two suppressed shots whistled from Flathman's rifle,

punching through muscle, gristle, and organs. One of the infected creatures thudded to the ground quickly, but the second beast stumbled backward, bony arms windmilling. It hit the edge of the building but didn't fall—yet.

Beckham held his breath and his fire, afraid another shot would send the beast tumbling to the ground. The crack of bones on pavement was far louder than the suppressed crack of his gun and would alert more creatures to their presence.

Apparently Flathman hadn't thought that far ahead. Another bullet from his M4 slammed into the center of the monster's forehead, crunching loudly on impact. The force flung the creature's skull backward, and its entire body flipped over the roof's edge.

Beckham shot Flathman an angry glare and then hurried over with his gun at the ready. The shattering of bones boomed like a shotgun blast before he got to the ledge. Flathman joined Beckham and watched in shock as every blood-soaked face in the street flicked in their direction.

What the hell did you think would happen? Beckham thought, cutting a second vicious look at the lieutenant.

As the birds fled into the darkness, Beckham and Flathman hustled across the rooftop toward the door Beckham had pointed at earlier. They had no choice. Without a helicopter to evacuate them, they would have to fight through a building full of horrors if Beckham was to have any hope of escaping this new nightmare.

Captain Rachel Davis could still picture the attack as though it was happening in real time. Lance Corporal Nick Black had steered the Zodiac up to the USS *George*

Washington. Everything had been ready to go. Sergeant Sanders, Private First Class Robbie, Lance Corporal Katherine Diaz, and Davis had remained calm during the ride across the choppy waves.

Dressed in ROT uniforms, and with Diaz and Davis sporting freshly cut hair as part of their disguises, she and her team had thought all seemed to be going to plan. They would sneak on board, rescue any surviving members of her crew, and then blow the ship and every ROT soldier on board to kingdom come.

They had been close—just three hundred feet from the aircraft carrier's first ladder—when gunshots lanced in their direction. Davis still didn't know if some fault in their disguises had tipped off the soldiers on the deck or if they'd missed some important signal or sign.

It didn't matter.

Sanders and Robbie had been killed instantly, but Davis and Diaz were able to lay down return fire. The first of the shots killed two of the men on the deck and sent the other man lunging for cover.

When Davis had looked over at Black, he was clasping his stomach, blood pouring out under his hand. Another gush of blood trickled from a hole in his chest.

"Jump ship," he had muttered. "I got this."

Everything that happened after that was mostly a blur in Davis's memory. Davis and Diaz had narrowly escaped a blast that blew a hole in the side of her ship.

She wasn't even sure how long they had been hiding in the forest, waiting for the ROT patrols that still hadn't come. The eerie quiet sent a chill through Davis. For hours, she had been anticipating the barks of search dogs or the beams of spotlights hunting them. Instead, there was only the whispering of the wind through the palm trees, the hissing of bugs and croaking of frogs.

Davis decided to move again, waving Diaz under a

ridgeline along the beach. She stopped a few minutes later at the sight of bodies crucified to the wooden poles beyond the surf.

Marine Sergeant Corey Marks's scarred face was still slumped against his chest, his flayed body hanging like a scarecrow on the pole the ROT soldiers had constructed on the beach after catching him and two other marines days earlier.

Now she knew where the scent of rot was coming from.

Diaz covered her nose with a sleeve, but Davis pushed on, breathing in the stench of death as a reminder she was still alive, against all odds. There was no time to bury the marines as they deserved, there was only the mission.

She had to get back to the ship and finish the job that so many men and women had already given their lives for. In her mind's eye she remembered Black gunning the engine of the Zodiac after Davis and Diaz bailed. The ROT soldiers on the deck had riddled Black's body with bullets, but he'd still managed to slam the Zodiac into the side of the ship and detonate the C4 on board.

Davis shook the memory away, determined to get back to the ship. She continued leading Diaz through the maze of palm trees.

Quick and steady, Rachel. Quick and steady.

The mantra helped her focus. She scanned the area with her rifle's sight, keeping an eye out for any sign of spotlights and her ears perked for barking dogs.

They stopped a few minutes later at the lip of a ravine to scout the low-lying area beyond. The minutes ticked by as slowly as the bug crawling across Davis's arm. She didn't bother brushing it off. Her flesh was already covered in mud, bug bites, and scrapes. At least the creature was a distraction from the pain of her injuries and the queasiness of her stomach.

She lost the battle with her sour stomach and leaned over to dry-heave in the bushes. Diaz looked up, shaking from the cold, her freckle-dusted features ghostly in the night. She hadn't said more than a few words since they had emerged from the water, and her eyes searched Davis's for some sort of reassurance.

But Davis had nothing to offer the lance corporal.

They were in bad shape. On top of losing their comrades, along with most of their weapons and ammunition, Davis had lost the radio and satellite phone. There was no way to contact Command unless they got back to the ship.

Diaz broke the silence. "I can't believe Black..." Her lips quivered and her brown eyes widened. "I...I can't believe he sacrificed himself like that."

"He did his duty," Davis said quietly. "At the very least, I think the blast disabled their launching systems and their ability to move out of the harbor. It's only a matter of time before Central Command moves in to finish them off, assuming they're still watching out there."

"So Wood can't hit any more SZTs with the hemorrhage virus?"

"Not with the *GW*. If Wood could fire the missiles, wouldn't he have already fired them?"

Diaz shrugged helplessly.

"He doesn't strike me as the type of guy to bluff," Davis continued. "Black started the job, but we still have to finish his work."

"What do we—"

Davis grabbed Diaz and pulled her down at the distant *whoosh* of helicopter blades.

"Quiet," Davis whispered. She brought up the SCAR-L assault rifle she'd grabbed on the beach and pointed it at the canopy of palm trees. The shifting fronds provided momentary glimpses of the sky. Her first thought was to take off running for cover, but she knew they were better off staying put.

Diaz raised her Beretta M9.

The thump of rotors rose until it sounded as if the bird was right on top of them. Davis leaned from left to right for a better view, finally catching a glimpse of a Black Hawk shooting over the swaying canopy.

But the bird wasn't out here hunting for them. It was heading for the *GW*.

Davis flashed a hand signal, motioning Diaz back toward Fort Pickens and the harbor. They advanced through the trip-me vegetation, weaving between palm trees at a quick but cautious pace. There were plenty of hazards out here, including snakes. One of them squirmed across the dirt path. Davis maneuvered around a boulder and focused on the Black Hawk racing across the night sky. There was no doubt about its trajectory— the bird was heading for the *GW*. She leaped over fallen limbs and powered through a cluster of vines.

"Wait up," Diaz said.

Davis slowed her pace and caught her breath, muscles burning and injuries flaring. The salty scent of an ocean breeze filled her nostrils. Diaz caught up a moment later, and they crouched behind a tree, both of them panting.

"Slow down," Diaz said. "What if there's a patrol searching for us?"

"I know. I'm sorry." Davis looked back through the fence of palm trees. They were almost back to the place where they had ambushed the ROT soldiers.

"Okay, I'm ready to move out," Diaz said.

Davis could see the fight returning in the lance corporal's eyes. Diaz was ready to avenge Black and the crew of the *GW*.

"Come on," Davis whispered.

They slipped back through the woods, guided by the glow of the moon. Davis did her best to watch every step. Despite her efforts, she tripped and fell several times, scoring more cuts for her collection.

The clearing that overlooked the weathered walls of Fort Pickens was just ahead, and Davis balled her hand to halt their approach. She took a knee next to a stump and scoped the fence of palm trees at the border of the fort. There was no sign of movement in the green space beyond, nor on the stone walls—no sentries, no snipers, nothing.

"All clear," she whispered. The words sounded strange, and her gut told her something was off. Where the hell were the patrols? Maybe the ROT soldiers thought Davis and Diaz had died in the blast, but she didn't want to bet their lives on it.

A wall of smoke drifted away from the *GW* on the other side of the fort. Davis pushed herself to her feet and raised her SCAR. She would use the opportunity to sneak over to the fort, where she could have a better look at the aircraft carrier and the Black Hawk that had landed there.

"Cover me," Davis said. She went first, running in a hunch, keeping as low as possible. She hadn't seen a sniper, but that didn't mean there wasn't one lurking in the shadows.

Halfway across the field, she stopped at a stone pillar that had been sheared off at the top. The broken piece lay in the dirt to the right. Diaz showed up a moment later and pushed her back against the partition while Davis got down and used the cover of the rubble to scope the rest of the fort.

She played the barrel of the SCAR over the walls and walkways overlooking the ocean. Where there had been ROT soldiers before, she saw only abandoned ledges.

Where the hell are they?

A flicker of white darted across the top of one of the lookouts and vanished into the fort. Davis froze and waited for the contact to reemerge in the moonlight.

"Did you see that?" she whispered.

Diaz shook her head.

Pushing her scope back up, Davis zoomed in on the wall. Seeing nothing, she searched for their next position. She pointed at the wall about a hundred yards away.

"Watch my back," Davis said.

Diaz looked over, eyebrows arching over her wide eyes at the sound of a distant scream. It rose into a screech of agony and then faded away.

This wasn't the sound of a monster—it was the scream of a man.

Davis took point and flashed an advance signal.

Quick and steady, Rachel. Quick and steady.

She led Diaz toward a staircase and up the stairs with their rifles angled up. At the top, Davis hunched down and cleared the overlook. She crab-walked to the wall and waited for the screams to come again.

A seagull called out in the distance, and the lap of waves sounded on the beach, but she heard nothing else.

Davis worked her way up to the ledge and peeked over to look at the harbor. The *pop* of gunfire pushed her back down. Diaz crouched next to her. They exchanged a glance.

Several shouts followed the gunfire, and then came the unmistakable shriek of a Variant. The thump of rotors and a frantic shout joined the din.

"Get us back in the air!"

Davis lifted her rifle over the ledge and centered the barrel on the *GW*, ignoring the black hole in the metal siding that provided a glimpse into the guts of the carrier.

On board the ship, ROT soldiers ran toward the

aircraft housed on the deck, some of them firing over their shoulders at figures bolting out of the open hatches. At first Davis thought that maybe these were members of her crew who had seized the opportunity to take back the ship, but then the figures chasing the ROT soldiers dropped to all fours and skittered after the retreating men.

Not sailors—monsters.

Davis focused her gun on the Black Hawk that had passed overhead for a better look. Its wheels were already lifting off the deck. A crew chief grabbed the chopper's M240 and directed the barrel at the beasts. That was when Davis saw the missiles containing the hemorrhage virus scattered across the deck.

The blast from the C4 hadn't just disabled the MGM-140 Army Tactical Missile System delivery vehicles—it had blown several of the missiles to pieces, releasing the virus and infecting the soldiers and sailors on the deck. Now Davis knew why they hadn't been pursued by the patrols. The ROT soldiers were no longer human.

For the first time in six months, Davis was happy to see the creatures. The former soldiers tore into the men who had landed in the Black Hawk. Two of the men made it to the chopper. A third soldier leaped into the air and grabbed the side of the troop hold as it lifted into the sky.

Dozens of the galloping beasts fanned out across the deck. A pack skittered over the ship's F-18 Super Hornets, and another dashed between the Ospreys. Davis felt her heart catch when she realized that some of the infected were former members of her crew.

"No," she whispered. Tears blurred her vision. This was so much worse than if they'd been executed by the ROT soldiers.

The 7.62-millimeter rounds from the M240 tore

through her old friends as the Black Hawk pulled sky-ward. She locked her jaw and raised her SCAR at the bird. The soldier hanging from the side swayed back and forth with a beast attached to his ankle. Another soldier in the troop hold stomped the man's fingers until he fell back to the deck with the monster. The callousness of the action took her back as four more creatures pounced on the fallen man. They tore him to pieces in seconds, tossing entrails out like spaghetti to the others.

A guttural howl rose over the thump of the rotors.

It took every bit of restraint for Davis to hold her fire. She wanted to empty her magazine into the chopper, but she couldn't compromise her position. Their primary mission was complete: The missiles were disabled. Her crew had given their lives, but in the end, countless more lives had been saved.

Now Davis had a new mission: to fight her way back onto the *GW* and find a way to contact Central Command and the president of the United States of America.

1

Three days later . . .

Hatteras Island didn't have any of the comforts of the White House, but the view of the ocean under the stars was breathtaking—and, even better, it was quiet here.

President Jan Ringgold sat on the fallen trunk of a palm tree with her bare feet dug into the sand, listening to the waves lap the shoreline. This was the second time in her brief tenure as president that her White House had been relocated. The most recent command center, at the Greenbrier in West Virginia, was gone now, the grounds poisoned and her staff likely infected with the hemorrhage virus. She still didn't know the fate of Vice President George Johnson or anyone else who had been in the Presidential Emergency Operations Center, but each passing hour of radio silence told her with more certainty they were dead or infected. Her entourage, or what remained of it, was in the stealth Black Hawk behind her, combing the radio frequencies for information.

I told you there's always hope. Together, we will persevere. The war will be over soon, Ringgold had said to Doctor Kate Lovato not long ago.

The doctor stood ankle deep in the surf, hand on her swollen stomach, staring up at the stars. Ringgold wasn't the type of person to regret her words, but the line seemed hopelessly naive now.

How could she have known then that a madman like Lieutenant Andrew Wood was waiting in the shadows for a chance to strike? How could she have predicted that he would deploy the very virus that they had worked so hard to eradicate?

Ringgold shook her head and stood. The only remaining Secret Service officer in her detail, Tom King, followed her down the beach, keeping his distance.

She checked the silhouetted figures of her team above the beach. Most of them were clustered under the canopy of trees set on a grassy bluff overlooking the ocean. The Black Hawk was positioned to the right, a camouflage tarp thrown over everything but the troop hold. They had taken refuge at the southern tip of Cape Point, away from the roads and the Woods Coastal Reserve.

Ringgold joined Kate at the water's edge. She remained silent, not wanting to disturb the doctor but still trying to show she was here if Kate needed support. It had been three days since Dr. Ellis was killed and Kate's partner, Captain Reed Beckham, kidnapped.

Three days of hiding and listening to the communications channels as the country slowly collapsed into civil war. Three days of waiting helplessly as SZTs joined forces with ROT, and three days of hearing about the losses of American and European Unified Forces in Europe.

The human race wasn't just back on course for extinction—it was barreling right toward the black hole that would end them forever.

"He's out there," Kate said, turning away from the ocean to look at Ringgold. "Reed is out there looking up at this same sky. I know it."

Ringgold had figured that was what Kate was thinking about, and as much as she wanted to believe Kate was right, Ringgold was losing faith. There was chaos in every direction. She had thought they'd seen the worst possible threat in the Variants, but Wood was more evil than the monsters. At least the beasts didn't have access to weapons of mass destruction.

"I better get back to Tasha and Jenny," Kate said. She walked past Ringgold, feet slurping in the wet sand, but Ringgold reached out to stop her. "Madam President?" Kate asked.

Ringgold struggled to find the right words. After a moment, she let her hand drop. "It's nothing. Come on, let's go."

Side by side, they walked up the beach toward the Black Hawk.

Master Sergeant Parker Horn greeted them at the edge of the forest, his machine gun cradled across his broad chest, his strawberry-blond hair rustled by the wind.

"All clear up here," he said, voice gruff. He offered a brief nod, then strode out into the grass and took a knee to scan for hostiles.

Ringgold was used to having a dozen men protecting her, but now they were down to just Secret Service agent Tom King, Horn, former NYPD officer Jake Temper, and the two Black Hawk pilots, Captain Ivan Larson and Captain Frank Spade. Both of the pilots were holding security just to the north, watching for any possible juvenile Variants that might have fled Kryptonite by jumping into the ocean.

National Security Advisor Ben Nelson and Chief of Staff James Soprano were both armed, but she didn't trust them to do much in a fight. They were ideas men— men of strategy, not violence. Both sat on stumps listening to the radio.

Ringgold found her shoes and shoved her feet inside. A crunching sounded, and she looked over as Jake tried to fasten the tarp over the troop hold of the Black Hawk. She could see several sleeping figures inside. Jenny and Tasha were nestled up next to Bo and his mother, Donna. Timothy, Jake's son, was sitting up, wide awake. He waved at Ringgold, and she waved back.

She finished securing her shoes and checked the cluster of backpacks neatly arranged at the foot of the trees. Even in the moonlight she could see their contents had dwindled. They would have to find water and food soon.

"Have you heard anything from the PEOC?" Ringgold asked, joining Kate and the men by the radio.

Nelson and Soprano shook their heads.

"Whatever ROT did, they completely cut off the PEOC," Nelson said. "I'm guessing they used some sort of electromagnetic pulse."

"SZT Forty-Nine just declared loyalty to them," Soprano added. "That pretty much evens the playing field. Once we lose half of them, I'm sure the other mayors will quickly fall into line behind Wood."

"We need support from our forces in Europe," Nelson said. He removed his suit coat and rolled up his shirtsleeves. "I say we try to reach General Nixon and recall our troops."

"We don't know what side he's on," Soprano replied. "For all we know, he believes we're behind the missile attacks on the SZTs." He paused and wagged a chubby finger. "We're better off trying to find help Stateside."

"The moment we send out an SOS, we're toast," King said. It was the first time Ringgold had heard the Secret Service officer voice his opinion. It was good, though; she needed all of the opinions she could get right now.

Kate remained silent, her arms still folded over her stomach. She was shaking, but it wasn't from the chilly breeze. Ringgold could tell her friend was near her breaking point, and all of that stress was terrible for the baby.

"Kate, why don't you go get some rest?" Ringgold said.

"I'm fine."

Horn walked over and whispered something in Kate's ear. She huffed and walked away to the chopper. The bulky Delta Force operator hurried after her.

"Kate, wait up. I'm sorry," he said.

Ringgold watched them move toward the helicopter. The children stirred inside the dark troop hold as Horn and Kate spoke outside. When they had finished talking, Horn bent down to kiss his daughters.

All of their lives were in Ringgold's hands. They couldn't stay here forever. They were running out of food, and there was a risk of Variant juveniles in the area. It was either take a chance on finding help or wait to die.

"Send out the SOS to our forces here in the States," she ordered.

Soprano nodded in agreement, but Nelson raised a hand.

"Ma'am, there are several commanders who know our call sign," he stated. "If any of them are compromised, then we're giving up our position. We can't trust—"

Ringgold glared at her advisor. "Ben, I've made my decision." She wasn't sure if it was the right one, but she also knew General Nixon needed to focus on winning the war in Europe. Besides, he was too far away to help her right now anyway. America had started this nightmare, and they would help finish it, one way or another.

Soprano picked up the radio and scanned through the frequencies. Nelson sighed and neatly folded his suit coat. Then he gently set it over the stump and held out his hand for the radio receiver.

Nelson met Ringgold's gaze, and she nodded firmly.

"This is Black Cat calling all Eagles in the area, requesting assistance at the following coordinates…"

Ringgold walked away. The deed was done; now they just had to wait. She strode to the chopper with her hands tucked into her pockets. If ROT was going to come, she wanted to be with her friends when they did.

She sat at the edge of the troop hold between Kate and Horn.

"I keep thinking Fitz is going to drop in and save the day," Kate said with a sad smile. "Or that Reed will show up with a tank and whisk us all to safety. Kind of stupid, right?"

"Don't say that, Kate," Horn said quietly. "Fitz, Beckham, Apollo, and our other friends are still out there. We'll get through this, and we'll see them again."

Kate wiped her eyes but didn't reply.

An hour later, Ringgold began to feel the tug of sleep. It was late, probably after midnight. Horn had returned to the beach with King to hold security. Storm clouds drifted in from the west, crossing the moon and carpeting the island in darkness.

Ringgold felt a prick of water on her leg. The adrenaline had worn off, and her eyelids drooped, but she stood with Kate as Soprano and Nelson walked over.

"Well?" Ringgold asked.

Soprano frowned. "Not a single reply."

"My guess is that any friendlies who are listening are too afraid to show up here," Nelson said. "I think we should fire up the Black Hawk and be ready to move."

"And go where?" Kate whispered.

The president of the United States and her few remaining allies had nowhere to go.

"We don't have enough fuel to get far," Horn said, coming in from his rounds. He leaned back into the troop hold to check on Tasha and Jenny. "You should try and get some sleep, Madam President—and you too, Kate."

Ringgold sat back down and sighed inwardly, desperate for sleep but too afraid to close her eyes. The pain of her bullet wound was flaring up again.

"He's right," Kate said quietly. "We should get some rest."

Ringgold balled up her coat for a pillow and set it beside her on the floor of the troop hold. She had slept in worse places than this during the nights she had hidden from the Variants in Raven Rock. Each time she had closed her eyes while hiding there, she had wondered if she would wake up to the deformed face of a monster. Now she wondered if she would wake up staring down the barrel of a ROT gun.

The nightmares were bad tonight. She saw her cousin transforming into a raging beast. In her dream, Emilia contorted, her body cracking and jerking as the hemorrhage virus pulsed through her veins. Then came the blood oozing from her frightened, enraged eyes, then the pained shrieks, and finally the cracking of joints.

Ringgold's eyes snapped open. Wrapping her arms across her chest, she leaned back against the bulkhead and waited for the rain to stop. Waves slapped against the beach, then receded back to sea. It was almost pitch black now that the storm had moved over the island.

She had nearly nodded off again when movement in the darkness caught her eye. Six figures clad in black armor moved up the beach. Ringgold blinked, her heart kicking.

"Kate," she whispered. "Kate, wake up."

King, silhouetted out on the beach, suddenly crashed to the ground, two men in black tackling him from behind. A muffled shout came from the other side of the bird—from Jake or the pilots, Ringgold wasn't sure.

Horn ran over to the helicopter, his eyes wide. "We have to go, *now*."

The kids stirred awake, sleepily calling out for their parents. Ringgold kept her focus on the men in black. They were all carrying machine guns.

Horn turned and raised his rifle, the muzzle shifting from target to target. He cursed. Even Ringgold, who was no soldier, could see that they weren't going to win this fight.

One of the men stepped out in front of the others and shouted, "We have you surrounded. Drop your weapons and identify yourselves!"

"You first!" Horn yelled back.

The leader of the team continued to advance. "Drop your weapons and give up the president."

The moon spilled across the ocean, its light parting the waves like a highway running through an endless desert. Ringgold didn't see any sign of a ship out there— so where had these men come from?

"I'm not going to ask you again," the leader said, his voice rising. The other men all fanned out to surround the Black Hawk. Two more showed up around the front of the chopper, shoving the marine pilots and Jake into the sand, their hands already bound.

Horn shifted from target to target. Nelson was standing to his left with a pistol raised. Ringgold couldn't see Soprano.

"Last chance," the leader said. He balled his fist, and the other men stopped, all of them directing their guns at Horn. He blocked the front of the troop hold with his body, the only person standing between Ringgold and these men.

Tasha called out for Horn.

"Stay where you are, kiddo!" he yelled back.

Ringgold would not allow Horn to be slaughtered in front of his own children. Not if she could do anything about it. ROT wanted her, and only her.

"Put down your weapons," she ordered as she scooted out of the chopper.

Nelson moved in front of her. "Get back, ma'am. I'm not letting them take you."

"Me either," Horn said with a snort. "Just give me the word, Madam President, and I will light these bozos up."

"Get away from her," the leader said. She could see his features now. The whites of his eyes stood out against his dark skin. She wondered what was going through his mind.

Nelson took a step forward and aimed the gun at the man speaking.

"Put your gun down!" he yelled at Nelson.

Ringgold reached over and put her hand on the barrel of Nelson's gun, slowly pushing it to the ground.

"I'll go with you. Just let everyone else go," she said to the leader.

She strode past Horn and Nelson and prepared herself to be riddled with bullets, or at the very least to be whisked away to a dark prison cell to await execution later. If it was the latter, she hoped she would get to look Wood in the eyes before she was killed.

"Ma'am," Horn pleaded. He tried to move in front of her, but she turned and faced him. "It's okay. You did your job protecting me, but you have to look after your daughters now, and Kate."

Horn snorted like a bull, his gun moving from face to face. The men in black all watched her as she strolled from the chopper toward them.

"Stand down," the leader said, balling his fist.

One by one the rifles were lowered. All but Horn's.

The leader approached slowly, his eyes flitting from Ringgold to Horn. "These men are with you, President Ringgold?" he said.

Horn finally pointed his rifle's barrel toward the sand. She straightened her back. "Yes, they are."

"You could have just said so earlier," the man said in a gruff voice. "I'm Senior Chief Petty Officer Randall Blade with SEAL Team Four. We're here to evacuate you to the USS *Florida*."

Ringgold narrowed her brows. "You're SEALs? Why the hell didn't *you* say so earlier?"

Blade flashed a white grin. "We thought this could be a trap. ROT was on the airwaves warning of something like this. We took a risk by coming here—a pretty damn big risk, if you ask me, but someone above my pay grade thought it was worth it, and they were right. You still have some friends out there, President Ringgold."

Horn and Kate stepped up to flank Ringgold on both sides. "I'm Doctor Kate Lovato," Kate said. "Please, have you heard anything about Captain Reed Beckham?"

Shaking his head, Blade said, "I'm sorry, ma'am. Get your things. We don't have long." Blade nodded at one of his men, who pulled out a radio. He called in a ride over the channel.

The other SEALs unbound the hands of the marine pilots, Jake, King, and Soprano, who had also managed to get himself captured. The men took up positions along the beach while Ringgold and her friends gathered their belongings.

"Where exactly are you taking us?" Kate asked Blade.

"To the USS *Florida* and then to a small fleet of warships, boats, and a French research vessel two hundred miles to the east," he said.

"French?" Ringgold cut in.

"Yes, ma'am. Those friends I was talking about, they

aren't just Americans." Blade paused and looked at Kate. "They're also looking for help. Apparently, there's some new kind of monster in Europe."

Andrew Wood stroked his scarred chin as he watched his fortress come into view from the plush leather seat of his newly acquired Boeing VC-25. The military version of the 747 was nicer than he had expected. Although he had been hoping for better in-flight meals.

"An MRE?" he said, staring at the package set in front of him by a female soldier who was doubling in duty as a glorified flight attendant. She stuttered and batted long eyelashes over a pair of blue eyes.

"I-I'm sorry, sir," she replied. "That's all we have."

"No fresh fruit or grilled salmon? What is this world coming to?"

She shook her head ruefully, and Wood chuckled. With their ranks swelling, he hardly knew anyone outside his inner circle.

"What's your first name?"

"It's, um, it's Yolanda, sir."

"Yolanda—what a sweet name."

"Uh, thank you, sir."

She swallowed and took a step back. Wood loved making people nervous and paused for dramatic effect. Then he raised a hand and laughed again.

"I'm just messin' with you, sweetie, but I would like an alcoholic beverage. I'm assuming we have something on board. I'd like something stiff—stiff and cold."

"Yes... Yes, I can do that, sir."

Yolanda hesitated again and then backed up as he shooed her away like an insignificant fly.

He took a bite of dry beef and turned back to the view.

Snow-brushed forests peppered the terrain below, and crystal clear rivers meandered through the frozen tundra. At night, the temperature dropped far below freezing. It was one reason the hemorrhage virus had never made it here, and if Wood had to guess, it was for that reason Jan Ringgold and her staff had evacuated survivors from Anchorage and other cities to SZT 19, which was only about twenty miles to the west.

But this time Wood wasn't heading off to take over an SZT. His growing army was doing that for him. He was going home to the place where he had spent the majority of his career in the military.

Xerxes, the code name for the Resistance of Tyranny military base near the Knik Glacier, was one of the most secure places in the United States. That was obvious even from the sky. The five-cornered former military facility was nestled along the blue wall of a glacier.

The men and women living there now had spent the past seven months beneath the ice. It was one of the most inhospitable places in the world, too cold and isolated even for the Variants. That was why Wood had picked the base to be the ROT headquarters.

He continued stroking his scarred face and leaned closer to the window for a better view of the blue glacier in the distance. Tucked against the bottom were five circular structures peeking above the snow. Most of the base, however, was hidden beneath the ground. He had renamed the top secret facility after the great Persian king who had sought to take over the Greek empire— and much of the rest of the world. The story had always fascinated Wood, but where Xerxes had ultimately failed, he would succeed.

Before he did that, he needed to get General Nixon on the ROT team, and the general wasn't the easiest man to coerce. It was going to take some major convincing to get the United States military in Europe to ally itself with him. Luckily, Wood had the perfect plan to make it happen.

Yolanda returned with a vodka on the rocks. For a moment, he wondered what her story was. You didn't survive the apocalypse and get a job working for Wood by being a loser.

"Prepare for landing," one of the pilots said over the PA system.

Wood sipped the vodka and looked away from Yolanda, no longer interested in the young woman. He glanced down at the graveyard of armored vehicles on the southern edge of the base, recalling the cold nights he had spent on patrol down there thirty years ago, waiting for the Soviets to invade. That experience—and working for a paranoid, borderline schizophrenic commander— had prepared Wood for a different type of invasion.

Wood didn't see the monsters populating the earth as the end of humanity. He saw them as an opportunity— an opportunity to finish what his late brother, Colonel Zach Wood, had started while working with the Medical Corps.

Before he could finish their work, he had to take down the most dangerous enemy of all—Jan Ringgold. The former president was an outlaw who had escaped his attack on the PEOC. He had been chipping away at her power and credibility with an intricate web of lies for the past few weeks, but the time for playing games was over.

His masterstroke had been attacking SZT 15, in what was once Chicago, and blaming the hemorrhage virus outbreak there on Ringgold. Once he'd discovered that Ringgold's nearest living relative, a cousin, was sheltering there, SZT 15's fate had been sealed. After all, who in their right mind would support a woman who had knowingly turned her own family member into a monster?

Wood resisted the urge to chuckle, fearing it would make the wrong impression on his inner circle. He was to be supreme ruler of the new world order, but he didn't want to be seen as an eccentric despot. If there was one thing Wood hated—other than Reed Beckham and his band of tyrants, of course—it was a stereotype.

The men who made up Wood's team sat in front of him. Three days earlier there had been four advisors, but Wood had lost Jack Johnson when he'd sent the man to check on the USS *George Washington*.

Someone had gotten to the aircraft carrier, blowing a gaping hole in the ship and destroying several of the hemorrhage-virus missiles. Wood wasn't sure who, but it didn't matter now. The bastards were undoubtedly all dead or infected.

The VC-25's pilots circled the base, providing an aerial view of a lake and the glacier below. Wood could even see SZT 19 in the distance, although it was hardly anything to look at—basically just a run-down fort built to house a couple thousand survivors. It had only taken one visit to get them to align with ROT. Most of the mayors of the SZTs were spineless cowards. And those who weren't, Wood would dispose of when the time came.

"Sir, sorry to interrupt, but I have news," said the rough voice of Michael Kufman.

Wood looked up at a pair of ruthless black eyes. The former Delta Force operator stood six feet, three inches tall, with linebacker shoulders and the massive biceps of an Olympic arm wrestler.

"Well?" Wood said. "What's your news?"

"I just got word that Coyote has been captured at the SZT in Los Angeles." Kufman didn't smile or show any hint of emotion as he gave the news.

"That's excellent," Wood said. He smiled, and Kufman returned the gesture with something that looked more like a scowl, his thin lips parting to show the gap between his two front teeth. Wood wasn't sure the soldier was capable of smiling.

"Have you ever cracked a joke, Kufman?" Wood asked.

"Your brother wasn't one for jokes, sir," Kufman said stiffly.

Wood took another sip of vodka, welcoming the burn. His older brother and Kufman had been good friends. The best of friends, in fact—there wasn't any other man Zach would have wanted at Andrew's side to see him through to the end.

"Tell the pilots to keep the plane hot. It seems I'm headed for La La Land shortly," Wood said. His smile was gone, and he turned back to the window to watch the tarmac rise up to meet the plane. The wheels hit the snowy asphalt with a jolt.

He finished off the vodka and waited for the plane to come to a stop. In moments like this, when he had nothing to do but wait, he would contemplate his revenge. Beckham was dead, but he was still looking for Master Sergeant Joe Fitzpatrick, the cripple who had blown his brother's head off at Plum Island.

At first, Wood had thought Beckham was his King Leonidas, but the Spartan king who had stood with three hundred of his warriors against the Persian masses was not Beckham after all. He had been far too easy to kill. In Wood's eyes, his great nemesis was Fitzpatrick, and Wood would have his revenge soon.

He walked through the plane's open door and stood at the top of a ladder overlooking the icy terrain. Gathered on the tarmac were a hundred men dressed in black parkas, automatic rifles slung over their backs and helmets with goggles atop their heads.

Sure, they weren't a million-strong Persian army, but they would have to do.

Despite the rage swirling through his veins, he forced a smile and waved at his men, imagining what Xerxes, the King of Kings, must have felt when he walked off his ships before the invasion of the Hellespont.

"You ready, sir?" said Kufman.

Wood nodded, but he knew the swearing-in bullshit was just words. Actions were more important than petty titles like "President Wood" or "King Whoever." He would never feel truly in control until he had taken revenge on the man who killed his brother. He was ready to lead the world into a new age—but first, he had a score to settle.

2

Master Sergeant Joe Fitzpatrick sat at the war table thinking of his friends back home and everything that had happened over the past seven months. He raised the coffee mug in his hand and eyed his trigger finger that had taken so many lives.

He had a hard time accepting the truth of his situation. None of it seemed real.

And why would it? The world was overrun with monsters, and he was in France, of all places. He'd always wanted to visit it, but not like this. There weren't even any pretty French girls to flirt with.

He took a sip of the coffee. It was cold, but it still tasted like liquid gold. He had just gotten back from Greenland twelve hours ago and needed the caffeine. Most of the members of Team Ghost were sleeping in their cots halfway across the camp. They were physically and mentally exhausted from facing the hybrid Variants in a remote Inuit fishing village. And although the mission had been a success, Sergeant Hugh Stevenson had almost lost his life. He was still recovering from a concussion.

Fitz hadn't lost a member of Team Ghost yet, but he wondered how much longer that would be true. He was sitting in the command tent at Forward Operating Base 5, just thirty miles inland from where Marine Expeditionary Unit 24 had landed a few days before.

Thirty miles of fighting and three hundred dead marines.

He took another slug of coffee, wishing it was spiked with whiskey. All around him were the heads of the other units making up what was left of the Twenty-Fourth MEU. Sergeant Jeni Rico sat to his left, twirling a tip of frosted blue hair around her finger and chomping on a piece of bubble gum.

She's not French, Fitz thought, *but she sure is pretty.*

He shook the thought away. Beckham had given him a lot of advice about leadership when he had nominated Fitz to take over Team Ghost, but they didn't need to talk about how to handle a situation in which Fitz might be attracted to one of his subordinates. He knew it went against regulations and was unprofessional. Fortunately for Fitz, there were plenty of other things to focus on besides Jeni Rico's good looks.

"I hope General Nixon authorizes the second phase of Operation Reach so we can get out there and start kicking some mutated ass," she said. "The sooner we start the march to Paris, the sooner we get to go home."

"We're going to find out in a few minutes," Fitz whispered back. He glanced at the men and women around them. Together, they were a hodgepodge of soldiers and sailors from different military branches. But they all wore the same mask of fatigue and despair, like football players after a brutal team loss.

No, that wasn't a good comparison at all, Fitz realized, taking a second look at the hardened features of those around him. Losing a game couldn't compare to losing a battle by any stretch of the imagination. It was an insult to think that.

Team Ghost had been lucky after Greenland and

the mission that had taken them to the Basilica of St. Thérèse, at Lisieux, after the invasion—much luckier than most of the soldiers in this tent, and luckier than the leader of the Ombres, Mira, and their captain, Michel. The boy had died in Fitz's arms, still wearing his Superman cape.

Fitz struggled to get his head straight as Colonel Roger Bradley ducked under the flap of the tent. Major Rick Domino followed him inside. Everyone rose to salute, but Bradley hardly seemed to notice. He dragged a sleeve across his mouth and then waved at them to sit.

"At ease," he muttered, sounding annoyed and maybe a bit drunk. "Got bad news, bad news, and more fucking bad news."

Bradley paced in front of the table while Domino spread out the maps. Fitz tried not to look at the gaping cavern where the old colonel's eye had been. Fitz hated to be stared at. But like Fitz, Bradley didn't shy away from the attention either. He never wore a patch, as many soldiers who had lost an eye did.

"Ready, sir," Domino said, smoothing out the wrinkles in the map.

"I'll start with the *really* shitty news." Bradley palmed the table. "The second phase of Operation Reach is still on hold for now."

Several men muttered under their breath, but Bradley didn't call them out for it.

"The radioactive dirty bombs dropped during Operation Reach didn't have the effect we thought they would," he said. "We're hearing all types of reports from recon units, and it sounds as if the bombs actually made things a whole hell of a lot more tricky for the United States Marine Corps and our allies."

Fitz squeezed the Styrofoam coffee cup in his hand. Team Ghost's mission to the Basilica of St. Thérèse had been supposed to help destroy the mutated army. Had it all been for nothing?

"If that shit weren't bad enough, we're getting more information about what's happening in the United States," Bradley said. He folded his arms across his chest and snorted at Domino.

"Resistance of Tyranny, a mercenary group that made a name for itself during the War on Terror, is leading the effort to bring down President Ringgold and her cohorts. They've been recruiting SZTs to their side," said the major. "Ringgold has allegedly deployed the hemorrhage virus on several of the SZTs that were challenging her legitimacy as president."

What? That can't be true. Fitz shifted in his seat anxiously, waiting for more info and holding back his own questions.

Bradley huffed. "I don't know what to believe, to be frank, but our focus right now is on the fight in Europe."

"Sir, with all due respect, President Ringgold would not kill Americans," Fitz chimed in, unable to resist. "I know her. She's not a murderer."

Bradley's remaining eye roved back toward Fitz. "The leader of ROT, Lieutenant Andrew Wood, says it's true, and half the SZTs are rallying behind the ROT flag."

Wood. The name sent a wave of anxiety through Fitz. He levered himself out of his chair, ignoring the hand on his shoulder. He knew it was Rico trying to calm him, but he gently brushed her aside.

Fitz was afraid to ask, but he needed to know. "Is this Lieutenant Andrew Wood any relation to Colonel Zach Wood, sir?"

Bradley nodded and said, "Yeah. Now sit your ass down, Fitz. I'm trying to give a damn briefing here."

Fitz slowly sat, his mind racing. He gripped the edge of the table so hard his knuckles turned white.

Rico tapped his leg with her boot, but he continued to ignore her.

Bradley grabbed a folder from the table and cracked the seal. "In front of you is a report from the fringe science division about the Variants in France," he continued. "As you can see, irradiation seems to speed up the process of the epigenetic changes caused by VX-99. The result is a metamorphosis of the monsters in—"

The whine of an air-raid siren cut Bradley off.

The tent flaps were pushed aside as two lance corporals stepped inside.

"Reavers, sir. We've got a sky full of 'em," one of the men said. "There's got to be hundreds!"

Fitz, Rico, and the rest of the team leads all hurried outside. The muddy road bisecting the columns of tents had broken into a flurry of motion. Marines, Army Rangers, army infantry, and a dozen other soldiers emerged with their rifles raised to the sky. One man still had shaving cream on his face.

In the glow of the rising sun, an armada of dark figures flapped across the sky, swooping low like fighters coming in for a bombing raid.

"Get your asses in gear, marines!" Bradley shouted with his hands cupped over his mouth. He turned to the lance corporal standing to his right and said, "Go grab Bertha."

"Air support should be on the way," Domino said.

Bradley spat in the dirt. "Yeah, but by the time the flyboys get here, we're going to be dead. Now go get me *my* air support!"

The other members of Team Ghost, except Stevenson, came bounding around the corner of the tent. Staff Sergeant Blake Tanaka and Specialist Yas Dohi unslung M4s. Apollo trotted over, his tail between his legs.

"Get to the MATV!" Fitz yelled. He turned just as

the lance corporal emerged from a tent with Bradley's "air support," aka Bertha. He handed the sleek FIM-92 Stinger surface-to-air missile launcher to the colonel.

"There's my lady," Bradley said with a toothy grin. He looked at Fitz. "When this is over, find me. I've got a new mission for Team Ghost."

Fitz nodded and took off after his team. The Reavers were starting to fan out as they neared the base. From the sky they had a perfect vantage of the four sections of the FOB nestled against a southern rocky backdrop.

A road bisected the camp and led out into the farm fields to the south. On the west side of the base were tents housing soldiers and supplies. To the east was a vehicle lot, and the north side of the camp consisted of trenches and artillery zones that were already spewing fire into the sky.

The Reavers speared through the barrage of missiles, mostly managing to avoid the tracer rounds that lit up the morning sky.

Otherworldly shrieks sounded over the bark of automatic gunfire and the thump of the M777 155-millimeter Howitzers. Surface-to-air missiles streaked away, marked by spiraling exhaust trails.

Apollo barked at the sky as he ran by Fitz's side.

"It's okay, boy," Fitz reassured the dog. The Reavers, of all the Variants, seemed to frighten Apollo the most.

"Follow me!" Fitz yelled to his team. They took a detour into an alleyway between two green tents and made a run for the west vehicle lot. Tanaka was already climbing into the turret of their MATV. The Reavers, numbering in the hundreds, reached the other end of the camp. One of them pulled into the sky with a screaming marine in its talons.

A missile hit the creature's wings, and the marine dropped on top of a tent, collapsing it.

"Come on, Fitzie!" Rico shouted. She opened the back door of the MATV and gestured frantically. Apollo hopped inside, and Fitz jumped in after him. Fitz closed the door just as a Reaver crashed into the other side. It flapped away, a stream of blood flowing from its warty, bulbous nose.

Tanaka turned the turret and fired a volley of rounds that shredded its wings to pulp. Fitz climbed over the seats as the vehicle lurched forward.

"Give 'em hell up there!" Rico shouted.

Dohi floored the truck and sped away from the fleet of vehicles. They were the first MATV out, but the other drivers quickly followed. Humvees and Bradley Fighting Vehicles too peeled out of the lot to engage the beasts.

Fitz looked out the windshield. Rounds of all calibers as well as missiles streaked into the sky, but there were so many of the Reavers. Dozens had already landed and were tearing apart soldiers who had been caught out in the open.

Something large and green hit the windshield with a thud. Cracks ebbed out around the impact point. Blood filled the web of cracks as a dead soldier's body slumped down the hood of the truck.

"Jesus!" Rico said.

Fitz shook away the shock. "Get us into this fight, Dohi!"

Overhead, Fitz spotted the Reaver that had dropped the man on their truck. He chambered a round in his MK11. The bark of the M240 above suddenly ceased, and Tanaka slid back inside, sealing the hatch with a click.

"Too many up there, man," Tanaka said, his voice shaking.

"Then let's take some down!" Fitz shouted.

"What if this is the start of a bigger attack?" Rico said. "What if there are more on the way?"

Fitz knew the answer, but he kept his mouth shut. If the Reavers were just the advance party, then the Twenty-Fourth MEU was screwed.

"Suck it up, Team Ghost!" Fitz pulled up the joker bandanna around his mouth, rolled down his window, and jammed his rifle between the metal bars while Dohi pulled back onto the road.

A squeeze of the trigger sent a round into the spine of a Reaver making a run for the southern side of the camp. It shrieked in pain, reaching back with a winged arm before flopping to the ground.

One down. A hundred to go.

Apollo jumped into the front seat with Fitz, snarling. A wave of fur trembled across his body, not from fear but from anger. The dog wanted back into the action.

Me too, boy.

Fitz centered his rifle on a Reaver perched on a mound of sandbags, hunched and snacking on the neck of a dead soldier. It pulled away ribbons of flesh just as Fitz fired a round into its meaty chest. Dark blood gushed out, and the creature slumped over the soldier's corpse.

Dohi took a left and gunned the engine toward the front lines. Only about half of the Howitzers and miniguns were still firing. Beyond the base's defenses, he could see the lush green stretch of farmland left untended.

"Watch out!" Tanaka shouted in the back. The MATV jolted from the impact of a Reaver crashing into the side. The vehicle weighed two tons, but the beast still shook the frame.

Fitz watched in the rearview mirror as the Reaver stood and let out a high-pitched scream at the escaping truck, ready to charge again. The MATV behind them smashed into the creature, flattening its body and wings like roadkill.

As soon as their truck rounded the last row of tents, Fitz saw the trenches and artillery zones. His breath caught in his chest. The Howitzers had all gone silent, and the soldiers along the trenches were down to their bayonets. Dozens were fighting in single combat against the overwhelming Reaver forces.

"Oh my God," Rico said. "Hurry, Dohi!"

Fitz turned to the back seat. "Get back up on the turret, Tanaka!"

The man had pulled out his Wakizashi, but sheathed it over his shoulder and climbed back up into the turret without uttering a word. Fitz was starting to worry about Tanaka, who seemed determined to use his blades when a gun was the better option. If they survived this battle, he'd have to talk with the staff sergeant.

"Fitzie," Rico choked. She pointed at the soldiers scrambling from the trenches. One of them was caught halfway out of the ditch. He clawed at the dirt, trying to get away from the Reaver holding him fast by the ankle. The man let out a scream as the beast yanked him back into the trench and out of view. A geyser of blood shot up over the dirt as his screams died.

Dohi parked the truck along a row of sandbags. In the rearview mirror, the other vehicles were all speeding down the road, dust pluming behind them. Reavers swooped in to claw at the turrets. None of them were firing back, and the hatches were all sealed.

"We need to get a bird in the air!" Rico shouted.

Fitz could see the choppers sitting idly to the west, but he shook his head. The skies were too hostile for the pilots to navigate. The Twenty-Fourth MEU was going to have to fight this one on the ground.

"On me!" Fitz opened the door, jumped out, and then shut the door to seal Apollo inside. The dog barked and clawed at the window.

"I'm sorry, boy," Fitz said. He hesitated for a second before turning to the battle. This fight was too hot for his loyal friend.

"Keep them off us, Tanaka!" Fitz yelled.

The M240 barked overhead as Rico and Dohi came running around the MATV with their M4s blazing. Fitz shouldered his MK11 and searched for a target, but the entire zone was a mess of white flesh and camouflage. There had to be at least thirty Reavers on the ground and even more in the skies.

The other vehicles jerked to a stop behind them and soldiers piled out. They all ran after Fitz, leaping over sandbags and screaming their fury. The sight of marines running toward a fight was familiar, even in the face of an unprecedented enemy.

Fitz lined up his sights on a Reaver that was pulling a marine into the sky and fired. The creature let go, and the man fell back to the ground, twisting his ankle, and then scrambled to safety.

Shots eight and nine of the twenty rounds in Fitz's MK11 lanced into the spiny back of a Reaver that had landed on a marine. It crashed to the ground, wings fluttering. The man managed to crawl out from under the beast and wiped blood from his face just as another Reaver barreled into him from the side.

Dust exploded into the air as the marine was pulled into a trench on the other side of the artillery guns. Another man came crawling out, soaked in blood, tattered fatigues hanging off his body. He was covered in lacerations from his ankles to his neck, exposing bone in several places.

The marine didn't beg for help or scream in agony. He pushed himself to his feet, staggered, and then turned with a pistol to fire on the spiked backs of the Reavers in the trenches before one of them reached out and yanked him back inside.

There wasn't anything Fitz could do but watch.

All across his line of fire, Fitz saw dying marines and Army Rangers fighting with their bayonets, knives, and side arms. Some of them were down to their fists, punching, kicking, and screaming. The Reavers were more agile, stronger, and faster than the men, and they pulled their prey into the ditches or into the sky.

The memory of Mira being pulled into the sky surfaced in his mind. The mother of the Ombres who had hidden in the Basilica of St. Thérèse had given her life to protect her adopted children.

Fitz gritted his teeth and fired two rounds through the wings of a massive beast. The two men it carried fell back into the violence below.

Rico and Dohi now knelt to Fitz's left, firing three-round bursts that dropped the Reavers headed for their position. The men from the other vehicles formed a solid line along the sandbags.

"Watch your fire zones!" Fitz shouted, realizing how crazy it sounded. Even if they fired with calculated precision, it was hard to find a clean target in the chaos. A cloud of dust swirled like smoke in the battle zone. Reavers advanced, leaving the dead behind to pursue the living, always in search of fresh meat.

Fitz finished off his magazine and slung the rifle across his back. He pulled Meg's hatchet and his Beretta M9. Rico was down to her sawed-off shotgun. She pumped in a shell and nodded at Fitz.

"You ready to get up close and personal?" she shouted.

Fitz tightened his gloved fingers around the hatchet. All around him, the men and women of the Twenty-Fourth MEU prepared to stand their ground. Several officers drew their ceremonial sabers, and everyone else fixed bayonets at the onslaught of hungry beasts moving in on all fours, wings tucked along their backs, stamping over the dead and dying.

The M240 fire thinned the two dozen remaining monsters by half, but those that made it through jumped over the trenches and galloped toward the line of soldiers.

"I'm out!" Tanaka shouted.

Fitz glanced over his shoulder to see Tanaka climbing down from the turret. That was when Fitz noticed several teenagers running down the dirt road: The Ombres were joining the fight. A Reaver sailed in from the north, claws extended like an eagle's as it swooped down to grab one of the girls.

"Watch out!" Fitz shouted. He turned to aim his pistol, but someone beat him to the punch. A missile slammed into the side of the Reaver, blowing it into hunks of meat.

Fitz made eye contact with the marine who had fired the missile—it was Bradley, and he was holding Bertha in both hands, grinning like a madman.

"Give 'em hell, marines! Hold your ground!" he shouted.

Fitz turned back to the Reavers making a final push for their position. Several more crashed into the dirt, flopping and jerking in pain.

Tanaka, now on the ground beside the vehicle, drew both his Katana and Wakizashi when he got to Team Ghost's position. He twirled the blades and shouted something that Fitz couldn't make out. Several of the Ombres took up position next to Rico and Fitz.

From the cloud of smoke and dust, ten of the beasts emerged, all of them peppered with bullet holes. Behind them, the bodies of dead soldiers and Reavers littered the ground.

It was ten injured monsters against fifty men, women—and children. For the first time since they landed in France, Team Ghost and the Twenty-Fourth MEU had the numbers.

Fitz fired off several shots from his M9 and then holstered the gun. He switched the hatchet to his right hand.

Everyone seemed to be screaming as he took a step forward with Meg's trusty weapon firmly in his hand. He joined the war cry with his own shout as he ran toward the fray: "All it takes is all you got, marines!"

Sergeant Piero Angaran sat in the dirt with his back to a wall polished smooth by hundreds of years of exposure to the elements. He tore off a bite of jerky and looked down at his only friend in the world. The mouse sat in the crook of his arm, chewing on a morsel of its own.

The tiny creature wasn't just his friend but also his early-warning system. He chirped whenever Variants were close, but tonight he was quiet.

Piero finished off his snack and stood to look out over Rome from their hideout atop Palatine Hill. A cool breeze that carried the scent of burning flesh rustled his filthy fatigues. His injuries were slowly healing, although his ankle still hurt. It would be a long journey back to 100 percent health, but at least he had food and medicine.

Ringo climbed up Piero's arm and perched on his shoulder, black eyes roving the darkness below. The moon hovered in the sky, but the light wasn't bright enough to see the tile roofs, terraces, and cobblestone streets with any degree of clarity.

He flipped down his night-vision goggles and studied

the ancient city. For over a millennium, Rome had played an important role in the development of modern culture in Italy and the world. Founded on the very hill where he stood now, the city had expanded in every direction, becoming a hub of Western civilization.

Weeks ago, the Italian military had sent its best—the Fourth Alpini Parachutist Regiment—to save the capital from the Variants, but the soldiers had been no match for the mutated monsters. Piero was the only survivor and perhaps the only living person in all of Rome.

A silhouette crossed the moon—a lonely Reaver, wings outstretched like an osprey. It let out a forlorn, high-pitched wail that seemed to echo over and over. Another creature answered the call somewhere across the city.

Varianti.

There weren't many of the winged monsters hunting tonight. A good number of the Variants had perished when the EUF bombarded the city with radioactive dirty bombs three days earlier, and the others all seemed to have vanished.

After escaping the bombs by hiding in the Vatican, Piero had bolted for his old shelter, where he made contact with the EUF.

Piero pulled out the radio. It was his only line to the outside world, and his conversation with the EUF radio operator in Spain had saved his life. He had been able to escape the Vatican and avoid the areas of the city hit by the radioactive bombs. They had even promised to send support when they could, but he wasn't holding his breath.

Hunker down. The radiation will kill most of the Variants. We will send in troops when their numbers have fallen.

The last transmission replayed in Piero's mind. He moved to the other side of their stone lookout, with Ringo riding on his shoulder. At the wall, Piero stopped and raised his Beretta ARX160 assault rifle to his night-vision goggles. In the green hue were the scattered corpses of the monsters caught outside during the bombing. Their armored shells flickered in the optics. He flipped up his NVGs and scoped the corpses with naked eyes. The juveniles glowed like fireflies.

There were far fewer than he'd expected. So where were the others?

Ringo chirped, and Piero ducked down, heart pounding. He heard the *click-clack*ing a moment later. With his back to the wall, he slowly shifted his gun into position. He already had a round chambered but flicked the safety off while Ringo darted down his arm, leaped to the dirt, and dashed into a small hole in the stone wall.

A low groan replaced the clicking sound, and he waited for the clatter of hooves on the cobblestone streets or the flapping of wings.

None of the familiar sounds came.

Piero waited in silence for several minutes, his heart rate slowly returning to normal. When he was confident there wasn't anything moving toward his location, he flipped his NVGs back into position and peeked back over the wall with his rifle.

The slope on the other side was clear of contacts. Whatever he'd heard was gone now. He backed away and moved out of the roofless shelter to the dirt path that led to the other side of the hill. Ringo remained in the hole, dark eyes no doubt fixed on Piero's back.

That was fine; he didn't want the mouse to follow him out here. In the eerie green of his optics, he studied the white jasmine bushes that blocked his view of the other side of the hill. Though he couldn't see their colors now, purple and light blue flowers framed the dirt path. He halted near an ancient fountain, where he heard a cracking sound.

This wasn't the snapping of joints or clicking of armor. This sounded more like the noise an egg made when cracked on the side of a pan.

He slowly moved past the fountain. On the other side was a breathtaking view of the city and the excavation area where Italian archeologists had uncovered the ancient walls of early Rome. Pillars, graves, fountains, and statues dotted the terrain below. Behind him was the Colosseum. If he turned to look, he could just see the high arched walls surrounding the circular structure that had once been the pride and joy of the Roman capital.

The cracking sound pulled him toward a grove of trees to the south. He followed it slowly, moving heel to toe, with the Beretta's barrel angled at the spindly trees ahead. He knelt with deliberate care, cautious not to scrape his kneepad on a rock, and pushed up his NVGs. Tucked among gangly branches, like a pearl in an oyster, was a glowing white cocoon that squirmed from side to side.

The cracking grew louder, and with it the pace of Piero's heartbeat. His eyes widened as he watched.

What the hell kind of monster was this?

It was curiosity that drove Piero forward. He slowly walked toward the trees, finger hovering outside the trigger guard of his gun.

A moaning stopped him midstride. The groan seemed to come from a slit that had opened in the middle of the cocoon, revealing the pale curved flesh of some sort of creature.

He took another step closer, bringing a hand to his nostrils against the rank rotting-fruit scent of the cocooned monster. The slit in the silky skin of the cocoon peeled back farther. This time he could see what looked like the black outer shell of a bug. A bony belly and smooth plates writhed inside.

This definitely didn't look like a Reaver—this was something different.

It moaned again and thrashed in its fleshy prison.

The creaking continued, but it wasn't coming from the beast in front of him. Piero raised his rifle's scope and zoomed in on a terrace to the west, where he saw another one of the cocoons. He did a quick sweep but couldn't see any others from his vantage point.

By the time he turned back to the cocoon in front of him, it had opened completely. A beetle the size of a man wiggled out and sloshed onto the dirt. A curved, misshapen head emerged. The multifaceted eyes, centered on the shell, darted back and forth. They focused on him, and serrated mandibles opened to release a low hissing.

All at once the city seemed to come alive with the same noise. Piero swallowed hard, taking a step back. The din was like the call of cicadas in the summer, an almost mechanical sound that rose and fell in waves.

The Beetle pushed itself up onto long limbs lined with jagged spikes. It stumbled, fell, and rose up again on all fours, plates clattering across its armored body. Clawed feet gripped the dirt.

Piero fired a burst into the thing's left eye. A green fluid exploded out and peppered his boots. Desperately, he fired again into its right eye. He backed away and stared in horror as the blind, insectlike Variant flopped to the ground. It snapped its mandibles together.

The hissing of the other mutated monsters rang out in all directions. Piero stumbled away, turning to run back down the path. He wheezed for air, flinging glances over his shoulder and nearly stumbling. He had to get to Ringo. They needed to get out of here.

The EUF had been wrong. The radiation didn't kill the beasts: It mutated them into abominations from the very pits of hell. Now Piero knew why most of the monsters had vanished. They weren't dead—they were just hiding as they morphed into these...demons.

The next step of the Variant evolution was happening all around him, and he was stuck right in the middle of the transformation.

3

Captain Reed Beckham had survived another day, but he felt like a can of expired sardines. The tiny apartment reeked of something sour and rotted, which made it nearly impossible to sleep. Add to that the wails of the infected outside and he had probably only snagged an hour or two of rest.

Beckham stood and stretched his aching muscles. His clothing, saturated with sweat, clung to his skin. He cracked his neck from side to side and the scarf Flathman had given him fell from his nose and mouth, allowing the rancid smell to fill his lungs.

The rotted corpse of a man was curled up on the mattress in the other room, skeletal hands still gripping the gun that he'd used to blow his brains out and splatter them on the ceiling. It was a common way out from the first days of the outbreak for people to take their lives instead of face the monsters.

This guy, whoever he was, had inadvertently helped save Flathman and Beckham. One of the infected beasts had sniffed right outside the door in the early-morning hours but then continued on, uninterested in the rotting body inside. It wasn't the first time Beckham had used the scent of the dead to camouflage himself, and it wasn't getting any more pleasant.

"Sun's up. You ready to make a move for that Humvee we spotted on our way here?" he whispered to Flathman.

"We got time to stop and get a coffee?" Flathman asked with a shit-eating grin. "I'm all out of whiskey."

"I wish, LT. I could use ten shots of espresso right about now." Beckham settled for a drink of water from his bottle. He chased down a handful of Tylenol with a long slug. The warm water would help with his dehydration, but what he really needed was an IV.

Flathman watched with a curious eye. Beckham knew he was being sized up, but he couldn't blame the lieutenant. Beckham, wounded as he was, was a liability, but for some reason, Flathman had made it his personal mission to help Beckham get back to Kate and President Ringgold.

"Thank you, sir," Beckham said quietly after dragging his sleeve across his lips.

"For what?"

"Saving my ass."

"You can stop thanking me and pay me back when my time card is punched." Flathman wagged his head. "'Ten Lives' Flathman they called me. 'The Running Man.' Pretty sure my ten lives are up, and I'm sure as shit tired of running."

Flathman pulled out his map, draped it across the couch, and motioned for Beckham to join him.

"We're on the corner of Fourth Street. This is how far we've come in three days." Flathman dragged his finger over approximately twenty blocks of the city. Then he moved his finger across the map to the outskirts of Chicago. "This is Outpost Forty-Six, aka Deadwood, aka home. It's thirty miles east of us. We have to find a vehicle to get there, otherwise this is going to take forever. And no more bank trucks."

"Yeah," Beckham agreed, recalling the last vehicle they had commandeered. The armored truck had ended up breaking down after two blocks, and the backfire had attracted a dozen infected. Flathman had had to help carry Beckham when his prosthetic leg fell off during the escape.

Beckham looked down at his prosthesis, now held together by duct tape, screws, and a makeshift brace. The damn thing sounded squeakier than a bed frame in a whorehouse and felt twice as rickety.

"That thing going to hold?" Flathman whispered as he folded up his map.

"It had better."

Flathman crouched down to check the brace.

"Looks okay, but we need to find you something for your…" Flathman's words trailed off as his eyes flitted up to Beckham's stump.

"I can still fight," Beckham said with more confidence.

"I know, Captain. Let's get moving."

They checked their weapons, loaded up their gear, and moved to the door. Flathman tightened his Cubs hat on his head and put his ear up against the wood to listen.

The lieutenant motioned for Beckham to get into position as he slowly unchained the first lock and twisted the dead bolt. Beckham wasn't sure why they had risked the noise in the first place. The chains and locks wouldn't do much to hold back the infected, and a juvenile could splinter the wood like a toothpick in seconds.

Flathman pulled open the door and strode out into the hallway with his M4 sweeping the shadows. Sunlight flooded through broken windows as they moved down the carpeted passage to the stairs. This time Beckham went first, pointing his M4's muzzle up and down to clear the stairwell. It was darker here, and the vision in his right eye continued to fail.

Would he even see a threat in the shadows?

He made his way cautiously down the stairs toward the first floor, stopping at each landing to listen. A beam groaned somewhere inside the century-old building, but there was no sign of the infected.

At the first floor, Beckham stopped to rest. He hated the fact he couldn't keep up. His entire body was swollen, and every time he pissed it felt as if he was passing a kidney stone.

Flathman waited patiently for a few minutes while Beckham took in more water and checked his prosthetic blade. When Beckham was ready to move, Flathman held up his fingers one at a time.

On three, Beckham opened the door to the lobby, and Flathman strode out to sweep for contacts. Sunlight funneled in through the missing windows, spreading over a carpet stained with brown splotches of old blood. An overturned table and couch on its back furnished the open space that reeked of mold and rot.

Flathman pointed at the skirt of glass where the double doors had been. They carefully navigated the broken shards. Vehicles covered in soot and dust littered the street outside. There were a few bodies crumpled on the sidewalk, mostly just bones and tattered clothing now.

Flathman motioned toward the sidewalk. Beckham rested his carbine on top of his stump. Even that hurt. It was also incredibly awkward. He had lost his trigger finger and knife hand.

They should have just killed me, he thought. Beckham quickly pushed the morose sentiment aside, but such thoughts had become more and more common lately. Every day it was harder to keep fighting.

He filled his lungs with clean air and pushed on.

A terrace full of trees was just around the next corner. Two birds sat on the naked branches, watching Beckham and Flathman as they crept along the metal fence.

Beckham stopped and directed his gun's suppressed muzzle toward the vehicles at the end of the road. Trash swirled by, but there wasn't a single infected in sight. The bright sun was keeping them at bay, for now.

But that didn't mean they weren't watching. Beckham looked at the rooftop above, wary of the sensation of eyes on his back. Flathman took a knee and pushed up the bill of his Cubs hat to follow Beckham's gaze. Nothing stirred along the stone ledges. Both men ran the muzzles of their weapons over the dozens of windows on each side of the street to look for the sucker faces of the infected beasts.

Seeing nothing, Beckham and Flathman continued forward. They increased their pace as they closed in on the Humvee.

Halfway down the block, another sound brought them to a halt.

The shriek of a juvenile rang out in the distance. Beckham raked his M4 from left to right, but this sound wasn't coming from the road or the buildings towering over them. It was coming from the sewer grate to his right.

Another creature answered the call, this time from inside a building to their left. Glass shattered, and the high-pitched wail of an infected followed.

Beckham froze at the sound of feet slapping the ground.

Infected and juveniles. It's a goddamn party.

Flathman jerked his head toward the Humvee, but Beckham was already running, blade squeaking like a rusty bicycle chain. The intersection where the truck was parked on the curb wasn't far, but the sound of the approaching monsters was closing in from all directions.

The whistle of a suppressed round came from the left. Flathman was firing at a pair of infected that came bounding out of a storefront. The male beasts were covered in blood from self-inflicted bite wounds covering their exposed arms and legs. They looked just as surprised as the soldiers.

To the right, an infected boy came bounding across a terrace on all fours. He leaped over the metal fence and landed on the sidewalk.

"Shoot it!" Flathman yelled.

Beckham squeezed off a burst that missed and bit into the concrete sidewalk instead. The creature roared and leaped at Beckham. He brought his gun up and fired a blast that killed the creature instantly. The body slapped the ground, infected blood pooling across the pavement. It wasn't the first time since the outbreak began that Beckham felt a stab of regret.

It's just a child, he thought, looking down at the corpse.

Three more monsters came skittering around the corner of the intersection ahead. One of them jumped to the roof of the Humvee, where it stood on two feet and let out a long wail. Behind them, more of the creatures joined in the war call. They streamed out of windows and down the exteriors of buildings, anxious for a chance to feed.

"Fire your damn weapon, Captain!" Flathman yelled. "I got our six, you take point!"

The order snapped Beckham's fatigued mind back to reality. He took a knee next to a car, placed his stump on the hood, and propped up his carbine. The first two shots whizzed past a dark-skinned beast running on two feet. The third cracked its skull, dropping the monster like a rock.

Two more took its place, and Beckham shifted the muzzle, bringing them down with shots to their vital organs. Another three infected emerged, all of them in tattered army fatigues, with helmets still atop their heads and blood dripping down their weathered features.

"Changing!" Flathman said. He was firing directly behind Beckham now, their flak jackets just inches apart.

A wave of motion flooded the intersection. Five beasts, all of them former soldiers, darted around the vehicles. The figures were blurred in Beckham's disabled right eye. He closed it and focused with his left.

"We're drawing too many of them out," Beckham said. "We have to retreat."

Flathman shouted back, "No, we have to get to the fucking Humvee!"

Rounds exploded from his M4, shattering bone and tearing through muscular flesh. Bulging veins burst and painted the street red. Beckham killed two more before his magazine went dry. He didn't have time to change the mag and drew his M9 instead. The shots popped, echoing through what had been a deserted street just moments before.

Three former soldiers dashed down the road, and two more crawled across the pavement, dragging bullet-riddled legs behind them.

Beckham shot one of the runners in the neck, ending its screeching. It took three more bullets to bring the next creature down. It fell face first, skidding over the pavement.

The other two beasts scattered. He clipped one in

the shoulder and followed the hairless head of the other creature with the iron sights of his M9. Leading it just a hair, he pulled the trigger. The shot blew its infected brains out.

His pistol clicked dry on the next squeeze. He removed the spent magazine, put the gun in his right armpit, pulled another magazine from his vest with his left hand, and pushed it home.

"Our six, our six!" Flathman yelled.

As Beckham worked on chambering a round, he turned to see what the lieutenant was screaming about. A sewer cover popped open and then clanked back down on the pavement. An armored head with saucer eyes emerged from the hole in the center of the street.

Beckham and Flathman were trapped between the enraged infected and the monster offspring of the Variants.

Beckham finally chambered a round and turned just as a creature hurtled itself into the air and body-slammed him into the car door. The impact knocked the air from his lungs, but he managed to roll away before the monster could slash his face.

A butt to the nose from Flathman's M4 dropped the thing onto its back, blood dripping out over its cheeks.

Beckham covered his eyes with a sleeve as Flathman fired a burst into the monster's chest. Despite his best efforts to keep it off, hot blood soaked Beckham's fatigues.

Flathman grabbed Beckham and yanked him upward. The first thing he saw was the pair of juveniles in the street behind them. Curved heads emerged and pointy ears perked. Almond-shaped eyes roved for targets, followed by the popping of dinner-plate-sized lips.

Armored plates clicked as the beasts moved, their massive paws clattering over the pavement like hooves.

After a quick scan, the beast on the left, which had to weigh at least four hundred pounds, rolled its head back to let out a guttural screech.

The infected creatures that had surrounded Beckham and Flathman all halted in their tracks. Yellow, slitted eyes homed in on the juveniles, and they sniffed the air like wild dogs.

For a fleeting moment, the entire street fell into silence.

Instead of attacking, the infected took off running on all fours like monkeys. One of the juveniles barreled after the retreating monsters, but the other creature snorted out a bulbous, warty nose, and focused on Beckham and Flathman.

Beckham swallowed hard, but Flathman just mumbled, "Run."

The infected scattered in all directions, fleeing the mutated monsters, and Beckham followed, stumbling away, his blade wobbling. He kept his eye on the Humvee and his ears on the pounding of hooves behind them as he attempted to run.

The juvenile chasing them was a fast son of a bitch. There was no way he was going to make it to the truck. Flathman must have had the same thought.

Gunshots cracked, but they sounded farther off than Beckham expected. He risked a glance over his shoulder to see that Flathman was still standing in the same spot. Apparently his order to run was just for Beckham.

The lieutenant stood his ground, firing his carbine at the armored monstrosity barreling toward them. Rounds chipped at its armor but did little to slow the beast down.

Flathman jumped onto the hood of a car to avoid the armored skull that smashed into the wheel well with such force it sent the vehicle careening onto the curb. Losing his balance, Flathman fell onto his back.

He kicked at the beast and fired at its unprotected eye sockets.

"Get the Humvee!" Flathman shouted at Beckham.

As he ran, Beckham wondered why the infected were fleeing the juveniles. Perhaps there was some scientific reason the beasts acted this way, something to do with the pack hierarchy, or perhaps it was just raw fear. Kate would probably be able to explain it. Either way, it didn't matter as long as they didn't turn on him.

Flathman slid off the car and onto the sidewalk as the juvenile held a clawed hand to a gushing wound on its face. The lieutenant was putting up one hell of a fight.

By the time Beckham reached the truck, his head was pounding, and his vision had started to fail in his left eye too. The infected creatures blurred into the exterior of buildings. Beckham blinked rapidly and staggered toward the front door of the Humvee. A deep pain settled behind his sinuses, burning as though he'd inhaled hot sauce.

He opened the door and yanked out the skeletal remains of the previous driver, a donut-sized hole in the top of his skull. Beckham scooted onto the seat and slammed the door shut.

He reached for the key in the ignition and twisted it until it made a coughing sound. The engine rattled but wouldn't turn over.

"Come on." His words were slurred, and when he looked out the absent window Flathman had split into three figures. The juvenile was a blob of white. He closed his right eye, but this time it didn't help.

A deep pain stabbed his gut, and his wounds were burning.

Beckham knew the symptoms all too well by now. Blurred vision, headaches...

No, no, no. You can't be infected. You can't.

He twisted the key again and again. Each time the engine would rattle but wouldn't commit.

"Please," Beckham mumbled. He wasn't a begging man, but desperation had set in. He had to get back to his family.

Kate, he thought, trying to fix her face in his mind. The image twisted aside, morphing into his mother and then a Variant.

"Beckham!" another voice called out. This time it wasn't in Beckham's mind. Flathman was screaming at the top of his lungs. "BECKHAM!"

At the other end of the street, another shape bounded onto the sidewalk outside a storefront with something hanging from its maw.

Beckham held his breath, twisted the key, and exhaled as the engine finally caught. He put the truck into gear and pulled off the curb. His vision seemed to clear momentarily, and he saw the second juvenile had returned at the other end of the road and was munching on an infected arm.

Flathman was on the move now, running like a madman. He fired the M9 at the armored creature over his shoulder. The second beast tossed its snack away and dropped to all fours to join the pursuit of the more appealing meal.

Only five hundred feet separated the Humvee and Flathman, but the juveniles were closing the gap. Both used their armor to deflect rounds as they prepared to move in for the kill.

Beckham steered with his stump and opened the passenger's door with his left hand. He locked eyes with Flathman. Now Beckham saw why his men called Flathman "The Running Man." For an old guy, he was moving like a high school track star, sprinting so fast he had to hold his Cubs hat down to keep it from blowing off.

The two juveniles galloped after him, tucking their heads down like bulls preparing to spear a matador. Streaks of red bled down Beckham's vision, nearly blinding him as he tried to drive.

You're not infected. You're not…

A hundred thoughts were racing through his mind all at once: Sergeant Tenor back at Building 8 when he was first infected—his mom in Rocky Mountain National Park the day he'd realized she wouldn't survive the cancer—Kate placing Beckham's hand on her stomach when they decided to name their child Javier Riley. The image of Kate suddenly became a nightmare as he pictured their child clawing its way out of her stomach.

"NO!" Beckham shouted. He forced his eyes open as wide as he could and focused on Flathman. The soldier was just twenty feet away, but the juveniles were so close.

Beckham grabbed the parking brake and then twisted the steering wheel. The truck fishtailed toward the monsters and Flathman, who jumped backward at the last moment.

The back end of the truck jolted from an impact that sent the two armored creatures flying backward. Beckham felt the air rush from his lungs again, the crash rattling his entire body. It snapped him completely alert, and the red vanished from his vision.

He could see again.

For now.

The juveniles clamped into balls and rolled away, screeching armor and wails so loud they hurt Beckham's ears. Flathman stood on the sidewalk, staring in shock. He reached up for his baseball cap, but it was gone.

"Get in," Beckham wheezed.

Flathman didn't follow the order. Instead, he ran to grab his hat on the sidewalk. The monsters were pushing themselves up now, stunned but recovering.

"LT!" Beckham yelled.

Flathman spat at the monsters and let out a victory whoop as he bolted around the truck and onto the passenger's seat.

"Go, go, go!" he shouted.

Beckham put the truck into reverse and pushed down on the gas pedal. When he had enough momentum, he pulled up onto the curb and back onto the street. As soon as the tires hit asphalt, he punched down on the gas, peeling out in front of the monsters.

Both men gasped for air as Beckham sped away. The creatures pursued, but their speed was no match for the Humvee's.

Flathman looked Beckham up and down, focusing on his blood-streaked face.

"You okay, Captain?"

"I...I think so," Beckham said. He watched the juveniles give up their pursuit in the rearview mirror. Then he looked over at Flathman and eyed the Cubs hat. "You risked your life for that hat."

Flathman chuckled. "It's a goddamn lucky hat, Captain. I couldn't leave without it."

Kate sat inside the cramped operations compartment aboard the USS *Florida*. Javier Riley had kicked several times over the past hour. It was as if her son could sense something happening out there and wanted to help.

She felt a large hand on her shoulder. "How are you feeling, Kate?"

Horn sat down next to her. He was chomping on something, like a horse eating hay.

"I'm fine." She patted his hand with a reassuring smile.

"Do you want anything else to eat?"

Kate shook her head. "I'm full. Those peaches really hit the spot. I think the baby is enjoying them too."

They both looked to the front of the compartment, where President Ringgold was meeting with her staff. Kate couldn't hear most of the discussion, but she did catch fragments, including something about General Nixon and Europe.

"Are Tasha and Jenny okay?" Kate asked.

"Yeah, but…"

Kate already knew the end of the sentence. "They've been asking where Uncle Reed is?"

Horn dipped his head solemnly. "Look, Kate, I *know* he's not dead. My guess is Wood's keeping him somewhere. We just need to find out where so I can bust him out and bust Wood's skull in."

"How? Wood has an army. And if—if Reed is still alive, he's somewhere we can't reach him."

She massaged the outside of her stomach. The uncertainty was the worst part. It was slowly driving her crazy, but she had to remain strong for Javier Riley, for Jan, and for all of the other survivors she had worked tirelessly to save.

"Doctor Lovato, can we speak with you?"

Kate and Horn both stood as President Ringgold walked over. Soprano, Nelson, and several submarine officers joined her.

"This is Captain Steve Konkoly," Ringgold said.

A man with brown eyes and close-cut, graying hair extended a hand. "It's an honor to meet you, Doctor. Your work has helped save the world."

"The world is far from saved," Kate replied, shaking

his hand. "Wood has single-handedly destroyed everything we've fought for. We have to find the *GW* and the *Zumwalt* and then stop Wood before he can deploy more of those missiles."

Konkoly nodded brusquely. "Trust me when I say Wood will pay for what he's done. As you know, the USS *Florida* was assigned to the *GW* strike group. It didn't take long for us to determine Wood was behind the attack on the *GW* and the SZTs despite the counter-information campaign. The problem is convincing others of that fact. We decided to dive until we could figure out who our allies—"

Ringgold interrupted him. "We still don't know who's on our side?"

"Those loyal to you have formed a fleet and are preparing to take a stand against ROT. We're heading to their location now. It's about two hundred miles east of here."

"What about General Nixon? Has he sent any ships from Europe?" Kate asked.

"No, so far he's remained neutral," Konkoly said. He gestured for them to follow him into another compartment. "I want you to listen to something we intercepted."

They walked out of the main control room and into the radio room, where several officers were listening to headsets.

"This was from two days ago," Konkoly said. He nodded at the comms officer, who reached forward to relay a transmission over the speakers. A voice that Kate hated crackled from the speakers.

"General, this is Lieutenant Andrew Wood of ROT. I hear the war efforts in Europe aren't going too well."

"Sounds as if things back home aren't going too well either," Nixon replied.

There was a mirthless laugh over the comms that made her skin crawl.

"That depends on you who you ask. President Ringgold has decided to wage war on the SZTs that don't support her. It's my duty as a retired soldier to take up the work of my late brother and help lead the effort to bring her down and restore order to the republic."

There was another pause before Nixon's rough voice replied, "I'm here to win a war, so I'm going to focus on that until the commander-in-chief tells me otherwise. So far, I haven't heard from President Ringgold, and I will remain neutral until I do. But I have a very hard time believing she would attack our own SZTs."

"Then you would be wrong, General. When the time comes, you should pick your side *very* carefully," Wood replied.

The transmission ended, and Konkoly looked at Ringgold with a raised brow. "That man is a bigger weasel than his older brother."

"I know," Ringgold replied. She sighed. "He must have thought I would reach out to Nixon. That's why he tried to trap me in the PEOC. It was the perfect plan."

"Until you escaped," Nelson said.

Soprano wedged his way closer to the president. "He figured Nixon would rally to our cause, so he attacked the PEOC and made it look as if you attacked those SZTs."

"But it sounds as if Nixon doesn't buy that lie," Konkoly said. "Maybe now is the time to contact him."

Ringgold looked to Kate for her opinion. She didn't hesitate in giving it.

"Like I said, finding the *GW* and the *Zumwalt* should be our primary objective. We have to destroy the hemorrhage virus. We can't let Wood infect any more safe zones."

"We know where the *GW* is," Konkoly said.

Ringgold turned to the captain. "How far?"

"It's in the harbor near Pensacola Beach in Florida, not far from Fort Pickens. The carrier hasn't moved for several days. We intercepted an encrypted SOS transmission when they were attacked."

"And Wood hasn't launched any more attacks on SZTs?" Ringgold asked.

Konkoly shook his head. "Why would he kill more people and risk getting caught? He's already got half the SZTs on his side."

"So why are we headed east to meet up with these other ships if the *GW* is west of us?" Kate asked. "We have to go finish it off, just in case you're wrong about Wood."

"The *GW* isn't going anywhere," Konkoly said. "Right now, my focus is on getting President Ringgold to safety, where we can protect her, and getting you to the French research vessel that has anchored with our allies. The monsters in Europe are continuing to evolve, and the scientists on board the *Thalassa* need your help."

Kate looked at Horn, who shrugged back at her.

"So we're just going to run away and leave the *GW* in Wood's grasp?" Kate huffed. She wanted to also scream about leaving Beckham behind but feared it would come off as too biased.

"Madam President, with all due respect, I think this is a bad idea," Kate continued. "We should finish off the *GW* before rendezvousing with your allies."

Ringgold directed her gaze toward Konkoly and said, "Captain, are you sure the *GW* has been disabled?"

"I listened to the transmission myself. Someone blew a hole in the side of the ship, and ROT ordered it abandoned."

"It must have been Captain Davis," Ringgold said. "I sure hope she made it out of there."

Kate suddenly felt guilty for her comments. Rachel Davis was a friend, and she was trapped out there in an awful situation.

Ringgold glanced at Kate. "I'm sorry, Kate, but I'm going with Konkoly's advice on this one. We head east to regroup with this fleet and come up with a plan."

"Aye-aye," Konkoly said. He turned to talk to Lieutenant Commander Bonner, his second in command. Both men left the room, still deep in discussion. Kate had begun to follow them out when the president called out for her. Ringgold gestured her into a corner where they could talk privately.

"I know you've done everything you can to save our species, Kate, but we need you again." Ringgold held up a hand before she could reply. "I know working with the French team in the middle of the ocean isn't ideal—"

"I've done this kind of thing before, and I'll do it again," Kate said, trying to smile. "It's just that with Pat gone and Reed missing...it's tough. But don't worry."

"Worrying is all I've been doing lately. But we've been given a second chance. I'm not going to waste it, and I'm certainly not going to underestimate my enemy ever again. I promise you that."

A commotion sounded from outside the compartment. Konkoly ducked back through the open door and motioned for Ringgold.

"You better see this, ma'am," he said.

He ushered them to the radar compartment. A female officer was sitting in front of the equipment. She twisted in her chair to look at Captain Konkoly.

"We're picking up multiple contacts. Looks like a squadron of aircraft bearing down on our location."

Konkoly pushed his headset to his lips. "Bonner, emergency deep!"

He watched the blips on the screen with his arms folded across his chest for several seconds before stepping away and looking at Ringgold and Kate in turn.

"Better follow me," Konkoly said. "Things may get a bit rough in a few minutes."

4

Captain Davis and Lance Corporal Diaz had been playing hide-and-seek with the infected for the past three days. One head shot at a time, they were slowly eradicating the monsters that had taken over the *GW* from the walls of Fort Pickens.

"Maybe we should have tried to get back to the truck," Davis whispered, her resolve faltering. Even if they managed to clear her ship, it was possible that the radios had been damaged in the explosion.

Or maybe there's no one out there left to listen, she thought.

Diaz, her face covered in mud, shook her head. "Negative, Captain. This is the *only* way."

Davis scratched a bug bite on her head. Three days of fighting and sleeping in the dirt had her second-guessing her initial orders. She was starving, itchy, and dehydrated—all the more reason to get back on the ship as soon as possible.

"Okay, you know the drill," she whispered.

"Yup," Diaz said, grinning. Davis almost laughed. They were both covered head to toe in filth; between that and their roughly chopped hair, they looked savage.

Davis raised the Remington MK21 precision sniper

rifle she had plucked off a dead ROT soldier, while Diaz grabbed her M4 and the bag of grenades. They parted ways to take up separate sniping positions on the walls of Fort Pickens. The nests provided a 360-degree vantage of the entire area. No one was going to sneak up on them out here.

The late-afternoon sun beat down on Davis with a vengeance. She wiped at her forehead, but that only provided momentary relief. Every inch of her skin itched and burned. At this point, she would have cheerfully murdered a whole army of infected former ROT soldiers if they stood between her and a cool shower. She set up her bipod on the top of the ledge that provided her a view of the beach below.

Dozens of corpses littered the sand, some of them ROT soldiers, others *GW* sailors. Carmine blood stained the formerly pristine beach.

Davis zoomed in on the deck. There were bodies there too, just above the massive crater where Lance Corporal Black had sacrificed his life. It was amazing the ship wasn't rusting on the bottom of the bay, but the blast had occurred just above the waterline. If it had taken on any water, those compartments must have been sealed off before the virus infected the sailors and ROT soldiers aboard.

One of the infected stared back at her from the hole, yellow eyes blinking, before retreating inside the vessel. The beasts were seeking refuge inside the *GW* like a turtle hiding in its shell.

It was time to draw them out.

Diaz ran across the lawn below with a pair of grenades in each hand. She worked her way to the edge of the beach, where she stopped to pluck the pin from one of them. She tossed it through the air like an outfielder throwing a baseball to the catcher at home plate. After lobbing the second one, Diaz turned back to run for her sniping location.

The explosions rocked the water, sending geysers into the sky. Davis pushed the butt of the rifle against her arm and settled the cross hairs on the deck. It wouldn't be long now.

A pair of seagulls took off for deeper waters, traversing the skyline. The birds knew what was about to happen.

Davis resisted the urge to scratch her itchy forehead and kept her eye behind the scope of her rifle. Nothing moved on the deck or in the gaping hole in the side of her ship.

There wasn't even a single screech.

Davis lowered the rifle and shielded her eyes from the sun to look at Diaz, who was standing on the tower to the right. The lance corporal shrugged and then directed her M4 back at the ship.

Are they really smart enough to know what we're doing? Davis wondered.

It was a fair question, but she decided there had to be another explanation. Perhaps it was the sun, or perhaps...

She mumbled a curse. If there were juveniles in the area, the infected beasts wouldn't show their faces. That had to be it, she decided.

Davis motioned for Diaz to join her. They had only seen one of the juveniles over the past few days, but that didn't mean they weren't out here. Black had spotted an entire field of them on the drive to the fort.

Davis scoped the ship again while she waited for Diaz. She centered the M4's muzzle on the crater. Ribbons of twisted metal protruded from the blast site like the maw of a Variant.

The beast she had seen earlier scrambled back into

view. Two more sets of yellow eyes emerged from the darkness. She zoomed in on the beasts, who cautiously sniffed the air for prey but did not leave the ship.

She felt a hand on her shoulder and whispered, "Watch our six, Diaz. I've got an idea."

If the bastards weren't going to come out to play, she was going to do this the old-fashioned way. Davis chambered a round with a click, lined up the sights on the first beast, and pulled the trigger. The round found a target, severing an arm at the elbow. The injured creature raised its gushing stump and stared for a moment before clamping its bulging lips around the wound to suck down its own blood.

Shots two and three hit one of her former sailors. She held her breath as the creature fell out of the opening and plummeted toward the water. A jagged piece of metal impaled it through the gut. The creature squirmed like a minnow on a hook.

Davis felt her courage flood away as she focused the scope on the monstrous face that had once belonged to Paul Conway, the chief engineer of the *GW*. He was one of the nicest and most gentle men she'd ever met in her life.

They aren't your friends anymore, Rachel. That's not Paul. That's a monster.

"I'm sorry," Davis whispered. She lined up her sights and ended the creature's suffering with a round to the skull.

More infected scrambled onto the deck of the *GW*, a dozen emerging from between the aircraft. In moments, the dozen had turned into twenty. Ten more skittered up the side of the ship.

Davis focused on the former ROT soldiers first. She shot one that was perched on the wing of an F-18 Super Hornet. Two more lost their grip on the side of the ship as rounds lanced into their backs. They thrashed in the water, and she didn't waste ammo on the drowning beasts.

Diaz crouched next to her and lifted her M4. "Our six is clear, ma'am. Want some help?"

Davis nodded. "But just kill the ROT bastards," she replied. "I'll take care of the sailors."

"Are you sure?" Diaz asked.

"It's my responsibility as captain."

Diaz pushed the scope of her gun to her eye and fired on a target. Side by side, they slowly thinned the pack of infected. Each shot that killed one of her former crew members took a piece of Davis's tattered soul. She wasn't sure how many pieces she had left.

It was going to be a long, painful day, but by nightfall, they would be ready to board their ship and see if the comms were still working. In the end, all that mattered was her duty and her mission. As long as Davis had that to hang on to, she could hold it together.

Quick and steady, Rachel.

Lining up another target, she pulled the trigger.

Piero smacked the side of the radio. The sound echoed inside the stuffy vault. He and Ringo were sealed inside a nearly airtight room about a block from the Colosseum. The stuffy space wasn't just hot and cramped—it was blocking the radio signal. He wasn't worried about the Variants hearing him down here, he was worried about reaching his contact at the EUF.

"This is Sergeant Piero Angaran of the Fourth Alpini Parachutist Regiment, calling Lieutenant Jorge Fortes. Do you copy? Over."

Static buzzed from the speakers. Either the signal

was too weak or something had happened to the EUF base in Barcelona.

He batted his head against the wall, frustrated. Ringo scampered over and pushed its tiny nose against Piero's hand as if to say, *Don't do that, friend.*

"I know, but I'm mad," Piero whispered. He waited a few minutes and then scanned through the other channels. He picked a different frequency and repeated his message, adding in English, "I'm holed up a block east of the Colosseum in Rome, requesting..."

A response crackled back.

Piero looked at the radio in his hand as if he couldn't trust his ears. He stood and held it toward the ceiling, hoping for a better signal.

A voice speaking English surged over the channel. "Sergeant Angaran..." Static. "This is Corporal Dominique Zales with EUF HQ in Paris."

"Copy that, Corporal. I was starting to think I wasn't going to hear from anyone again."

"Things are chaotic," Zales said. "We've taken heavy losses recently."

Piero looked down at Ringo. The mouse perked its ears and tilted its small head.

"My contact, Lieutenant Jorge Fortes at the EUF base in Barcelona, said things were going well," Piero said.

There was a pause, and then: "I doubt he would say that now. That base fell to the Variants yesterday."

Piero bowed his head at the news. Another fallen friend.

"I'll serve as your new EUF contact," Zales said. "It will be my honor, Sergeant. You're practically a legend. They call you the Italian Stallion."

"Hah!" Piero said, a bit too loudly. The smile felt unnatural on his face, and his lips quivered. "I'm not a legend. I'm a survivor."

"The *only* survivor in Rome, that we know of. What I'm about to tell you is of the utmost importance."

Piero waited in silence.

"The radioactive dirty bombs that we dropped on highly concentrated pockets of the juveniles are having the opposite effect from what we hoped. The creatures are going to be more dangerous than ever."

"I know," Piero replied. "I've seen it with my own eyes. They are turning into something like insects. I came across what looked like a beetle, and I've also seen the winged demons."

There was another pause, longer this time. "One moment, Sergeant—I've got someone else here who wants to talk to you."

A different voice came online, speaking in Italian this time. "Sergeant Angaran, this is Lieutenant General Christoforo Piazza. It's great to hear you're still alive, son."

Piero sat up straighter. He knew Piazza—not personally, but everyone in the Italian military knew the war hero. "Hello, sir. Thank you."

"I've been relocated to Paris," Piazza continued. "We've got a new mission for you. Those monsters have Central Command on edge. They need to know more about them if we are to have any hope of taking Europe back. The problem is we don't have many people in the field."

Reconnaissance, Piero thought, not surprised.

"The Beetles you spoke of have armor like tanks, and another variation, the Wormers, can tunnel. They work together, although we're not sure exactly how yet. No place is safe, Sergeant. The only hope is to stay on the move," Piazza said.

Piero reached for Ringo and nudged the mouse. It had dozed off and looked up with exhausted eyes. "Time to get up, little friend," he whispered.

"Understood, sir," Piero said into the receiver. "I'll move as soon as I receive my new orders."

"The orders are simple: Send us any and all intel on these new monsters in Rome. And stay alive. You're the only one there, son. It's up to you. I understand what I'm asking you to do is dangerous, but you have proven you can survive."

"I won't let you down, sir. I will report back anything I can learn about these demons. You have my word." Piero thought of the Wormers and the other types of monsters that were out there, some of which he'd never even seen. The images gave him a quick chill, but he remained confident and upbeat, thrilled to be talking to Lieutenant General Christoforo Piazza.

"Good luck, Sergeant. When this is all over, I'll make sure you get the recognition you deserve."

Piero smiled again, his mouth watering at the thought of what he really wanted. "Sir, I'll settle for some carbonara and a bottle of pinot noir. And some cheese for my friend."

Piazza chuckled a little uneasily. "Son, if you make it through this, I'll make sure you get it. But who is your friend?"

"You still have blood in your hair," Rico said.

Fitz raised the small mirror for a better look. His freshly shaved face was smooth and clean, but he couldn't seem to get the sticky Reaver blood out of his hair. He had never been any good at science but he knew that meant the Reavers had high concentrations of glucose in their blood. Some scientist in a bunker somewhere was probably studying the reason behind it right now. Maybe even Kate...

He missed his friends—missed them so badly it hurt like the dull pain of a headache. If it weren't for Apollo, Fitz would have been worried about relapsing into the depression and pain of PTSD. Having the dog by his side had kept the darkness at bay for a while.

But that darkness had suddenly returned like a wave with the news of Andrew Wood. There hadn't been much time to contemplate what it meant before the Reaver attack, but now that it was over, Fitz couldn't stop thinking about Wood's effort to bring down President Ringgold.

He picked a ribbon of dried blood out of his shaggy hair and lowered the mirror.

"You okay, Fitzie?" Rico asked. She sat on the cot across from him, cleaning her M4.

Dohi, chewing on a piece of licorice, eyed Fitz with a flat expression that nevertheless missed nothing, and even Tanaka looked up from sharpening his precious blades.

"I'm just exhausted," Fitz lied.

Dohi stopped chewing. "You're a terrible liar."

"Yeah, I know."

"'Cause he's a Southern gentleman," Rico said, swatting him playfully on the arm.

Fitz took a swig of water and looked at his watch. "Shit, we need to move. We should stop at the medical tent and see Stevenson before our mission briefing."

Team Ghost stood and followed him out of the barracks, keeping quiet as they passed beds of men and women trying to snag a few minutes of shut-eye. Outside, a Humvee rumbled past. The soldier in the turret focused the barrel of the vehicle's M240 on the sky, half of his face covered in a yellowing bandage.

Team Ghost walked together in silence. Even Rico was unusually quiet. Apollo trotted in front, tail wagging every time Fitz reached down to pat his head. The dog was the only one of them who seemed to be in good spirits.

Each soldier they passed wore the same solemn mask. Morale had tanked further after the Reaver attack. The Twenty-Fourth MEU had arrived in Normandy with a sense of excitement and pride, ready to help their European allies fight against monsters as their grandfathers had done during World War II, but the past week had been one loss after another.

Poor morale wasn't the only issue. Virtually everyone had an injury of some kind. Crews were still cleaning up the battle zone and trying to salvage what weapons they could. Bulldozers pushed the winged abominations into the ditches, and the soldiers who could still fight were back to the trenches, where they watched the sky.

Those who weren't on detail were preparing for the next stage of Operation Reach—the stage that would send the allied forces on a march east of Paris to reclaim the once great cities of Europe. Rome had fallen. Moscow had fallen. Berlin had fallen. Barcelona had fallen. Fitz wondered if there was anything left out there worth saving.

He steeled himself as they walked toward the medical tent. A macabre chorus of pained voices drifted out of the open flaps. A nurse ducked through the opening with a bucket in hand. Bloody water sloshed over the sides as she waddled to a ditch on the left side of the tent and tossed the contents in.

Fitz could smell festering wounds as he approached. Nothing could prepare a man for the inside of a medical tent after an attack by the Variants, but at least this time there were no injuries from the toxic juvenile acid. Beckham was lucky to have survived his wounds. Most men died in agony.

Like Michel, Fitz thought, remembering the brave boy who'd died in his arms outside the basilica.

Team Ghost stopped outside while Fitz walked toward the tent. Apollo attempted to follow.

"Stay here," Fitz ordered.

Rico took a seat on a barrel and checked the brace on her leg while Dohi and Tanaka folded their arms across their chests. Apollo sat on his hind legs, eyes following Fitz.

He held his breath and bent down under the open flaps. The long tent was about thirty beds deep, and the lack of airflow made the heat and smell almost unbearable. Flies buzzed through the air, one of them landing on his cheek. After brushing it away, he brought his bandanna up to his nose and held it there. Some of the injured soldiers squirmed and moaned in pain, others had already passed out from it. Each body he saw had suffered terrible lacerations. One man had a bandage covering his face, two circular bloodstains marking where his eyes should have been.

But he was alive, which was more than could be said for the fifty marines and soldiers who had lost their lives during the attack.

Fitz pushed on, wedging his way through the narrow aisle, past nurses and doctors working on patients. He looked for Stevenson's dark skin and saw the man sitting at the edge of his bed, wide shoulders hunched as he helped a nurse tie a bandage around an injured woman's leg.

As he approached Stevenson, Fitz saw Sergeant Allan Bird, a marine who had served with his brother overseas. He stepped up to the nurse who was working on Bird. The sergeant was unconscious, his chest slowly rising up and down.

"Is he going to make it?" Fitz asked.

"Not sure," the nurse whispered. "He's in septic shock. Those Reaver claws are covered with bacteria."

Fitz swallowed hard when he saw Bird's leg, or what was left of it. "Did the Reavers do that?"

"Friendly fire," she said, shaking her head. "It was chaos out there."

Fitz closed his eyes. His brother had been killed by friendly fire. He said a prayer for Bird and then walked over to Stevenson.

The hulking marine turned when Fitz put a hand on his shoulder.

"Master Sergeant, what are you doing here?"

"Checking on you," Fitz said. "How are you feeling?"

"I'm good. Doc says I have a concussion, but I'll be fit for service in a few days."

Fitz glanced at the woman in the bed to their right. Her short-cropped red hair, freckled nose, and determined gaze reminded him of Meg Pratt, the firefighter he hadn't been able to save.

"Master Sergeant?" Stevenson asked.

Fitz forced himself to look away from the woman and took a moment to scrutinize Stevenson. "You're sure you're good?"

"Yeah..." His words trailed off as realization settled over his dark eyes. "We're going back out there again, aren't we?"

"Yes, and we don't have any extra days to recuperate. Colonel Bradley has another mission for Team Ghost. We're headed to the command tent now."

Stevenson stood and grimaced. "I had a feeling. I'll get my shit together and meet you there in a few minutes."

Fitz looked at the red-haired woman again before he left. Her eyes were closed now, but she was breathing steadily. Surrounded by wounded warriors, he walked with his head down, saying prayers for each of them. There was nothing he could do for anyone here anymore. His mission was to keep soldiers out of these beds.

The other members of Team Ghost were chatting outside in hushed voices. They all looked at him. Apollo stood, tail wagging.

"Stevenson's meeting us at the briefing tent," Fitz said. He didn't wait for questions and jogged down the dirt road. A Humvee drove past, the armored sides dented and stained red from the Reaver skulls that had plowed into them.

Bradley was smoking a cigarette outside the command tent. He had his good eye turned in the opposite direction, and Fitz cleared his throat as he approached.

"Colonel, Team Ghost, reporting for duty," he said.

"About time," Bradley said. He tossed the cigarette in the dirt and smothered it with his boot. The lance corporals guarding the tent opened the flaps for everyone to pass through. Inside, they all took seats around a metal table.

Major Domino was already seated in front of a pile of maps. He scowled when he saw Apollo.

"Who invited the dog?" Domino asked.

"Stow your shit, Major," Bradley said. "Apollo is just as much as part of this team as anyone."

Fitz held back a smile. He was really starting to like the colonel.

"This all of you?" Bradley asked.

"We're just waiting on Sergeant Stevenson—should only be a few minutes," Fitz said.

"He's back on his feet?" Bradley asked. "Good to hear. You're going to need everyone where I'm sending you."

Rico caught Fitz's gaze. She blew a bubble that popped, covering her mouth and part of her chin, and then slowly plucked it away, her cheeks flaring red when Bradley looked at her.

"Sorry, sir," she said quietly.

Bradley palmed the table, shaking his head at Rico, and studied the maps with Domino. They spoke in whispers about the resources the Twenty-Fourth MEU still had at their disposal. From the sound of it, the expeditionary unit was in worse shape than Fitz had thought. Despite the news, his mind still locked onto Andrew Wood.

"Colonel, sir?" Fitz said.

Bradley glanced up with his single eye. "Yes?"

"I was wondering if I could ask a few questions about what's going on back in the States," Fitz said.

Bradley shifted his brows upward, a cue for Fitz to go ahead.

Fitz licked his lips. "Do you have any more intel on what's going on with this Lieutenant Andrew Wood?"

Bradley clasped his hands behind his back. "Why are you so curious about Lieutenant Wood?"

Fitz considered his next words carefully, but Rico beat him to it.

"Fitz blew his brother's head off," she said.

Fitz and Bradley both glared at her.

"Sorry," she said, then added defiantly, "but it's true."

Bradley snorted. "I do remember hearing about how that went down from Captain Beckham, but he didn't mention that you were the one who pulled the trigger."

"If Andrew Wood is anything like his brother, then he's going to be out for revenge," Fitz said. "I'm worried about Captain Beckham and my other friends back home, sir."

"Well, you better get your head out of the shitter, because there's nothing you can do to help them," Bradley said. "You're in Europe now, and Captain Beckham can take care of himself."

The other members of Team Ghost all looked at Fitz, but he said nothing.

"You let General Nixon worry about what's going on back home, Master Sergeant," Bradley said. "Until we're told otherwise, our focus is winning the war here."

"Yes, sir," Fitz said after a split second of hesitation.

The tent flaps opened, letting in the bulky frame of Stevenson.

"Welcome back to action," Bradley said. "Have a seat and we'll get started."

Stevenson lumbered over and pulled out a chair. He was moving slower than normal, but at least he was back on his feet.

Bradley drew in an audible breath and said, "Brass has been shitting their pants about the radioactive bombs we dropped during the first stage of Operation Reach. Long story short, the radiation is causing the Variants to mutate in some pretty horrifying ways. But you already know that because you saw it firsthand. The monsters you encountered at the Basilica of St. Thérèse were the result of leaked radiation from the nuclear power plants that the French government blew up."

"So we just made it worse by dropping more dirty bombs?" Rico asked.

"Unfortunately, yes," Bradley said. "Our orders are to figure out where that army of creatures is now." He pointed at a regional park on the map called the Parc naturel régional du Perche. "This is where we dropped the majority of the bombs."

"The Ombre leader said something about that place," Fitz said.

Bradley tilted his head. "What's that?"

"She said if there's one area to avoid, it's that place. She said we should set the forest on fire," Rico replied.

"We did," Bradley said. "We bombed the shit out of that entire area. But much of the mutated army seems to have survived. Our drones and fighter jets have only been able to find about ten percent of the original army."

"We don't know how accurate those numbers are,

though." Domino leaned over the map. "EUF Command hasn't been able to get a single recon unit on the ground within twenty miles in any direction. It's a complete dead zone."

After a short pause, Bradley said what everyone already knew was coming.

"Your mission is to find that Variant army and relay its coordinates. General Nixon has a limited supply of bombs and missiles, so we need to make the next run count."

"You won't have air support after we drop you off," Domino said. "Once you slip behind enemy lines, you're on your own until you complete the mission."

"We have reinforced your MATV, though," Bradley said. "You've got enough armor to protect you from the juvenile acid."

"That's reassuring," Stevenson said.

Dohi stroked his silver goatee. Tanaka shot Fitz an anxious glance.

"In the meantime, the second phase of Operation Reach is on hold," Domino said.

"And the EUF? What are they doing?" Stevenson asked. "I still have yet to see one of their uniforms in France."

"What are they doing?" Bradley said incredulously, his eye bulging. "They're trying to survive, Sergeant, just like us. They just lost the HQ in Barcelona, and the HQ in Paris is being hit every hour by Reavers and Wormers. I'm not sure how much longer they can hold out."

"You can count on Team Ghost," Fitz said, standing and saluting before Stevenson could get them in any more trouble. Apollo stood and wagged his tail as if saluting as well.

The other members of Ghost stood at attention.

Bradley shifted his gaze from Stevenson and nodded at Fitz.

"I know I can count on you, son. That's why I'm sending you out there. Now go get your shit ready. Team Ghost moves out in four hours."

Apollo's tail stopped wagging, and the dog looked up at Fitz with anxious amber eyes.

Fitz started to say everything would be okay, but he paused to reconsider his words. Lying to Apollo felt like lying to himself. "Come on, boy, let's go."

5

Captain Reed Beckham was, as ever, a lucky man. His splitting headache and blurred vision hadn't been the early stages of the hemorrhage virus after all but rather a slight concussion. For now, his humanity was still intact.

He stood sentry on the street while Flathman worked on putting fuel in the Humvee's tank. They had run out of fuel about five miles west of Outpost 46, leaving them exposed in an old industrial area.

Gray rain clouds blocked out the sun, and the steady drizzle of rain saturated Beckham's fatigues. It was the closest thing to a shower he'd had in days, but it did little to wash away the sticky sweat and blood.

Dozens of warehouses and other buildings in disrepair hugged the road. Sagging roofs, broken brick veneer, and shattered windows provided possible dens for Variants.

Beckham scanned the area with his rifle for hostile contacts.

"Hurry up, LT," he whispered.

"Almost finished," Flathman replied. He was using a funnel to pour the diesel into the tank, careful not to spill a drop. Beckham went back to checking the rooftops. He hoped the infected hadn't made it this far from

SZT 15, but that didn't mean there weren't juveniles or adult Variants in the area. Scientists had calculated that around 5 percent of the monsters would have survived the radiation attacks by going underground after Operation Extinction.

"Got it. Let's go," Flathman said. He set the empty canister back inside the vehicle and then climbed into the front seat. It took three tries before the truck started, but as soon as it did, he pushed the gas pedal down and jerked back onto the road.

A cloud the color of a Variant's eyes passed overhead. Beckham chased down some pain meds with the last of his water. Between the pain of his pulsing headache and the fatigue aching his bones, he was having a hard time concentrating.

"Hope there's water at the outpost," Beckham said. "I'm out."

"I still have a bit, and we have a well at the post, so don't worry." Flathman pointed at a canopy of oak trees in the distance. "I'm going to park about a quarter mile away. We'll use the forest to trek in on the west side of the outpost, to make sure it's clear."

Beckham pulled out the partially spent magazine in his M4 and exchanged it for a full one. "You sure there isn't anyone left there?"

"All my men are dead."

There was a fleeting moment of silence that didn't feel right. They were both too tense, too tired. Beckham and Flathman both had stories to tell, and this seemed like a good time to tell them, if for no other reason than to keep them both awake and alert.

"Before the outbreak, I'd never lost a man under my command," Beckham started. "Since Building Eight, I've lost all but one of the original members of Team Ghost."

Flathman took one hand off the steering wheel and pulled out his flask from his vest pocket.

"I had a good thing going here," Flathman said. "We held this post for months. Now my boys are all gone, and I've got nothing left but this."

He held up the flask and shook it. The liquid sloshed inside, and Flathman drained it in one pull. "I've got vodka hidden back at the base. It ain't whiskey, but it'll do. Tonight, we drink to our fallen brothers."

It wouldn't be the first time Beckham had toasted the memory of his men. It seemed like just yesterday he was sharing a bottle of Jameson with Riley and Horn after the massacre at Building 8. He prayed that Horn was still out there somewhere, keeping an eye on Kate and the girls.

Flathman pulled down another road that curved through a city block of warehouses. Train tracks divided the end of the street. He took a right at the next intersection to take the back way to the woods. He eased off the gas and stopped around the next corner, where the road was blocked by a semitrailer.

"That wasn't here a few days ago," Flathman said.

Beckham bent down to check the three-story buildings on both sides of the road. This time he wasn't as worried about a juvenile staring back at him as he was worried about an ROT sniper.

"Move it, LT," Beckham said. He twisted in his seat to look at the road to the west.

Flathman performed a U-turn and sped away from the roadblock. He hung a right at the next street, which took them over the railroad. The tires thumped over the tracks.

"I got a bad feeling about this," Flathman said. He pulled down another street and slowed as they approached a four-story brick building built around the turn of the twentieth century. Vines snaked up the side, twisting around windowsills framing shattered glass.

"Why are we stopping?" Beckham asked.

Flathman's eyes were focused on the rooftop. "I just remembered this place. Used to have a guard stationed here at all times because of the vantage. Something tells me someone's taken up residence at my former outpost, and I want to have a look."

He parked outside the building and opened the door.

"As long as it's quick," Beckham said. His blade creaked as he stepped onto the concrete, piercing the afternoon quiet.

Flathman bent the bill of his Cubs hat and stuffed it back on his head. He flashed a hand signal toward an old fire ladder on the side of the building, directly over a pair of Dumpsters. When they got to the ladder, Flathman glanced at Beckham's blade.

"You're going to sound like a wind chime in a tornado on this rusty piece of shit. You stay here and watch the truck. I'll take a look," Flathman said.

Beckham eyed the rusted metal rungs and decided not to argue. He put his sleeve to his nostrils to hold back the putrid rot drifting from the Dumpsters. The smell didn't seem to bother Flathman. He scrambled up the side and reached for the ladder. The screech of rusty metal sounded as he pulled it down into position.

"And I'm the one who makes too much noise?" Beckham muttered under his breath. He walked back to the Humvee and held guard while Flathman climbed. It took the lieutenant several minutes to get to the top, but when he did, he gave a thumbs-up and then vanished.

Beckham flicked the safety off on his M4. He rested the gun on his swollen stump of a forearm and kept the barrel trained on the road. A bug buzzed from the shadows cast by the building, and a crow cawed in the distance, but besides that, the industrial zone was devoid of noise.

The trees growing on the shoulder of the road hardly moved in the weak breeze. A single brown leaf fluttered to the ground.

Beckham checked the building across the street. Shattered pieces of glass lined the windows like the teeth of a Variant. Nothing moved in the dark rooms.

He raised the carbine and scoped the intersection at the other end of the road. There was only a single vehicle there. All four tires on the pickup truck were deflated, and a skeletal body hung out the open door.

The rain increased, splattering the street and funneling into a sewer grate. Beckham took a few steps away from the Humvee and pivoted to look at the other side of the road. That was when he noticed the insects and birds had all gone silent.

He stood there in the eerie quiet, listening for anything besides his own breathing. Between his damaged vision and hearing, he was starting to feel like a blind, deaf dog. For a Delta operator, it was beyond frustrating—it was humiliating.

A low thumping broke the silence. Beckham slowly turned to locate the noise and recognized the drone of helicopter rotors.

Flathman's baseball hat suddenly emerged over the edge of the roof. He slung his rifle over his back and started climbing down. Halfway down the ladder, he put his boots out on the sides and slid down to the ground.

He pointed at the Dumpsters. "We have to hide, Captain."

Ah, hell no, Beckham thought. The brain-rattling *whomp whomp* of the rotors grew closer, so close it was as if the bird was right overhead.

Flathman dove into the first Dumpster. Holding his breath, Beckham climbed in right after Flathman, who pushed Beckham down into the mound of trash as the chopper passed over the building. They waited in the stink for several terrible seconds before finally getting up to peek out over the side.

A Black Hawk traversed the skyline, lights blinking as it moved higher into the gray sky.

"Who the fuck is that?" Beckham asked.

"Who do you think?" Flathman replied. "It's ROT. Bastards were at my outpost."

Beckham nearly choked on the putrid scent of trash as he watched the helicopter. "Did they see you?"

"I don't think so." Flathman's voice was confident, and Beckham kept his mouth closed, not interested in arguing with the lieutenant anymore. Whatever was in the Dumpster smelled like stagnant swamp water. His blade sank into something that had the consistency of bony salmon, both horribly soft and crunchy at the same time.

He moved his blade to see the decayed corpse of a Variant, bulging sucker lips deflated like the tires of the pickup on the road. A pair of hollow eye sockets stared up, the yellow eyes gone.

"Aw, shit," Flathman said. "I forgot about those."

"Forgot?"

"My men helped clean this street of dead Variants after Kryptonite killed most of them. They don't half stink, do they?"

As soon as the thump of the chopper had faded away, Beckham climbed out of the Dumpster. He exhaled a long breath and then heaved up what was left of his lunch.

Flathman dragged his boots on the concrete, leaving behind a blackened paste.

"What do we do now?" Beckham asked, wiping off his mouth.

"Go to the outpost and see if ROT left anything behind." Flathman pulled off his Cubs hat and examined the fabric. "Goddamnit, I got shit all over it."

"LT, stop worrying about that damn hat. Are you sure the outpost is empty now?" Part of Beckham was hoping there were a few ROT soldiers left behind to kill, but the mission right now was to find a radio and supplies, not seek revenge. That would come later.

"No, but what other option do we have?"

Beckham nodded. "Then let's get our asses moving."

They climbed into the Humvee, but Flathman hesitated before starting the engine, narrowing his eyes at the windshield.

"What?" Beckham asked.

Flathman asked the question Beckham had also been wondering about.

"Why the hell would ROT pack up and leave right now? Do they know something we don't?"

Pregnant during the apocalypse: It wasn't exactly the way Kate had planned things. In fact, she had never thought she would be a mother at all.

She stirred in the cramped bunk. The jets searching for them had given up, but no matter which way she positioned her body, she couldn't get comfortable. Javier Riley did not want to sleep.

She couldn't sleep either, what with the rattle of Big Horn snoring in the bunk above her. He sounded like a pit bull having a bad dream. His muscular arm hung over the bunk, twitching in the darkness.

The snoring didn't seem to bother his daughters. Tasha and Jenny were curled up together in the bunk across from Kate. Both of them were exhausted from being on the run for so long.

Kate was still trying to grasp everything that had happened. After settling into their new home on Plum

Island, she had thought they would all be safe—that they would have a chance to start over.

Now she was on a submarine heading for a fleet of ships in the middle of the Atlantic Ocean, and once again people were assuring her that she would be safe. There was only one place she felt safe anymore, and that was in Reed's arms. A thousand miles separated them, assuming he was even still alive.

Thinking about Plum Island reminded her of Pat. They'd had to leave his body behind when they fled the island. She imagined Pat rotting in the sun, his dark black hair blowing in the wind.

It was all too much. She just wanted to shut it all off, to disconnect from the memories. But since being evacuated to the USS *Florida*, she had only managed a few minutes of sleep. She knew it wasn't good for the baby, and that knowledge only made her feel worse.

For the next several hours, she lay there staring into the darkness, thinking of everyone she had lost. Were her parents on that list? She had written them off as dead, and after hearing what was happening in Europe, she almost hoped they were. The mutated monsters sounded more terrifying than anything she had experienced in the States.

A knock on metal snapped her out of her trance sometime in the early-morning hours. Horn nearly fell off the top bunk. He swung his legs over and jumped down.

"Who the hell's there?" he grumbled, disoriented. "Girls, where are you?"

"Over here," Jenny said.

The privacy curtain hanging over the doorway peeled back.

"Doctor Lovato?" asked a voice.

The curtain opened farther and let in a ray of light

that captured Horn's hulking frame. He was wearing a pair of white briefs—and nothing else. Kate looked away, choking back a snicker. Unlike Horn, Kate slept fully clothed, prepared to get up at a moment's notice.

"It's okay, Horn." She sat up with a hand on her stomach.

Horn grabbed his pants and put them on as Ben Nelson opened the curtain all the way. Tasha and Jenny squinted into the light.

"My apologies for waking you," Nelson said, "but President Ringgold would like you to meet her in the operations room."

Horn slipped a navy T-shirt over his disheveled hair. "Hang on just a sec."

"It's okay," Kate said again. "You stay here with the girls and get some more rest."

"You sure?" Horn said, one of his arms stuck in the shirt.

"I can walk on my own," Kate said with a reassuring smile. Horn sat down on the bed with his girls and watched Kate leave.

Nelson shut the curtain behind Kate and handed her a cup of coffee. Kate took it with thanks, but she didn't drink any. As a scientist, she knew a moderate daily intake of caffeine was perfectly safe for pregnant women, but as a first-time mother, she didn't want to take any chances.

Sailors passing by kept to the sides of the passage to allow Kate and Nelson through, as if they were something special. Kate sure didn't feel like anything out of the ordinary. If anything, she felt useless.

Nelson didn't speak during the short trip through the submarine. Outside the operations room stood Chief Petty Officer Ivan Petrov, a short man with a five o'clock shadow and bushy eyebrows.

"Welcome, Doctor Lovato. Please follow me," Petrov said with a slight Russian accent.

Kate and Nelson followed him into the operations room, where Captain Steve Konkoly and President Ringgold were looking at several monitors in the dim lighting.

"I had no choice, General Nixon," Ringgold was saying.

Nixon's rough voice came over the speakers. "If I had known about Wood earlier, I could have sent a few ships back to stop him. But we're in quite the mess, President Ringgold. I'm losing the war in Europe, and now you tell me the United States is headed for civil war."

Ringgold looked over her shoulder but didn't signal for Kate to join her at the comms.

"We've taken heavy losses in Italy, France, Spain, England, Germany. The EUF has retreated to a handful of strongholds. I'm afraid if we pull any troops now, Europe will be lost forever," said Nixon.

Ringgold leaned down closer to the comm system. "We can't afford to let Europe fall, but we can't help anyone if we lose the United States of America."

"I understand, Madam President," Nixon replied promptly. "I can send you two destroyers and a sub to help track down Wood and finish him off, but that's all I can spare without jeopardizing our mission here."

Konkoly nodded and whispered, "We need as many ships as we can get to capture the *Zumwalt*."

"Thank you, General," Ringgold said. "I'll have my people send you the coordinates."

"Nixon doesn't know about the fleet we're heading for?" Kate whispered to Nelson.

"It's a secret. We can't risk ROT sympathizers leaking that information."

Kate nodded, but she didn't feel any safer. It seemed Wood had spies everywhere.

"Stay safe, President Ringgold," Nixon said.

"Give 'em hell in Europe," Ringgold said. She turned to Kate. Judging by the dark circles under the president's eyes, she hadn't slept much either. "I'm sorry to call you in so early in the morning, but I wanted to discuss something with you before we meet the fleet."

"It's okay, I wasn't sleeping anyway," Kate said.

Ringgold cut right to the chase. "I've spent the last hour being briefed on the Variants in Europe. General Nixon is losing the war."

"Yes, I heard."

"The Variants there are undergoing"—Ringgold paused to search for the word—"mutations."

Ringgold glanced down at her empty coffee cup and frowned. She looked around for Nelson, but he was hanging back with Soprano near another station.

"Here," Kate said, offering the president her cup.

"Thanks. I've been living off this sludge," Ringgold said, wincing. "Worst coffee I've ever had in my life."

"I probably shouldn't be drinking any anyway," Kate said, placing a hand on her belly.

Ringgold nodded and said, "The reason I bring up the Variants is because we're about to join the *Thalassa*, a French research vessel that I'm told is studying the creatures in Europe. Maybe you can help them design another weapon?"

Kate stopped the president before she could go any farther. "I don't know how much more I can do. I've been researching the hemorrhage virus for seven months now. I helped design two bioweapons that killed ninety percent of the world's population."

Kate flinched at a pain in her stomach. Javier Riley was moving again, responding to her agitation. "The truth is, I'm done designing weapons. I just don't think I can do it again. I didn't become a scientist to destroy; I became a scientist to save lives."

"But you *have* saved lives, Kate. The weapons killed monsters, not innocent civilians. You shouldn't feel guilty about that."

Kate frowned. She hadn't told many people about her brother, Javier, who had been infected early on during the outbreak. Her first bioweapon had almost certainly killed him. No matter how many times people told her she wasn't to blame, the guilt weighed heavily on her conscience.

"Maybe a bioweapon isn't the answer," Ringgold said. "Either way, the researchers aboard the *Thalassa* need you in the fight against the new monsters in Europe. You're the brightest scientific mind in the world, Kate. And I'm not just saying that to stroke your ego."

"I don't know," Kate said, shaking her head. "Ellis had a few theories about the juveniles and mutating monsters in Europe, but he's gone now. I ..." Her voice trailed off at the memory of her friend and lab partner. She still couldn't believe he was gone. "I'm sorry, but I just don't think I can."

"I understand, Kate, but I hope you'll reconsider," Ringgold said.

Kate didn't have a chance to reply. Captain Konkoly walked over, clearly waiting for an opportunity to speak.

"Yes, Captain?" Ringgold said.

He bent down next to her and said, "Ma'am, the radar is clear. Do I have your permission to surface?"

"Go ahead. And Kate? You can take the day to think about it. But I need your answer tonight. The French are going to head back to the mainland tomorrow morning."

Kate sighed. "I'll give it some thought."

A few stations away, Konkoly stood with Chief Petty Officer Petrov and his bulky second in command, Lieutenant Commander Bonner.

Bonner sat down at the comms. "Prepare to surface," he said into the mic. The message played over the master intercom system. Sailors rushed through the passageway to their stations. Petrov repeated the message over the ballast control panel.

He looked up at Konkoly. "The board is all green."

Konkoly gave a nod to Bonner. Now that the ballast tanks were all confirmed closed, the order to blow the tanks was given. A moment later, the Klaxon sounded three times. The ballast tanks blew, and the submarine slowly rose from the frigid depths.

The hull creaked as the pressure on the rising vessel reduced. Kate knew that if anyone were listening on the radar out there, they would hear everything.

She tried not to worry and turned to Ringgold with a question that she was frightened to ask but needed to have answered before she tried to sleep again.

"Have we picked up anything on the comms about Reed?" Kate asked.

"I'm sorry Kate, but if ROT does have him, they're not talking about it."

"What if he's not with ROT? What if he's somewhere else? What if he's trying to find me?" Kate knew how crazy it sounded, but she couldn't stop the words from spilling out.

Ringgold seemed to contemplate the question for several moments. "I suppose we could send something out over the channels that would tell him you're alive, but not where you are. A message only he would understand."

The sound of the tanks blowing echoed through the submarine.

"Steady," Konkoly said across the space.

"What about just the words 'Javier Riley'?" Kate said.

Ringgold gestured for Konkoly, who stepped over.

"Captain, I'd like to send a brief message out over the comms to a friend who might be out there listening," she said.

"I'm not sure that's the best idea, Madam President."

"No one will know what it means besides the person we're looking for," Ringgold said.

Konkoly pursed his lips, clearly unmoved.

"Javier Riley is the name of my unborn son," Kate said. "His father is somewhere out there, and he could be looking for me. Please, Captain. Please send out a comms message to let him know we're still alive."

"Two words, Captain," Ringgold said. "That's an order."

6

Davis hadn't seen an infected for over an hour. She pressed her sweaty face back to her rifle's scope and zoomed in on the corpses. Davis and Diaz had killed more than fifty of them that day. The sight of old friends and colleagues sprawled over the beach and bobbing in the water had made Davis sick twice now. She couldn't afford to throw up again. They were about to make their move, and she needed all of her energy.

"The water looks as though it's calmed down," Davis whispered. She glanced over at Diaz. "You ready?"

The younger woman scratched at a swollen mosquito bite on her neck. "I'm ready."

Davis stood and swung her MK21 rifle over her back. She pulled out her M9 instead and limped away from the lookout. Diaz followed her down the stairs, and they set out across Fort Pickens toward the *GW*.

The two women strode out across the terrace and halted at the edge of the beach. They had to pass through a minefield of corpses to get to the water and then wade through the surf with more of the scattered dead. After swimming to the carrier, they would then climb a ladder to the deck, which was littered with yet more bodies.

Davis pushed onward despite the gruesome sights

ahead. She hated delaying things that were hard. She had learned at a young age to take on the hard tasks first, to get them out of the way. Today was no exception.

When they reached the beach, Davis took point, navigating among the bloated corpses as quickly as possible. Some were badly disfigured from the virus, and others had taken rounds to the skull, erasing their features. But Davis did spot several people she recognized. She passed Tom Miller and Rebecca Hamman halfway down the sand. Eric Michaels and Jay Sopa were lying by the water's edge, staring up at the sky. She mentally apologized to each of them as she passed.

The surf brought what appeared to be a log onto the beach next to Jay. The object rolled across the sand and came to rest a few feet from Davis's boots. She took another step closer and saw it was a muscular arm with a skull tattoo—the same tattoo she remembered seeing on Lance Corporal Black's arm.

Diaz put a hand to her mouth, cupping her lips and bending down as if she was going to throw up when she saw it. Davis put a hand on her friend's back.

Quick and steady, Rachel. Quick and . . .

The mantra helped Davis concentrate. She led Diaz away from the gore, both of them preparing their weapons as they walked. They didn't have any dry bags to put their gear inside, so they waded out into the surf with their rifles above their heads. As soon as they were deep enough, they started treading water and moving toward the ship, using one arm to swim and the other to hold their weapons in place. Under normal conditions Davis would have used fins, but normal conditions no longer existed.

Small waves lapped at Davis's face as she worked her way through the surf. She breathed through her nose, careful not to swallow any of the salt water. Five minutes out, her legs were already starting to cramp. Her right arm was locking up too, the injuries starting to burn. Normally swimming would have been therapeutic, but not in choppy water, and not while holding a twelve-pound rifle over her head.

Diaz was struggling a few feet away, but she managed to keep her head and weapon above the surface.

Something brushed up against Davis. She panicked for a moment, thinking at first it was an infected, or worse, a juvenile. The creatures were known to be expert swimmers. But as she kicked away, nothing tried to pull her beneath the surface.

Just a fish, she told herself. *Get a grip.*

She could see the ladder hanging from the deck ahead. Only about a hundred yards separated her from the ship. Paul Conway, the chief engineer, still hung from the jagged piece of metal that had impaled him through his torso. His head was bowed to his chest, at peace now. It hurt her heart that she couldn't bury her sailors.

They weren't people in the end, Rachel. They were monsters.

No matter how many times she reminded herself of this, she still saw the dead as her friends. She was going to make Wood pay for this, when she finally reached the bastard, and she was going to do it in the worst possible way.

Determined, Davis kicked harder, glancing over her shoulder every few yards to check on Diaz. Her freckled face was barely above the water now, but the lance corporal's eyes were steely with determination.

Davis finally grabbed on to the ladder and pulled herself up. The rungs were slick beneath her soaked boots, and she clutched the bars tightly after securing her rifle over her back. Keeping her M9 in her right hand, she began the climb to the deck.

Diaz coughed as she made the final stretch, inhaling water. Davis continued climbing, eyes on the prize overhead. Halfway up the ladder, the coughing stopped, replaced by the lap of water against the side of the ship. When she glanced down, bubbles frothed over the area where Diaz had been just a moment earlier.

"Shit," Davis said. She waited a second for the lance corporal to surface, hoping she had just cramped up, but when she didn't appear, Davis started climbing back down.

She paused on the next rung when she saw the ripple of water about fifty yards out. A rigid white shell like a turtle's crested the water.

"No," Davis choked out. She holstered her pistol and unslung her rifle. Then she looped an arm around a rung and grabbed the rifle with both hands, aiming it at the juvenile that was dragging Diaz away. It was a nearly impossible shot, since the rifle was so heavy and the beast on the move, but she didn't have time to climb to the deck and set up. Diaz wasn't going to last that long!

A head popped above the water and then an arm, flailing wildly. The violent flurry of motion was hard to lock onto, and it took Davis a second to realize it was her friend and not the monster. The juvenile had Diaz pinned under the water.

The small woman managed to keep her head above for a moment and shout, "Help!"

Blood flowed from a slash on her freckled face, and her other arm was mangled. Davis did her best to aim, knowing she was only going to get one shot at saving her friend.

Positioning the scope and steadying her wet boots on the rungs, Davis prepared to fire. One shot to make the juvenile let go of Diaz, and then another for the kill.

She directed the sights toward the creature, leading

it slightly, but captured Diaz's face instead. Davis locked onto her terrified brown eyes before moving the barrel back to the beast.

"CAPTAIN!" Diaz shouted.

"Hold on," Davis said through clenched teeth, waiting for the right moment to fire a shot. She moved her finger to the trigger and prepared to fire just as the creature pulled Diaz under the water. Waves rippled outward, and within seconds the surface calmed.

"NO!" Davis shouted. She raked the barrel back and forth over the water for the outer armor of the monster, her arms burning from the weight of the rifle. Taking another step down, she considered jumping in after Diaz, but that, Davis knew, was suicide.

Her eyes flitted back and forth, searching the murky water for her friend. After a few agonizing minutes, she knew it was too late to help the lance corporal.

Davis was alone now.

Another minute passed, and she finally secured her rifle over her back, grabbed the rung above her, and then started climbing back toward the deck. Tears streamed down her face as she moved. They had been so close—so fucking close!

On the fourth rung, Davis heard a splash. She looped her arm inside a rung again and turned to see the tall, armored figure of a fully grown juvenile emerge from the water, standing in the shallow surf. It was cradling something in its muscular arms like a mother holding a baby: the mangled remains of a human torso.

Davis swallowed hard and grabbed he rifle. She quickly zoomed in on the monstrosity standing in the surf, anger pulsing through her veins. It pulled its sucker lips off what was left of Diaz, ribbons of flesh hanging off razor-sharp teeth.

The beast glared at Davis with eyes darker than a tar

pit. For a fleeting moment, they stared at each other, or perhaps into each other's souls, human versus nature's most magnificent killing machine, neither of them backing down.

Davis was the first to act. She pulled the trigger and slipped in the process. The round punched into the beach, kicking up sand. She held on to the rung with her arm, muscles screaming from the exertion.

Stupid, stupid.

She fought to get her right boot back on the rungs. The abomination let out a screech and scrambled away for the ruins of Fort Pickens, leaving Diaz's remains behind.

Davis managed to regain her footing and raise her rifle again, but the beast was already moving into the old fortress, and at this distance, she would just be wasting ammo. Before she could stop it, the bile rose in her throat and she threw up over the side of the ladder into the dark water. She wiped off her mouth, slung her rifle over her back, and continued climbing.

She had a mission to complete, and she was the only one left to do it.

A few minutes later, Captain Rachel Davis, the only survivor of the *GW*, pulled herself onto the deck and limped toward another ladder that led to the island, the command center for flight operations. She had a message to deliver to the president of the United States: The USS *George Washington* was back in the hands of the United States Navy.

Ringo ran along the railing, squeezed through the window of the fifth-floor apartment, bolted right up Piero's arm, and sat on his shoulder.

"You see anything out there, little buddy?" Piero asked.

The mouse sniffed the air, his way of saying the coast was clear. Piero knew that Ringo wasn't really talking to him. The mouse wasn't smart enough for that, but if there were mutated Variants outside, Ringo would have darted into a hole instead of climbing onto Piero's shoulder.

"I'm not crazy," he said out loud. "I just like to talk to you."

Ringo did not reply.

Piero picked up his Beretta ARX160 assault rifle and checked the magazine even though he knew it was fully loaded. It was an anxious tic that he had developed over the past few months.

"Time to move, Ringo," Piero said. He pushed the kitchen door open cautiously, doing his best not to make any noise. Then he moved out onto the tiny balcony that was crowded with ceramic pots. Flowers and vines grew up the side of the building's cracked stone exterior, eating at the veneer, as they had done for over a century.

This had been someone's oasis before the war. The plants were now overgrown and covered with Reaver waste. A human femur bone protruded out of a muddy pile.

It looked fresh, still swathed with gristle.

Piero pointed his rifle at the tile roof above, just to make sure there weren't any monsters perched there. Sections of tile were broken away where the beasts had once landed, but the roof was clear.

He turned back to the city to search for anything that might be prowling the skies. Historic buildings lined the horizon. From this vantage point, he had a breathtaking view of the city's landmarks. Castel Sant'Angelo was to the west. The Vatican and St. Peter's Basilica were just beyond that. One of his favorites, the Colosseum, was just three blocks away. Ancient arched entrances defined the ruins of the three-story stone structure. He had only been inside the amphitheater a few times in his life, but today he was making the trip again.

He set off down the twisting fire ladder to the cobblestone street with the mouse still sitting on his shoulder. Several small cars stood where they had been abandoned months earlier. Debris covered the sidewalk where a food cart had spilled its contents.

Piero cradled his rifle across his chest. He wasn't sure what good it would do against the newly mutated monsters, but he felt better having the weapon.

Just before he got to the street, the wail of a Reaver echoed through the city. When the Reaver was answered by another call, Piero realized it was a message.

Varianti. Two of them.

The beasts had been communicating more frequently over the past few days. Piero had only a rudimentary knowledge of biology, but he had a feeling the calls were a kind of language. Were they smart enough to talk to one another?

He hurried down the ladder and took up position under the shadows of an awning. Ringo had the right idea, climbing down Piero's shoulder and into his pocket to hide. No matter how hard Piero tried to flatten his body against the wall, he was still exposed in the sunlight.

He pulled his boots back into the shadows and scanned the sky for the monsters, ready to fight or flee at a moment's notice. The otherworldly cry came again, but it was farther off this time, somewhere in the direction of the Vatican.

The Varianti were on the move, and so was Piero. He stepped out from under the awning cautiously to look for contacts, and then set off for a narrow alleyway tucked between two apartment buildings across the street.

Piero had never taken this route before, but he'd seen a stairway leading to another street below. The Colosseum wasn't far.

He bolted for the alley after a final skyward glance. He made it across the street and slipped into the alleyway, where water dripped from a fountain and flowed down the stairs.

Ringo chirped at him to stop, and Piero let the mouse down to drink. He didn't risk filling his bottle with the water. It might be contaminated, and the last thing he needed was the shits.

As they neared the bottom of the steps, Piero saw the next street was littered with police cars and military vehicles. He remembered this place now, the site of an earlier battle. Several bodies rested where they had met their doom months ago. They were all picked dry, nothing but tattered clothing and skeletal remains. The last time Piero had seen them, there had still been flesh on the bones of most of the corpses.

He checked the sky several times, raising his hand to shield his eyes from the glare of the sun. It was clear, but he hesitated, performing several scans of the street and buildings for whatever mutated monsters might be hiding here.

Stay focused and stay alive.

He repeated it to himself in his mind, never forgetting that a single mistake, a second's lapse in concentration, meant death. Even when he was exhausted, he would keep his eyes and ears alert for any sign of the monsters hunting him.

The wails of the monsters and the flap of wings were absent, and the sky, streets, and buildings were all clear.

There was only the whistle of the wind in a city that had been a hot spot for tourists and travelers for centuries.

He longed to hear a human voice. Talking to the EUF operators wasn't the same, and despite Ringo's friendship, Piero felt a void that the mouse couldn't fill. He'd made a promise to Ringo to find a mouse colony at some point. Or was it rats that lived in colonies? Piero wasn't sure, but eventually he would find a good home for his furry little companion.

Most creatures should be with their own kind. It wasn't good to be alone.

He hurried across the intersection and moved one block closer to the Colosseum. It was just on the other side of the next street. Behind him was Palatine Hill, the place where he had seen the Beetle monster emerge from the cocoon.

The mouse pushed its pink nose into the air and sniffed. Before the creature could protest, Piero grabbed him and stuffed him into his vest pocket.

"Sorry, little buddy, this is for the best."

Ringo safely inside his pocket, Piero set off to cross the street, keeping low and alert. The Colosseum rose above them, casting arched shadows over the street.

Piero ran past a police car, noting its charcoaled exterior riddled with bullet holes. The Italian military had attempted to defend citizens seeking refuge in the Colosseum many months ago.

The Varianti had won.

The Varianti always won.

Piero stopped halfway across the road and took a knee behind a military truck. He peeked around the corner to look for a way into the building. The ancient site's twelve-foot metal fence was already down, but he would still have to cross over the razor wire that topped it.

He took off running and leaped over the coils of wire. His boot snagged, but he made it over the top and continued running under an arched ceiling.

Three stories of concrete and stone towered above him as he stepped into the shadowed mezzanine. Piero shouldered his rifle and swept it back and forth over the passage, listening for the *click-clack* of joints or the screeches of the Reavers. He habitually checked the ceiling every time he entered a structure, after seeing the creatures nesting like bats under the domed roof of St. Peter's Basilica.

There was nothing on the ceiling and no sign of droppings on the floor.

He continued up a staircase, moving heel to toe, trying not to make any noise. Ringo stirred inside his vest pocket but kept silent. The mouse knew the drill.

They advanced through the dim vestibule toward the entrance of the amphitheater. Rays of light shone through the arched doorway ahead.

He stopped just shy of the entrance to take in the view. Thousands of spectators had once watched violent battles here. The structure was said to hold up to fifty thousand people, but every time Piero had been here, the Colosseum seemed too small for that.

He carefully made his way through the entrance, where he stepped in sticky white goo. He scraped his boot on the floor to remove the tarlike substance.

The remains of a cocoon hung from the ceiling. The skin was flayed open, and whatever had plopped out was long gone.

He followed the gooey streak out into the amphitheater. The brilliant glow of the sun blinded him, and he squinted, his rifle still pushed against the sweet spot of his shoulder. When his vision cleared, he had a view of the arcades. He took it all in, scanning every floor, row, and arch in the arena where so many men and beasts had fought to the death.

Ringo chirped, and Piero quickly put his hand against his pocket to silence the mouse. Collapsed tents, trash, and clothing littered the bottom of the amphitheater where civilians had sought refuge during the early days of the outbreak. But the corpses were all gone now, replaced by the remains of cocoons that had disgorged mutated Variants.

It didn't take Piero long to see where the beasts had gone. The gooey trails led down the seats, into the battle arena, and across the dirt to a large iron gate that stood ajar.

"No," he breathed. "Not down there."

Ringo squirmed inside Piero's pocket again. The mouse might not have been able to understand what was happening, but it must have sensed something was wrong. After all this time, Piero and his friend were going to have to go back underground to find the demons.

He aimed his rifle at the gate and set off down the stairs, his head held high, like a gladiator preparing for battle.

7

The MATV wasn't just their transportation; it was going to be Team Ghost's living space for the intermediate future. They had everything but a kitchen sink and shower inside the armored vehicle—so much gear and armor that the King Stallion helicopter carrying them through the dark skies was struggling for altitude.

Colonel Bradley hadn't been lying when he said his engineers had added armor to the vehicle. They had welded large plates over the already two-inch-thick armor in several strategic spots, including the hood. It would stop an acid attack from the juveniles and protect Team Ghost against any suicidal Reavers that decided to nosedive into the truck.

The black paint had been Fitz's idea, however, as was the Team Ghost logo of a skull surrounded by smoke on the hood. He doubted it would scare off any Variants, but it sure made him proud.

Rico twisted her blue-tipped hair with one hand and gripped the steering wheel with the other. Fitz had reassigned her to the driver's seat for this mission due to Stevenson's injuries.

She reached into her vest pocket and dug out a piece of gum.

"You got any for me?" Stevenson asked from the back seat. He sat between Dohi and Tanaka. Apollo was resting on the floor at their feet.

Rico shook her head. "I'm down to my last pack— sorry."

"And here I was thinking you had an endless supply," Fitz said.

He turned his attention to the sky. The hazy clouds stretched across his field of vision. Two Apaches flanked the MATV, and even though he couldn't see them, it felt good to know they were there. But Fitz also knew they would need more than some Hellfire missiles and .50-caliber rounds if the Reavers showed up. That was why they were flying at a higher altitude, hopefully out of reach. If Fitz had to guess, he would put them somewhere around five thousand feet above sea level.

Of course, if the steel cords connected to the MATV snapped, the fall would crush everyone inside the vehicle, regardless of its thick armor.

Fitz was trying not to think about it. He looked out the passenger's window at the checkered farmland below. Motion distracted him a moment later, his heart flipping at the silhouette in the clouds to the right.

He reached for the M4 propped next to the MK11 on his right but hesitated before sounding an alarm. The shape in the clouds was too big to be a Reaver—it had to be one of the Apaches.

He relaxed and pushed the black bead of his minimic to his lips. "Raptor One, Ghost One. How far are we from the target?"

The primary pilot of the King Stallion replied almost instantly. "Thirty minutes, Ghost One. As soon as we're in position, we're going to make a quick descent to avoid any potential hostiles in the air."

"Roger that," Fitz replied. He twisted in his seat for

a final briefing—and, more important, a final chance to check his team. Everyone wore the same anxious look, and Fitz didn't blame a damn one of them.

"Look, I know what you're all thinking about this mission, but we have a job"—Fitz corrected himself—"no, we have a *duty* to give this all we got. A lot of lives are riding on the line again."

Rico stopped chewing her gum and said, "I've heard that line before."

"Yeah, I know, Rico. We were told the same thing last time, and the coordinates that we sent up the food chain ended up making things worse. That's why we're out here again. This is our chance to make up for it."

Rico shrugged, signaling that she accepted his answer. Stevenson, on the other hand, let out a huff.

"When I was reassigned to Team Ghost, I didn't realize I was signing up to be cannon fodder," he said. "I've nearly died on the past two missions, and it's all been because of faulty intel from the EUF. And I still have yet to see one of those fuckers."

Tanaka shot him a cockeyed look and then glanced at Fitz. "I thought we all volunteered for Team Ghost?"

"Not everyone," Fitz said.

"Apollo didn't volunteer either," Stevenson said. "I don't know what you're thinking, bringing an animal into—"

Fitz twisted around so he was looking Stevenson in the eyes. "Sergeant, you're starting to get on my nerves. Apollo is a trained warrior, and he understands more than you think. I don't see him complaining."

Apollo wagged his tail and licked Fitz's hand.

"I know, boy. Stevenson is sorry," Fitz said. "*Right*, Sergeant?"

Stevenson folded his muscular arms over his tactical vest and nodded. Before he could open his trap again, Fitz continued the mission briefing.

"The pilots are going to put us down close to where the dirty bombs were dropped. The radiation has a very short half-life, unlike the fallout from a nuke, and it should already be at minimal levels by now. But we have CBRN suits and a Geiger counter just to make sure."

Dohi pulled the device from his rucksack and held it up wordlessly.

"Once we're on the ground, Dohi and Apollo are going to track down this missing army," Fitz added. "We'll determine its location, relay the coordinates, and then call in our evac."

"Maybe I'm a dummy, but how the hell did an entire army go missing?" Stevenson asked. "And wouldn't it make more sense to use drones or aircraft to find them?"

Fitz sighed inwardly while Tanaka explained.

"You were hit pretty hard in your thick head back in Greenland, so you missed out on some stuff, including the fact that we already tried using drones and aircraft. Here's the deal—we're low on fuel, ammo, and boots. Think back to World War Two, when my grandpa was using this sword." Tanaka reached back and gripped the handle of his Katana, pulling it out just enough for Team Ghost to see the blade.

"Yeah, yeah, I get it," Stevenson said. "We're cannon fodder, just like the doughboys were."

Fitz shook his head. Stevenson had a real attitude problem.

"Let's wrap up all final gear and weapon checks," Fitz said. "Once we start the descent, things could get hot. I want Tanaka up on the big gun just in case there are any Reavers in the area."

"You got it," Tanaka said. He moved into position under the hatch access that opened to the turret and the M240.

The comms crackled with a message from the King Stallion's pilots.

"Ghost One, Raptor Two. I have a visual of the park."

Fitz leaned closer to the window for a look at their target. The checkered fields were gone now, replaced by the edge of a dense forest.

"Ghost One, I have eyes on a fire at two o'clock," reported Raptor Two. "Looks pretty big."

Fitz could vaguely make out the blaze through the thick cloud cover. It appeared as a glowing ball to the east. He realized the MATV wasn't passing through a storm cloud—they were flying through smoke haze.

"Beginning the descent," Raptor One said.

The MATV dipped slowly, the cords that tethered it to the King Stallion groaning. Fitz looked up at the roof, his heart rate spiking.

"Easy, Raptor One," he said. "Take us down slowly unless you got eyes on hostiles."

"Roger that, Ghost One."

Rico gripped the steering wheel with her tactical gloves. "That shit's gonna hold, right, Fitzie?"

He dipped his helmet in acknowledgment even though he wasn't sure. He hadn't had much faith in engineers or scientists since the hemorrhage virus had escaped Building 8. Every time they said something was impossible, it seemed to turn around and happen anyway.

As they descended, the smoke choked out the view, shrouding the vehicle in darkness.

"I can't see shit," Rico complained.

"Hopefully the Reavers can't either," Stevenson said. "You sure I can't have a piece of gum?"

The groaning of metal echoed in the MATV as they dipped toward the ground. For several minutes, Team Ghost remained silent and still.

Rico looked over her shoulder and then tore a fresh stick of gum in half with deliberate care. She placed them side by side to see which was bigger, looked over her shoulder again, apparently to make sure Stevenson wasn't looking, and then handed the bigger piece to Fitz.

"Here," she whispered.

Fitz almost turned her down, but he could see that it meant something to her. He put it in his pocket. "Thanks. It'll be my lucky charm."

"Almost clear," said one of the pilots over the comms.

The thick smoke suddenly lifted. Fitz finally got a view of the forest that Mira, the leader of the Ombres, had warned him about. For miles, the trees were flattened as if a tornado had whipped through the area.

But Fitz knew this wasn't natural. Command had listened to the French woman after all. The dirty bombs and a second attack of Hellfire missiles had destroyed the terrain, leaving behind a smoldering graveyard of trees.

Fitz heard more than a hundred aircraft from the EUF had taken part in the raid, which was still small compared to some of the bombing runs of World War II.

Rico chewed her gum slowly as she studied the park. "Everything I always wanted to see in Europe is ruined."

"Better get used to it," Tanaka said.

The comm line crackled with a message from one of the Apaches. "Raptor One, this is Arrow One. Sky looks clear, no sign of hostiles."

"Fox One reporting clear skies too," said the other Apache pilot.

Fitz looked down, expecting to see corpses, but all he saw was a bed of sparkling embers in the cooling, likely radioactive dirt.

"Arrow One, Fox One, can you get lower to check for any crispy critters down there?" Fitz asked.

"On it," Fox 1 replied.

The Apache swooped down and out of view. Meanwhile, the King Stallion's pilots lowered the MATV toward a road that wound through the devastated landscape like a dry riverbed through a lava field.

The cords tightened on the front of the vehicle, coming taut right before Fitz's eyes.

Please hold, baby, please hold. He didn't want his team to see his anxiety, but he couldn't help but clench his jaw.

"Ghost One, Fox One—I got eyes on what look like corpses, but I don't see anything moving down here."

"Copy that," Fitz replied. "Put us down, Raptor One."

The big gray bird lowered the MATV toward the road framed by burned trees. Rolling hills dotted the horizon, providing a refuge for small islands of forest that had been spared from the fires.

"Get ready, Ghost," Fitz said.

The click of magazines being palmed into weapons and final gear checks sounded all around him. He checked his helmet strap, tightened it, and then did the same to the straps on his blades.

The charcoaled ground rose up to meet the tires of the truck, and a moment later they connected with the dirt. The King Stallion's pilots set them down as gently as possible, allowing Rico plenty of time to start the vehicle before the helicopter detached the cords.

"Ropes away," said Raptor 1. "Good luck, Ghost. Call us when you need evac."

"Stay safe," Fitz said. He ducked down to watch the big gray bird and the two Apaches pull away, leaving Team Ghost alone in the devastated landscape.

"Stevenson, do a thermal scan," Fitz ordered. "See if anything's alive out there."

Fitz climbed into the back seat and began putting on his CBRN suit while Stevenson moved from window to window with his thermal scope.

"I don't see anything besides the heat from the fires," Stevenson said. He moved into the passenger's seat and checked the windshield next. "Nope, nothing alive out there. Pilots were right."

"Good," Fitz said. "I'm going to detach the ropes so we're not dragging them behind us. Dohi, get a reading with that Geiger counter. The rest of y'all, cover us."

The other members of Ghost prepared their weapons while Dohi and Fitz changed into their suits.

"Stay put," Fitz said to Apollo. The dog whined but sat back down.

Rico helped Fitz secure his helmet. Her hands lingered for a moment, and she looked into his eyes.

"Be careful," she said.

Fitz patted her hand. "I will," he promised.

He took in a breath and made sure everything was tight before reaching for the door handle. Dohi finished putting on his gear and grabbed the Geiger counter. He nodded at Fitz, who opened the door and stepped outside with his M4, blades crunching over the hardened dirt. He quietly closed the door and did a sweep with his rifle.

Blackened trees protruded out of the drab landscape. The bark of the once towering maples, oaks, and spruces was burned, and their leaves had all turned to ash. Their naked branches swayed gently in the wind, creaking eerily.

To the north, the forest fire continued to spread, clogging the already gray sky with impenetrable smoke. It was hard to believe anything could have survived out here, but he got the sense that something was watching them.

Fitz hurried to the front of the vehicle and unfastened the cables while Dohi turned on the Geiger counter. The device began to tick. A flake of ash landed on Dohi's helmet. He brushed it away, leaving a black streak. It was coming down like snow from the dark sky.

By the time Fitz had finished unlatching the ropes, the Geiger counter was quiet again. Fitz coiled the steel cords and met Dohi at the back of the truck.

"Command was right," Dohi said. "Radiation's minimal."

"First good news I've heard in a while," Fitz said. "To be honest, I half expected this place to be a radioactive night-light."

Dohi shrugged and began to stow the Geiger counter back in its case.

"Let's get back inside before our luck runs out. I've got a bad feeling something's still out here."

Dohi slowly turned to scan the terrain. "Don't see anything."

"Come on," Fitz said. They were walking over to open the back door when a voice rang out behind them.

"Hey!"

Dohi and Fitz whirled and aimed their weapons at a head peeking around the back end of the truck. The person pulled back, taking refuge behind the bumper.

Fitz flashed a hand signal to Dohi. Dohi turned and moved toward the front of the vehicle to flank the contact, while Fitz slowly walked to the back. When he got there, he found a figure crouching under the bumper.

He bent down to see a teenage girl wearing camouflage fatigues that were too big for her.

"What the hell are you doing out here?" Fitz said, lowering the barrel of his M4. He crouched for a better look, recognizing her as a member of the Ombres. But how was that possible?

Fitz reached down to grab her. "Get out from under there."

Dohi moved in from the other side, and the girl

crouched lower, staying out of their reach. Her brown eyes flitted back and forth. She was trembling, but Fitz could see it wasn't from fright. Her teeth were chattering...from cold? Had she hitched a ride on the back of the MATV?

He glanced at the vehicle's storage area, where a tarp hung loose from the gear.

"Holy shit," Fitz said. "Were you back there this entire time?"

The girl nodded.

"Come on, kid," Dohi said, holding out a gloved hand.

Rico opened the back door and poked her head out. "What the hell is going on out here?"

Fitz motioned for Rico to come out. He figured the girl might respond better to a woman. Rico gasped when she saw the girl.

"Don't think she speaks much English," Dohi said.

The girl brandished a knife and said, "I speak it better than you."

Rico got down on her knees and extended a hand, but the girl ignored her too.

"Come on, kid, it's dangerous out here," Fitz said. "We need to get back inside the truck, where it's warm and safe."

The girl's eyes flitted from face to face.

"Come on," Fitz said forcefully.

She looked at him and replied, "I'm not a *kid*. My name's Alecia and I'm here to fight with you."

The girl sheathed her knife, and then wriggled out from under the MATV at last. Fitz eyed the blade and the pistol holstered on her belt. Both weapons were almost as big as her forearms.

"Looks as if we have a new member of Team Ghost," he said with a sigh.

"They're all dead."

Hearing the voice of Captain Rachel Davis should have been a thing to celebrate, but nothing President Ringgold had heard the captain say so far seemed worth celebrating. Ringgold stood between Captain Konkoly and Kate in the cramped radio room aboard the USS *Florida*, where they had just made contact with Captain Davis. Ringgold still couldn't quite believe it.

"Is this frequency safe?" Ringgold whispered to Konkoly.

"Yes, ma'am. It's encrypted."

Ringgold cleared her throat and leaned down to the mic. "Captain Davis, this is President Jan Ringgold. I'm truly sorry to hear about your crew."

There was a long pause before Davis replied. "I had to kill them."

Ringgold exchanged a worried look with Kate.

"They were infected with the virus," Davis continued.

"Captain, are you in control of the *GW*?"

"I wouldn't say I'm in control," Davis said. "The ship's disabled. It's not going anywhere, and I can't bring any of the weapons systems online. We blew a hole in the side with C-Four a few days ago. The attack resulted in the destruction of several missiles loaded with the hemorrhage virus on the deck. Every surviving member of my crew and the ROT soldiers who had commandeered the craft were infected."

"My God," Kate whispered.

"I've cleared the ship, but there are juveniles in the area. They're…changing." Davis paused again, and her voice broke from what sounded like a sob. "One of them got Lance Corporal Diaz. I couldn't save her. It's just me now."

The pain in her voice made Ringgold's heart ache. "You're alive, Captain; that's what matters right now. We need you to stay focused," Ringgold said in her most presidential voice.

Konkoly motioned for the mic. "I need to ask her a few questions."

"Go ahead," Ringgold said, relinquishing her spot.

"Captain Davis, can you account for all of the hemorrhage-loaded missiles?" he asked.

"Yes, sir. I did a check," Davis replied. "None of the missiles are missing, but several of them were damaged in the explosion."

Kate squeezed next to him and whispered, "Ask her how she's protecting herself from infection."

"Have you taken the proper precautions to protect yourself from potential infection?" Konkoly asked.

"I'm being cautious, sir."

"Ask her—"

"Doctor Lovato, please," Konkoly said.

Kate elbowed Konkoly out of the way, and Ringgold bit back a smile. "Captain Davis, this is Doctor Kate Lovato. Are you sure all of the infected are dead?"

"Yes, Doctor."

"Have any of the infected made it out of the area?" Kate asked.

There was a short pause, and then: "I don't think so." Davis paused again and then added, "Actually, Lance Corporal Diaz and I did see an ROT helicopter land on the deck of the *GW*. They took off shortly after landing. I'm not sure if anyone who made it into the troop hold was infected or not."

Kate shook her head and looked back to Ringgold. "Chicago, New Orleans, and now Florida. We can't allow the infection to spread again. This time we'll lose everything."

"What do you suggest we do to stop the spread?" Rinngold asked.

Kate thought for a moment and then said, "We have to destroy those missiles. We can't take any chances. The entire ship needs to be blown sky high. The virus won't survive the heat."

Ringgold trusted the doctor, but destroy the *GW*? They needed that ship and the aircraft on its deck to fight the coming war with Wood. Still, she knew the most important thing right now was keeping the virus out of enemy hands, and besides, attempting to fly those aircraft off the ship was too risky.

Taking a seat, Ringgold exhaled and leaned toward the mic. "Captain Davis, we have new orders for you— destroy the *GW* and destroy those missiles by any means necessary, and then get the hell out of there. Captain Konkoly will relay the coordinates to a rendezvous point shortly. We're bringing you home, Captain."

"Understood . . . Madam President." There was a short hesitation in Davis's response, only a few milliseconds, but Ringgold knew the captain would do what it took to carry out the order, no matter how difficult it was for her.

The connection broke, and Ringgold stood to face her team. "I guess there are miracles after all. With the *GW* out of the picture, we just have the *Zumwalt* to worry about."

"Not necessarily," Kate said. "What if Wood moved some of his missiles off the *Zumwalt* to a loyal SZT or some other ship?"

Konkoly cut in. "We would know it. I've got my people listening on those comms twenty-four-seven. If he moved a missile, we would have heard about it."

"I sure hope you're right, because the biggest threat to our country right now isn't a civil war—it's the spread of the virus," Kate said.

"We won't let Wood hit any more SZTs with the virus," Ringgold said firmly, thinking of Emilia. "I'll give myself up before I let that happen."

Konkoly and Kate exchanged a glance, but neither replied.

"Send out a team to get Davis back," Ringgold said. She reached for her empty coffee cup but didn't ask for a refill. She was running on empty herself. Caffeine wouldn't fuel her forever—what she needed was sleep.

"I'm going to my quarters for a few hours. Kate, please consider what we talked about earlier."

"I will," Kate said. "I hope you can get some sleep, ma'am."

"Me too," Ringgold said with a sigh, knowing the chances weren't good.

8

Outpost 46 was impressive by anyone's standards. Boxed in by twelve-foot-tall electric fences, it looked secure from Beckham's point of view through the scope of his M4. He began to see how Flathman's men had survived out here for months after the outbreak without reinforcements.

The field around the eastern barrier was pockmarked with holes from exploded mines. Flathman claimed there weren't any left and hadn't been for months. The juveniles had apparently set off the last of them.

Four guard towers equipped with M134 Gatling guns were positioned one hundred feet behind the three levels of fences in each corner. A fifth tower with an M260 rocket launcher, protruding from the center of the outpost, overlooked a second barrier of fences topped with razor wire. The sight of the weapons gave Beckham hope that ROT hadn't stripped the outpost of the radio equipment that Flathman promised was inside.

The shipping containers and supply crates stacked outside the three buildings also appeared undisturbed. A forklift, a bulldozer, and a Humvee were parked next to a metal shed to the right of the buildings. Rows of sandbags formed a perimeter.

Absent were the soldiers who had manned this post since Medical Corps scientist Jim Pinkman had arrived at the O'Hare International Airport carrying the hemorrhage virus in his bloodstream. For seven months, Flathman's ragtag crew had held this place against hordes of the infected, the Variants, and later the juveniles.

But they were all gone now, and apparently so were the ROT soldiers who had been here just hours earlier.

A third and final chain-link fence formed a wall around the three buildings across the outpost. It was more of a cage than a fence, with a ceiling that connected to the rooftops of the buildings.

Beckham pulled his eye away from the scope when Flathman returned from a quick recon of the woods. He gave the all clear with a hand signal. Wincing, Beckham rose and limped over to the lieutenant.

"Doesn't look as if anyone's home," he whispered.

Flathman nodded. "No sign of juveniles either. Nothing to indicate why ROT packed up shop."

"Maybe they were deployed elsewhere," Beckham said. "We've been out of radio contact with anyone for a while. It's possible Wood is going after his other enemies and needed the troops."

"Who knows," said Flathman. "All I know is that I need a drink. Let's move."

Beckham limped after the lieutenant. He was starting to wonder if this was how Apollo felt when he followed his handlers. The thought of the German shepherd was just what Beckham needed to kick his tired ass into gear. Apollo, Fitz, and his other friends were out there fighting, and Beckham would be damned if he would let them down now.

He moved quickly through the shadows of the forest, ducking below branches and stepping over fallen logs covered in moss. His twisted prosthetic leg was hanging together by nothing more than a few pieces of tape and a prayer at this point, but at least it wasn't creaking.

Flathman halted ahead, balled his hand into a fist, and dropped behind a bush. Then he pointed at the guard tower on the western electrical fence.

"Stay here, I'll be back," he said before Beckham could protest.

Beckham rested his back against the bark of an oak tree and scanned the outpost, while Flathman slipped out into the meadow. Keeping low, the soldier bolted across the grass for the fence.

Damn, he's fast.

The lieutenant was also one of the worst—or best, depending on your perspective—high-functioning alcoholics that Beckham had ever met in his life.

It took Flathman less than five seconds to get to the edge of the first chain-link fence. He dropped to his knees and then got down on his belly.

Beckham turned to check the woods while he waited. The afternoon sunlight could barely penetrate the canopy. Shadows shifted beneath the trees like the ghosts of the dead soldiers from Outpost 46. When he turned back to the outpost, Flathman was gone.

A single cricket chirped in the still forest as the shadows closed in around Beckham. He waited for his blurry vision to adjust. Clicking sounds drew his attention, and he whirled with the barrel of his M4. Another shadow darted across the forest floor and vanished behind a tree.

Beckham moved to the right for a better view.

Other noises seemed to ring out from all directions: the crunch of a stick, the hiss of an insect, the caw of a crow.

A minute passed. Then two.

Beckham froze at the snapping sound that could have been a branch or the joints of an infected. He searched the canopy of changing leaves above, recalling the beasts at Fort Bragg that had hidden in the trees.

Nothing moved in his vision.

He turned back to the outpost and raised the M4's scope to his good eye. The ankle-high grass shifted in the wind on the other side of the fences. He moved the cross hairs back to the area where he'd last seen Flathman but only saw more of the overgrown grass.

Beckham took a step out into the meadow and, keeping low, set off for the fence, refusing to wait here any longer. His blade sank in the mud, resulting in a creak so loud that he cringed.

He could feel something watching him from the woods. The sensation of eyes on his back forced him to turn, but he still didn't see any yellow eyes staring back at him.

Pushing on, Beckham limped to the fence and angled his rifle at the area where Flathman had disappeared. He bent down in the dim light and found a hole just wide enough for a human. At first he thought Flathman had been pulled into a Variant-dug tunnel, but then he saw the metal plate that had been used to block the entrance lying a few feet away.

A low whistle came from the outpost.

Beckham aimed his rifle at a figure on the other side of the fences.

"Holy shit—hold your fire, Captain," Flathman said. He grinned as he unlocked a gate. Once through, he jingled a key in his right hand and jerked his head toward the gate to the first fence.

"Welcome to Deadwood, Captain Beckham—also known as Outpost Forty-Six. How about a drink?"

"I'd prefer a radio. Did you see one of those yet?" he asked as he slipped through the gate.

"Haven't checked yet to see if the ROT pricks took it with 'em. Figured I'd let you in first."

He locked the gate behind Beckham, and they set off for the buildings.

"So I'm guessing these fences aren't live, right?" Beckham asked.

"Correct. They need power, and we're out of fuel. I'll check on the generators in a bit, but first things first."

Vodka, Beckham thought, resisting the urge to shake his head. At least Flathman had let him inside before going to find the bottle.

"Had that tunnel dug a month after the outbreak," Flathman said. "Figured it might come in handy if we needed to escape. Never thought I'd use it to get back in."

"You should have told me what you were doing. I got worried."

Flathman shrugged off the rebuke and pulled out the key ring. He held it up and fingered through the keys.

"I think it's this one," Flathman said. He inserted the key into the door, and it clicked open. Pulling out his flashlight, Flathman angled the beam into a dark room furnished with several metal desks and a leather couch. Two offices and a small kitchenette were off to the right, and a bathroom was to the left.

"Radio room is over there," Flathman said, directing the light to the office on the far right.

They walked over and Beckham opened the door, anxious to see if ROT had left anything behind. His heart flipped when he saw several radios and a desktop computer inside.

"They didn't take the equipment," he said with a smile.

"That's more than I can say for my two ex-wives," Flathman muttered. "ROT left in a hurry, just like them two lovely ladies. Question is, why?"

Beckham sat down at one of the desks and began checking the equipment.

"I'll see if I can get a generator working, but we should have a battery-operated radio in here somewhere," Flathman said. "Check those cabinets."

He walked back out into the main quarters without waiting for a response, and Beckham opened the metal drawers of the cabinets to his right. The first was empty, but the second contained a radio that was both battery operated and outfitted with a hand crank. He couldn't use it to send a message, but he would be able to listen to anyone transmitting over the AM/FM channels.

A ruckus came from the other room—drawers opening and shutting, the tap of boots on tile, and the clank of metal. It sounded as if a wild animal was ransacking the other offices.

"Hell yes!" Flathman finally shouted. "They didn't find my loot!"

The lieutenant reappeared, cradling a bottle of vodka as if it was a newborn baby. He screwed off the cap and took a gulp, then another, and finally sat the bottle down on a desk.

"I'll be right back," he said, again leaving without waiting for a response.

Beckham turned back to the radio. He flipped it on and began searching the stations. The speakers fuzzed with static, but it didn't take long to find a broadcast. There were dozens of active stations, but most of them were too difficult to make out due to the crappy signal.

Beckham stopped the knob when he heard the first clear voice and slowly turned it back to listen.

"This is Coast-to-Coast Resistance," said a male operator, "bringing you the latest news from North America and Europe."

Beckham waited impatiently for a wave of static to pass. Each second that ticked by felt like an hour. It finally cleared, and the broadcast continued.

"We're just receiving word that another EUF base in Spain has fallen to the Variants. The EUF troops pushing east are facing mutated creatures unlike—"

White noised flickered over the man's voice. Beckham tapped the radio on the desk and then pushed the antenna up toward the ceiling.

"…in news back at home, the hunt for Jan Ringgold, the disgraced former president, continues. Anyone with information regarding her whereabouts should go to their local SZT embassy immediately. Anyone aiding her is subject to execution by hanging."

The *former* president? Had the other SZTs all sworn loyalty to Wood? Another flurry of static rolled from the speakers, and Beckham tapped the radio harder on the table.

"…has promised that all mayors of SZTs aligning with his administration will receive—"

The transmission cut out again, and Beckham cursed. He was about to shatter the damn radio but he managed his anger by taking in a deep breath.

"We also received word today that President Wood has signed an executive order drafting all citizens over the age of eighteen into the Resistance of Tyranny army. Eligible citizens should immediately report to their local recruiting station."

Beckham had to place his hand flat on the table to stop himself from throwing the radio across the room. Not only was Wood apparently president now, he was also building an army. It made sense, all of it, but Beckham didn't want to believe the news. It was as though he'd woken up in an alternate universe.

Static broke over the frequency again, and no matter how many times he tried to get a better signal, he couldn't make out the rest of the broadcast.

Beckham set the radio back down and continued through the channels, his heart pounding faster and faster. For the next ten minutes, he skimmed through broadcasts from other SZTs. There was a guy transmitting from Banff National Park in Alberta, Canada, about a rogue juvenile pack patrolling the forest, a woman from the Deep South in the States reporting a missing aid shipment in a Southern drawl, and multiple FEMA broadcasts on repeat. There were a dozen more channels broadcasting news Beckham didn't care about or couldn't make out due to the poor signal quality.

What he didn't hear were messages from the American military.

That meant either they were lying low and waiting to make a move against Wood or, worse, they had already aligned with ROT. Beckham had no idea how many troops were even still out there, but Wood couldn't have manipulated everyone.

The bank of lights suddenly flickered on overhead. Beckham put the battery-operated radio away to save its juice and turned on the main radio and transmitter. It would pick up broadcasts from all around the world, and he would be able to send his own transmission when the time was right.

He skimmed through the channels as he waited for Flathman to return. Another ten minutes passed, and then ten more of listening to the broadcasts from SZTs and survivors out in the wastelands of the United States. There was even a young woman from Canada who had spent the past five months in her grandfather's Cold War–era bunker with her father. Neither of them seemed to believe the world had ended.

Beckham wasn't going to be the one to convince them. There were plenty of other people out there for that.

A click from the other room distracted him, and he looked over his shoulder. The front door was still shut. He trusted the lieutenant to watch their backs, but he'd been gone for a while. If it weren't for the shit Flathman had pulled earlier with the tunnel under the fences, Beckham might have stepped outside to look for the other soldier.

Instead, he kept scrolling through the transmissions until he heard two words that made his fingers lock up. With the utmost care he scrolled back to a message that was on repeat.

The door burst open in the other room, but Beckham didn't turn to see why Flathman was panting.

"Quiet," Beckham said, holding up his hand. Then he reached down and turned the volume up, listening to the two words that were being repeated by a male operator.

"Javier Riley. Javier Riley. Javier Riley…"

"Holy shit," Beckham said. It was from Kate. It had to be from her, right? He pushed himself up with a groan and turned to look at Flathman with a smile. But the lieutenant's weathered face was set in a mask of horror.

"Captain," Flathman said. "We got a big fucking problem."

Beckham made it halfway to the other room before he heard a high-pitched screech in the distance. Another answered the call, and all at once a dozen of the distant, otherworldly shrieks seemed to surround the outpost.

"I guess we know why ROT left," Flathman said, gasping for air. He shut the door behind him, locked it, and turned off the lights.

"The infected," Beckham said quietly. "ROT knew they were coming."

Flathman nodded. "The creatures must have left the SZT to find food. And we're it, Captain."

"Wood's declared himself president?" Ringgold said in a voice bordering on a shout.

"And he's declared a draft to build his army," Konkoly explained. "ROT will be unstoppable soon if we don't do something."

The submarine captain's words were met with silence. Kate held back what she was really thinking—that it was actually a brilliant move to add to ROT's already swelling ranks. "Wood's insane," she said instead.

Horn popped his knuckles. "I'll crush his head in when I find that son of a—"

Kate shot him a glance, and Horn looked over at President Ringgold sheepishly and said, "Sorry, ma'am."

"No apology necessary, Master Sergeant," Ringgold said. She sighed and looked at the monitor in the operations room. The cramped space was filled with naval officers, Ringgold's staff, Kate, and Big Horn.

On the screen was their first look at the fleet still loyal to President Ringgold. Kate recognized only the USS *Abraham Lincoln*, an aircraft carrier, and the French research ship *Thalassa*. But there were other ships out there: one naval Ticonderoga-class guided-missile cruiser and one Arleigh Burke–class guided-missile destroyer. She also saw a smaller ship with US Coast Guard insignia, a container ship, an oil tanker, several yachts, and a large fishing boat.

Kate almost shook her head at the motley fleet. This was the resistance that had come together to help

President Ringgold take back the country from a psychopath? Weren't there more people out there to help?

She studied the screen in despair, having expected so much more.

"SEAL Team Four is en route to pick up Captain Davis and confirm the destruction of the *GW*," Konkoly reported.

"The same team that evacuated us from Hatteras Island?" Ringgold asked.

"Yes, the mission is being spearheaded by Senior Chief Petty Officer Randall Blade."

"Good," Ringgold said. "Hopefully they'll have her by the time I arrive on the *Abraham Lincoln*."

Konkoly ran a hand through the graying hair on the side of his head. "Ma'am, I really think you should stay on board the sub for your safety."

Ringgold shook her head. "Not a chance, Captain. I need some fresh air, so that's where I'd like to move our command center."

"I'd highly recommend listening to the captain," James Soprano said. "I don't trust this 'loyal' fleet," he said, using his fingers to trace quotation marks around the word.

"I'm with Soprano and the captain on this one," Ben Nelson chimed in.

Ringgold thought on it for a moment and then looked at Kate. There was something in the president's gaze that made Kate wonder if she was holding back information. It could have been fatigue, but Kate wasn't so sure. The president looked as if she was hiding something.

"Have you given any more thought to working with the *Thalassa*'s team?" Ringgold asked.

Kate nodded. "I have, Madam President, and I won't be joining them."

Ringgold held Kate's gaze but accepted her answer

with a nod and then turned away. "All right, ladies and gentlemen, let's get ready to move command to the USS *Abraham Lincoln*. I'm anxious to meet with the men and women who will be taking back the United States of America."

Everyone stood and began to file out of the room, but Ringgold waited and walked over to Kate.

"I understand your decision and respect it. Perhaps you'll join me on the *Abraham Lincoln*?" Ringgold said. "We can move the children there as well. I'm sure they're all getting anxious for some fresh air and sunshine."

Horn nodded his head, but Kate could see reluctance in his eyes. Despite the promise of sunshine and a better view, she couldn't help but feel they were safer beneath the ocean.

Ringgold placed a hand on Horn's shoulder, smiled at Kate, and then followed her staff and the navy officers out of the room.

Horn watched them leave with his muscular arms folded across his chest. "I'm glad you decided not to go aboard that French ship," he said. "I don't trust 'em, for one, and two, you've done everything you can for science. It's time to pass the torch, right?"

"I don't know," Kate said, suddenly unsure. The guilt was already eating at her, but feeling Javier Riley move reminded her why she had made the decision. He was her future now, and she had to protect him at all costs.

"Let's get back to my girls," Horn said. "I want to break the news to them that we're leaving."

They returned to the quarters where Tasha, Jenny, Bo, and Timothy were playing a game of cards with Donna. Jake stood outside the privacy curtain, not quite standing guard but watchful nonetheless.

"What's the word?" he asked.

Horn stopped to talk to Jake. They had become friends over the past few days, and Kate had heard them talking about Beckham the night before—something about mounting a rescue mission when the time came. She appreciated the idea, but what could they possibly do against Wood's growing army?

She walked into the room and forced a smile despite her rising despair.

"Pack up your things, kiddos. We're going on a field trip," Kate said.

Tasha stayed focused on the game, but Jenny beamed. "Do we finally get to see the sun again?" she asked.

"I want to go fishing," Bo said.

Horn laughed from the passage and ducked back inside. "I might be able to arrange that, little buddy."

"Are there sharks out here?" Tasha asked, looking up.

"I sure hope so!" Bo said. He smiled so wide that Kate could see his teeth.

The Klaxon sounded, erasing the smile from Bo's face.

"It's okay," Kate said. "That just means we're moving."

Footfalls pounded the passageway, and Kate looked out to see Ben Nelson ducking under the pipes. He gestured for her to join him outside the quarters.

"We received a message from Outpost 46, just outside of Chicago, in response to our broadcast," he said.

"What did the message say?" Kate asked.

"'Say hi to the kid.'" Nelson lifted a brow. "That mean anything to you?"

Kate's eyes flitted to Horn, whose grin rivaled Bo's earlier smile. "I told you Reed was still alive!" Horn shouted, hooting and clapping his hands together. The children in the room all turned to glare at him as if he was crazy, but Horn bent down to scoop Jenny off the ground. He twirled her around, laughing.

Kate placed one hand on her pounding heart and the other on her belly. "You hear that, Javier Riley? Daddy says hello."

9

Davis couldn't believe the radio transmission. The secure message gave her hope in a time when she had thought there was none left.

"Come again?" she said. "Please repeat your last."

"After the rendezvous, you will be rerouted to pick up Ghost One. Stand by," said Chief Petty Officer Ivan Petrov from the USS *Florida*.

Davis wiped the crud from her eyes, a combination of tears and mud. Ghost 1 was the call sign for Beckham, and if he was still alive, then he was even harder to kill than she'd thought. She replied over the handheld radio she'd taken from the *GW* and then prepared to duck out from her hiding spot in the ruins of Fort Pickens.

The sun was already setting on the horizon, and more juveniles would be coming out soon. As the twilight approached, the sounds of the animals and insects quieted; even they knew what the darkness brought. It was amazing how dark it was without the power on. Soon it would be nearly pitch black.

For the past hour, she'd been waiting to make her move. The juvenile that had killed Diaz was definitely out there, prowling, but the monster didn't know

Captain Rachel Davis, a woman hell-bent on revenge, was also on the hunt.

She wondered if the creature could comprehend something like revenge. Did it think that way? Did it think at all, or did it rely on basic predatory instincts? It was hard to guess what kind of changes had occurred in the latest evolution of the beasts.

Davis *did* know that she was running out of time. She had spent an hour burying Diaz and Black—what was left of them, at least. Piles of rocks marked their shallow graves overlooking the beach. SEAL Team Four would be here soon, and she had a mission to complete before they arrived.

She moved around the stone wall and pushed up her MK21. The fading orange glow of the sun cast little light over the terrain, but she used what there was to guide her, cautious not to stumble and give away her position to the juvenile. She hoped the juvenile hadn't already smelled her adrenaline.

She slung the rifle across her back and slowly crept out into the grass, boots squishing in the mud. Suddenly, a wail gave away the monster's position. It leaped off a stone tower and landed in the dirt about two hundred yards behind her.

Davis took off running through the maze of ruins toward the woods where she had hidden with Diaz after their failed attempt to destroy the *GW*. The sound of clicking joints and plates of armor shifting over leathery hide followed her through the fort.

The beast was tracking her.

Good, you bastard. You've got about two minutes left to live.

Davis ran harder despite the pain flashing through her body. She leaped over a crumbled pillar and focused on a slanted wall of stone. On the other side was a ravine that separated Fort Pickens from the forest.

She charged across the terrain at a breakneck pace, pushing as hard as she could, muscles tightening and stretching to their max. The sound of joints and armor grew louder.

The wall wasn't far, maybe just fifty feet or so, but the juvenile was gaining on her. She could hear its nose sniffing the air. Its lips popped over a maw of razor-sharp teeth.

Quick and steady, Rachel!

She hurdled the fallen pillar and ran as fast as she could toward the three-foot wall of stone. She was going to have to clear the top if she wanted to avoid becoming this creature's next meal.

The second before she jumped, she pulled the detonator from her vest. As soon as it was in her hands, she threw herself over the wall, her boots narrowly clearing the chipped stone.

She landed on her butt, sliding toward the stream below. A second later, she heard the creature slam into the wall, armor shattering rock. Davis pushed the button on the detonator as the juvenile let out a high-pitched screech that was soon drowned out by a boom.

The explosion and subsequent shock wave hit her in the back, pushing her helmet over feet. She lost her rifle in the process and landed on her stomach with such force it knocked the air from her lungs.

Dirt and rock rained down around her. She gasped and continued sliding down the hill until her gloves hit the water. Her face went in next, and salt water gushed up her nose, burning her sinuses. She pushed at the muck to right herself. Chunks of rocks splashed into the water and landed nearby.

After wiping the dirt from her face and spitting on the ground, she looked at the debris rolling down the hill. What was left of the wall and the juvenile was still tumbling down the slope. An oval head with narrow eyes and curved ears rolled toward her. It stopped at her boots, slurping into the water.

The C4 she had planted had blown the juvenile into a dozen pieces. It seemed like fitting revenge, but she felt no relief or satisfaction. Her mind was already focusing on her next mission.

She calmly retrieved her rifle and climbed back up the bank. There was a smoking black crater where the wall had been, surrounded by a ring of blood and gore.

Davis moved into the field of swaying grass. Somewhere in the distance came the *chop chop* of a helicopter. The sight of a Seahawk traversing the purple sky greeted her as she made her way back toward Fort Pickens. The radio tucked inside her vest crackled to life.

"Victor One," said a voice. "Victor One, do you copy?"

"Roger that—this is Victor One. I'm at the rendezvous point," she replied. "It's all clear."

The helicopter lowered over Fort Pickens, disgorging the team of Navy SEALs that had come to rescue her. Little did they know she had just saved them the trouble of putting down a three-hundred-pound juvenile.

She jogged over to them with the C4 detonator still in hand. An African American man led the team out across the grass. The other men fanned out to set up a perimeter. The senior SEAL gave her the elevator-eyes treatment. Then he checked the smoking hole in the stone wall behind her.

"Captain Davis, I presume," he said.

"You presume correctly."

"I'm Senior Chief Petty Officer Randall Blade with SEAL Team Four. I was under the impression that the *GW* would be destroyed. You had specific orders to—"

Davis held up the detonator. She pushed the second

button and stepped to the side so Blade could see the aircraft carrier out on the water. A blast exploded on the deck where the hemorrhage-virus missiles were scattered. F-18 Super Hornets and millions of dollars' worth of other precious aircraft were blown to pieces by carefully placed charges.

Three more blasts tore through the inside of the ship, blowing holes in the bow, center, and stern all at once.

Blade ducked as the fireballs burst into the night sky. The other men all whirled and flipped up their night-vision goggles to shield their eyes from the explosions.

"Happy now?" Davis asked. She dropped the detonator on the ground and took off for the troop hold of the chopper. She'd finished what Black, Diaz, and so many other members of her crew had started. But scuttling her ship—her home—still felt like blasting a hole in her own heart.

It's done, she thought grimly. *Now what's next?*

Piero wasn't sure how long he'd been scouring the moist tunnels under the Colosseum. It felt like an entire day, but it was hard to tell without any sign of the sun.

Keeping low and hugging the walls, he continued into the darkness guided by his flashlight. Every few minutes, he would cup his palm over his light and stop to listen for the mutated monsters.

Ringo sat on his shoulder, providing an extra set of eyes. If the mouse sensed anything, he would jump back into his pocket, and Piero would know to haul ass or hide. But so far, the only sign of the beasts was the gooey trails leading deeper into the tunnels. Piero wasn't sure exactly where he was, but it had to be somewhere under the arcades, in what appeared to be the intestines of an old sewage or water system.

He stopped when he heard a strange sound. It started as a long, guttural croak like the call of a bullfrog and was followed by a clicking like that of a rattlesnake's tail.

The sound seemed to be coming from everywhere and nowhere. The rattling was followed by the chilling *click* and *clack* of skittering, many-legged creatures, and something else that sounded like the wet hide of a snake wiggling across the ground.

Ringo dove into Piero's breast pocket, and Piero crouched behind a pillar. He held his rifle, ready to fire. As he had so many times before, he waited for the sounds of the monsters to pass and wondered if this time they would find him.

It wasn't all that long ago that he had been losing his mind beneath the Vatican. Seeing the sun again and contacting the EUF had brought him out of the grips of madness, but every step he took down here threatened to transport him back into the mental darkness.

The beasts eventually retreated until once again there was nothing but the sound of his stilled breathing. He waited for his heart rate to return to normal and repeated the mantra that had kept him moving all day.

You have a mission. You have to keep going.

Piero pressed onward, flitting his beam up and down the passage. The cracked walls had been spared from the graffiti that he was used to seeing under other historic buildings throughout the city, but there was something else smeared on them.

He reached out and fingered a gelatinous white material. At first glance, it looked like the same stuff from the cocoons, but it had the consistency of drying glue. He brought it up to his nose and caught a whiff of sour fruit and acid. The glue webbed out between his thumb and index finger and then popped back together.

Piero scraped the gunk on the wall, but some of it had already hardened onto his glove like plastic. His heart kicked back into overdrive. Was this some sort of toxin, like the juvenile spray?

Instead of risking contamination, he took off his glove and tossed it on the ground. That was the last time he would be touching anything down here.

He followed the white streaks deeper into the tunnels. Several round holes the size of a basketball peppered the ceiling. Water dripped from the openings, plopping into puddles on the ground. This place had to be some sort of sewer and water system, he was sure of it now, and he had a feeling the noises from earlier had emanated from the sewage drains.

The openings were likely connected to old latrines for the fifty thousand spectators who had once watched the games in the arcades far above his head. It was amazing that the Romans had been so advanced two millennia ago. That amount of time was hard to fathom. Would humans still be here in another twenty years—or even two?

He continued toward the intersection ahead. If he lost his life to help save the human race, then that was a good death—far better than what had come to those who had died overhead as gladiators in brutal combat for a few minutes of entertainment.

He stopped a few feet from a junction and crouched before shining his beam into the passage. It crossed over more of the circular openings in the ceiling. Concrete troughs were built underneath to catch the sewage before they continued draining into the lower levels.

Piero listened, waited, and then ducked under a low

arch. He played his light over a faded drawing on the wall to his right and saw the familiar outline of a gladiator helmet etched into the stone.

He cursed under his breath as he roved the beam toward more of the drawings, all of them depicting warriors from the past with swords, spears, and bows. They were beautiful, but they were also familiar; he'd been here before, which meant he was walking around in circles.

But if that was the case, then where were the monsters?

Piero slowly turned to look for a way out of the room. There were three connecting corridors—or two if he didn't count the one he'd just come from.

He picked the one to his right, ducked down, and shone his light over the walls, ceiling, and floor, where the streaks of white goo continued. He was almost certain this was a new passage. It had a lower ceiling and narrower walls than the sewage tunnels. Perhaps this was an old aqueduct. The Romans were some of the first to engineer such a system in ancient times, Piero recalled from school. Surely they had fitted the mighty Colosseum with the technology.

Ringo popped up out of Piero's vest pocket, sniffed the air, then pulled up and scrambled onto Piero's shoulder to watch. They entered another tunnel that seemed to end at a central circular space. This was definitely new. After a few sniffs, Ringo decided it was safer back inside the pocket. He jumped inside, leaving Piero to navigate the room himself.

He caught a draft of whatever the mouse had smelled a moment later, an acidic and sour smell.

Varianti.

Piero raked his beam over the cracked walls and holes overhead that looked like portals in the bulkhead of a spaceship. They all drained into this one central area.

He flitted the ray back to the floor. In the middle of the room was a large oval opening the width of a small pool. The circular grate was pulled to the side, exposing a gaping hole into the earth.

Raising his rifle, he approached the opening, keeping his footfalls as quiet as possible. Ringo stirred inside his pocket, a signal that Piero ignored. He kept his light on the hole. A few steps later, his boot scraped against the grate.

Lowering the flashlight, he carefully stepped off the rusted metal. A faint rattle sounded, and Piero froze like a statue.

Another long, low croaking sound echoed through the tunnel system, but this time he was certain of the source's location. It was coming from the massive hole right in front of him.

He shut off his light and backed away.

The *click-clack* of four-legged monsters followed the croaking. It was as if an army of crabs was marching underneath the Colosseum, preparing to do battle.

Piero moved away in horror, nearly stumbling. He steadied himself and angled the flashlight's beam toward the nearest overhead hole just to make sure there weren't any monsters that were going to drop down on him. The tunnel was empty, void of any slitted eyes staring down at him.

He willed himself to take a cautious step forward toward the hole in the center of the room. The ray of his flashlight couldn't penetrate the darkness, which meant the space below was very deep and very dark.

If he'd had a grenade, he would have already tossed it into the oversized toilet bowl.

As he took another step forward, the beam captured a yellow flicker. He raked the light back and forth, illuminating what looked like yellow diamonds.

The croaking sound came again, and this time it was so loud it could have come from a bullfrog next to his ear. He took two steps back, then a third, but more of the yellow orbs glimmered in the massive hole in front of him.

They were eyes, he realized.

Hundreds of them.

10

Ringgold was guided through the USS *Abraham Lincoln* by an armed entourage that included Master Sergeant Horn, Secret Service agent Tom King, Captain Konkoly, and a team of marines from the USS *Florida*. There was a lot of firepower and muscle around her, but she was still on edge.

After taking a Zodiac from the submarine to the aircraft carrier, she had enjoyed a few minutes of sunlight and the view of the ocean before entering yet another dimly lit quarters. There, she would meet the leaders of the makeshift fleet.

More marines met them outside the flag bridge, where Captain Konkoly coordinated the introductions. She first shook the hand of Captain Bill Ingves, a short Latino man with salt-and-pepper hair and an iron grip. Next came Rear Admiral Dan Lemke.

"Pleased to have you aboard the USS *Abraham Lincoln*, President Ringgold," he said. Dimples dotted his cheeks, and she found herself smiling back at him. "My duty as the ranking officer is to destroy ROT and to take back our country, and I am proud to fulfill it."

"Thank you. I feel lucky to be here," she said.

Turning to her staff, or what was left of it, she introduced Soprano, Nelson, Kate, and Horn.

Lemke gestured to the conference table. The flag room, normally reserved for an admiral's confidants, was furnished with only a table, a few chairs, and a wall-mounted monitor at the head of the room. Lemke had given it a personal touch by hanging pictures of the places the aircraft carrier had visited over the years since its commissioning.

She paused to look at a photo of three men in uniform standing on the deck of the ship, arms around one another. Lemke stepped up next to her.

"Those are my brothers, Lenny and Nate. They both serve—" He corrected himself. "They both served in the navy. I miss those days."

The Lemkes had been much younger men when the photo was taken, at a time when wars were fought in far-off lands.

"I miss the old world too," Ringgold said quietly. "Come on, let's go get everyone up to speed."

"Absolutely, Madam President," Lemke said.

They all took seats around the conference table, and Ringgold addressed everyone for the first time.

"These past months have been full of trials and tribulations for everyone. Time is not on our side, but we still have much to celebrate. We have a chance to make things right—we have a chance to take back our country and rebuild..."

Ringgold didn't mean to let her words trail off, but she had given this speech before. She realized, even as she spoke, that now wasn't the time for inspiring words. Now was the time for action.

"I want a plan to find the *Zumwalt* and destroy ROT before they can poison our country further," she said firmly, more as an order than a request.

"We've put something together," Lemke said. He

nodded at Captain Ingves, who handed out a stack of folders around the table.

"Inside the folder you will find data about which SZTs are loyal to ROT and which we think we can still swing our way. The resistance to your administration is growing, and we fear that Wood will launch another attack soon," Lemke said.

Ringgold took a moment to read the briefings. There wasn't as much information as she was hoping for. For the next hour, Lemke and Konkoly discussed potential plans for finding the USS *Zumwalt*, but with limited aircraft and supplies it seemed as though the task would be nearly impossible.

"Do we have any spies out there? Anyone who can infiltrate ROT?" Nelson asked.

"We've tried, but all of our agents have been killed," Lemke said. "We know ROT has a base in Alaska, but we don't know the location."

"We've also tried to lure Wood out, to no avail," Ingves added. "Much of the ROT leadership is former military, and some are even Special Forces. They know how to move without detection and when to strike. He also has a very loyal inner circle."

Konkoly snorted derisively. "Loyal only from fear, I'm sure."

"Not necessarily," Soprano replied. "From what we've seen, even Wood's ground soldiers seem to be unwavering in their support."

Lemke folded his hands together. "Wood is really good at manipulation. We need more than weapons and aircraft to fight ROT—we need to change the narrative. We need to bring SZTs back on board by explaining what really happened to New Orleans, Chicago, and the White House at the Greenbrier. We need to prove it wasn't you who attacked those SZTs, ma'am."

"We need Vice President Johnson," Nelson said. "He's the key to selling that story."

"Not selling it," Ringgold said. "*Proving* it."

Soprano started nodding. "If we could prove what happened at the White House, then the mayors of the SZTs would have no choice but to believe us."

"But would they fight for us?" Ringgold cut in. "Why would they rally to our cause when they know they could be punished with the hemorrhage virus?"

The room went silent for several moments. Horn raised one of his massive hands.

"Go ahead, Master Sergeant," she said, curious to hear his thoughts. Sometimes it was the enlisted soldiers who had the best perspective.

Horn cleared his throat and stood. "Uh, Master Sergeant Parker Horn. I've got an idea—a risky idea, but in my mind it's the only way to fix things."

"Go ahead," she urged.

"We have men and women we can trust out there right now. SEAL Team Four has gone to rescue Captain Davis, Captain Beckham, and Lieutenant Flathman. What if we divert them to the Greenbrier to see if the vice president or anyone else is still alive?"

"That's...not a bad idea. If Johnson is still there, we can ask him to send out a radio message over the channels and broadcast the message that Wood sent before the SZT went dark," Nelson said.

Kate looked up at Horn, who glanced back down at her and whispered something. He redirected his gaze to the president.

"I'd like to volunteer to lead a team to rendezvous with the others at the Greenbrier," he said.

Nelson gave Horn a reluctant look. "It's going to be dangerous. The area was hit with the hemorrhage-virus missiles. There will be infected there."

"Have the French scientists on the *Thalassa* found the cure for the hemorrhage virus yet?" Soprano asked. "If they have, perhaps Horn and his team could bring it with them."

Kate nearly shot out of her seat. "Cure? What cure?" She looked to Ringgold for an answer. "Is this true, Jan? Are they working on a cure?"

"Yes, it's true. The French have been working on a cure for the hemorrhage virus since the outbreak started, apparently. I was recently informed of their work and I'm told they're very close."

Kate shook her head incredulously. "Why didn't you tell me this earlier?"

"I thought they were just studying the Variants in Europe. By the time I learned of the nature of their work, you had already made up your mind. I respected your decision."

An officer walked into the room and whispered in Lemke's ear. He nodded back and said, "General Nixon is sending the USS *Forrest Sherman* and the USS *Ashland* our way. The *Thalassa* will also be departing in the morning."

Horn, still standing, looked to President Ringgold. "Madam President, may I lead a team to the Greenbrier?"

Ringgold took a moment to study Kate before answering Horn. The doctor's blue eyes had regained their sparkle after learning Beckham was still alive, but they seemed dimmer again now. Kate looked as if she'd been betrayed, and this time Ringgold felt responsible. It seemed that no matter what she decided, someone ended up getting hurt. And now she was faced with yet another life-or-death decision.

"Yes, Master Sergeant," she said at last, knowing that she might be sending Horn to his death. "Pick your team and get ready to head out."

"I haven't seen this shit city for years," Andrew Wood said into his headset. "God, I hate LA. Most of these self-righteous pricks deserved to die."

"I still think coming here is a bad idea," Michael Kufman replied. "The mayor may be allied with us, but there are thousands of people here, and I haven't been able to oversee security details."

"And I'm going to show 'em exactly what happens if you fuck with ROT," Wood said. "If there are people down there who aren't loyal yet, they will be soon."

Despite his hard talk, Wood was feeling anxious, and that always made him angry. Normally, he didn't venture far from Xerxes or the *Zumwalt*. This time he had no choice. ROT had captured Coyote, a high-level target who needed to stay here in order for the ROT's plan to work. Moving Coyote would jeopardize everything, and so Wood had been forced to leave his stronghold.

"Rest assured, every soldier in those Black Hawks is ready to die to protect you, sir—but I still wish we'd had more lead time."

Wood glanced over his shoulder and checked the other birds before turning back to the City of Angels. He was piloting an MH-6 Little Bird himself toward the silver skyscrapers. It had been a while since he'd flown one of the small helicopters, but he was sick of sitting in troop holds and the plush leather seats aboard the Boeing VC-25. Sitting with nothing to do gave him too much time to think, and thinking made him mad.

Flying helped him focus. He checked the skyline again for any sign of a threat, but the only other aircraft in the area were the two Black Hawks packed full of ROT soldiers behind them. They flanked his chopper, as they flew low over ruined suburbs. Some of the mansions below were nothing but charred rafters and concrete foundations. But there was one that seemed to have survived on top of a hill.

Wood looked down as they passed over a modern three-story house with large glass windows overlooking a swimming pool and sprawling gardens. A corpse sat in a lawn chair along the water's edge. The Little Bird was low enough for Wood to see the bag of bones was still wearing a pair of sunglasses.

He burst out laughing and pointed. Kufman followed his finger, but his features remained a mask of stone. Wood's right-hand man and bodyguard didn't share his sense of humor. He kept telling Kufman to lighten up, but he was starting to think it was a lost cause.

Wood regained his composure and gripped the controls. They were heading into the city now where, unlike in the suburbs, no building had been spared from the damage of Operations Liberty and Extinction.

"LA was hit harder than I thought," Kufman said, finally speaking. "Looks like hell on earth down there."

"I'm going to take a quick detour for a better look."

Wood flew toward the heart of the city. The Black Hawks hovered, unable to follow through the gauntlet of slanting buildings.

"Meet you at SZT 19," Wood said over the comms.

He pushed the cyclic to the right and swooped around one of the few skyscrapers still standing. The glass of the first thirty floors had been blown to pieces, and debris had drifted up against the foundation, piling there like snowbanks. Vehicles, now rusting black hulls, littered the streets.

"Lots of people trapped down there during the evacuations," Kufman said, pointing at the skeletons.

"They were the lucky ones," Wood said. "I'd take that over turning into one of the monsters. I don't know what my brother and Colonel Gibson were thinking. They should have used nukes like Lieutenant Colonel Kramer wanted."

Kufman didn't respond beyond a nod. His ruthless eyes roved behind his aviator sunglasses like an assassin's searching a crowd for a target. His attention to detail was one of the things Wood appreciated about Kufman. Even at fifty-five, the former Delta operator was still deadly.

"I should have let you kill Beckham," Wood said almost wistfully. "I know you hate him as much as I do. Maybe even more..."

Kufman turned slightly, his silver brows forming a solid line over his glasses. "It would have been an honor, sir. He betrayed his country."

Wood smiled. He had never doubted Kufman's loyalty, even when it came to executing a fellow Delta operator. Although it was easy for Kufman to say that he wouldn't have hesitated. Perhaps a little test was in order, just to make sure.

Wood glanced out the window and down at someone who hadn't understood the meaning of loyalty. Sergeant Dave Price, a former ROT soldier, had been found guilty of treason after calling Wood a psychopath and a bastard. Price was now dangling from a rope wrapped around his ankles and attached to the skids of the MH-6. The man's weight was starting to pull on the left skid.

"This fucker is heavier than I thought," Wood said. He carefully moved the cyclic to keep them steady as he prepared to head to the SZT. He was a bit rusty at flying, but he evened the bird out in a few quick motions, and they soon left the charred buildings behind.

Wood chuckled again when he spotted the iconic Hollywood sign—or what was left of it. The crooked H and Y were the only letters still anchored to the dirt. The rest were scattered downhill among the green bushes and drab terrain. Beyond the hill, Wood got his first view of the safe-zone territory that Ringgold's administration had constructed.

It wasn't very big compared to the rest of the city, just five blocks surrounded by concrete walls topped with razor wire and machine-gun nests—an island, really, amid a sea of death, the same as most of the SZTs.

What was different was a cluster of three buildings centered in the middle of the territory that looked like silos. Wood had heard they were turning the silos into farms and growing different types of plants on each level. This hippie shit amused him. Everyone knew LA couldn't grow its own food even before the apocalypse. The place was practically a desert and full of shallow people afraid to get their hands dirty. What made them think they could do it now?

The Little Bird descended toward the tarmac, where the other Black Hawks had already set down. ROT soldiers were pouring out of the troop holds.

A muffled shout sounded over the noise of the rotors just before Wood touched down.

Price was screaming and begging for his life, from the sound of it. The gag they had over his mouth had slipped. The sergeant knew what fate awaited him—a shot to the head, if he wasn't crushed by the skids of the chopper—but Wood decided at the last second to change those plans. He couldn't bear to hear a man begging like a dog. It was so undignified.

"Hold on," Wood said.

Kufman stiffened as Wood banked hard to the left. The bird pulled away from the tarmac and headed toward the tallest silo structure. Price swung like a pendulum from the rope attached to the skids.

"Careful, sir," Kufman said.

"Don't trust me?"

"I do, sir, it's just..." Kufman reached out to brace himself when Wood moved the cyclic again. "Pull up! What the hell are you doing?"

Price was hollering like a little schoolgirl now, his high-pitched voice louder than the rotors. Gritting his teeth, Wood pulled up on the cyclic one last time, and after a short delay, the bird's nose and skids pulled upward. He circled with Price dangling below, waving at the workers who were tending their gardens. They all stopped and walked to the ledge of the silo to watch.

Wood flashed a peace symbol to a short, elderly woman, who dropped a tomato plant and stumbled back from the ledge when Price's body smacked against the side of the building.

"That should shut him up!" Wood yelled.

He jerked the cyclic so the bird rolled away from the structure. But to Wood's shock, Price continued screaming.

"What the fuck," Wood mumbled. He looked down and saw Price was somehow still alive. His legs were both shattered, but his upper half was squirming. Price screamed again as Wood flew the Little Bird back toward the silo.

He couldn't hear Price's body slap into the side of the building this time, but he felt it and was grimly satisfied. Taking life thrilled him in a way nothing else could. He eyed the bloody dent where Price's body had impacted.

"That should do the trick," Wood said.

The bird pulled away from the building with Price's mangled body hanging from the rope like a dead fish on a line. Wood waved a final time at the farmworkers, who were still staring in horror.

Kufman looked shaken. It was the first time Wood had ever seen the retired operator show any sign of fear, and it was also the first time Kufman had ever told him to be careful.

Wood frowned and said, "The true test of trust between two men is the ability to look the Grim Reaper in the face together and not flinch." After a brief pause, he firmly added, "You failed that test, Kufman."

Kufman took off his aviator glasses and put them in his vest.

"Open your door," Wood said.

"Sir?"

"Open your goddamn door," Wood growled.

Kufman looked out his window at the ash-covered street hundreds of feet below. Then he grabbed the door handle, opened it, and met Wood's gaze with fearless black eyes.

"There it is," Wood said, a half smile forming on his face. "Your don't-give-a-single-fuck attitude is one of the things my brother liked about you. That and your brutality with your enemies. I, however, value loyalty above all else. Understood?"

Kufman continued staring at Wood, silent and calculating. It was, Wood had to admit, a bit intimidating.

"Jump, or I'll shove your ass out," he said.

Unbuckling his belt, Kufman scooted over to jump out the door so fast that Wood hardly had enough time to grab his arm.

"Jesus Christ, Kufman, I'm just fucking with you," Wood said.

Kufman didn't reply and continued studying Wood as if this was still part of the test.

"Close the door!" Wood yelled. He put his other hand back on the cyclic and directed the bird toward the tarmac. "And I'm supposed to be the crazy one," he grumbled.

They flew over a single-file line of people looking up

at them outside the embassy building. They were dressed in civilian clothes but were standing at attention. *They would make good soldiers if they kept that up*, Wood thought.

"Looks as though my draft is working," he said. His grin returned. All of his plans were coming together.

Price's broken body and the skids smacked against the tarmac a minute later. Kufman remained in his seat for a second before he opened the door again. Wood clapped him on the shoulder to relieve the tension. "I'm sorry about that stunt, but I've got to know if you're loyal."

"I am, sir."

"You know me—I like testing people."

The rotors slowed, and Wood jumped out onto the tarmac. A group of ROT soldiers, all of them armed to the teeth and wearing black tactical gear, surrounded the Little Bird to form a perimeter.

"Come on, let's go meet Coyote," he said to Kufman.

They kept low and walked away from the bird toward two ROT soldiers checking Price's ruined corpse. Wood's half grin spread into a full-fledged smile.

Back when he was a kid, he would toss frogs like baseballs against the barn out back of their house. The splat and crunch had always produced the same thrill in him. Sometimes, when he'd grown bored with that game, he would hack off a leg or two, then tape them back on and apply Neosporin to see if the frog would survive.

But no amount of Neosporin would save Price, even if Wood had been inclined to help the man. He was as dead as a doornail.

Wood knew he was a psychopath. But, being a psychopath, that truth didn't bother him. Xerxes, the King of Kings, was a psychopath too. Many of the world's finest military minds were just like him: Napoleon, Genghis Khan, Adolf Hitler, Mao Zedong, Pol Pot, Alexander the Great. History didn't always look favorably on them, but historians failed to see that sometimes it took a psychopath to make great changes in the world.

Bending down, he looked at Price's dead eyes, picturing Xerxes hovering over King Leonidas after the Persian army had riddled him and his men with arrows. The Persian king was said to have cut off Leonidas's head and put it onto a pike, a grave insult to the Spartan warrior.

Wood had even better plans for Joe Fitzpatrick. The crippled marine was going to pay for what he had done to Wood's brother. Years of killing other men, and women, across the planet had given Wood plenty of experience in coming up with unique ways of executing men. Especially during his time leading ROT. Now all he had to do was capture the son of a bitch.

"But first," he said to himself, still smiling, "Coyote."

11

Fitz had a hell of a headache. He still couldn't believe that Alecia had snuck onto the back of their MATV. No wonder she was freezing. She'd flown over fifty miles, with nothing but a tarp covering her, at five thousand feet above the ground.

Rico had wrapped a blanket around the girl and was talking to her in the back seat of the MATV. Apollo sat on the floor in front of them, allowing Alecia to stroke his fur without complaint.

She hadn't said much over the past few hours, but she was starting to talk now that the sun was going down.

"She wants to fight with us," Rico said. "That's why she risked her life to come out here."

"I can fight," the girl said.

Fitz snorted a laugh as she pulled out her knife. "Better be careful before you cut yourself."

Alecia twirled the handle impressively before sheathing the weapon again.

"She's good—maybe she'll take your place, Stevenson," Tanaka joked. He had taken over for Rico and was driving through the remains of an old forest.

"How old are you, Alecia?" Rico asked.

The girl sat up straighter. "Almost fourteen."

"Do you know how to fire a gun?" Stevenson asked.

Alecia glared at Stevenson as if he was slow. She pulled out a pistol that was the size of her forearm from a satchel she kept on the seat next to her.

"Well, okay then," he replied. "I hope you're a better shot than Tanaka."

"Hah," Tanaka said, making a face. "I bet she's got bigger nuts than you, bro. Hell, she came out here voluntarily."

Stevenson shot Tanaka an angry glare.

"Cut the shit," Fitz said. He changed the subject by pulling out his map and saying, "Dohi, you got any idea where we're at?"

Their primary navigator held up a finger, signaling for Fitz to wait. Despite the tension in the vehicle, Dohi was busy working. He was staring at the screen of the Geiger counter. His brows knit together at the ticking of the device.

"Higher rads here," he reported.

"How bad is it?"

"Better find an alternate route."

Fitz turned back to the windshield. The sun retreated on the horizon, leaving behind a sky striped with orange and blue.

"Hold us here for a minute, Tanaka," Fitz ordered.

The MATV eased to a stop on the dirt road. Fitz snatched their thermal scope and roved it back and forth over the landscape, searching for even a flicker of a heat signature. There were several cars parked on the road ahead, but besides that he didn't see much sign of civilization.

"Where did this so-called army go?" Fitz said, frustration rising in his voice. "They couldn't have just disappeared, and they didn't make it out of this forest, so where the hell are they?"

Tanaka tapped the steering wheel. "Could they be camouflaged? Remember the beasts that killed President Mitchell at Cheyenne Mountain? I've seen multiple reports of Variants that can blend in with trees."

Fitz studied the rigid bark of an oak tree to the right of the road. He half expected to see a pair of yellow eyes staring back, but there wasn't anything but charcoaled branches and bark.

He shook his head. "If they are out there, why wait to attack us?"

"Could they have gone underground?" Stevenson asked. "Maybe the Wormers tunneled away from the forest."

"I thought of that," Fitz admitted. "Colonel Bradley told us to keep our eye out for any tunnels, but so far I haven't seen shit, and we've been out here for hours."

"Yeah, but how would thousands of the Variants escape into tunnels during the bombing?" Rico asked. "Those Wormers can't work that fast, can they?"

Fitz massaged his chin. They'd seen the Variants as they'd flown away from the Basilica of St. Thérèse. There had been thousands of the pale monsters below their helicopter, their ranks so thick they looked like a carpet of pallid flesh.

He could count the amount of corpses they had found out here on his hands, and there was zero evidence of tunnels. Seeing nothing, Fitz grabbed the radio and brought the receiver to his lips.

"Lion One, Ghost One, do you copy? Over."

Static fuzzed out of the speaker for several minutes before Colonel Bradley replied.

"Copy, Ghost One, you got a sitrep?"

Fitz reluctantly relayed the lack of intel, then waited through another long pause.

"We've got just a few hours before General Nixon

gives the green light for all troops to advance to Paris, son," Bradley replied. "The EUF HQ is under attack from all directions, and they're not sure how long they can hold the lines."

"Roger that, sir. We'll find the creatures. Over and out."

Fitz pointed at the road. "Keep driving. We're running out of time."

Tanaka put the truck back into gear. The engine hummed and the vehicle lurched down the road.

Fitz propped his M4 up against the door and grabbed his MK11. He was getting anxious for multiple reasons, not the least of which was his uncertainty about what was happening back in the United States. General Nixon was preparing for the second phase of Operation Reach to Paris, and America was on the brink of a civil war.

How had things gotten this bad?

He had thought coming to Europe was the beginning of the end, but now it seemed like a detour from an even bigger problem back home.

Fitz breathed deeply and pushed away his other concerns. He focused back on the terrain.

One mission at a time.

The MATV crested a hill, and Fitz saw life for the first time since they landed. The green canopy of a forest surrounded a sparkling lake in the next valley. Rays of waning sunlight danced over the oasis in the center of the scorched landscape.

"Anyone thinking what I'm thinking?" Fitz said.

"You think the Variants went for a swim when the bombs dropped?" Rico said.

Fitz lifted a brow. "Only one way to find out."

"On it," Tanaka said. He pushed the gas pedal down and accelerated along the winding road. Rocks and other debris had fallen from a bluff hanging over the right side of the road. Chunks of juvenile armor were strewn around the scree. Fitz spotted more bones protruding out of the dirt to the side of the road.

Tanaka rolled up next to the lake a few minutes later.

Fitz grabbed his MK11 and turned back to Dohi. "Do we need our suits?"

"Not if we make it quick."

"Okay, let's check this lake out," Fitz replied. He opened the door and took in a breath that smelled of charred firewood, pine needles, and sour fruit. Dohi joined him in front of the truck.

"You smell that?" Fitz asked.

"Was just about to ask you the same thing. Smells like dead Variants to me."

Fitz opened the back passenger's door and gave the rest of the team orders to stay put.

"Stevenson, get on the two-forty if we run into trouble. We'll be back in thirty minutes, okay?"

"Someone else should go out there with you," Rico said.

Apollo jumped up and moved toward the door, eyes pleading with Fitz to let him go.

"Fine," Fitz said.

Apollo leaped out into the dirt. Fitz shut the door and scanned the sky with the thermal scope. If there were Reavers up there, the scope would pick them up. The dog checked the sky too, sniffing the air.

"Looks clear," Fitz said.

Apollo confirmed it with a tail wag, and the trio set off for the lake, leaving the rest of Team Ghost and the girl behind.

Dohi took point and moved slowly, cautious with every step. Fitz crept behind him, watching for contacts. Apollo sniffed the ground for a scent as he trotted next to Fitz. They didn't have a full radiation suit for Apollo, but the dog was wearing protection over his paws. Fitz almost told Apollo to return to the MATV, but they needed him out here. Countless lives might depend on the dog's keen senses.

They moved into the forest on the northern side of the lake. Tree branches shifted in the breeze. A leaf cartwheeled to the ground in front of him and crunched under Fitz's blades.

He scanned the bark of the trees for the outline of hidden Variants, but nothing stirred. Dohi stopped every few feet, bent down to look for tracks, then kept moving. He paused longer at a clearing overlooking a brown beach and the calm lake. The setting sun had receded behind storm clouds, and with the smoke choking much of the sky it was difficult to see.

At the grassy overlook, Dohi took a knee to scope the area and then motioned for Fitz. He crossed over the meadow and joined the laconic marine.

"Look," Dohi said quietly. He pointed at dozens of corpses below. A pincher claw stuck out of the sand, and armored carapaces littered the beach like seashells.

Dohi scooped up a handful of dirt. He let it filter through his fingers and then looked up at Fitz. "If they can tunnel through rock, they can tunnel through this."

Fitz nodded back and walked closer to the beach. Dohi was a stoic man, always calm, always thinking. Fitz trusted him to find the creatures, but so far even Dohi seemed stumped.

Apollo, on the other hand, seemed to be onto something. He trotted away, muzzle to the ground. Fitz and Dohi took off after the dog. They moved along the grassy bluff overlooking the beach and then back into the woods.

The dog was zigzagging around rocks and foliage, definitely onto a scent. He weaved back and forth as he followed whatever clue his nose had picked up.

They came upon another sandy clearing set about a hundred yards away from the beach. Grass grew in patches around the perimeter. Apollo stopped at the edge of the clearing, sniffing, and then backed away. He trotted along the sandy ground and then began to circle as though he had lost the scent. Fitz and Dohi swept their rifles over the area while Apollo hunted. The dog moved to the edge of a rocky outcrop above the beach, where his back suddenly went rigid.

"What's wrong, boy?" Fitz said as he approached.

The dog looked back at him and then toward the water.

Dohi flashed a hand signal to Fitz, and they retreated to the safety of the trees on the edge of the clearing. The wind whipped the branches, creaking eerily, as Fitz finally saw what had spooked Apollo. About halfway across the lake, a ripple broke across the water, and a fin poked through the surface.

"Master Sergeant," Dohi said.

"I see it," Fitz replied.

A dozen more of the fins poked out of the water. They hadn't found the army, but they had discovered some of the monsters.

"Looks like juveniles," Fitz whispered. He watched for a few more seconds and then jerked his chin to the north. "Let's get back to the MATV."

The men had only taken a few strides when Apollo yelped. Fitz turned to see the dog standing in the sandy clearing on the other side of the trees.

"Come on, boy," Fitz said, waving.

Apollo tried to lift his left paw, but it was inexplicably stuck in the sand. He let out a low whine and then barked. Fitz rushed over to him and bent down to grab Apollo's leg. The first tug did little to move his paw, and the dog yelped in pain.

Fitz moved to the other side to get a better grip. The vantage point gave him a wide view of the lake—and the monsters still moving beneath the water. A humanoid head surfaced. It was connected to a long back that looked eerily like an alligator's. The juvenile, not really a juvenile anymore, was a monstrosity, with scabby armor protecting most of an elongated body.

"Hurry," Dohi said. He was standing on the other side of Apollo, rifle aimed at the creature.

"Hold your fire," Fitz said. He finally freed the dog's paw from the sand. Apollo bolted away toward the grass. Fitz went to stand, but his right blade was now stuck to the wet sand where he had knelt to help Apollo.

"What the hell?" Fitz muttered.

"I'm stuck too," Dohi grumbled. He stood a few feet away from Fitz, his left boot sunk into the sand and his right in the grass, where Apollo was now rolling as if trying to get something off his fur.

Static buzzed over the comms, and Rico's panicked voice came over the frequency in Fitz's earpiece.

"Fitzie, where the heck are you guys? We've got multiple contacts back here!"

Automatic gunfire cracked in the distance, and Fitz looked to the north. Tracer rounds from the M240 shot into the sky.

"We're on our way," Fitz replied. "What's going on back there?"

"Reavers! Get back here pronto!"

Fitz cursed and pulled as hard as he could to free his blade. It finally popped out of the sand and he fell on his rear. He pushed himself up and took another step, but this time both of his blades sank in the muck.

He looked down at some sort of quicksand, realizing he and Dohi were right on the border of the deadly pit.

Dohi shouldered his rifle and squeezed off a three-round burst into the water as his left boot sank. The rounds punched into the monster's shell, and it dove beneath the surface.

More gunfire cracked to the north.

"Fitz, hurry!" Rico shouted over the comms.

In the lake, another row of fins emerged, attracted by the gunfire. There were now at least three of the monsters swimming toward the beach.

"Apollo, get back to the truck," Fitz ordered.

The dog barked in defiance.

"That's an order, boy!" he shouted.

The dog took a few steps back in the grass, growling, and then stood his ground. Fitz cursed again and tried to free his blades, but they were being sucked down into the sand.

Dohi set his rifle in the grass and then reached down to untie his boot and yank his foot out of it. He managed to free his leg and hopped backward. The sand swallowed his boot with a slurp.

Scooping his rifle off the ground, Dohi extended it to Fitz.

Fitz tried to reach it, but his fingers came just inches from the carbine.

Was this how he was going to die? Sucked into the earth while his team was slaughtered and forgotten?

Hell no, it's not, he thought as he pulled harder to free his blades.

Dohi searched for a longer stick to hand to Fitz. By the time he found one, Fitz's blades were almost completely submerged. The force of the suction was stronger than the grip of a Variant.

The world slowed as if he had been stunned by a flash

grenade. The Reavers swooped through tracer rounds over the road. Fitz turned back to the lake, where one of the juveniles emerged from the water. It clambered onto the beach and shook the water from its armor.

Apollo's barking pulled Fitz back to real time. The dog stood on his hind legs and pawed the air as if he was trying to reach out and help Fitz.

The creature on the beach focused a pair of almond-shaped eyes on the dog.

"Dohi, shoot the juveniles!" Fitz ordered.

Dohi dropped the stick he was holding and brought up his rifle. Fire blossomed from the barrel and lanced into the creature's leg, splattering blood on the sand.

Another beast scrambled out of the water and tilted its head in Fitz's direction. It cracked open a wide mouth, revealing jagged teeth.

"Fuck this," Fitz said. Reaching down, he unfastened the straps of his blades. "Dohi, hand me that stick!"

The other soldier tossed it to him between gunshots. Fitz grabbed the end with one hand and then used his other to unfasten the final straps of his blades. He fell forward and hit the sand with a grunt, leaving his precious carbon fibers behind.

Dohi dragged Fitz toward the grass. He didn't bother looking back at his blades, which were as good as gone. Instead, he did the only thing he could do and pulled his M9 from his holster to fire at the beasts on the beach. He pushed himself to a sitting position as Dohi continued to fire with his M4. The first shot Fitz squeezed off chipped at its thick, armored back, but the second shot hit the creature scrambling toward them in the eye.

It trumpeted like an elephant and swung its head from side to side, blood sloshing out of the shattered socket. Dohi hit it in the forehead with two more rounds, killing the monster instantly.

Apollo licked Fitz's face and then nudged his side as if to say, "Let's go!"

Dohi grabbed Fitz up under his armpits and then hoisted him over his shoulder. He wasn't used to being carried, but Fitz wasn't going to protest.

Dohi lumbered across the grass to the woods separating them from the MATV. Fitz couldn't see the truck, but the gunfire continued. It meant his team was still alive.

A projectile came crashing through the branches of the forest somewhere in the distance. Fitz caught a glimpse of a Reaver tumbling through the canopy, flapping and squawking in its otherworldly language.

The bark of the M240 drowned out his voice, and the chatter of at least two M4s joined the battle. Fitz fired his pistol at a humanoid face that emerged from a bush. The beast plowed through the vegetation and slammed into a tree. Fitz searched for an unprotected hunk of flesh and popped off two shots that ripped through the slimy skin above the monster's neck. The creature crashed to the ground, screeching in rage.

A voice crackled over the comms. "We're stuck!"

The transmission from Rico prompted a flood of adrenaline-induced heat that prickled through Fitz. If the MATV was in quicksand as well, then they were all doomed. Losing the vehicle out here was a death sentence.

"Hold on, we're almost there," Fitz said into the comms. He bobbed up and down as Dohi carried him back to the road, winding around trees and powering through underbrush. The rumble of a strained engine soon joined the sound of gunfire.

"The Reavers are retreating, but we can't move!" Tanaka said over the comms.

Fitz tried to look over his shoulder, but he couldn't see the truck. He forced himself to keep his pistol trained on the trees, realizing the M240 was no longer firing.

Dohi took a few more steps and then lowered Fitz to the ground. He was crawling from the moment he touched the grass, and Dohi spun to fire quick bursts from his M4. Fitz pushed away at the ground, propelling his now useless lower half up the rest of the embankment to get a look at the MATV.

Tanaka had reversed into the field on the left side of the road, and from the look of it, they were indeed stuck in another quicksand trap. The front tires were still above the ground, but the back of the vehicle was submerged.

"Get out of there!" Fitz shouted.

Tanaka was already climbing out the front driver's side window. He pulled himself onto the hood and then reached back for Alecia. The girl jumped off into the dirt and scrambled away to safety.

"Changing!" Dohi yelled.

Rolling to his back, Fitz squeezed off three quick shots at a juvenile that skittered around a tree. The rounds ricocheted off its armor.

Dohi slammed in a fresh magazine and fired off another burst that brought the monster down. The other creature sank back into the shadows.

Fitz flipped back to his stomach and dragged himself toward the road. Alecia and Tanaka were standing on solid ground, but Rico was still climbing out onto the hood, and Stevenson was nowhere in sight.

"Hurry!" Fitz shouted.

The back of the MATV was buried up to the passenger's window, but the front wheels were still on solid ground and kicking up dirt. The sand gurgled and slurped around the armored doors as Stevenson fought to keep the vehicle above the muck. The engine groaned, filling the air with the scent of smoke and burned rubber.

Drawing his Katana, Tanaka ran over with the blade in one hand and his pistol in the other. Alecia raised her pistol and fired into the forest, scoring a hit that prompted a screech from one of the monsters.

"Stevenson, you gotta bail!" Rico shouted.

Dohi was firing again behind Fitz, and Apollo was barking up a storm.

"Stevenson, get out!" Rico yelled again.

Fitz dragged his body a few more feet. He changed the magazine in his M9 and searched for a target. The wall of smoke to the south had completely swallowed the setting sun, and darkness spread over the land. In the woods separating him from the lake, three juveniles were prowling the shadows, darting between trees.

Apollo took off running toward the forest, and Fitz reached out to stop him. "*No!* Get back!"

Behind them, there was a loud sucking sound followed by a *pop*. Apollo retreated, and Fitz squeezed off three more shots into the woods before turning to look at the road.

The MATV was gone—with Stevenson still in it.

12

To say they were surrounded was an understatement.

Beckham finished sending the SOS and their current GPS coordinates over the channel that had broadcast the repeating message "Javier Riley" and turned to look at the monitors in the radio room.

Outpost 46, or Deadwood, as Flathman called it, was an island in a sea of infected. There were hundreds of the beasts, some of them clothed, others naked and covered in pus-oozing bite marks and deep gashes. Flathman watched the security footage from a chair in front of a table covered with magazines, boxes of bullets, and the single bottle of vodka.

They had plenty of ammo, but not enough weapons to fire it. Between the two of them, the soldiers had two M4s, two M9s, and a twelve-gauge shotgun—hardly enough firepower to hold off the horde beyond the gates.

"They definitely know we're here," Flathman kept saying. He took another swig of vodka.

Beckham almost slapped the drink out of his hand.

"At least the fences are live," Flathman continued. "Those will keep the bastards out for a while."

"How long is a while? I just sent an SOS to whoever

is sending out the repeating message. Maybe we can hold them back long enough to get evacuated."

After another swig, Flathman shrugged a shoulder. "Two, maybe three hours."

"And then what?"

Flathman shrugged again. "They get in."

"Fuck," was the only word Beckham could think to say. He looked down at his blade. He needed to find a replacement or fix it before the monsters breeched the outpost. There was no way he could run with the condition it was in now.

"Does that Humvee work?" Beckham said. He didn't want to leave the base, just in case President Ringgold sent them a bird for evac, but so far there had been no answer to his SOS, and he couldn't wait around for one either.

"I filled the generators with the last of the diesel," Flathman said.

"How about that M260 and the Gatling guns? Do any of 'em have ammo?"

Flathman shook his head. "My men burned through it weeks ago. That's probably why ROT left them behind."

"Is there another tunnel to get out of here?"

"Nope."

"Make it too tough for the enemy to get in and you can't get out," Beckham muttered under his breath. The old saying had been drilled into him during his training, but he hadn't thought of it in years.

"Be polite, be professional, but have a plan to kill everybody you meet," Flathman said with a chuckle. "I've never been a great soldier, Captain. I've spent my life failing at the first two parts of Mad Dog's advice, and now I've failed at the third."

Both soldiers stood for several minutes in silence, listening to the shrieks of the hungry monsters.

"We have to do something," Beckham said. "I'm not going to sit here and wait to die. Kate needs me."

"Your lady is still alive out there?" Flathman went to take another drink, but Beckham reached out for the bottle. He clearly hadn't been listening to anything Beckham had said about the radio transmissions.

"You've had enough, LT. I need you sober when those fences come crashing down."

Flathman clutched the bottle to his chest. It was already a third gone, but his gaze was still sharp, and his reaction time seemed normal.

"Come on, hand it over," Beckham said more firmly. He motioned for the bottle with two fingers, but Flathman turned his body to shield it like a kid protecting a stolen candy bar.

Beckham balled his left hand into a fist. His eyes flitted to the monitor where the infected were prowling outside the eastern electric fences. One of them galloped through the field, making a run for the chain-link fence. It leaped into the air and latched onto the top, earning itself a jolt for several seconds before it released its grip and fell back to the dirt, pale flesh smoldering.

"Stupid little bastard," Flathman chuckled. "My men and I used to watch this shit all night long. Then we met the Badger, an Alpha who figured out how to tunnel beneath them. The sly fucker killed four of my soldiers before we brought her down. But at least we got a tunnel built for us. It's the same one I used to get inside."

Beckham grabbed the bottle as Flathman brought it back to his lips and yanked it away. He backed up out of the lieutenant's reach.

Flathman stood, his chest heaving and eyes crooked with rage.

"You do not want to get into a pissing match over that bottle," Flathman growled. "Trust me."

"I need you sober, sir. A lot of people are counting on us, including the commander-in-chief. You may not take orders from me, but you do from her, and she told you to hold this post. Did she not?"

Flathman took a step forward, and Beckham saw raw anger in the lieutenant for the first time since meeting him. The lieutenant was a strong and brave man—a man who had suffered as Beckham had, losing men under his command. But unlike Beckham, Flathman had chosen to drink his sorrows away.

"It's over, Captain. I'm sorry. There's no way in hell we can hold back that many. Now give me my damn booze."

Beckham could see taking away his self-medication wasn't going to be easy, but he wasn't going to let Flathman give up. Not now, not after fighting for survival for so long—and especially not after learning Kate was still alive.

"You asked if my lady is alive, and she is," Beckham said. "I sent an SOS over that channel while you were over here drinking your sorrows away. If it gets through, then maybe President Ringgold will send a bird in time to get us the hell out of here."

Flathman snorted. "Your message is more likely to get through to ROT, Captain, and the moment Wood finds out where you are, he's going to send cruise missiles to finish the job. My guess is you just made things worse for us." He fingered the air, motioning for the bottle. "Now hand that over, or we're going to have a *major* fucking problem."

A shriek sounded outside the front door. Flathman had taken a step forward to grab the bottle, but at the noise he drew his M9 and pointed it at the door.

"Shit, one of 'em must have made it past the defenses," he grumbled. "Those fucking moles."

Beckham sat the bottle down on the table and grabbed the M4 resting against the wall. They walked out into the dark main room, side by side, the tension from their argument subsiding as the threat of the monsters loomed.

A shadow flashed by the gap in the window curtains to Beckham's right. Another darted past the window on the left.

Not one infected, but two.

Flathman held up two fingers and then directed Beckham to the right.

The lieutenant stepped up to the window and slowly pulled the drape back. He then pushed the drapes together and walked back to the operations room to look at the monitors. After a quick scan, he muttered, "You have to be fucking kidding me."

"What?" Beckham said, stepping up for a look. He didn't need Flathman to answer his question. On-screen, several infected were climbing into the tunnel that Flathman had used to get back into the outpost.

"Fuck, fuck, fuck," Flathman said. "You didn't seal it off?"

"Me? So this is my fault?"

Flathman cursed and then kicked a chair, sending it crashing into the wall.

Beckham glared at him and brought a finger to his lip. He'd never seen the lieutenant act like this. "Calm down, man."

Flathman took in several deep breaths. He released a sigh and wiped his nose with his sleeve.

"I'm sorry, Cap," he said. "I don't know what got into me."

Beckham furrowed his brows. He had a pretty good idea of what had gotten into the lieutenant: about three gills of vodka. "We have to seal this end of the tunnel then. Where does it come out?"

Flathman pulled off his Cubs hat and fluffed it over his head. "There are two places. One is the central guard tower, and the second is by the machine shed."

"Do you have any explosives?"

Flathman shook his head and then followed Beckham's gaze toward the bottle. "Oh, fuck no."

"Sorry, LT, but we don't have a choice," Beckham said, grabbing it off the desk. "We need to make a Molotov cocktail or at least set that tunnel on fire to keep out any more of the infected until we can find a way out of here."

Beckham thought he was going to have to fight Flathman, but a wave of calm seemed to suddenly pass over the man. He drew in a deep breath, exhaled, and then reached out. "I'll do it, Cap, but it's going to take more than a single bottle of vodka."

Beckham reluctantly handed him the bottle.

"Don't worry, Jim 'Ten Lives' Flathman has one last trick up his sleeve." He took a swig and winked at Beckham.

"I'll watch your six from the top of the building," Beckham offered, wondering if he'd made a terrible mistake.

They loaded up on magazines, grabbed their weapons, and checked the radio one last time to see if there was a reply to their SOS, but all they heard were the same two words on repeat.

"Javier Riley, Javier Riley."

Flathman exchanged a glance with Beckham, and then a nod. They proceeded to the back entry that led to a ladder up to the roof, pausing at the door.

"Good luck, sir," Beckham whispered.

Flathman twisted his lips to the side in a pained frown. After a moment of silence, he said, "I'm sorry about earlier. It's truly been an honor fighting with you,

Captain. I'll do everything I can to make sure you make it out of here and see your lady and, someday, your son."

"Thank you, sir. It's been an honor fighting with you too. Good luck out there."

Another nod, and the men parted ways. Beckham's final words to Flathman seemed absolute, but he still held on to hope they could both get out of this alive. He slung his suppressed M4 over his back and climbed carefully, while Flathman took off around the building.

The monsters surrounding the fences to the south shrieked when they saw him and several rammed the fence, earning jolts that sent their smoking bodies into the field.

Beckham made it to the roof and crawled to the sandbags on the ledge. The third chain-link fence was just below. An infected prowled outside the door that led into the building.

The creature had been a brunette woman not long ago, with hair that hung down to shoulders hunched like a cat's. Razor-sharp claws still bore traces of purple fingernail polish. Beckham ducked lower when the beast glanced up at his position, blood oozing from its eyes, ears, and nose. A long, swollen tongue flicked over bulging lips, licking them dry, before the beast dropped to all fours.

He charged his rifle, then pulled out his M9 and placed it on the ground. Next he lined up his magazines. When he was finished preparing, he bowed his helmeted head.

Instead of saying a traditional prayer, he spoke to the person he knew was looking out for him.

Mom, I could really use your help now. I gotta go meet your grandson. Feel free to move mountains to get me out of this one!

That's what it was going to take—or something on

the same level, he realized as he peeked again over the sandbags. A tsunami of pallid flesh was flowing in from all directions. More of the infected were still darting out of the forest. Their noses had brought them straight to Outpost 46 to kill the last two men left in Chicago.

Kate, baby, if I don't make it, please know that I loved you and our boy more than anything on this earth.

It was torture knowing that Kate was still alive out there but not being able to get to her. At least he could die knowing she still had a chance—even if it was without him.

But that didn't mean he wasn't going to fight tooth and nail to return to her side.

He magnified his scope's sights on the tunnel entrance Flathman had used to get into the base. Several of the beasts were crawling into the hole, but most of the others were either too dumb or too distracted to notice the back door into the outpost.

Beckham counted five infected in the fenced-in area outside the buildings: three to the east near the Humvee, a fourth sniffing the metal building to his right, and the fifth moving around the corner below, right toward Flathman.

The lieutenant glanced up and met Beckham's gaze. They exchanged a nod, and Beckham propped his M4 on the sandbags. He pushed the butt against his shoulder and aimed for the creature moving toward Flathman.

The beast crossed in front of his sights and Beckham got a magnified view of the lacerations covering its naked back like whip marks. Several chunks of flesh were missing, teeth marks surrounding the wounds.

A double pull of the trigger dropped the creature into the dirt with nothing more than a faint thud. Flathman took off running for the central guard tower with a shotgun slung over his back. In his right hand was the bottle of vodka turned Molotov cocktail, and in his right hand was a small camouflage bag.

Apparently the lieutenant had made a pit stop to gather some extra gear. He attracted the attention of a sinewy creature still wearing a pair of jeans and a T-shirt. It jerked toward him, every limb seeming to contort as it tilted its head and snarled.

Beckham lined up the sights on its back as it gave chase. A burst of 5.56-millimeter rounds punched through flesh and painted the ground with infected blood. He fired a single shot that hit it in the skull once it was down, silencing it before it could cry out.

Flathman stopped at the next gate and unlocked it.

So far, so good.

The shrieks around the outpost disguised the clatter from his suppressed M4, and Beckham shifted the barrel toward the three beasts stalking around the Humvee. They all looked at Flathman, yellow eyes homing in on the soldier.

The largest of the bunch, a male with a heavy gut covered in blue veins, let out a screech just as Beckham fired a shot into its puckered lips. The beast collapsed to the ground face first. The females flanking the dead monster dropped to all fours and darted away. They used their back legs to propel their naked bodies after Flathman. Beckham led them with the sights of his scope and fired a shot that hit one in the rib cage, throwing her off-kilter. She tumbled across the dirt. His next shot missed, kicking up dirt in front of the beast making a run for Flathman.

The creature was almost on him, but Flathman didn't turn to fight. He was trusting Beckham to take the shot. He squeezed off three shots, the second trimming the monster's skull. The female collapsed inches from the duffel bag.

Flathman picked up his gear and grinned at Beckham. Then he turned and hurried over to the bottom of the guard tower inside the second fenced-in area. Beckham didn't see any beasts inside the zone. The others outside the building must have all used the exit near the machine shed.

So why the hell was Flathman going after this entrance? Unless he was trying to stop them from getting under the third section…

"Smart thinking, Lieutenant," Beckham whispered.

Flathman moved under the guard tower and got down on his knees outside the hatch. He set the duffel bag down and pulled out a car battery and what looked like a land mine. He spent a few minutes fiddling with the materials and finally lit the rag hanging out of the vodka bottle.

Flathman reached for the hatch and opened it just as a pair of infected hands shot out, grabbing him by the arm. He pulled back, and Beckham squeezed off a shot that hit the monster in the temple.

Blood and gore exploded onto Flathman's face.

He spat and dragged his sleeve across his mouth, still holding the burning Molotov cocktail.

"Shit," Beckham whispered, pushing the scope away. The lieutenant remained on his knees for a moment before dropping the vodka bottle inside the hatch. Then he placed the car battery and mine inside.

"Get out of there," Beckham whispered.

Flathman pushed himself to his feet and then shut the hatch over the tunnel. He retreated to the gate, but instead of walking through, he closed it and locked it.

"What the hell are you doing?" Beckham pushed the scope back to his good eye and zoomed in on Flathman's face. It was covered in so many flecks of gore that it looked like a pepperoni pizza.

"Oh God," Beckham said, realizing what he'd done.

Flathman raised a hand and traced a finger across his neck—a request that no soldier ever wanted to receive from a brother. Beckham had already doomed Flathman with the messy shot that splattered inflected blood on his face, and now the lieutenant wanted Beckham to finish the job.

He aimed the sights on Flathman's heart and moved his finger to the trigger. An explosion boomed in the tunnel. Dirt caved into the earth, and flames spewed outward.

Lieutenant Jim Flathman rolled away from the blast, his fatigues catching fire. He did indeed have one last trick up his sleeve, but in the end, it looked as if the officer had run out of lives, using up his tenth to save Beckham's.

13

Davis could hear the chatter between the Seahawk pilots, but it was just white noise, like the rotors and crackle of static in her new comm-link earpiece. Her mind and heart were still back at the *GW* with the remains of her crew—her friends, her family, all of their lives had been destroyed by the actions of a madman.

The Seahawk had been flying north for over an hour now, but time, like the voices in the cockpit, was lost to Davis. She had received a quick briefing when the SEALs picked her up, but she was having a hard time paying attention to anything.

Across the troop hold sat Senior Chief Petty Officer Randall Blade, helmet bowed. Davis had spent years picking up on the subtle signs of emotion in posture and expression—a shaky hand, a twitch of an eye, a lowered helmet like Blade's.

Davis recalled a similar sight just a week into the outbreak, when she had led a rescue mission with more than two dozen soldiers. Only four of them had made it back, and the survivors they had attempted to rescue had perished, dragged beneath the city streets and entombed in a Variant meat locker.

The SEALs around her were just as tired, broken, and scared as she was.

Blade looked up and caught her gaze. He crab-walked over to Davis. He took a seat next to her and pulled out a water bottle.

"You look more tired than a nerd after pulling an all-nighter."

She raised a brow. "Interesting analogy."

Blade shrugged it off. "I have another one about the prom queen, but..."

"Yeah, probably not a good idea. I *was* the prom queen."

"Well, damn, Captain." He laughed and pushed the water bottle toward her. "Splash some on your face. Trust me. It will help."

She pulled off her gloves and palmed water onto her flushed cheeks. Blade reached into his collar and pulled off a black shemagh.

"For your face," he said.

She couldn't see her reflection, but if her filthy uniform was any indication, her face was covered in a layer of shit. Her clothing reeked of body odor and death— something she had gotten used to over the past few days.

"Thanks," she said, low enough that he probably couldn't even hear her over the rotors. She wet the scarf and wiped the muck from her face, a combination of mud, blood, and sweat.

"Feel better?" he asked.

She took a swig of water and nodded. "You got a sitrep?"

"Yes, ma'am."

Davis cracked her neck from side to side and tried to get her head back in the game.

"President Ringgold has been moved to the USS

Abraham Lincoln, sailing two hundred miles to the east," he said. "As you know, SEAL Team Four has been tasked with finding Captain Reed Beckham and Lieutenant Jim Flathman at Outpost Forty-Six. Command made the decision not to warn them we're coming, for fear that ROT would intercept the message."

Davis recognized the name of the outpost, a memory surfacing. "I've been there, back before Operation Earthfall. Impressive place. Let's hope it's still intact and our boys are still there."

Senior Chief Blade nodded and continued the briefing. "Once we evacuate them from Outpost Forty-Six, we will head to the White House at the Greenbrier, in West Virginia, to infiltrate the PEOC and determine the fate of Vice President George Johnson. He's the key to stopping Lieutenant Wood."

He glanced at her for a moment, sizing her up. At least that's what she figured he was doing, checking to make sure she wasn't too broken after blowing up her own goddamn ship.

"You can count on me," she assured him.

"I know, Captain, and you can count on us. Let me introduce you to my men." Blade jerked his chin at each man as he introduced them. "This is our medic, Petty Officer Third Class Brandon Melnick."

The SEAL scratched at his beard and nodded. He had sharp green eyes like Davis's.

"This is Petty Officer Third Class John Tandy," Blade said, gesturing to the second man on his left. Tandy was by far the tallest of the group. He raised a gloved hand.

"Next are Petty Officer Second Class Robert Larson and Chief Petty Officer Dave Watson."

Larson and Watson nodded. They were similar in appearance, with athletic builds, tan skin, and mustaches. Each carried an MK16 fitted with an Advanced

Armament Corporation SCAR suppressor and an Aim-point CompM4 sight.

"Finally we have Petty Officer First Class Andrew 'Papa Smurf' Dixon."

Dixon was the shortest of the group, which Davis assumed had something to do with his nickname. He was the only SEAL to offer a reassuring smile, and Davis forced herself to return the gesture. It was good to be back in the company of the SEALs. The men were some of the finest warriors on the planet, and they were going to be vital assets in her eventual mission to find and kill Wood.

Blade looked toward the cockpit. "That's Colonel Pressfield and Captain Omstead," he said. "Call signs are Scorpion One and Two."

The crew chief sitting at the other end of the troop hold raised a hand when Blade pointed in his direction.

"That's Ronaldo," Blade said.

Davis nodded at the crew chief and looked back at Blade. "How far out are we?"

"Not far," Blade replied. "Should be there shortly."

Davis took a final swig from the water bottle and handed it back to Blade.

"Keep it," he said.

Davis tucked the bottle into her pocket and rested her helmet on the vibrating bulkhead. It was amazing what a clean face and a few sips of water did to lessen her anxiety. But as soon as she closed her eyes, images of monsters surfaced. She saw her crew, of course, but there were other familiar faces in the horde. She pictured her husband, Blake, and her nephew, Ollie, transformed into hideous, sucker-faced infected. She had left them behind when the outbreak happened, sailing away on the *GW* while they remained holed up in her tiny apartment.

She hoped they'd died quickly, or at least that they'd

lost themselves the moment the infection took hold. She couldn't imagine how horrible it would be, knowing that you were turning into a monster but being unable to stop it.

She lost herself in the memories, slipping away until Colonel Pressfield reported they were coming up on the target.

"Lock and load, boys," Blade said. He handed Davis a new M4, while his men palmed magazines into their weapons and finalized their gear prep. "And ladies," he amended.

"Thanks," she said with a smirk.

"I have no idea what we're going to find at Outpost Forty-Six, but better to be prepared," Blade said.

She grabbed the carbine and slapped in a fresh magazine. A few minutes later, the helicopter began its descent through the clouds.

"Target sighted," said one of the pilots.

"Holy shit," added the other. "You better have a look at this, Captain Davis."

Most of SEAL Team Four moved to get a view out of the windows, while Blade and Davis maneuvered into the cockpit. Pillars of smoke rose from a fire burning under a guard tower centered in the base.

"Looks like trouble," Blade said.

"Where the fuck did all of those Variants come from?" Melnick asked over the comms.

Davis stared at the base. Its three rows of electric fences were surrounded by hundreds of the beasts.

"Hand me your binos," she said to Blade.

He gave her the binoculars, and she zoomed in on the southern side of the fence. But what she saw wasn't the Variants she was used to. These beasts were bleeding from their eyes and ears.

"Infected," she said. "Those are all newly infected!"

"What?" Blade said, reaching for the binos to see for himself.

"Looks like hostiles inside," said Captain Omstead, pointing down.

Davis spotted the beasts inside the third fenced-in area, but she didn't see any in the first or second lines of defense. How the hell had those gotten through?

"Get us closer," she ordered.

The pilots dipped lower, providing a better view of the three buildings.

"Look at that," Blade said.

Davis followed his finger to a beast draped in flames, rolling in the dirt. Another creature came running around a shed and slammed into an electric fence. It flew backward from the electric jolt and sprawled on the ground, sizzling.

"Gunfire on the rooftop at two o'clock," Blade said.

Davis leaned closer for a better look. Sure enough, a soldier was lying in a prone position behind a mound of sandbags. The man continued firing at the infected below the buildings without so much as glancing up at the bird. A man that determined could only be Flathman or Beckham. But there was just one man on the rooftop. Where was the other soldier?

"Anyone got eyes on other survivors?" Davis said.

"Negative," reported both of the pilots.

"I see where those things are coming out," Blade replied. "Check out that machine shed."

Davis pivoted for a better look. Sure enough, one of the burning monsters came crawling out of a hole in the ground. It stomped out the flames and then made a run for the fence behind the concrete building where the soldier was camped out.

Blade looked to Davis for orders. She had forgotten, briefly, that she was the commanding officer.

"Keep them away from that soldier," she said firmly.

Another monster leaped onto the fence surrounding the building. This one wasn't zapped and continued climbing.

"Shit," she whispered, realization setting in. The power had gone out, and it was only a matter of time before the other barriers fell.

14

There were a few memories seared in Fitz's brain that would never fade. They weren't happy memories: the moment he got word his brother had been killed by friendly fire, losing his teammates and his legs to an IED in Iraq, hiding under a pile of rotting corpses in New York.

And now this one: sitting on a rock, staring at the stumps of his legs in the middle of a radioactive wasteland in France.

Things weren't looking good for Team Ghost. They were stranded, and they'd lost Stevenson. Their MATV, radio, and CBRN suits had been sucked into the bowels of the earth. Tanaka and Dohi held a perimeter on the outskirts of the woods, waiting. Rico stood nearby, her weapon at the ready. Alecia was stroking Apollo's coat, while Fitz sat helpless on a boulder and tried to figure out their next move.

"What are we going to do, Fitzie?" Rico asked. She fiddled with her blue locks as she paced in front of him.

"Don't call me that," he snapped.

Fitz immediately regretted his outburst, but the damage was done. Rico's huge eyes gleamed with hurt, and she turned away to stare at the spot where the MATV had disappeared.

A few feet away lay the corpse of one of the juveniles. The beast's oddly humanoid head and misshapen eyes seemed to stare up at Fitz. Ghost had killed all of the monsters that had attacked them, but Fitz had a feeling there were more out there. He could feel their presence, and Apollo could sense them too. The dog's eyes were alert, roving back and forth while Alecia ran her fingers through his fur.

"Better start walking," Dohi said. "Come on, Master Sergeant, I'll carry you."

When Fitz didn't respond, Rico walked over and hunched down in front of him.

"Fitzie—Fitz—he's right. We gotta move," she said. "Stevenson is dead, and our MATV is gone. If we stay out here, it's a race to see what kills us first—the Variants or the radiation."

Fitz balled his hands into fists. He wanted to scream and lash out and punch the closest tree, or stomp the dead Variant in front of him, but he couldn't even do that. A wave of despair swept over him. He hadn't felt this helpless since he'd landed at Walter Reed.

"I'm falling apart," he said, so quietly that only Rico could hear him.

She put her gloved hand on his. "You are stronger than this bullshit," she said. "You're the strongest man I've ever met. Now let that big Indian pick you up, and then let's get moving."

Fitz almost laughed. "And you're the craziest woman I've ever met."

Before she could answer, Apollo walked over and shoved his snout under their hands, clearly feeling left out.

"Pack up," Fitz said. "We're moving out."

Dohi did another sweep of the woods with Tanaka before walking over. Rico grabbed Alecia's arm and pulled the girl to her feet. The teenager didn't seem all that rattled by recent events. If anything, she appeared anxious to get back into the fight.

"Where will we go?" she asked.

Fitz didn't have an answer. None of them did, so they headed west, with Apollo on point and Dohi carrying Fitz over his back. Tanaka took rear guard, and Rico walked with Alecia in the middle of the group.

"Stay on the road just in case there are more of those sand traps out there," Fitz said. He tightened his grip around Dohi's neck. Being unable to defend himself was probably the worst part of being carried.

No, he decided. The worst part was feeling like a burden.

If it came down to it, Fitz would order his team to leave him behind. He wouldn't be responsible for their deaths. When he'd taken off his blades, he'd known what he was doing—but that was before the MATV had been swallowed.

"What do you think those things are?" Rico asked. "The sand traps, I mean."

"My guess is the Variants created 'em. Remember the beaches at Normandy? They set a trap for our mechanized units," Tanaka replied.

"Yeah," Fitz said. His mind drifted as they walked out of the burned valley. The scent of charcoal floated around them, and ashes fluttered in the moonlight.

Team Ghost continued up a hill, and Fitz twisted to see the valley they were leaving behind. Alecia looked up at him. There was no hint of fear in the girl's eyes. She had already lived through so much in her short life. Today was just another day in a world overrun by monsters.

"Get me a reading with the Geiger counter," Fitz said.

Tanaka, who'd taken over the duty from Dohi, pulled the device from his cargo pocket. It ticked so rapidly Fitz didn't even need to look at it to know they were still in danger.

Apollo halted and snarled.

"What is it, boy?" Fitz asked.

The dog whined and paced, his tail held low. Something had him spooked.

"Set me down and form a perimeter," Fitz said.

Dohi did as ordered, and Fitz unslung his rifle. Team Ghost formed a phalanx around him, with each of them angling their rifles in different directions. Alecia gripped her pistol, a World War II–era 1935A semi-automatic, a beautiful gun that fired 7.62-by-20-millimeter cartridges. They had plenty of weapons and ammo to hold back a small Variant attack, but without their MATV there was no way they would last long out here if they ran into multiple contacts, no matter how brutally they fought.

Clouds shifted across the moon, carpeting the valley in darkness. To the east, the glow from the fires warmed the dark horizon. Fitz and the other members of Ghost flipped their night-vision optics into position.

"Stay close to me, Alecia," Rico said.

"Anyone got eyes on hostiles?" Tanaka whispered.

"Negative," Dohi reported.

"I've got nothing," Fitz said. He scanned the meadow to the left of the road below them where the MATV and Stevenson had been swallowed. Then he zoomed in on the woods surrounding the lake.

Apollo continued to growl. The dog was slowly roving his head from the meadow to the forest.

Fitz was squirming over for a better view when he

felt a slight vibration under his butt. Dohi glanced at his boots.

"You feel that?" he whispered.

Apollo suddenly bared his teeth.

"Where's that sound coming from?" Rico asked.

Alecia pulled out her knife and held it up alongside her pistol. She looked ready to take on the entire missing army of Variants and juveniles, even without a pair of night-vision goggles. Tanaka and Dohi moved their M4 barrels back with calculated precision to search for targets.

"Two o'clock," Dohi said.

Fitz roved his rifle to a field of burned vegetation. The earth bulged, something moving beneath the surface. He swallowed and chambered a round inside his carbine.

"Get ready," Dohi whispered.

Team Ghost came together, back-to-back, with Fitz on the ground between them. If the Wormer or Beetle or whatever was large enough to shake the earth, he doubted their bullets would do anything against it.

"You have to run," Fitz said. "Everyone get the hell out of here."

"No fucking way, Fitzie," Rico said.

"That's an order," Fitz said, his voice rising. "I'm just going to slow you all down. Get Alecia out of here."

"I can fight!" the girl yipped.

Dohi and Tanaka exchanged a glance.

"I'm not leaving a man behind," Tanaka said.

"We all die together," Dohi added.

The ripple in the dirt was spearing in their direction now, but it wasn't moving erratically, like the subterra-nean beasts Fitz had witnessed from the bell tower of the Basilica of St. Thérèse. Whatever was beneath the surface was coming for them in an almost completely straight line.

"Prepare to fire," Fitz ordered.

Every gun was aimed toward the dirt. The mound suddenly sank, the dirt folding inward, creating a hole like a mouth opening. From the gaping darkness came a strange humming sound.

Fitz zoomed in just as a massive black object exploded from the dirt. The *pop* of gunfire broke as Alecia fired her pistol. The round pinged off the armor of what looked a lot like their missing MATV.

"Hold your fire!" Fitz said.

Tanaka lowered his rifle. "Well, fuck me sideways. Is that what I think it is?"

"Shit," Dohi said. He kept his barrel on the filthy MATV that was driving up a dirt ramp leading out of the hole. The oversized tires kicked up chunks of soil and mud.

"How is this possible?" Rico said.

Stevenson—at least Fitz assumed it was Stevenson— drove the MATV into the meadow. The vehicle halted for a moment, wipers streaking across the mud-caked windshield.

Fitz caught a glimpse of Stevenson's bulky frame through the glass, and for a moment he was sure it was a ghost or a hallucination. The MATV lurched forward and turned toward the road.

Team Ghost all backed away as Stevenson eased to a stop next to them, propping open the driver's door. He looked at Tanaka first, then down at Fitz.

"So were you guys going to leave me back there or what?" Stevenson asked.

"We thought you were dead!" Rico said. "How are you not dead?"

"Everyone get inside," Fitz said. "Explanations can wait."

Dohi picked up Fitz and placed him in the passenger's

seat, while the rest of the team piled in the back of the truck.

"You didn't happen to find my blades, did you?" Fitz asked.

Stevenson looked over at him, a wide grin on his face. "Nope—but I found something better."

Rico squeezed between the front seats.

"What's that?" she asked.

"I know where the Variant army is," Stevenson said. "Wait till you see it, Master Sergeant."

"See what?" Fitz asked.

Stevenson's features turned serious. "The highway to hell."

Kate stood on the deck of the USS *Abraham Lincoln* in a tight-fitting NAVY sweatshirt and jeans, looking out over the sparkling purple water. She had only seen the sun for a few hours before darkness rolled in.

The USS *Florida* had slipped back below the surface, and the *Thalassa* was long gone. She stared at the horizon in the direction of Europe, wondering if the French scientists were going to accomplish what she and Dr. Ellis hadn't been able to do—to cure the virus that turned men into monsters. Had she known that was what they were doing, she would have—but no. She'd made her choice. She was going to focus on Javier Riley and Beckham and leave playing god to other scientists.

Behind her, the deck was alive with activity. Sailors and soldiers prepared for the arrival of the ships that General Nixon had deployed. Everyone was ready to move out at a moment's notice. As soon as Lieutenant Wood's stealth ship was located, Ringgold had authorized a mission to destroy or neutralize all ROT targets.

Kate walked over to a group of Army Rangers preparing their gear behind an Osprey. Horn was briefing the men who would serve under his command on the mission to the Greenbrier.

"Our job is to link up with SEAL Team Four, Captain Davis, Lieutenant Flathman, and Reed—I mean, Captain Beckham," Horn said, correcting himself. "We're told there will likely be hostiles and infected in the area."

"Infected?" said a handsome young man with a freckled face. "Do you mean with the hemorrhage virus?"

Horn looked at Kate. She zipped her sweatshirt up to her chin.

"Yes. That's why we have CBRN suits," Horn replied to the young man.

"Is there reason to believe ROT soldiers will be at the White House?" asked another soldier.

"It's possible, but I'm more worried about infected," Horn said. "ROT launched a missile over the Greenbrier and the White House before some of President Ringgold's staff could get inside."

"That's all the intel we have?" asked another man with a thick beard.

"Yes it is. Do you have a problem with that, Sergeant?" Horn asked.

The soldier massaged the tip of his beard and shook his head.

"This is a volunteer mission," Horn said. "America needs you now more than ever, but if you're having doubts, I'd rather you stay behind than slow me down once we get there."

"We're with you," said the younger man with the freckles.

Several firm nods followed his vote of confidence, and Horn concluded the briefing with a whistle. "All right, then—we move out in fifteen."

Horn strode over to Kate wearing black fatigues under matte armor that covered his chest, knees, and elbows. A dark helmet topped with night-vision goggles covered his strawberry-blond hair. He tightened the skull bandanna around his neck as he approached.

"Look after Tasha and Jenny while I'm gone, okay, Kate?" Horn didn't wait for a reply. "If something happens to me, the girls have no one left. I know you got your own kid to worry about soon, but I'd feel better if I knew you would look after them. Will you do that?"

"Of course, but nothing is going to happen to you. You're going to bring Reed home, and Javier Riley is going to grow up with his cousins, Tasha and Jenny, and his big uncle Horn. One big, happy family, right?"

Horn beamed, revealing his row of crooked lower teeth.

"Sounds like a dream," he said.

"Make it a reality. Go get Reed back."

He embraced Kate in a hug that was a bit too tight, but she didn't complain. When they parted, Horn looked up at a group of sailors hurrying across the deck. Among them were President Ringgold, Captain Ingves, and Rear Admiral Lemke.

"Doctor Lovato," Ringgold said, waving.

The president's tone and her use of Kate's title did not bode well. She knew before Ringgold got to them that something was wrong.

"What is it?" Kate said, shivering despite her sweat-shirt.

"SEAL Team Four and Captain Davis have reached Outpost Forty-Six," Ringgold said. She hesitated for a second, eyes flitting from Kate to Horn. "They were able to rescue Captain Beckham, but he's been exposed to the hemorrhage virus."

The news took the breath from Kate's lungs. Her

knees seemed to wobble, and she reached out to grab on to Horn. He put an arm around her back, steadying her despite the fact that his own breath had quickened.

"I'm afraid we're going to have to ask your team to stand down, Master Sergeant," Lemke said. "SEAL Team Four and Captain Davis are on their own right now until we can confirm Beckham isn't infected."

"They will proceed with their mission to the former White House, but for now, I'm not risking sending anyone else out there," Ringgold said. She continued talking, but it was just noise to Kate.

Horn's face instantly took on the color of a tomato, and his nostrils flared, an indication he was about to blow a gasket. Kate put a hand on his arm, a subtle hint to choose his words carefully. Then she pivoted back to the view of the ocean, looking out over the waves in the direction the *Thalassa* had sailed. She could have been on the ship working on a cure, but instead she had remained here, doing nothing. If Reed was infected, if he died because the cure didn't get finished in time, it was on her.

"President Ringgold," she said, turning back to face her friend. "I made a mistake. I need to get to that research ship right now."

Piero could hear the monsters roaming the streets, but he didn't dare look out his window. He didn't need to see them to know what kind of beasts they were anyway. The noises they made gave them away. Full-grown juveniles hunted in the streets, and a Reaver perched on a nearby balcony, squawking at the creatures below.

He and Ringo had spent most of the night and the early-morning hours hiding in a small bedroom while the mutated beasts crawled out of the Colosseum and brought food back to their nest like an army of ants. Sometime around midnight, he had seen the Variants with crablike hands for the first time. The sand-colored chitinous double claws looked as though they could cut off a human limb. The beasts were what the EUF had called Pinchers, he realized. Piero was going to make a special point to avoid tangoing with any of those abominations. The last thing he needed was to lose a leg. Running had saved his life a hundred times now.

There were also several Black Beetles and even one of the Wormers moving beneath the buildings across the street. He could feel the tremors as it tunneled under the ground.

Each and every monstrosity below was a creature of nightmares—morphed from different types of animals, insects, and reptiles. Piero had no idea how the mutations occurred, but he was making a mental note of every creature he saw to pass to Command. Hopefully some scientists a hundred times smarter than him would know what exactly these things were and how to kill them.

There was one thing he remembered from school: Insects worked together in a hive, and the Variants seemed to be doing the same thing. He peeked out the window to watch them in the street below. A sinewy Variant moving on all fours had a snake hanging from its maw. Another beast had several big black birds. He even saw a juvenile carrying a limp cat. They were heading back to their colony in a nearly single-file line, like drones.

A human scream filled the night. The sound snapped Piero to his feet. He knew it was a risky move, but he couldn't help but look. It was the first human sound he'd heard that hadn't been transmitted over the radio in... he wasn't even sure how long.

The scream faded away.

Piero remained standing, looking desperately for the human survivor. Across the street, the Reaver turned in his direction, forcing him back down.

"Please, no!" a woman screamed in English. "Let me go!"

Slowly raising his head above the windowsill, Piero spotted an armored juvenile dragging a woman by her hair across the cobblestone street.

He ducked back down before the Reaver could see him looking.

"Help!" she yelled.

Piero was almost more surprised to hear the pleas in a foreign language than to see the woman at all. Had she been a tourist? If so, how had she survived all of these months? Were there more survivors out there?

The questions ping-ponged in his mind. But there was one that was more important than all the others.

What could he do to help her?

Nothing. You can't do anything, he realized. The magazines sticking out of his vest wouldn't even put a dent in the mutated army. By the time he killed the Reaver watching over them, another would have heard him and attacked his hiding spot.

Your mission is to document and relay information to Lieutenant General Piazza. That is your only mission, Sergeant, and you can't—

"Please, somebody help!" the woman screamed in a strangled voice. "They have my daughter! They have my—"

A guttural screech and crunch silenced the woman. Piero jumped up with his rifle at the ready. He couldn't just let a little girl die. He was a soldier—his job was to protect the innocent.

Keeping to the side of the window, he pulled the drape

back to look at the Reaver across the street. The beast was still perched on the balcony, wings folded against its sides, as still as a gargoyle. It appeared to be watching the unconscious and possibly dead woman below with interest. A lizard tongue shot out of its puckered lips, leaving behind a strand of saliva. The beast suddenly flapped into the air, shrieking in its otherworldly voice.

Piero scanned the street for the little girl, but there was no sign of her, only her unconscious mother, who was now being dragged by her wrists. The juvenile halted and craned its neck toward the sky before letting out a long screech.

Four more of the juveniles galloped past, cracking the stones beneath their feet as they moved into position beneath the Reaver.

Another squadron of Reavers was flapping across the skyline. A Beetle came crashing out of a storefront across the street, shattering wood and glass. Another hissed in the distance, answering the call.

Bricks burst outward near the sidewalk where one of the Wormers was tunneling. Tentacles shot out of the opening.

It took Piero a second to understand what he was witnessing. What had been an organized migration back to the colony had broken into all-out chaos—the monsters fighting over the flesh of the woman and possibly her child, although he still didn't see the girl.

A battle was about to occur in the street right below Piero's hiding spot. The creatures were starving, and while they seemed content to bring back animal meat for the good of the colony, they were ready to tear one another apart for a chance at human flesh.

Piero ducked and placed his back against the wall, gripping his rifle so tightly his knuckles popped. Armored plates collided below, and then the screeches began. Hissing, wails, croaks, shrieks, and the clank of armor and scratching of nails rose into a din that hurt Piero's ears.

For several minutes, the monsters tore into one another. Piero closed his eyes, telling himself that there was nothing he could do for the woman or her daughter, wherever the little girl was.

But you still have to do something.

He forced his eyes open to a sliver of light streaming in through the apartment window. The sun was rising over the ancient city, golden light warming the tile rooftops.

A long, guttural croak, louder than those of all of the other monsters combined, rang out. The sound was followed by the same rattlesnake clicking he'd heard back at the Colosseum.

Piero slowly stood and pulled back the drape to look at the carnage below. The street was flooded with blood and hunks of gore. Armored plates, ripped off like scabs, lay surrounded by pools of red.

A Reaver staggered down the sidewalk gripping its leathery shoulder where a wing had been attached. It halted, along with every other Variant on the street, to tilt its head in the direction of the rattling noise.

He had thought the noise was a warning, but this was something else—it appeared to be a command.

All at once, the monsters that still could walk began to march in the direction of the Colosseum. They moved robotically, as if nothing had happened, leaving their dead and dying behind in an urgent and organized fashion.

Piero watched with grim interest, his heart hammering in his chest as the juveniles dragged the helpless woman away. It pounded even harder when at last he saw her daughter, a girl no older than his sister had been when his family visited Rome years ago. She too was unconscious, but that didn't make Piero feel any better.

It took several minutes for his heart rate to return to normal. When he could breathe again, he pulled Ringo from his pocket and sat him on the window ledge, then he pulled out his radio.

Piero had a message for Lieutenant General Piazza. The mutated Variants in Rome had a leader, something that was controlling the army, and Piero knew exactly where it was hiding.

15

Beckham awoke with a splitting headache to find himself lying on the floor with half a dozen guns pointed at his face. But it sure beat waking up to a Variant slinging him onto some sewer wall. As long as these men weren't ROT soldiers...

He tried to move his legs, but his boot and blade were bound. When he moved his hand, a chain rattled from the handcuffs that were attached to the bottom of a metal seat.

The cold metal beneath his body vibrated, and he realized the loud thumping noise wasn't the sound of his heartbeat in his ears but the chop of a helicopter's rotors. There were voices too, all muffled. Beckham saw why when his vision cleared. Six men, all wearing black CBRN suits, were sitting in the troop hold of a Seahawk helicopter. His rattled brain finally managed to focus enough to remember what had happened on the rooftop.

He'd been pinned down at Outpost 46 with Lieutenant Jim Flathman, surrounded by the infected from the SZT. The Seahawk he was in now had descended from the sky to pluck Beckham from the rooftop. He recalled the team of soldiers fast-roping all around him and laying down covering fire to hold back the hordes of infected.

One of those soldiers had asked Beckham a series of questions—questions that Beckham had apparently answered incorrectly. The last thing he remembered was the butt of a rifle to his head.

Now they were pointing their guns at him in the dimly lit troop hold, their eyes watching him.

This wasn't the first time Beckham had had weapons pointed at him by friendly forces. Back on the USS *Truxtun*, he had stared down the barrel of Staff Sergeant Jay Chow's rifle. It wasn't the kind of thing that got easier with repetition.

Beckham looked down the row of seats and saw a woman who wasn't in a CBRN suit. It took him a few seconds to recognize her.

"Is that you, Rachel?" he slurred.

Davis ran a hand through her short-cropped hair. Instead of a CBRN suit, she wore a frayed uniform that was ripped and soiled with blood and mud. She watched him sadly and stood, only to be forced back into her seat by one of the soldiers in a CBRN suit.

"He's not infected," she said.

Beckham glimpsed her holstered side arm. If Davis was armed, then Beckham knew these soldiers weren't aligned with ROT—if they were, Beckham and Davis would already be corpses.

"Captain Beckham," said a man with dark skin covered in camouflage paint. "I'm Senior Chief Petty Officer Randall Blade, with SEAL Team Four. Can you understand me?"

Beckham focused on the man's eyes behind his plastic visor. This was the SEAL who had given Beckham a hard tap with his rifle on the rooftop.

"Where's Kate? Where's Horn? Where's President Ringgold?" Beckham said. He tried to push himself off the floor with his stump, but fell back down to his stomach.

"Stay still, Captain Beckham," Blade said.

Though his voice was calm, Beckham knew the man wouldn't hesitate to blow his brains out if he suspected Beckham was infected.

"Do as they say," Davis said. "You were exposed to the virus, Captain."

"I'm not infected," Beckham said. "Please, please tell me where Kate is."

Instead of answering him, Blade asked, "Captain, do you have a headache, fever, nausea, itching, or abdominal pain?" Blade asked.

Beckham recalled hearing these exact questions from the Medical Corps doctors at the decontamination facility where Team Ghost had been examined right after the raid on Building 8.

"Captain, please answer the question," Blade repeated. "Do you have a headache, fever, nausea, itching, or abdominal pain?"

"I have all the above," Davis said before Beckham could reply. "And I'm not infected. Come on—he's clearly still in his right mind. He needs water, a couple of bandages, and some chow, not an interrogation. The man's a Delta Force operator, for god's sake."

Blade wasn't swayed. He kept his weapon trained on Beckham, and so did the other SEALs. The crew chief unholstered his M9 and chambered a round.

"Captain Davis, you know this is just protocol—" Blade had started to say when Beckham looked up and said, "I have a headache because you hit me in the face with your rifle, Senior Chief."

The thump of rotors filled the troop hold with a

rhythmic din. Beckham kept his face raised to meet Blade's gaze, hoping his answer was enough for the SEAL.

It wasn't.

"My men are alive today because we never break protocol. So either you answer our questions or I'm going to be forced to put you down again. Don't make me do that, Captain."

Beckham lowered his head and looked at himself for the first time since waking. His tattered uniform was covered in blood and gore.

"I'm not infected," he said. "I would be experiencing symptoms by now."

"You know that's not necessarily true," Blade replied coldly. "The incubation period ranges from minutes to hours."

"Fine," Beckham said. He knew the last thing he should do right now was argue, but he did have questions that he needed answered. "You got a family, Senior Chief?" Beckham asked, raising his head again.

After a brief pause, the SEAL said, "Yeah, I do. My wife and son are at SZT Nineteen in Los Angeles, but my daughters were both killed in the outbreak. What's that have to do with anything?"

"I'm sorry about your daughters," Beckham said. "I have a son on the way myself, and I'd really like to get back to his mother. I want . . . I *need* to know where she is and if she's okay."

Blade and his team remained silent. Beckham scanned their faces, or what he could see of them behind their visors. They were all in their early or midthirties—not the greenhorn grunts Beckham had fought with on other missions, but not hardened, half-dead veterans like him either. These SEALs were probably some of the most experienced and capable warriors left in the American military.

Captain Davis looked to Blade, her eyebrows drawn together in a straight line. "I'm pulling rank here, Chief. The man lying on the floor in front of you is a national hero, and I'm not going to treat him like a dog."

Blade grunted when she crouch-walked across the troop hold. "Captain Davis, please do not approach—" he began to say.

Davis cut Blade off with a glare and then sat down beside Beckham. She reached into a gear bag for a bottle of water and screwed off the cap.

"Go ahead," she said, holding it out so he could drink.

Beckham lifted his mouth and greedily accepted the water. She gave him half the bottle and then screwed the lid back on.

"Kate's safe," Davis said. "She's with President Ringgold, Master Sergeant Horn, and the rest of your friends at an undisclosed location."

Beckham heaved a long sigh, unable to contain his relief. He relaxed on the cold floor. "I heard her message, and I knew she was still out there."

For a few seconds neither of them said a word, but Beckham could see she wanted to talk about something.

"They're all dead," Davis finally said.

It was hard to hear over the rotors. "What?"

"My crew. Every single soul aboard the *GW*. I had to put them down after the infection spread," she said.

"I'm sorry." Beckham thought of all the men he had killed over the past seven months. "I had to put Flathman down. He saved me, and I killed him."

"He was infected?" Davis asked.

Beckham nodded. "It was my fault. I panicked and made a rookie mistake, took a shot without thinking, and he ended up covered in infected blood."

"I feel as if this pain is getting worse," she said. "I've lost everyone."

"I wish I could tell you it gets better."

Blade waved at Davis and yelled across the troop hold so she could hear. "We're two hours from our target, Captain."

"Let's get him uncuffed and off the floor," Davis said. "We're going to need his help."

"With all due respect—" Blade began.

She cut him off with, "That's an order, Senior Chief."

Blade bent down to unlock the cuffs, but he kept the zip tie around Beckham's boot and prosthetic. Davis helped Beckham up into the seat. He winced in pain as he sat down but quickly said, "I'm fine, it's just my arm."

"This is a bad idea," Blade said. He returned to his seat and motioned for his men to keep their guns on Beckham.

"When's the last time you ate?" Davis asked.

"A real meal?" Beckham shrugged. "I have no idea."

"Ronaldo, hand me one of those MREs," Davis said.

The crew chief grabbed a pack from a bag and tossed it over to Davis. Beckham knew he needed the energy to get back to Kate. He tore into the MRE and downed the food like a Variant, the SEALs watching from across the chopper anxiously.

By the time Beckham finished his meal, the shock of the attack on Outpost 46 had finally subsided. He still had the pounding headache, but knowing Kate and his friends were safe helped relieve the pain of his other injuries. Having a belly full of food helped too. He almost felt as if he could fall asleep.

"Where are we headed?" he asked.

"The Greenbrier," Davis said. "The PEOC, specifically."

Beckham finished chewing and narrowed his brows. "What? I thought it was hit by a missile loaded with the hemorrhage virus."

"It was," Davis said. "We're going to see if anyone in the PEOC is still alive. Vice President Johnson is the key to rallying the SZTs."

"He's dead," Beckham said. "Everyone there is dead."

Blade finally lowered his rifle. "That may be true, but we need to get inside the PEOC to obtain proof of what happened there. Our mission is to find evidence and relay it over the radio channels to the SZTs. They have to know what Wood has done."

"Did he really declare himself president?" Beckham asked.

Davis nodded gravely. "The bastard has convinced most of the SZTs to rally behind the ROT flag."

"What about General Nixon?" Beckham asked.

"He's got Wood believing he's remaining neutral and focusing on the war in Europe for now. But Nixon has sent President Ringgold's fleet two destroyers to help find the USS *Zumwalt*," Blade said. "Who knows how long we have until Wood discovers that, though."

Davis stroked her long, chiseled chin, as if in deep thought. "At least we were able to neutralize the *GW*."

Beckham looked at Davis, seeing the pain in her features. He didn't ask how it had been destroyed, because he had a feeling he already knew.

"I don't like the idea of raiding the PEOC," he said. "Why not just try to find Wood and take him out?"

"And turn him into a martyr? No. We have to bring the SZTs back to our side before we kill him. Our orders came from President Ringgold," Blade said. "She feels this is the best option."

Beckham nodded. There was only one thing he could do now, and that was to help. "Someone give me a gun. I can still fight," he said.

Blade smiled wryly. "Sorry, Cap. You may not be infected, but you sure as hell aren't coming with us."

"So what do you expect me to do while you break into the PEOC?"

"Crew Chief Ronaldo and Captain Davis are going to watch you," Blade said.

"Like hell," Davis said. "I'm coming with."

Blade shook his head. "You're both from the same breed, aren't you?"

"That's how we survived out here this long," Beckham said. "You have a better chance of surviving if you bring us with you."

Blade glanced down at Ronaldo and, after a brief pause, said, "Get Captain Davis a CBRN suit, but Captain Beckham stays with you after we put down."

"I really don't think this is a good idea," said Horn. "You should stay here, Kate."

Kate finished stuffing a shirt in her bag and turned to face Horn. He was standing in the entry hatch to the quarters Kate had been assigned on the USS *Abraham Lincoln*, still decked out in his tactical armor and carrying his M249. A second rifle was strung over his back, and two pistols were holstered on his thighs. There was also a blade that could have passed for a small sword in a sheath across his black chest armor.

She went back to packing her bag, talking as she worked. "You heard President Ringgold. Reed is out there and he may have been exposed to the virus, and even if he wasn't, there are thousands of newly infected people at the SZTs from ROT attacks. Those researchers need my help."

"I still think it's a bad idea to leave this ship. Why the hell did *Thalassa* leave the fleet, anyway?"

"Maybe they didn't feel safe here," Kate said. "Not that I blame them. Ringgold is a wanted woman."

Horn scratched at the red stubble on his chin and ducked into the room. He walked over to the bunk. Standing over six feet tall, he towered over her.

She had a feeling he was also thinking about Tasha and Jenny, whom Kate had promised to look after, but Kate had already talked to Donna, Bo's mother. She was going to look after the girls while Kate was gone.

"Think about all the people we could save," Kate said. "Think about what would happen if Wood uses another missile loaded with the hemorrhage virus. I have to do this. I should have gone in the first place."

"But going back to the lab could put the baby at risk, right? Reed would want—"

Kate shook her head. "I'm not going to be inside a lab. I promise."

Horn let out a half snort, half cough. "Fine, but I'm going to escort you to the ship with my team. I'm not letting you go by yourself."

"You sure?"

"Absolutely. I'm not letting you go by yourself. Besides, no one's vetted those scientists. I'll be coming on board to make sure they're not a bunch of looney tunes."

"Okay," Kate said with a chuckle.

"Wait," Horn said. "Are you sure this shit isn't all just a ruse? I mean, I'm no expert—hell, I hardly even passed high school chemistry—but I thought you said a long time ago there is no cure."

Unlike Kate, who had almost immediately started designing a weapon after the outbreak, these French scientists had focused on finding a cure. She'd never looked for one because the evidence she'd seen pointed to the epigenetic changes being irreversible.

But what if she'd been wrong? What if she could have found a cure months ago? What if she could have saved her brother?

"What were you going to say?" Horn asked.

"I don't know all the answers, okay?" Her words came out fast and snippy. She shot him a rueful look. "I'm sorry. These pregnancy hormones are a roller coaster."

Horn held up a hand. "Okay, but explain this to me. A cure would mean they could make someone infected with the hemorrhage virus normal again?"

"Theoretically, yes."

"What about the juveniles, or the monsters we're hearing about in Europe?"

Kate shook her head. "Not those. They aren't human anymore. I'm not sure they ever were. Maybe the cure could stop future mutations. I simply won't know until I see what these scientists are doing."

"I won't lie—I don't understand a word you just said," Horn said.

"Just leave this to me, okay?" Kate zipped up her bag and patted him on the shoulder. "Come on, let's go say good-bye to the kids."

Less than an hour later, they were in a Seahawk flying east toward the *Thalassa*. Kate sat next to Horn in the troop hold along with the Army Rangers he had planned to lead to the White House before Ringgold told him to stand down. Kate could see these men were all itching for a fight. They wanted to go after ROT, and Horn wanted to bring his best friend back.

The farther the pilots flew east, the farther Kate felt from Beckham.

I'm going to make sure your dad makes it home safe, she thought to her baby.

Horn smiled at her and then crossed the troop hold to sit next to one of his men. He talked privately over a comm channel with the rest of the team. Kate wasn't tapped into the frequency and couldn't hear any of the conversation, but it probably would have made about as much sense to her as her science spiel had made to Horn.

It was almost midnight by the time Kate saw the outline of the *Thalassa* on the horizon. The white boat with a yellow stripe and blue hull stood out in the dark waters. She could even see the dolphin painted on its side in the moonlight.

"Prepare for drop," one of the pilots said. He maneuvered over the bow of the ship, and Horn helped Kate walk over to the open troop hold. The pilots weren't able to land, but they got close enough that Horn jumped out. He turned around and helped Kate down. The other Rangers hopped out after them and followed them toward the deck as the pilots pulled back into the sky.

A woman in a black trench coat stood on the deck waiting, coattails and silver hair whipping in the wind.

"I'm Doctor Adriana Bruno," the woman said with a thick Italian accent. She held out a hand.

"Doctor Kate Lovato."

Bruno looked over Kate's shoulder at Horn and his men. "I wasn't informed President Ringgold was sending an armed escort." The Italian scientist glanced once more at the weaponry Kate's entourage had brought on board and said, "Please follow me, Doctor Lovato, but the muscle must stay put."

"No way," Horn protested.

"Horn's with me," Kate said. "It's not negotiable."

Bruno shrugged. "Fine. He comes, the rest stay."

"Park it here," Horn instructed his men.

The Army Rangers did as ordered, while Horn and Kate hurried to catch up with Bruno. She was already walking toward a hatch that opened to a ladder. At the top was the operations room, where several officers were watching over the control panels and monitors.

After brief introductions to the ship's captain and crew, Bruno led Kate and Horn down to the labs.

"These have all been retrofitted," she said. "The primary function of the *Thalassa* before was as a fisheries research vessel. A few days after the outbreak, we brought our labs here, and we have been sailing for the past seven months."

She showed them a clean room and two labs. Each was sealed off with translucent plastic walls. There were various tables and equipment set up inside, but Kate saw only one other scientist working in the space.

"Where is everyone?" Kate asked.

Bruno pointed at the scientist in a CBRN suit working in the lab. "It's just me and Doctor Orlov."

Kate had a dozen questions she wanted to ask, but she remained silent, letting Bruno do the talking.

"There were a dozen of us, all from different countries, at the beginning. The French were leading the project, but one by one we lost members of our team while testing our work."

Alarm bells started ringing in Kate's mind. Horn stepped up next to Kate, apparently sensing something was off, just as she did.

"What do you mean, exactly?" Kate asked.

Bruno pivoted away from the labs so she could look at Kate and Horn in turn.

"We had to use ourselves as test subjects in order to get where we are," Bruno said. She shrugged. "There was no one else. It was a risk we all took because of the importance of the project. Make no mistake, complete eradication of the hemorrhage virus is the only goal that matters. Anything less would mean extinction."

"You tested this shit on yourselves, Doctor Bones?" Horn said, stepping forward.

"Bruno," she corrected.

"Right," Horn said. "Listen, Kate is a special lady, and she's six months pregnant, so I don't want her working in those labs. And I sure as hell don't want you using her as a lab rat."

"We're not going to do anything to jeopardize her health," Bruno said. "And I believe the decision is hers, not yours, Mr. Horn."

Kate did another scan of the labs. They looked secure, but this wasn't an ideal place to be doing any sort of research. Had she made a mistake in coming here?

"Our object here is twofold," the researcher continued. "First, to find a cure, and second, to study the monsters and help the EUF fight them in Europe."

Dr. Orlov took off his CBRN suit and joined them. He eyed Horn suspiciously after sealing the hatch.

"No, no, no. I said no soldiers," he said in heavily Russian-accented English. "I told you this how many times, Doctor Bruno?"

Horn held up his hands and moved in front of Kate. "Whoa! The Cold War's over, bro. I'm here to help."

Orlov fastened his thin gray hair into a ponytail and raised his upper lip in a snarl. "If it were up to me, no American would be allowed on this ship."

Horn shot him a cockeyed look as Kate moved between the two men. "Go wait upstairs with your men," Kate said to Horn.

"Men? There are more of them?" Orlov said, turning to Bruno.

"They are waiting on the upper deck," Bruno said, stepping in. "I made sure of that."

"I don't like this, Kate," Horn mumbled.

Orlov raised a brow on his wrinkled forehead at Horn, sizing him up.

"We were told there would be no soldiers," Orlov said.

Kate, sensing things were going to spiral out of control, gently put a hand on Horn's arm. "It's okay, you should wait upstairs with your team."

He hesitated, and she gave him a reassuring nod before he reluctantly retreated back to the ladder, where he watched for another minute, then moved up the steps.

"I'm Doctor Kate Lovato," Kate said, holding a hand out to Orlov in an effort to smooth things over.

He watched Horn leave and then reached out. "Doctor Andrei Orlov. Pleased to meet you, Doctor."

"Likewise," Kate replied.

After a brief moment of awkward tension, Bruno waved Kate toward a computer monitor and a desk that held radio equipment. "Now that that's over, there's something I want you to hear before we get started."

Kate sat in a leather chair in front of the desk and waited while Bruno fired up the computer.

"We've been working with the EUF in multiple cities," she said. "There's a soldier in Rome who has been documenting the ongoing metamorphosis of the creatures there. We've learned a lot from him."

A message played over the speakers in Italian. Bruno translated for Kate.

"The monsters are emerging from inside cocoons. I've come across all sorts of different types, but they all seem to migrate to a colony beneath the Colosseum. They act very much like insects and seem to be obeying a strange rattling noise. I believe there might be some sort of leader or hive Queen controlling them."

Kate considered the implications. If the soldier's observations were correct, then it wasn't necessarily the radiation that was morphing the monsters in Europe.

There was something else going on too, something that had a scientific explanation. Her duty on the *Thalassa* had just become two missions—find a cure for the hemorrhage virus and figure out what the hell was commanding the mutated armies in Europe.

16

Calling it the "highway to hell" wasn't an exaggeration. Fitz sat in the radio operator's seat of the MATV, staring in awe at the tunnel, which was wide enough for two armored trucks to drive side by side.

"Turn on the headlights," he said.

Stevenson switched them on as they drove down a dirt ramp into the tunnel. The high beams cut through the darkness and illuminated a road that Wormers had carved under the earth—hundreds of them, judging by the fifteen-foot ceiling and wide dirt walls.

"This shit is bananas," Rico said.

Fitz agreed. For a moment, he had almost forgotten that he was still missing his blades. The grim view was that breathtaking.

This wasn't just an escape tunnel—it was a graveyard. The monsters that had died from the radiation bombs were everywhere. Some were burned beyond recognition, making it difficult to identify the beasts.

A mangled Variant lay sprawled in the middle of the tunnel, the headlights sweeping over sucker lips and filmy yellow eyes.

Stevenson used the cowcatcher to plow the charred

bodies out of the way. Bones crunched under the weight of the two-ton armored vehicle.

"This is amazing," Tanaka said.

"Amazing isn't exactly the word I would use," Stevenson said dryly.

"My ancestors had legends about places like this," said Dohi. The normally quiet man sat in the back seat with his fingers around a necklace with a black stone that Fitz had never seen before.

"I hate it when you say shit like that," Stevenson said. "You know how much it gives me the creeps."

"Maybe the Variants aren't man-made monsters. Maybe they're demons," Dohi continued. "The Lakota tell of a creature called Two-Face—a half man, half demon with one face that is human and one that is a monster. In some of the legends Two-Face is a cannibal, but in all of them he kills and disfigures his victims to feed his endless appetite. Sounds familiar, doesn't it?"

Rico shuddered. "I think I liked it better when you didn't talk so much," she said.

"The hemorrhage virus caused this," Tanaka chimed in. "Sorry, brother, but that's science."

They fell into silence as they drove deeper into the tunnel. The headlights illuminated a mound of dirt that looked like the gritty sand Fitz had lost his blades in. Stevenson eased off the gas pedal.

"Is that one of the sand traps?" Rico asked.

"Yup," Stevenson replied. "They're everywhere. I almost got lost trying to find my way out of here earlier."

"Keep going," Fitz said.

Stevenson maneuvered around a ramp of dirt that nearly reached the ceiling and continued deeper into the passage. A veiny, wrinkled arm protruded from the bottom of the pile, the claws reaching out for the approaching MATV.

"Christ," Stevenson said. "Do you see that?"

"Keep going," Fitz said when Stevenson slowed.

"You want me to call Command?" asked Tanaka.

"No, I'll do it, but I want more intel before I do," Fitz said. He couldn't quite believe his eyes as they continued forward. The creatures seemed to have evolved into something that more closely resembled insects than humans.

"The Wormers must have dug the tunnels and then created openings above to let the other beasts through," he said.

"So those things aren't traps then?" Tanaka asked. He leaned forward between the seats for a better view.

"They're doors," Dohi said. "Doors to the underworld."

"Ba-na-nas," Rico said, cracking her gum with each syllable.

"All y'all shut up," Stevenson grumbled. "I'm trying to drive here."

Fitz took out his compass and waited for the needle to settle. They were still headed north, not toward Paris, but that didn't mean they wouldn't intersect the zones through which General Nixon planned on leading his advance toward the capital.

"You got any idea why these tunnels would be heading north, Dohi?"

Dohi studied the laminated map on his lap for several moments. "There's not much between us and the ocean besides some towns that were all evacuated months ago."

Fitz tried to relax in his seat, but seeing the stumps sticking out of his fatigues reminded him how helpless he was without his blades.

For the next thirty minutes, they drove down the winding passages until they came to an intersection that split off into three smaller passages like veins from an artery.

"Which way?" Stevenson asked.

Fitz held up the compass. He pointed to the tunnel on the right that was heading east, toward Paris.

The MATV chugged forward, headlights flitting over roots hanging from the dirt ceiling like skeletal chandeliers. The new tunnel was much narrower, and there were no corpses here.

A few minutes into the drive, Fitz saw something else hanging from the ceiling.

"Halt," he said.

The truck's headlights penetrated the inky darkness and captured the bottom of a white sac attached to the dirt roof. Apollo let out a low growl and sat up in the back seat.

"What is that thing?" Rico asked.

"Dohi, Tanaka, check it out," Fitz said.

Apollo bared his front teeth in a warning growl as the two men stepped out of the MATV. They turned on the tactical lights attached to their suppressed M4s and moved in front of the vehicle, where they directed the beams at the translucent sac. In the glow, Fitz saw what looked like a snake inside a cocoon.

Suddenly, it moved.

Rico gasped and cupped her hand over her mouth.

"Sweet baby Jesus," Stevenson whispered.

Fitz didn't know what to say. He scooted forward as Tanaka and Dohi raked their lights back and forth, revealing more of the sacs. The entire tunnel was covered with them. Goo dripped off the skin of the cocoons and webbed to the ground.

"Looks as if we've figured out how the Variants are mutating," Rico said quietly.

"How do you mean?" Fitz whispered back.

"It's like when a caterpillar turns into a butterfly," Rico replied. "Somehow, the radiation must be speeding up the changes we've been seeing all along. What doesn't kill them mutates them."

Tanaka and Dohi moved farther away from the MATV, their lights crossing over the cocoons that clung to the walls, ceiling, and ground like eggs. The skin of the sac hanging in front of them bulged as the soldiers approached. The snakelike creature inside slithered and wiggled. Several of the other cocoons had already burst, leaving behind hollow skins that looked like plastic.

"There have to be hundreds," Stevenson said. He glanced over at Fitz. "We should start thinking about getting out of here, man."

Fitz scooted his thighs up to the edge of his seat. He put one hand on the dashboard and signaled to Tanaka and Dohi with his flashlight.

"Are those the monsters?" Alecia asked.

"Yeah, sweetie, those are the monsters," Rico said.

"Cut one open," Fitz said over the comm link.

Tanaka pulled out his Katana and approached the closest cocoon. Quickly, he sliced it open and backed away as a tiny Wormer sloshed out. It crashed to the ground in a waterfall of goo.

"Kill it, bro," Stevenson whispered.

Tanaka impaled the monster through its misshapen head, pinning it to the dirt like an insect thumbtacked to a board. Blood gushed out into the pool of yellow goo.

The dying creature let out a high-pitched screech that reverberated down the passage. Tanaka and Dohi raked their beams across the darkness. All at once, the other cocoons wriggled.

"Get back to the truck," Fitz said.

Tanaka and Dohi backed away with their rifles shouldered. When they were back in the vehicle, Fitz turned in his seat and said, "Get the flamethrowers."

Both men climbed into the back and prepared the weapons while Fitz pulled out the radio receiver. The sacs were all moving now, the creatures inside stirring.

"Turn off the lights," Fitz said.

Stevenson did as ordered, and darkness flooded the tunnel. He flipped his night-vision goggles over his eyes and watched Tanaka and Dohi slip back into the tunnel wearing their flamethrowers.

They stood on the left and right side of the MATV, where they lit the torches on their gas-operated weapons. Small flames shot out, appearing green in Fitz's vision. The glow flickered eerily over their armored features as they stepped away from the MATV.

"Hold for orders," Fitz said over the comms. Then he lifted the radio receiver and pushed it to his lips. "Lion One, Ghost One. Do you copy? Over."

A cocoon stuck to the wall about a hundred yards away on the right side of the passage split open, exposing the shell of the monster inside.

"Are they going to kill those things or not?" Alecia whispered.

"Shhh," Rico said. "It's okay. We're safe in the truck."

"That's not a Wormer," Fitz said when he saw the creature fighting to free itself from its sac.

Stevenson strained to get a better look over the steering wheel. "Looks like one of them Beetles to me."

The speakers crackled with the response from the Twenty-Fourth MEU. "Ghost One, this is Lion Three. Go ahead, over."

Fitz wasn't expecting Major Domino's voice.

"Sir, I have new intel for Lion One," he said after a brief pause.

"Copy. Go ahead with that intel, Ghost One."

Fitz hesitated as a claw burst through the skin of a

cocoon to the left of Tanaka. An arm popped through, and a second claw tore another opening in the sac.

"Lion Three, we've located a tunnel heading northeast," Fitz said. "And we've come across what appear to be cocoons—hundreds of them, containing mutated monsters."

He lowered the receiver. The other members of Ghost all waited anxiously for their next orders. He could hear their heavy breathing in the darkness.

"Ghost One, this is Lion One. You found that army?"

It was Bradley, and he sounded more short-tempered than normal. Fitz was about to respond when the MATV jolted.

"Stand by, Lion One," Fitz said.

"What the hell was that?" Stevenson asked.

Fitz lowered the radio, knowing exactly what was under the truck.

"Dohi, Tanaka, watch your six," he said over the comm frequency. Then he grabbed his M4 and rolled down the window. He looked through the bars covering the open window to see a mound of earth rising past his door, the fins of a Wormer cutting through the dirt. The beast was heading right for Dohi.

Fitz pointed his rifle through the bars and fired a three-round burst at the fins. The floor split open and a trio of tentacles thrust outward, writhing in the open air. One of them shot toward Dohi, who ducked at the last second.

"Shoot it!" Stevenson shouted.

"No!" Rico yelled back. "They might hit us!"

Both of the soldiers outside backed away from the Wormer as it worked to free its body from the ground. An armored head crested, followed by the long, wrinkled body with shriveled arms hanging from its sides. It stood on two muscular legs and whipped its tentacles at Tanaka.

He countered the attack with a slice from his blade that cut one of the six-foot-long tentacles in half. It gushed green blood like a fire hose, painting the MATV with the sticky substance.

Fitz moved his gun, but he couldn't get a clear shot with the bars in the way. He opened the door and propped the gun in the gap, lining up his sights on the Wormer's back, just below the armored fins. It screeched in agony as Fitz blew gaping holes in its soft flesh.

A tentacle hit Dohi in the leg, wrapping around his calf, and then pulled him to the ground. Another cocoon split open on the wall, then another. One by one, the monsters burst from their white coffins.

"Ghost One, Ghost One, do you copy?" asked a voice from the radio.

Fitz went to line up another shot, but the Wormer that had Dohi whipped another tentacle toward the MATV. Stevenson pulled Fitz back into the truck, saving him from a slap to the face.

Tanaka engaged the Wormer with his sword, slicing Dohi free and opening the beast's gut and chest with three quick thrusts.

On his feet again, Dohi turned with his flamethrower, and together, the two men torched the tunnel. Fitz closed the door, rolled up the window, and flipped up his NVGs to watch the long orange flames coat the walls.

The beasts that had managed to make it out of their cocoons thrashed in the dirt, flesh sizzling in the heat, while the thin, fleshy walls of the cocoons that hadn't yet hatched sizzled and then exploded like popcorn.

"Toast those fuckers," Stevenson grumbled.

Fitz finally brought the receiver back to his mouth. "Lion One, Ghost One. Sorry about that. Over."

"What the hell is happening out there, Ghost One?" Bradley said.

"Sir, those cocoons started to hatch. My men are torching the tunnel now."

Dohi and Tanaka were slowly retreating to the truck as they continued to spray fire over the passage. There was another long pause of static before Bradley came back online.

"Ghost One, what are your coordinates?"

Rico handed Fitz their GPS, and he relayed the coordinates over the comms while he kept an eye on Dohi and Tanaka. One of the beasts struggled to its feet even as flames licked the creature. It raised an arm with a pincher-like claw, snapping it shut once before dropping to its knees and finally succumbing to the burns.

"Roger that, Ghost One," Bradley said. "When you finish burning the tunnel, get topside. You have an hour to get the hell out of there before we drop an MOAB on those motherfuckers. Stand by for coordinates."

Fitz appreciated the blunt use of force, but the biggest bomb in the US military besides a nuke sounded a bit like overkill.

"Guess they aren't taking any chances this time," Fitz said.

"What's an MOAB?" Alecia asked.

"The mother of all bombs, kid," Stevenson said. "Better get Dohi and Tanaka back here, Sarge."

The men returned to the MATV and climbed inside, letting in smoke and the scent of scorched flesh.

"There's an EUF mechanized unit about forty miles west of you in Hardanges," Bradley said over the radio. "I'll send you the coordinates shortly. The Twenty-Fourth MEU is heading there now."

"Nixon ordered the advance?" Fitz asked.

"Phase Two of Operation Reach is a go, Ghost One,"

replied Bradley. "The HQ in Paris is evacuating. We're out of time."

Fitz watched the flames outside and the monsters still wriggling and fighting the fire down the tunnel.

"Roger that, sir," Fitz said into the receiver. "Oh, one more thing—can someone bring me a spare set of prosthetic blades?"

Davis eyed Beckham's broken blade as she slipped on her CBRN suit, thinking of Master Sergeant Joe Fitzpatrick. She had fought alongside the disabled veteran at the Earthfall facility, and she owed him her life. She had no idea where he was now or even if he was still alive. But Beckham was still fighting, despite all odds, and she had a feeling Fitz was too. Both men had proven to be extremely difficult to kill.

"You sure you're up for this, Captain?" Blade asked.

At first Davis thought the senior chief petty officer was talking to Beckham, but he was focused on her.

"Yeah," she said, palming a magazine into her new M4.

Blade glanced over at Beckham. "And you?"

"I'm fine," he replied gingerly.

"Check him again, Melnick," Blade said.

SEAL Team Four's medic got up from his seat and moved over to Beckham. He had already checked him three times, but Blade wasn't taking any chances, especially since Beckham was still displaying one sign of infection: a headache. No matter how many times Davis told Blade he was giving *her* a headache, he insisted on being cautious.

"Prepare for landing in five minutes," one of the pilots said over the comms.

"Any sign of contacts?" Blade asked.

"Negative, Chief," replied one of the men.

"All right—listen up, everyone," Blade said in a voice loud enough to reach everyone in the troop hold, even Beckham, who didn't have a comm-link connection.

The SEALs finished their gear checks and turned toward the senior chief petty officer as the helicopter shot over the dark landscape.

"Larson, Dixon, as soon as we hit dirt you two head out for recon. There were marines trapped outside when that missile hit the White House with the hemorrhage virus," Blade said. "Once we figure out what we're dealing with, we're splitting into two teams. I'm taking Alpha with Captain Davis, Dixon, and Melnick."

Great, she thought.

"Watson, you've got Bravo team with Larson and Tandy," Blade said. He gestured toward Crew Chief Ronaldo. "You keep an eye on Beckham while we're gone. No offense, Captain."

Beckham shrugged. "At least give me a gun."

"Sorry, but that's not going to happen," Blade said.

Davis patted Beckham on the shoulder and turned to look out the window. Bare branches reached up toward the chopper. A creek snaked through the landscape. In the springtime, it was probably pretty. Now the grounds of the famous resort were a barren, almost alien, landscape.

She took a swig of water and then secured her helmet. Beckham leaned his head against the bulkhead, accepting that it was his fate to stay behind on this mission.

The pilots circled the field near the forest's edge until Blade instructed them to put down in a meadow. The rotor wash spread the overgrown weeds outward like ripples in a pond.

Larson and Dixon jumped out and took off for the

trees along the western edge of the field, while the other SEALs set up a perimeter as ordered.

Davis exchanged a glance with Beckham as she got out of the bird. He remained in his seat with his foot still bound to his prosthetic blade. The crew chief had out his M9, and once the two pilots finished powering down the bird, they pulled out their own weapons to watch Beckham.

It was an insult, the way they were treating him. She held rank and could have forced the issue, but maybe Blade was right. Beckham wasn't in any condition to go anywhere anyway. His battered body needed a break from fighting.

"Stay safe," he said.

Davis nodded her helmet and joined Blade out in the grass. She shouldered her M4 and aimed it at the trees that Larson and Dixon had vanished into.

The men returned a few minutes later, and Dixon hurried over with his MK16 cradled.

"All clear, Senior Chief," he reported. "Thermal and visual scans revealed zero contacts in the vicinity."

"Good," Blade said. He pulled out a map of the sixty-five hundred acres surrounding the Greenbrier.

"All right, gents, listen up. Alpha will take this wing, and Bravo will take this wing," Blade said, pointing. "Once we clear the grounds and gardens, we move in. Access to the PEOC is here, but we're going to have to turn the power back on first. Bravo, that's your job."

"Roger that," Watson said.

"Think we should get a message through to Command before we move in?" Blade asked Davis.

She shook her head. "I don't want to take the risk of ROT intercepting anything."

"Good idea, Captain," Blade said. "Same goes for this mission: radio silence. Hand signals only, unless it's an absolute emergency, and by emergency I mean, unless you're about to become Variant chow."

Six nods acknowledged his order.

"Okay, let's move out," Blade said. He turned to look at Beckham one more time, then jogged away from the bird. Davis exchanged a nod with Beckham before she too turned and left the Delta operator behind.

17

President Ringgold managed to sleep for a few hours before she was awoken by her reoccurring nightmare about her cousin Emilia. For several minutes after waking, Ringgold lay in the small bed, staring in horror at the bulkhead, her heart pounding. This time it took longer to shake the terror of the dream.

A knock sounded on the door to her quarters.

"One moment," Ringgold said groggily.

She threw on some clothes and opened the door to see Nelson standing in the passage, dressed impeccably as ever, not a wrinkle visible on his suit.

"Did you find an iron somewhere on the ship?" Ringgold asked.

Nelson tightened his red tie proudly. "No, ma'am, but I learned a few techniques while traveling back in the day."

"I imagine you did," Ringgold said. She could tell by his casual tone that whatever he had to say wasn't an emergency. "Give me a second to freshen up."

Ben nodded and retreated into the passage while she splashed frigid water on her face. It helped her shake off the fog of sleep and the horror of the nightmare.

When she was presentable, she followed Nelson to the

aircraft carrier's island, a command center for flight-deck operations on the USS *Abraham Lincoln*. Rear Admiral Lemke was standing stoically at the window with a pair of binoculars angled at the ocean.

All around him, a team of sailors worked at their stations, surprisingly bright-eyed despite the early-morning hour. She followed Nelson to the panoramic viewpoint set six stories above the flight deck. Captain Ingves was nowhere in sight, but the bridge was above the island, and he was probably watching from his leather chair.

"Ah, President Ringgold," Lemke said. "Did you get some sleep?"

"Yes, I got a few hours," Ringgold said.

"Sorry to wake you, but I thought you would want to be here when the USS *Forrest Sherman* and the USS *Ashland* arrive," Lemke said. "My communications team has picked up the destroyers and an advance team of three Sikorsky SH-60 Seahawks carrying General Nixon's men."

"Excellent," Ringgold said.

Soprano walked into the room behind them, attempting to tuck in his shirt. He fetched a mug of coffee without needing to be asked and handed it to Ringgold, while Lemke spoke to one of his officers. She tried to listen to the conversation, but truthfully, she was having a hard time focusing, and not just because she was exhausted. She still felt terrible about Kate leaving in the manner she had, not even saying good-bye before boarding a chopper to the *Thalassa*.

"Want to have a look?" Lemke asked.

Ringgold took the binoculars. She glassed the ocean and the ships making up the fleet. The water sparkled under the reflection of the moon, illuminating the shapes of the USS *Bunker Hill* and the USS *Fitzgerald*, which flanked the aircraft carrier. She pivoted to get a view of the civilian ships. The oil tanker and container ship carved through the water on the starboard side of the aircraft carrier, but she didn't see the dorsal fin of the USS *Florida*.

"Where's Captain Konkoly?" she asked.

"Submerged right now, just in case we run into trouble," Lemke said. "We have hundreds of early-warning systems to detect threats and plenty of firepower to combat them, but Konkoly is our final out if something goes awry."

Ringgold took a seat next to the rear admiral. He had put his life and the lives of everyone in the strike group on the line by backing Ringgold.

"Why did you do it?" she asked bluntly.

Lemke turned slightly toward her. He was a handsome man with a full head of hair and dimples, but he also had the face of a warrior, with a crooked nose clearly broken and not set right, and a scar cutting through his right eyebrow. He arched that brow and said, "Pardon me, ma'am?"

"What made you risk everything to stand against Wood?"

Lemke grinned. "Simple answer—I knew his older brother."

"Ah," Ringgold said. "Zach Wood was a monster too, but Andrew seems to be even worse."

"Yes, he is." Lemke paused, his smile gone. "That's not the only reason, though. I followed your career as secretary of state and have a lot respect for you, ma'am. I saw what you were doing with the SZTs, and I knew you wouldn't hit one with the hemorrhage virus. My duty is to do what's right, and protecting you is the greatest honor of my life."

"I wish the other commanders back in the States and the mayors of the SZTs shared your sentiment—which I appreciate very much, by the way."

"Some of them do, but Wood, unfortunately for us, is a sadistically brilliant bastard. He played his cards perfectly, waiting for the right opportunity to rise to power and then using WMDs to strike fear into all those who opposed him."

"History shows that men who are willing to use WMDs don't need the strongest army to win a war," Ringgold said. "Look at World War Two. If we hadn't dropped the atomic bombs on Hiroshima and Nagasaki, we might have been fighting for years against the Japanese."

"Indeed, but President Harry Truman wasn't a crazy SOB like Wood, and the hemorrhage virus is more than a WMD. It's a species ender."

"I know," Ringgold said. "Forgive me if my analogy wasn't appropriate. I'm exhausted."

"Nothing to forgive, ma'am. As I said, I have a lot of respect for you and will give my life to protect you. So will my sailors."

Ringgold reached out and patted Lemke on his shoulder. "Thank you, Admiral."

"Call me Dan," he said. His dimples deepened again with a warm smile that reassured Ringgold she'd made the right decision by coming here.

"Ma'am," Nelson said. He was still waiting by the porthole windows with Soprano.

"I've just got a few updates for you while we wait for those destroyers," Nelson said. "Mind if I borrow some of your time?"

"You can use the flag bridge to meet," Lemke said. "I'll send someone to get you when the Seahawks arrive."

"Thank you, Ad—" Ringgold corrected herself. "Thank you, Dan."

He pushed the binoculars back up to his eyes as they made the trip two decks below to the admiral's personal command center. She eyed the pictures on the wall as she walked in, noticing again the one of Lemke and his two deceased brothers.

Don't give up hope, Dan, she thought. *We can get back what we lost.*

Once she sat at the conference table, Soprano got right to it. "Doctor Lovato has landed at the *Thalassa* with Master Sergeant Horn's team."

"How close are they to a cure?" Ringgold asked.

"We don't know yet. We're waiting for a sitrep from Doctor Adriana Bruno, the lead scientist."

"Good. I want you to keep Horn and his men there for a while until we're sure it's safe for Kate," Ringgold said.

Soprano nodded, and Nelson loosened his tie, an indication that the next bit of news wasn't going to be good.

"We haven't heard anything from SEAL Team Four and Captain Davis yet," he said, "but they should have arrived or should be close to arriving at the White House at the Greenbrier."

"So we don't know if Captain Beckham is infected with the virus?" Ringgold asked. "Should we be worried that we haven't heard from them?"

"We don't know about his condition, but we do know the team was under strict orders to monitor him for infection. They were also told to keep radio silence, so I wouldn't worry too much," Nelson replied.

"Okay. What else?" Ringgold took a sip of her coffee and reached for the folder Soprano pushed across the table.

"We lost SZT Two and SZT Four yesterday."

She opened the folder and read over the list of SZTs that still hadn't aligned with ROT, her heart sinking. After all she had done to start the recovery and rebuilding efforts, seeing how short the list was made her nauseous.

"That means Wood now has the majority of SZTs on

his side, and the others will quickly follow suit," Nelson said gravely. "It's just a matter of time now."

Ringgold's heart sank even lower. A knock on the door interrupted their meeting. It was Lemke, with Captain Ingves right behind him.

"Sorry to interrupt, but I've got excellent news," Lemke said. He nodded at Ingves, who stepped into the flag bridge.

"We have a spy at SZT Nineteen in Los Angeles, and we just got word that Wood was spotted there," Ingves said.

Ringgold flipped the folder closed and stood. "How sure are you?"

"Pretty sure," Ingves said. "Our spy was working in one of the farm silos and claims to have seen Wood piloting a Little Bird with a prisoner hanging from the skids. Apparently he smashed the guy into the side of the building in front of everyone."

"Sounds like Wood," Ringgold said. "Scramble together whatever teams we can in the area. If we can get proof of my innocence at the Greenbrier, then this is our chance to cut the head off the snake."

"We're really in trouble now, Ringo," Piero whispered.

The mouse squeaked at him in acknowledgment. They were back in their apartment a few blocks from the Colosseum, waiting for a message from Paris.

It was late morning in Rome, and they had been tracking the monsters through the night. The creatures were gone now, having retreated into the ancient sewers below the Colosseum. And Piero knew it wouldn't be long before he had to go back down there.

He sat cross-legged on the floor, with Ringo on his

knee. The mouse was hungry, and so was Piero. He pulled out a granola bar, peeled back the wrapper, and tore off a small hunk that he placed in front of Ringo. The mouse greedily chomped onto the side of the morsel. He had already gained some weight back since Piero found supplies a few days earlier, but he could still see Ringo's ribs.

"Angaran, this is Piazza, do you copy? Over."

Piero fumbled for the radio, nearly knocking it to the floor. He turned the volume down and then pushed the radio up to his lips.

"Roger that, sir."

"Good to hear your voice, Sergeant. I'm told you have a report for me."

"I do, sir," Piero said. "Last night I observed something new—something that the scientists are going to want to hear."

He paused, recalling the mother and daughter he hadn't been able to save. Using his index finger, he stroked Ringo's furry head while the mouse ate.

There was a flurry of static, and then what sounded like gunshots.

"Sir, is everything okay?" Piero asked.

"We're under siege, Sergeant. The Variants have us surrounded at Sainte-Chapelle. I'm not sure how much longer we can hold out."

Piero didn't know what to say. All this time he'd been feeling alone, but he wasn't the only one risking his life. Piazza was talking to him during a firefight!

"I'm sorry, sir. Let me get right to it. The mutated monsters here are nesting beneath the Colosseum. Last night I saw them tear one another apart after capturing a woman and her daughter."

Ringo finished his morsel and looked up for more food. Piero tore off another small chunk of granola bar for the mouse as he spoke.

"I've heard your transmissions, Sergeant," Angaran said. "There must be a Queen or something controlling the beasts there, and you're the only man we have in Rome to kill it."

Piero swallowed at the new orders and, just to be sure, said, "Come again, sir? I didn't catch that last part."

"Sergeant, you're the only man we have in Rome, so I need you to find, and kill, this Queen if possible. It may be the only way to take back your city and win the war."

"Can't you just drop a bomb on the Colosseum? A bunker buster or something?" Piero asked.

"We need to figure out what we're dealing with first," Piazza said. "We've already depleted most of our arsenal, and we're running out of fuel for our birds."

There was a short pause on the other end, and then: "I know what I'm asking you to do isn't going to be easy, but we need you, Sergeant."

"Roger that, sir. You can count on us," Piero replied.

"Us?" Piazza said.

Piero hesitated and looked down at his only friend left in the world.

"I have a...a mouse with me. He's become a friend of sorts. Keeps me company."

He knew how crazy it sounded, and he expected Piazza to either laugh or tell him he was a madman. But instead, the lieutenant general simply said, "I don't care if you have a goddamn unicorn with you. Once this is over, I'm going to make sure you're both rewarded. Good luck. Over."

Piero slipped the radio back in his pouch and stroked Ringo's back with his finger, smiling for the first time since he had seen the EUF fighter jet days earlier. If the mouse could have smiled, he probably would have too. The furry little creature seemed to be in heaven just eating the granola bar.

"Maybe this time I should go on my own," Piero whispered. His mood suddenly changed, depression setting in. That got Ringo's attention. The mouse looked up with beady black eyes and nuzzled Piero's hand. Leaving the hunk of granola on the ground, Ringo ran up his arm and jumped onto his shoulder.

He grabbed his rifle, checked the magazine, and then slung his rucksack over his shoulder.

"Okay then, my little friend, if you don't want to stay here, let's go meet this Queen."

Kate cupped her hands over the radio headset and listened to the message again. It was just as unbelievable the second time. She sat in an uncomfortable metal chair outside the clean room set up inside the belly of the *Thalassa*.

"Reports detailing colonies of mutated Variants are all pointing at there being some sort of Queen controlling their activity. If these things are real, they are very elusive. The EUF is currently in the process of sending teams out for verification."

If only Pat could have been here to listen to this, she mused.

Her old partner had been fascinated with the metamorphosis of the Variants in Europe. Dr. Ellis had come up with his own theories on why the juveniles were mutating, but none of them had included a Queen or the colony behavior described by the European reports.

It still hadn't quite sunk in that Ellis was gone. She had grown so used to bouncing all her ideas off him; Dr. Orlov and Dr. Bruno were no doubt brilliant in their own ways, but it just wasn't the same.

Picking up a set of handwritten notes, Kate continued

reading over Dr. Bruno's documentation of their work. Somewhere above her, Horn and his men were eating breakfast. After talking with Admiral Lemke about the conditions on the *Thalassa*, Horn's team had been ordered to stay on the ship to protect Kate for the time being, an order that didn't sit well with the European researchers.

"That Italian lady gives me the creeps," Horn had said to Kate earlier that morning.

She agreed. Kate felt safer with Horn here, especially after their first conversation with Dr. Bruno and Dr. Orlov.

Kate continued reading over the documentation. Ten test subjects had perished from the hemorrhage virus over the past seven months, their bodies dumped into the sea. Each of them had been first injected with the hemorrhage virus and was then given an experimental cure for the virus. It had cured the Ebola symptoms in more than half of them, but not the transformations brought on by the VX-99 nanoparticles.

The transformations had continued in the other subjects, and each subject had been thrown into the sea, alive. It wasn't exactly murder, since they had agreed to being infected, but it still seemed...

Kate shuddered at the thought of what had taken place in this lab, but in the end, these scientists had given their lives to find a cure—something that her mentor, Doctor Michael Allen, had done during the first days of the outbreak, when he too had been infected. It was her job to help finish the work Allen and Ellis had helped her start.

After reading over the last of the pages, she looked up to watch Bruno and Orlov working inside the clean lab. They wore bulky white CBRN suits with battery-operated air-filtration units, but the clean lab was far from being up to the standard of the one Kate was used to working in. It simply wasn't possible to put something of the caliber of her old BSL4 lab on a ship.

The scientists had done a great job of securing the equipment to the floor, and they had taken extra steps to ensure sensitive samples weren't contaminated or broken if the ship hit stormy waters. They had a second air-filtration system, but they would have needed more fail-safe systems and a hundred other security measures to meet BSL4 standards.

Kate stood and walked over to the comm-link button. "Doctor Bruno, I've read through your lab notes and have some ideas about VX-99, but first, how about you explain to me where you're at in the process?"

Bruno looked up from her lab station. "As you know from those reports, the experimental cure for the Ebola virus works eighty percent of the time, which just leaves us with the problem of halting or even reversing VX-99's effects. Doctor Orlov has been focusing on that part."

Orlov finished with the pipette he was using and then secured his sample and stepped away from the lab station.

"In short, I used ultra-high-performance liquid chromatography to separate and identify the chemical compounds in VX-99," Orlov said. He used his gloved hands to gesture wildly as he spoke, kind of the way Ellis had done when he was excited. "That was a difficult and time-consuming project, but I was finally able to complete the separation just this morning. What I'm working on now is creating an antibody to target each of the VX-99 nanoparticles, just like you used when you were developing Kryptonite."

"Interesting," Kate said, her mind already racing with possibilities.

"That's where I'm stuck, however, as once the VX-99

particles mature, there seems to be a point of no return. When we talk about a cure, we're talking about one that can be used to stop and reverse only the beginning stages of infection."

"What's the point of no return?" Kate asked. Her thoughts were on Beckham, but she buried the worries and focused on the work ahead.

"We don't know that yet," Orlov said.

"Perhaps explaining how Doctor Ellis and I created Kryptonite will help us brainstorm a way to target those VX-99 nanoparticles," Kate said. Memories washed over her as she recalled her work with Pat. He had been a nerd, and a brilliant one. She wished he were here to help explain.

"Doctor Ellis and I identified a protein, which we called the Superman protein, attached to oligosaccharide chains on the cell membrane of Variant stem cells. The protein enabled better, quicker interactions with the biochemical cascade associated with wound healing. In short, we created antibodies targeting the Superman protein."

"How were the antibodies delivered to the cells?" Orlov asked.

"Chemotherapeutic drugs," Kate replied. "We encapsulated them and coated them with these targeting antibodies. These were delivered to the cells responsible for the Variants' fast healing. The Variant stem cells gobbled up the drugs attached via the targeted protein-antibody interactions and killed themselves."

"Genius," Bruno said.

Orlov spread his arms, indicating the lab equipment. "We have limited resources here, obviously, but we do have the ability to design our own nanoparticles that can attach to VX-99 within the blood system. That's where we're hoping you can help us."

"If we can find a way to do that, we're going to need a facility to produce the nanoparticles and manufacture a supply of the cure," Bruno said.

Kate did a quick scan of the computer equipment outside the clean room. "I can help with the development," she said. "I'll get started on some simulations to see which nanoparticles might work best."

Footfalls echoed down the ladder behind Kate. Horn made his way into the cluttered room outside the labs.

"How's it going down here?" he asked. His rifle was slung over his back, but she knew the other doctors and staff didn't appreciate the military presence. She pressed the comm-link button and said, "Give us a minute, please."

Orlov and Bruno looked at Horn but then went back to work at their stations inside the lab.

"Have you heard anything about Reed?" Kate asked.

Horn shook his head. "No news. He's been evacuated from Outpost Forty-Six and is on his way to the White House PEOC at the Greenbrier."

"When are you going to head back to the *Abraham Lincoln*?"

"I don't know. I'm worried about my girls, but I also don't feel good about leaving you here by yourself."

"They're excellent researchers," Kate said, not sure if she was trying to convince him or herself.

"As long as they don't try and experiment on you. But if they do..." He hit a fist into his gloved palm.

Kate didn't exactly smile, but her lips did turn up at the edges. "Don't worry, I'll be fine."

He looked through the plastic wall of the clean room and let out a snort. Kate imagined her friend was feeling much as she was—frustrated and missing his family. At least she felt a bit less alone with him here on the ship.

"Hey, Horn, can you do me a favor?"

He pivoted toward her and nodded. "Of course, Kate. What do you need?"

"If you hear anything else about Reed...if things go badly at Greenbrier..." She trailed off, not wanting to finish the thought out loud.

Horn understood what she was asking. "Don't worry, Doc—if I found out Beckham needed my help, I'd disobey an order from Jesus Christ himself to save his ass."

18

The sun was rising over France by the time Stevenson pulled the MATV onto a dirt road on the south side of the small farm village. The rendezvous point Colonel Bradley had sent them looked as though it was straight out of medieval Europe, with hedges framing the dirt road and wooden shacks built on top of stone foundations.

Between the woods and the hedges that provided easy hiding spots, this was the perfect place for an ambush. In his mind's eye, Fitz pictured Nazis attacking Allied troops and tanks during World War II.

He was honestly surprised they'd made it here without a fight. For the past hour, they had raced down dirt farm roads under the cover of darkness at the vehicle's max speed of sixty-five, stopping only when they detected a pack of juveniles prowling through the checkered farm fields.

A Reaver had spotted them an hour earlier, but Fitz took care of the beast with a round from his MK11. Now they were approaching the village of Hardanges, about forty miles west of the national park they had left behind.

As the warm globe of the sun crested the horizon, the

surviving American and EUF forces had started moving across the countryside. Most of the monsters would retreat from the light and return to their lairs, so the soldiers would take advantage of the daylight and trek through the ashes to prepare for war against the Variants.

In twelve hours or less, there would be all-out war, with almost fifty thousand human soldiers from dozens of countries participating in a final push to clear Europe of the Variants. For the first time since landing in Normandy, Fitz felt some confidence they would succeed. The air force was dropping everything it had left on the tunnels where the monsters had taken up residence.

By the sound of it, the bombs were falling right now.

A mushroom cloud rose above the Parc naturel régional du Perche. Alecia caught Fitz's eye in the mirror.

"Big bombs," she said with a smile. "Good."

Fitz had never seen or heard children speak of war as the Ombres did. Alecia reminded him of Michel. He shook his head at how fucked up it was for children to have to go through a hell like this. If Beckham and Kate lived long enough to have their child, the kid was going to grow up in a desolate, decaying world where survival would be a constant struggle.

Rico's friendly voice prevented him from slipping further into those dark thoughts.

"I don't suppose they have many MOABs left," she said, blowing a bubble that popped on her lips. Alecia watched Rico chew the gum with interest. Fitz reached into his vest and pulled out the half piece that Rico had given him earlier. He handed it back to the girl with a smile, narrowly missing Apollo's wet muzzle.

"Should have dropped nukes instead of MOABs," Stevenson said. "Radiation bombs were supposed to kill those ugly fuckers, and instead it turned 'em into even nastier fuckers. Nukes would have gotten the job done."

"Watch your language," Tanaka said from the back seat.

Stevenson shrugged off the suggestion.

"The radiation worked on the juveniles in the States, or did you forget that?" Rico said. "Besides, nukes would kill *everything*, and the fallout would poison whatever was left. The point of us coming here is to help the survivors of Europe."

Stevenson shrugged again. "I don't see any survivors out here. We should be Stateside, helping our own."

Alecia raised a hand before Fitz could respond. "What about me? I survived out here for months with only *Maman* and my Ombre brothers and sisters."

"Yeah, yeah," Stevenson said. He returned his focus to the road. Fitz smiled at the girl and then shot a sidelong glance at Stevenson that told him to keep his trap shut.

Tensions were high, and everyone was exhausted, even Team Ghost's four-legged friend. Apollo rested his head on his paws and let out a sigh. The thump and roar of the bombs continued behind them, the drumbeat of war.

"You hear that?" Fitz asked. No one answered the rhetorical question. "The real battle hasn't even started yet. Once we link up with the EUF mechanized unit and the Twenty-Fourth MEU, we're going to head out to join the main forces on a march to Paris. The worst Europe has to offer is standing, or slithering, inside the capital. We need to be prepared."

Another mushroom cloud rose into the air behind them, and the MATV vibrated from the shock wave.

"Wow," Alecia said. "Do you think that one killed all of the monsters?"

Rico shook her head. "Not all of them, but a lot."

Alecia chomped the gum and patted Apollo on his head. She seemed to be enjoying herself, like a kid on a very violent field trip. Fitz was going to see if he could get her evacuated as soon as they met up with the Twenty-Fourth MEU.

Fitz turned back to the front of the vehicle as the dirt road smoothed out into asphalt. The sun spread a blanket of orange over the village of Hardanges.

"Looks deserted," Dohi said.

The MATV passed the final row of hedges and drove down the narrow road lined by stone walls. Two armored trucks and a pickup bearing the white and blue colors of the EUF were parked at the end of the street, behind a barricade of barbed wire and concrete blocks. An old church rose above the barrier.

Stevenson drove at a snail's pace. Brick and stone buildings with moss-covered roofs and white shuttered windows lined the left side of the street; a garden of yellow and brown shrubs lined the right.

"Park it here," Fitz said when he noticed smoke fingering away from the rooftops to the east.

"I hope we're not too late," Tanaka whispered from the back.

Fitz brought his binoculars up and magnified the white pickup truck and the two armored vehicles parked at the roadblock, which were basically retrofitted United Nations vehicles.

"You see anyone?" Stevenson said quietly.

Fitz scanned the area and then lowered the binos. "Machine-gun nest and vehicles are empty, and that church is all boarded up. No sign of hostiles."

He directed Stevenson to keep driving. The MATV crawled down the street, passing a boarded-up building on the left with a white picket fence out front. On the passenger's side was a two-story brick structure of newer construction with a minivan parked out front. Judging by the deflated tires and shattered windows, it hadn't moved in a while.

About a hundred yards from the church, Fitz instructed Stevenson to stop. They sat in silence, watching the sunrise spread over the damp rooftops. A bird cawed in the distance, and Fitz slowly reached for the rifle that was propped up against the side of his seat. They were protected by several inches of armor, but he still felt exposed on the road.

Rico pumped a shell into her shotgun, breaking the silence. Something was off, and the other members of Team Ghost could sense trouble. It wasn't just the smoke and deserted streets.

Fitz picked up the radio and brought it to his mouth. "Lion One, Lion One, this is Ghost One. We've arrived at the rendezvous. Place looks deserted. Please advise. Over."

Static crackled from the speakers.

Fitz waited for several minutes before trying again. More white noise fluttered from the radio on each attempt.

"Shit," he mumbled.

"Want me to keep driving?" Stevenson asked.

"No," Rico said. "This road is far too narrow. We won't be able to turn around if it's a trap. Let me check it out on foot."

"Absolutely not," Fitz said.

"I'll go with her," Tanaka said.

"Me too," Dohi added.

Apollo sat on his hind legs, looking to Fitz for orders.

Fitz sighed. It was either wait here or let them check out the area, but this time he couldn't go out there with his team.

"We'll be careful," Rico said.

Dipping his helmet, Fitz reluctantly gave the order after another scan of the street. With Bradley not answering and no sign of the EUF, Team Ghost had to do something.

The three soldiers got out of the vehicle and walked around the front of the MATV. Apollo took point, with Dohi and Tanaka fanning out at combat intervals. Rico walked at the rear, her sawed-off shotgun at the ready and her M4 slung over a shoulder.

"Stay frosty," Fitz said to Stevenson.

He nodded and gripped the steering wheel. Fitz flicked the selector on his M4 to three-round burst and followed the four Ghost members anxiously while they made their way down the street toward the barricade. Apollo's tail was still up, a good sign.

Alecia popped up between the driver's and passenger's seats to watch.

"Come on, kid," Fitz said. "Put your seat belt back on."

She scowled. "I came out here to avenge my friends and family. *Maman*, Michel, all the other kids who died at the basilica."

Fitz had had a feeling this was coming. The girl hadn't hitched a ride out here for nothing—she wanted to fight, and the rage in her eyes told him he was going to have more problems if he continued treating her like a child.

She raised her pistol, and Fitz cracked a half grin. "Okay, kid, get ready. We might need you."

"You see that?" Stevenson asked.

Fitz followed his finger to the rooftops where the tendrils of smoke rose off charred rafters. Fitz put on his sunglasses for a better view in the glare of the sun.

"I don't see anything but smoke," he said.

"Thought I saw something—guess it was a shadow."

Dohi stopped about fifty feet from the barricade. He pointed to a building around the corner that Fitz couldn't see and then flashed hand signals to Rico and Tanaka. The three fanned out, with Apollo trotting behind Rico.

"What are they doing?" Fitz whispered, more to himself than Stevenson.

"This could be a trap," Alecia said, her head still wedged between the two seats. "You should tell your team to watch for the bat monsters."

Fitz had a feeling she meant Reavers, but he didn't correct her. She was right, after all: This could be a trap. He relayed the message over the comms.

"Eyes up, Rico."

Then he pushed his binoculars to his sunglasses and magnified the church just as a single EUF soldier staggered into view.

"Finally, someone in a white-and-blue uniform," Stevenson said with a huff. "Want me to move?"

"Hold," Fitz said. He centered the binos on the soldier limping down the road. The man was injured, and he wasn't carrying a weapon.

Dohi and the others were at the roadblock now, and they had lowered their weapons at the approaching soldier.

"We got a contact," Rico reported over the comm channel.

"I see that," Fitz replied. "What's wrong with him?"

"Looks hurt. Can't see much from behind this barricade."

Dohi and Tanaka prepared to move around the concrete blocks and barbed wire–topped fences. Fitz flitted the binoculars from his team to the EUF soldier.

"What's he saying?" Fitz asked over the comms.

"I don't know. He's speaking French," Rico replied.

Alecia leaned closer, nearly climbing into the front seats. "I'll translate."

"Rico, can you relay what's he saying so Alecia can translate?" Fitz asked.

"Uh, maybe it's not French," Rico replied. "It just sounds like gibberish."

Fitz zoomed in on the man's hands as the soldier pulled them away from his mouth. It was no wonder Rico couldn't make out the words: The man had no tongue. He stumbled into the other side of the barricade and tripped, falling into a barbed wire fence.

Tanaka and Dohi leaped over the concrete blocks to help. Apollo froze, tail between his legs and eyes on the sky.

"Oh no," Fitz whispered.

"What the hell is going on?" Stevenson said.

"Fall back," Fitz said.

There was a pause, and Dohi turned to look at the MATV as if to make sure he'd heard correctly. Tanaka had pulled out bolt cutters from his rucksack. He went to cut through the fence while the EUF soldier struggled and squirmed like an insect caught in a cobweb.

Fitz could hear the man's screams now, strangled, guttural screeches that sounded more monster than human. It was one of the most awful things he'd ever heard in his life.

"Get back to the truck!" Fitz said, his voice just shy of a shout. He reached for the door handle, forgetting for a moment that he had no blades to carry him.

"Oh shit—we have company," Stevenson said. Fitz saw the Reaver at the same moment Stevenson did. The beast flapped away from the smoke and spread its wings like a dragon.

The EUF soldier stopped struggling to look up at the sky. As soon as he saw the creature, he started squirming more violently, tearing his flesh on the razor wire.

The injured man was being used as bait by the Variants.

"Move," Fitz said to Stevenson.

Stevenson pushed down on the gas pedal, but instead of speeding down the road, the MATV caught and jolted. The pavement beneath the tires vibrated as if from a miniature earthquake. Fitz knew right away the vibration was too powerful to be the impact of another distant bomb.

A mound of asphalt rose in front of the truck as a Wormer moved under the earth toward the barricade.

"Floor it!" Fitz shouted.

Stevenson pushed the gas pedal down again, the engine roaring and the tires skidding. The vehicle heaved forward and then jolted backward, throwing Fitz toward the dash. The seat belt caught his chest, compressing the air from his lungs and setting him gasping for breath. Above them, the sky filled with Reavers.

"We're stuck!" Stevenson shouted.

Fitz looked in the passenger's side mirror and saw the tentacles wrapped around the back right tire.

"Give it some gas," Fitz said.

Stevenson pushed down, but the tentacles remained wrapped around the tire like a rubber band, yanking them backward each time he tried to move.

Everything slowed around Fitz, but his senses seemed to heighten. He could feel the sweat dripping down his brow, he could hear Alecia chomping on her gum and see the puckered lips of the first Reaver swoop down and pluck the EUF soldier from the barbed wire.

The crack of automatic gunfire snapped Fitz alert again. Dohi, Tanaka, Rico, and Apollo were retreating from the barricade, straight into the path of the tunneling Wormers.

Fitz unfastened his belt and pulled his body into the back seat, where Alecia was reaching for the door handle.

"Stay put!" Fitz ordered.

"We have to help your friends!" Alecia yelled back.

Fitz extended a hand up for the hatch but was unable to reach it. He said, "Actually, help me with this."

The vehicle jolted again as Stevenson tried to free the tires. Alecia stood on the back seat and helped Fitz push the hatch open. Using the handholds, he pulled himself up and climbed onto the roof, where he positioned his butt and stumps on the mesh net that would have to serve as a seat.

"Get us out of here!" Fitz yelled at Stevenson.

"I'm trying!"

Fitz looked to the right rear tire. Tentacles were wrapped around the MATV's axle, but Fitz couldn't get a solid shot at the Wormer under their truck. He grabbed the M240 and aimed it at the beautiful sunset in the backdrop of a sky filling with the winged abominations.

He fired a volley of 7.62-millimeter rounds at his first target, a Reaver with the wingspan of a goddamn osprey. It angled into a nosedive, clutching its wings against its side and preparing to pluck Rico up with its talons.

The rounds slammed the beast into the side of a building, killing it on impact. Rico pumped her shotgun, discarding a spent shell, and waved up at Fitz. Then she went back to firing blast after blast at the monsters swooping toward the street. Tanaka ducked, pulled out a sword, and sliced off a wing. The creature he'd struck slammed into a stone wall on his right.

Fitz led another creature in the sky with the M240's barrel and pulled the trigger. The rounds lanced into its spiky back, shredding vital organs and dropping the Reaver like a stone to the street, where it splattered in front of Tanaka.

The Wormers continued to break under the asphalt, the ground sagging where they had already tunneled. Fitz fired a barrage into the street and then raked the gun back and forth to keep the monsters in the sky off Team Ghost. Mindful of not wasting ammunition, he fired well-timed short bursts.

There were more than a dozen of the Reavers and at least three Wormers. A fair fight, for now, but they were running out of time, and Fitz had a feeling there were more of the beasts on the way.

"Hurry!" Fitz shouted to his team.

"Let me help them!" Alecia shouted from inside the vehicle.

"*No!* Stay put!" Fitz yelled back.

Stevenson was still trying to free the truck; it jerked back and forth, making aiming incredibly difficult. Fitz followed a Reaver diving toward Apollo and pulled the trigger just as the beast folded its wings to the sides of its leathery hide in a dive.

Rounds tore into its deformed face, and it hit the road with a boom that sounded like it had come from Rico's shotgun. The dog leaped over a mound of asphalt one of the Wormers had created and then stopped to bark.

"Get back to the truck, Apollo!" Fitz shouted in between gunshots. He ducked as a Reaver lowered its talons to grab him. The beast came so close, Fitz met its yellow, almond-shaped eyes for an instant. There was evil in its gaze, and he knew it would be back for him if Fitz let it live.

He swiveled the turret and riddled the winged monstrosity with rounds that sent it crashing into a tree. When he rotated the gun back toward the street, another Wormer had broken through—the largest Fitz had ever seen.

Ten-foot tentacles whipped out of the rubble like a giant squid's and slapped Rico and Tanaka to the ground. One of the tentacles wrapped around Dohi's leg as he fired at the Reavers.

A minute had passed since Fitz had climbed up top, and in that time, all three soldiers had been brought to the ground, shooting, screaming, and fighting for their lives. Apollo bounded over and bit at the tentacle holding Dohi's leg.

"I'm burning the tires!" Stevenson yelled, still unable to get the vehicle unstuck.

"Get out and shoot then!" Fitz shouted back. He focused the barrel on the Wormer in the middle of the street.

Gunshots sounded from the side of the truck, but it wasn't Stevenson obeying orders, it was Alecia disobeying them. In his peripheral, Fitz saw the girl jump out. She bent down and emptied her pistol's magazine into the Wormer under the truck.

"Die!" she was shouting in an enraged voice that made her sound like a woman.

"Get back inside!" Fitz screamed at her.

Alecia pulled out the magazine, put in a fresh one, and then further disobeyed his orders by firing down the street.

The southern wall of the church down the street suddenly exploded outward, raining bricks and stone. A Black Beetle pulled itself out of the opening and let out a ringing hiss that sent the Reavers fanning out in a frenzy.

This time Fitz didn't tell Alecia to retreat. They needed every gun in this fight. He directed the barrel of the M240 at the Beetle. The gun clicked when he pulled the trigger: A round had jammed. He reached forward and tried to work the bolt and eject the stuck round, one eye on the battle.

On the street, Dohi was thrashing as the Wormer tentacles pulled him toward the hole. Apollo clawed and bit at the thick, spiky appendage, and Rico was firing her M4 at the Wormer trying to free its sinewy body from the tunnel, but it was Tanaka who freed Dohi with a slash of his Katana. He swung both of his blades in graceful arcs that sliced through the long, wormlike arms.

The chorus of high-pitched shrieks from the Reavers, the hissing of the Beetle, and the screeching of the Wormers rose into a din that hurt Fitz's ears.

A Reaver plunged toward him and, unable to fire the M240, Fitz pulled Meg's axe from his belt and waited until it was about twenty feet away before he flung the weapon. It cartwheeled into the creature's right eye.

The beast jerked to the left, narrowly missing the front of the MATV, and collided with something meaty instead. A human scream joined the chorus of shrieking monsters.

Fitz glanced back at Stevenson, who had stepped out of the vehicle only to be hit by the Reaver. He landed on his back, helmet bouncing against the pavement like a ping-pong ball. The Reaver straddled him, wrapping its wings around his body to pin him to the ground.

Fitz pulled out his M9 and pointed it at the beast. From his angle, he could see Stevenson looking up at him, terror in his eyes. It was over before Fitz could fire a single shot. The Reaver pulled the axe out of its eye with one clawed hand and wrapped its other arm around Stevenson's neck. A crunch sounded as the monster snapped the marine's spine as if he was a turkey's wishbone on Thanksgiving Day.

"*No!*" Fitz didn't recognize his own voice at first as he kept yelling the word. He squeezed the trigger of his M9 as the Reaver plucked up Stevenson's limp body and flapped away. He followed it into the sky, squeezing off his entire magazine, heart kicking in his chest with each shot.

Fitz continued pulling the trigger even after the mag went dry. He finally forced his gaze away, knowing he had to help the others before they too joined Stevenson. He turned back to the M240, freed the round, and aimed for the Beetle. It was lumbering toward Dohi and

Tanaka, who were almost back to the vehicle now. Rico and Apollo were already inside, and she was shouting like a madwoman.

Fitz waited for a clear shot, but Dohi and Tanaka were both in the way. He couldn't risk killing them with friendly fire.

"Dohi, Tanaka, get out of—" His scream was interrupted by a thump. Halfway down the street, a red streak hit the black shell of the Beetle, sending the monster smashing into a brick wall. It exploded in a shower of gore.

An M1A1 Abrams tank rolled around the corner and smashed through the barricade. The sky filled with tracer rounds, shredding the remaining Reavers, including the beast holding Stevenson.

Stevenson's body plummeted to the ground, where it cracked on the pavement outside the church. The sound of diesel engines and tracks echoed through the village as Colonel Bradley and the Twenty-Fourth MEU arrived. For Sergeant Hugh Stevenson, the cavalry had been one minute too late.

19

Quick and steady, Rachel.

She crouched behind a wall of bushes about a quarter mile from the Greenbrier. From her vantage point, she could see why President Ringgold had selected this place as the new seat of government. The colonial-style architecture was classic, and its beauty seemed to provide a beacon of hope amid the destruction and chaos of the world. The main building was reminiscent of the old White House, but it was set in the perfect area, nestled between the mountains and forests of West Virginia. The hundreds of windows and sprawling grounds would be difficult to defend, though.

She brought her M4's scope to her night-vision optics and magnified the main structure, a six-story building with seven hundred rooms looking over a parking lot and stately English-style gardens. It was clear they had once been beautiful, with meticulous landscaping, geometric flower beds, fountains, and cobblestone paths.

She moved the sights toward the windows of the building, looking for any sign of ROT soldiers who might be waiting in ambush. Next, she checked the archways over the entrance.

Two scans revealed zero contacts, so she took a

moment to admire the gardens again while she waited for Senior Chief Blade to give orders to SEAL Team Four. Before the military, she had considered being an architect or teacher, but neither of those careers would have served her well—not enough adrenaline.

She felt the spike in her system saturating her nerve endings when she saw movement on the front lawn. Blade, who was standing next to a tree a few feet away, raised his rifle and directed it at the silhouette of a monster hunting in front of the resort.

Davis didn't need to zoom in to see the creature was infected with the hemorrhage virus. The beast moved on all fours across the grass. It still wore fatigues but was missing a weapon and helmet. The monster in the gardens ran toward a row of bushes and then pounced. Its humped spine rose above the leaves like the back of a whale surfacing in dark waters.

Three seconds later, the beast emerged holding a prize in its maw. Reaching up, it grabbed the rabbit by the head and legs and then tore it in half, warm blood coating the grass.

The low crack of a suppressed shot came from the trees to Davis's left, where Dixon had fired a round from his MK16. By the time Davis found the infected beast again in her sights, it was facedown in the grass, with a 5.56-millimeter slug wedged in its skull.

"Tango down," Blade whispered.

The six-man, one-woman SEAL team moved out of cover and fanned out into the gardens with calculated precision, at combat intervals. Gun barrels swept the shadows, covering high and low. Blade flashed hand signals as they crossed the wet lawns, breaking the team into two. Alpha headed toward the building's right wing, and Bravo moved toward the left.

Davis followed Blade, Dixon, and Melnick across a

driveway and through the grass set along the west side of a parking lot. The trees here were decorative and far too small to provide cover. But if there were more infected out here, cover wasn't going to matter much anyway.

Bravo team, led by Watson, made it to the right wing of the building without contacting any hostiles. That was where the hemorrhage missile had exploded, according to Ringgold's people. Premission intel was often shoddy, however, and Davis saw no evidence of any explosion.

She jogged through the maze of abandoned vehicles and Humvees left behind during the evacuation. Blade was on point, with his rifle shouldered, at the entrance of the building. He stopped at the end of the pavement, balled his hand, and flashed signals to take cover.

Davis picked a minivan and took up position next to Melnick. The medic was young, probably the youngest man on the team, with bright green eyes and a baby face to boot. He raised his MK16 and directed the AAC SCAR suppressor around the end of the minivan.

"Hostile at two o'clock," he whispered.

Two suppressed cracks sounded, and Davis followed Melnick back into the parking lot without even looking to see if the bogey was down. SEALs didn't miss, especially not this close to their targets.

They took off for the archways that led into the lobby of the building, passing another bed of flowers set in a stone box. Davis eyed the infected corpse lying outside the front doors, two bullet holes punched through its skull like an extra set of eyes.

It was another former marine, a female with wispy brown hair. Tattered fatigues revealed bite marks and self-inflicted lacerations. She felt sick at the sight. Davis had seen the infected cannibalize themselves, and it was one of the most horrifying effects of the virus. To be so blinded by hunger that you'd take a bite out of your own arm...it was truly monstrous.

Davis felt the spike of adrenaline soaking her muscle fibers as they entered the building. It was one thing to kill Variants from the earlier days of the infection, but these people should never have been infected. They should have been safe, just like the sailors from the *GW*. She still couldn't quite accept how pointless these deaths were.

Gritting her teeth, she looked away from the corpses and directed her anger at Wood. She would have her revenge. He would die at her hands soon. The fury drove her onward.

Blade moved through the door into a tiled lobby, while Melnick and Dixon took the right doors. The interior was decorated with paintings from early in the history of the United States, but Davis didn't take the time to admire the artwork. They moved through the darkness and down a narrow hallway containing wooden desks and leather chairs. The entrance to the PEOC wasn't far, if she remembered the map correctly.

Blade and Dixon took up position to the right and left sides of intricately carved oak doors with glass handles. Dixon tried one of them and then shook his head.

Davis and Melnick hung back, their rifles directed at the rear guard. With a nod, Blade gave Dixon the order to execute.

Dixon kicked the right door, splintering the wood but not opening the door. Another swift kick, and it swung off the hinges. Blade entered with his gun's barrel moving right to left and back again.

A suppressed shot sounded.

"Tango down," Blade said.

Davis was the last one into the hallway. The patterned

wallpaper was blotted with dark blood, and another corpse lay on the floor. This one wasn't a former marine; she was still dressed in a green polo with the Greenbrier's logo.

"Looks as if she was trapped in here," Blade said. He pointed at the scratch marks on the wooden door.

Davis knew what that meant: The hemorrhage missile had infected more than just the marines trapped outside. If it had gotten into the air-circulation system, then it was possible everyone in the PEOC had been infected.

They continued onward until they got to the elevator doors that led to the bunker.

"Going to break radio silence to see where the other teams are," Blade said.

Davis nodded.

"Bravo One, Alpha One, do you copy? Over," Blade said over the comms. The lights were still off, which meant Watson, Larson, and Tandy either had run into trouble or hadn't been able to find a way to get the lights back on.

"Bravo One, Alpha One, do you copy?" Blade repeated.

There was no response, and the senior chief looked at Davis. She couldn't see his eyes behind his visor, but she knew by the tone of his voice he was on edge.

"Get out the gear," he said to Dixon.

Papa Smurf placed his rucksack on the ground and pulled out a crowbar and rope.

"Alpha One, Bravo One." Watson's voice broke over the comms. "We've got multiple contacts in this wing and have been unable to reach the breakers."

"Roger," Blade replied. "We'll get in the old-fashioned way."

"Got it," Dixon said. The SEAL stood and made way for Blade and Melnick. Together, the two men pulled apart the elevator doors. Dixon dropped a rope into the shaft, and moments later, the team was rappelling down.

They landed on the top of the elevator box, and Blade crouched down to open the hatch. Davis waited while the other men dropped inside. Dixon was nearly silent while he worked on jacking the doors open below.

Quick and steady, Rachel.

As soon as Blade gave the order, she slipped down into the box and moved out into an empty tunnel. They all flipped up their night-vision optics and turned on their tactical lights. The beams penetrated the inky darkness and hit the final doors leading to the PEOC.

Blade balled his hand, and the team waited, listening and watching for any sign of movement, but the passage was empty. The heavy doors had been designed to protect against a direct hit from a nuke, and they couldn't hear any sounds coming from the other side. The double steel doors also rendered Dixon's tools useless, and Blade instructed him to get out the plastic explosive.

The rest of the team waited inside the elevator box while Dixon approached the doors. He carefully placed the C4 in several areas and then retreated.

Blade gave the order with a dip of his helmet.

A fiery explosion followed a beat later. The concussive sound rattled in Davis's ears as she followed Alpha team into the hallway that had filled with smoke and plaster dust.

Blade and Dixon dropped to one knee, while Davis and Melnick took up position behind the men. It took several moments for the smoke and dust to settle. The ringing faded away, and in its wake came a new sound.

"Hold," Blade said.

The *click-clack* could have been from pipes in the walls, wooden supports creaking above their heads, or perhaps even the groan of the walls themselves, but Davis knew it wasn't any of those things.

The beams from their lights speared through the smoke, capturing a single figure staggering out of the bunker, hands cupped to his ears.

"Stay where you are!" Blade shouted. The man, wearing a military uniform, stumbled a few more feet, hands still on his ears. "Don't move!" Blade yelled.

"He can't hear you, Senior Chief," Melnick said.

Davis moved her finger from outside the M4's trigger guard to the trigger. In the glow of the beams from their tactical lights, the man finally came into focus. The first thing Davis saw was the American flag on the man's lapel, and the second was his slitted yellow eyes. His face was covered in bulging blue veins, rendering him almost unrecognizable.

Almost, but not quite.

Vice President Johnson wouldn't be able to give them the intel they needed after all.

Before Blade could give an order, a half dozen figures exploded out of the smoke and bolted past the former vice president, jumping to the walls and ceiling like insects.

Davis stood her ground and yelled, "Open fire!"

Piero used the barrel of his rifle to pick up the shed skin of a Wormer. The flaky material was thicker than snakeskin, but not much more durable. It tore as he raised the clump that had been coiled on the ground like an oversized fire hose. It wasn't the only sample on the historic battlefield of the Colosseum. The dirt was speckled with shredded skins.

"Gross," he whispered.

Ringo's whiskers twitched, and he reared back in disgust.

The morning sun blazed overhead, cooking the remains of flayed cocoons and the skins that filled the amphitheater with an odor like sewer water.

Piero breathed through his mouth and dropped the fragile skin back to the ground. He navigated the minefield of organic litter and walked over to the open gate leading to the guts of the Colosseum.

The Queen was somewhere down there, but this time he wasn't heading back into the darkness. He knew exactly where she was hiding—the sewer system beneath the building. His mission was to confirm and/ or kill the abomination, and there was only one way to do that without getting himself and Ringo turned into monster jerky.

"We're going to draw this Varianti whore out," he whispered to Ringo.

Piero had spent the morning coming up with the plan after remembering something from his childhood. His family had spent many summers in Sicily. Those holidays were some of the best times of his life, but there was one summer he'd ended up in the hospital after a run-in with some killer hornets that had come over from Asia. His sister had insisted on knocking the nest down, but Piero, always the protective brother, had swung the bat himself.

Twenty minutes later he was on his way to the hospital, his skin swollen and red from the multiple stings that would have likely killed his younger sister.

Disturbing a nest of hornets was one thing, but disturbing a nest of mutated monsters made Piero pause outside the gate to reconsider his plan. He imagined he felt much as the gladiators did before they stepped out into the blinding sun in a crowded amphitheater, with citizens screaming in bloodlust from all directions.

Those men hadn't had a choice. Then again, Piero didn't have one either. This plan was all he had—and he was the only one who could carry it out.

He raised the radio to his lips, his decision made, even though it wasn't based on the full truth.

Ringo squeaked and paced on his shoulder while Piero sent Lieutenant General Piazza a message. It only took a few moments for a female operator to reply in English.

"Roger that, Sergeant Angaran. This is Crow One, go ahead. Over."

Crow One? Who the hell is Crow One? Piero thought.

"I'm in position at the Colosseum," he said, switching from Italian to English. "In about ten minutes, send in the best pilot you've got and target the heart of the structure. Drop everything you have . . . blow this place to kingdom come!"

"Have you located the Queen?" she replied.

"Yes, ma'am. In a few minutes, she's going to be in the open, let me assure you."

There was a pause that was long enough to make Piero nervous.

"Sergeant, this is Crow Two," said a new, male voice. "We need a confirmed sighting before committing any aircraft."

"Where's Lieutenant General Piazza?" Piero snapped, frustrated. He didn't have time to waste on these people. He wanted to talk to the man in charge.

"He's KIA, Sergeant," replied Crow Two, his voice cold and stern.

Piero stiffened at the news. He knew right away what it meant: He was about to be grilled about his plan— a plan that had sounded great earlier, but now seemed kind of crazy.

"We need a confirmation before sending air support,"

the man said. "Lieutenant General Piazza gave you specific orders, and—"

Piero cut the operator off. "The Queen is here," Piero said firmly. "I know she's here because I was in the bowels of the Colosseum and I heard her moving around down there."

There was a pause filled with more static.

"Roger that, Sergeant. My CO has given the green light to fire up a jet and send it your way in approximately fifteen minutes, with enough bombs to level the Colosseum, but they won't be dropping a single one unless you have a confirmed sighting, understood?"

"Roger that," Piero said.

Shaking with anger—and partly with fear—he placed the radio back in his pouch. He crossed over to the gate that led to the tunnels. A chain hung from the metal latch, and he looped it through several passes. After securing the gate with a lock, he retreated to the stairs leading up into the arcades.

This is the only way, he thought. *You are doing the right thing. If that woman and her daughter are still alive below, you're doing them a favor.*

Despite the reassurance, Piero still felt conflicted. The fighter jet would kill anyone and everything within a one-block radius of the Colosseum, including any other survivors who might be held prisoner beneath the structure.

The climb up hundreds of steps took him several minutes, and by the time he reached the top, his thighs ached. He didn't have time to stop and rest. Standing on the highest row in the arcades, Piero set his pack down and pulled out the ancient boombox he'd stolen from the apartment building earlier that morning. He blew off the dust and set it on top of the wall.

An hour earlier he'd changed the batteries and dug

through the CD collection the previous resident had left in the apartment. He held a CD of his favorite British band, Led Zeppelin. A smile curled on his face. He wasn't sure he was going to make it out of here alive, but if he was going to die, he wanted to go out listening to one of the best bands of all time.

Piero put the CD into the player. Ringo skittered over his neck and perched on his other shoulder to look out over the city. The view was remarkable from up here, with views of the Vatican, Palatine Hill, and the rooftops of thousands of ancient buildings. In a few minutes, he hoped an even better sight would show up on the horizon: an EUF fighter jet.

He drew in a breath of fresh air that didn't reek of rotting trash and closed his eyes for a moment to picture everyone and everything he'd lost: his family, his friends, the rest of the Fourth Alpini Parachutist Regiment. In his mind's eye, he was transported back to the last trip he'd taken to Rome with his family. His younger sister was standing next to him in the memory, and they were both complaining about being asked to pose for pictures every few feet. His mother had insisted they were making memories, and she had been right.

Now all he had were memories. But at least they were mostly good ones. He opened his eyes as a bad one threatened to overtake his mind—his friend, Lieutenant Antonio LoMaglio, being torn in half by a Reaver right in front of his eyes.

Piero ran a hand through his greasy hair and looked down at Ringo.

"You ready for this, little buddy?" Piero asked.

The mouse squeaked excitedly. It probably thought Piero was going to feed it. Piero heaved a sigh and pushed the Play button on the boombox. The speakers crackled for a few seconds before the opening notes of "Immigrant Song" blasted through the Colosseum. Ringo jumped back to Piero's shoulder, head tilting from side to side.

As soon as the music started playing, Piero reached for the mouse. "Time to get out of here, little buddy," he said, dropping his friend into his vest pocket. The song blared behind them as they worked their way down the stairs. They made it only a few steps before the Colosseum shook, the stone and concrete beneath his boots rumbling.

Piero kept moving. The Zeppelin song had been one of his favorites to listen to when running track in school, and it was always on the playlist for the Fourth Alpini Parachutist Regiment in the weight room.

The song started to crescendo. It hit the climax when he reached the bottom of the stairs. He took a right and hurried down the enclosed veranda toward the arched doorway leading out of the amphitheater.

He glanced over the side of the railing at the floor below. The wooden platform was rattling, and the empty bottles and other trash scattered in the dirt were shaking.

His plan was working. The beasts were moving from their nest.

Robert Plant continued to scream from the speakers. For an old stereo, it sure was loud—loud enough that Piero never heard the flapping wings of a Reaver until it was almost too late.

The beast landed on top of the arched doorway, giving Piero just enough time to duck before it reached down to claw at his face. The six-inch talons narrowly missed him. As soon as he hit the shadowed hallway, he slid to a stop and raised his rifle, firing a burst into the beast. It squawked and fell backward, wings flapping and hitting Piero with a draft of rotten air. He quickly turned and ran through the vestibule.

At the end, another Reaver prowled in the shadows, wings at its side and spiky back hunched. Both almond-shaped eyes focused on Piero, nearly stopping his heart in fright.

He pulled the trigger twice. Both shots found their target, puncturing fragile eyeballs that exploded like pus-filled zits. A screech of agony followed, and hot blood coated the ceiling. Piero considered firing another shot but decided to save his ammunition. The blind beast flopped on the ground, thrashing.

Piero pulled out his knife to finish off the monster as he moved into the dim passage. Two steps in, a pair of claws grabbed his pack and yanked him backward. He landed hard on his tailbone. The creature he'd fired a direct blast into earlier climbed on top of him, shrieking in rage and using its wings to pin his arms down.

He stared up at the ugliest alien face he'd ever seen in his life. Two crooked eyes bulged in pale sockets, and wormy sucker lips opened to blast him with hot, wretched breath that smelled like a thousand dead fish.

"*No!*" he screamed. "Get off me, you hideous turd!"

Piero fought violently, more worried about Ringo than himself. He could feel the mouse moving in his breast pocket.

The beast slammed his knife hand against the ground, knocking away his blade and cutting his wrist with sharp claws. Somehow he managed to hold on to his rifle.

Sunlight hit his face as the creature dragged him, kicking and squirming, onto the veranda. He caught a glimpse of the dirt floor below, where Wormer tentacles had burst through. Several sets of snakelike beasts wriggled as the tunneling monsters tried to free their bodies from the dirt.

At the gates were several full-grown juveniles. The lock held them back for all of two seconds before the creatures barreled into the open. Another gate across the Colosseum broke off its hinges, disgorging mutated monsters of all shapes and sizes: Beetles, Pinchers, and Reavers.

Piero fought the beast holding him, but every time he moved, the wings tightened around his body. Ringo squeaked inside his pocket, terrified and wiggling.

I should never have brought him with me, Piero realized. The thought of his furry friend ending up as a snack made him fight harder. He managed to fire a shot with his rifle that only pinged off the concrete floor.

The monster's grip suddenly loosened, and it flapped away, but before Piero could raise his gun, an arm wrapped around his neck, and a claw tightened around his wrist.

He screamed in pain and dropped the rifle.

Then he was rising into the air. Wings flapped to his right and left. He managed to move his head to see sucker lips the size of his head, and remembered Antonio LoMaglio's last minutes on this earth.

Not like this, Piero thought. "Fuck, not like this!" The words choked out of his mouth. He tried to punch the monster with his other hand, in a desperate attempt to injure the beast or at least startle it into letting go.

As it pulled him into the air he got a bird's-eye view of the Colosseum. It was filling with the monsters like a rush of ants leaving an anthill. His plan to lure them out had worked, but his escape had failed miserably.

The boombox had been the fishing hook, but Piero and Ringo had ended up the bait.

"N-no," Piero stuttered. "Let us go!"

He tried to reach down and let Ringo out of his pocket, but any movement only resulted in the Reaver tightening its grip around his neck.

Red encroached on his vision, blurring his view of the Colosseum. Another Zeppelin song was playing in the distance, but he could hardly make out the words.

Piero kicked the air helplessly, his boots a hundred feet away from the nearest rooftop. Over the music came a voice. Someone was calling his name.

It took a few seconds to realize it was the radio still in his pouch.

"Sergeant Angaran, Crow Two. Do you copy? Over."

Piero continued squirming, but the beast was three times his size, and it had the grip of a Greek Olympic wrestler. He dug his fingers into the tendons of its wrist, trying to break its hold, and miraculously, the creature let up slightly. Piero filled his lungs with a long, deep breath.

The stars and red faded away, his vision clearing to the sight of Rome beneath his boots.

"Sergeant, Crow Two. We have a jet en route, do you have a visual of the target? We need confirmation. Over."

Piero tried to pull his radio, but his fingers came up shy, and his captor increased its grip around his throat as it changed course, flying toward the Vatican.

This new angle provided Piero a view of the Colosseum again. The arcades and bottom floor were filled with the mutated flesh and armor of the monsters. Some of them took to the skies; a pack of Reavers flapped away to the south.

He wiggled a finger and gripped the pocket containing Ringo. As soon as the Reaver put him down, he would let the mouse go. It was something he should have done long ago—a selfless act that would be Piero's last.

He just had to survive the ride to wherever the monster was taking him. His eyes flitted from the rooftops back to the Colosseum, where a pillar of Reavers was climbing into the sky.

In the center of the column was a bright red beast twice the size of the others. As it rose, it whipped a black tail through the air and released a guttural croak that Piero recognized even from a distance. A clicking noise followed, and so did a small army of Reavers that flapped after the red monster into the sky away from the Colosseum.

"The Queen," Piero gasped.

The Reaver tightened its grip, choking off his oxygen supply. Piero's vision blurred once again while his cheeks flared with heat, then turned numb. He managed a breath through his nostrils, giving him a short reprieve. Over the rush of flapping wings around him came the scream of a fighter jet's twin engines that drowned out the distant clicking call of the Queen.

The EUF was right on time.

Piero fingered for the radio again and this time was able to pull it from his pouch. He hit the button on the side and sucked in several breaths through his nostrils.

"Crow Two, I have confirmation. The Queen is a red Reaver. Repeat, a red Reaver flying out of the—"

The Reaver choked off his vocal cords, and his last breath came out in a squeak like Ringo's.

"Roger that, Sergeant. Stand by," was the reply.

The jet appeared to the east, moving low over the city. He blinked and tried to focus on the black dot. The Reaver clutching him began to descend as the fighter jet closed in on the Colosseum.

Come on, brother. Nail this son of a bitch, Piero thought.

Missiles streaked away from the jet and side-wound through the air toward the target. They impacted the sides of the building a moment later in a brilliant flash of fire. Explosions tore the ancient structure apart, a wall of flames enveloping the heart of one of Rome's most historical structures in one pass, silencing both the music and the monsters still trapped inside.

The tendrils of flames and smoke reached toward the escaping Reavers, enveloping the column of flapping monsters.

The jet tore across the skyline, away from the destruction.

Piero blinked again, focusing on the rising smoke. His heart flipped when he saw several of the Reavers break through the top of the dark cloud, flapping through the smoke. One of the beasts fluttered back to the ground, wings smoldering. But the majority of the small army, including the Queen, rose into the sky.

"No," Piero choked.

He watched in horror as the EUF fighter jet vanished on the horizon, unknowingly leaving the Queen behind. The armada of beasts suddenly changed direction, turning in the same direction as the creature holding Piero— toward the Vatican.

The sight of the place where he'd spent months hiding filled Piero with rage, despair, and sadness. He didn't want it to end here. He'd hoped at least to die a free man under the sun.

But it was not to be. His fate, so it seemed, was to return to the place of his nightmares. He struggled for air as the Reaver gripping him descended toward the holy structure. It flapped toward a shattered stained-glass window below St. Peter's Basilica. They landed on the tile floor a moment later and wings began wrapping around Piero.

He didn't bother trying to fight the Reaver. His last

act was to free his furry friend trapped inside his pocket. The mouse climbed down his chest, jumped to the floor, and bolted for safety right before Piero was enveloped by the creature's wings.

"I love you, Ringo," Piero whispered. "Good-bye."

20

Kate sat in front of her computer desk inside the cramped quarters assigned to her, still reeling from an epiphany. She was supposed to be taking a nap, but she was too excited about her new idea to sleep.

The combination of excitement, worry, and fear had also made her sick to her stomach. The gentle rocking of the *Thalassa* didn't help. A half-eaten bowl of soup sloshed next to her computer. She had managed to eat a little to calm her nervous stomach, but the nausea was returning.

The tea Dr. Bruno had brewed earlier was helping. Kate took another sip. The warm liquid ran down her throat and helped clear her mind. She was thankful for Bruno's kindness. She seemed to be very mindful of Kate's health and pregnancy. Orlov, on the other hand, had hardly said a word to Kate since she arrived. She could tell he didn't want her here.

The other doctors were back in the clean room, testing the chemical components of VX-99. The work they had done to separate the components had taken months, and it was truly genius. The next step was just as difficult— but not as time-consuming, if Kate's idea worked.

Getting up from her computer, she left the quarters and walked back down a narrow passage leading to the clean room. Bruno and Orlov looked up from their stations when she pushed the comm-link button.

"I think I made a breakthrough," Kate said.

Orlov was the first to speak. "About time."

That earned him a glance from Bruno.

"Go ahead, Doctor Lovato, we're excited to hear it," she said.

"So, we know how to target the separate chemical components of VX-99 with nanoparticles. But that's not the problem. The issue is that the particles are still small enough to pass through the blood-brain barrier."

She paused to collect her thoughts and, confident in her idea, she said, "I've been looking for protein fragments or something to coat the particles to stop them from passing through the barrier. What if we coat the nanoparticles with a complementary protein fragment—say, C3bi? That would activate phagocytes that would devour anything harmful or foreign in the body—including the VX-99 chemical compounds."

Orlov and Bruno exchanged a glance.

"Massive phagocyte activation could also cause an adverse autoimmune response, but I guess it's worth a shot," Bruno said. "I'll prepare the rats for testing."

"It better work," Orlov said. "We have only a few rodents left. So unless you want to use fish—"

The crack of what sounded a lot like gunfire cut the doctor off.

"What the hell was that?" Bruno asked.

The clank of boots on steps came from behind Kate, and she turned to see Horn and one of his men hurrying down the ladder. Both of them were putting on their body armor.

"We got Variants incoming," Horn said. "The flying kind."

"Reavers?" Bruno said from inside the lab, her voice cracking.

"Yeah," Horn said. "Stay down here. My men will take care of them. Lock yourself in a hatch and stay there until I give the all clear."

Bruno and Orlov were already getting out of their suits in the staging area. By the time Horn lumbered back up the ladder, the other doctors were hurrying out to join Kate.

"Where's the safest place to hide?" Kate asked.

Orlov pointed down the passageway to their quarters. They hurried in that direction, and Kate followed them into a cramped, windowless room with a single bed and desk. A picture of Orlov and two small children rested next to a laptop.

"Stay calm," Bruno said, sitting next to Kate on the bed. "Everything's going to be okay."

Gunfire echoed through the ship. Orlov sealed the door and spun the handwheel until it clicked shut. Then he sat down at his desk and opened his laptop as if this were just another workday.

Kate rubbed her belly, trying to take deep breaths. In a lull in the gunfire, she heard a scream—a mixture of pain and terror. It was impossible to tell if it was human or monster.

"Get out the gun," Bruno said.

Orlov opened a drawer and pulled out a pistol. He handed the gun to her and she handled it like a pro, inserting a magazine and then chambering a round.

"Just in case," she whispered.

Another screech reverberated belowdecks. This time it was unmistakably Variant. The monster let out a cackle, almost a laugh. A human scream followed, and then crashing equipment and shattering glass sounded outside the hatch.

"That's coming from the lab," Orlov said. He walked over to the hatch and put his ear against it. "One of them must be inside."

"Is there another way into the ship?" Kate asked.

"Plenty of ways," Orlov said.

Bruno raised the pistol. "We can't let them destroy our work."

"If we die, it won't matter, but you're right," Orlov said. He gripped the handwheel and looked at Kate as if for approval.

"I agree," Kate said. "We can't let those things destroy the clean room."

Grinding metal echoed, and a crunching sound made its way through the lower decks of the ship. The frantic sound of nails scratching against metal, like the sound of a rat trying to escape its cage, seized the air from Kate's lungs.

It was growing louder, and it was headed in their direction.

Bruno pointed the gun at the hatch and nodded at Orlov. He was breathing heavily, and he used a shoulder to wipe the sweat from his wrinkled forehead.

"On three," Bruno whispered.

A sniffing sound came from the passageway. The beast was hunting them.

"One," Bruno said. "Two…"

Kate flinched at the sound of gunfire right outside the door. A mixture of human shouting and monsters screeching filled the passage. Grunts, the popping of joints, more screeching, and another gunshot followed.

Blood pooled under the hatch and flowed into the

room. Kate pulled her feet up as a loud thump hit the ground. An eerie silence loomed for several moments before a voice said, "All clear."

Orlov opened the door to reveal Horn bracing himself against the bulkhead with one hand, chest armor rising up and down as he panted. Behind him, on the ground, was a Reaver curled up in a fetal position.

Kate rose to her feet to look Horn over. "Are you okay?"

"Yeah, not a scratch." He pushed a finger to his earpiece. "Diamond One, sitrep."

Kate sagged against the bulkhead, relief washing over her.

"Roger that," Horn said a moment later. "Looks as if we got all of 'em. This one must have gotten in through one of the portholes. I'll make sure that won't happen again."

Bruno nodded and handed the pistol back to Orlov. She looked at Kate and said, "Time to get back to work," as if nothing had happened.

This is it, President Ringgold thought to herself. She stood in the flag bridge on the USS *Abraham Lincoln* with her fingers on her chin.

All around her, staff members and officers were monitoring the events that would shape history. Each of them had on a headset connected to the teams working inside the combat information center, where more sailors were monitoring the situation.

In Europe, the EUF and American forces were moving across the country to face mutated beasts straight from the pits of hell. In Los Angeles, an Army Ranger team was moving to capture another monster, Lieutenant Andrew Wood. At the White House in the

Greenbrier, SEAL Team Four was raiding the PEOC to search for Vice President Johnson and evidence of the attack perpetrated by ROT, and on the *Thalassa*, Kate was working on a cure for the hemorrhage virus.

Ringgold only had access to the video feed of what was happening in LA, but she was focused on the entire picture, her mind racing from one event to another. They needed victories across the board for success, and right now that seemed unlikely.

Everything comes down to this. Our species will look back on what happened today with pride...or there won't be anyone left to remember how we failed, Ringgold mused.

"Okay, we're live at SZT Nineteen," said Nelson. The national security advisor gestured to a wall-mounted monitor displaying a crowded street in Los Angeles. To the right and left of the man with the hidden camera were two soldiers dressed in civilian drab. Ringgold imagined they were packing major firepower beneath their coats.

"This feed is from Sergeant Major Pat Churchill of the Seventy-Fifth Ranger Regiment," Lemke said. "Churchill and his ten-man team have been all over the United States killing Variants in the past seven months."

Ringgold folded her arms across her chest. She had thought about asking for another SEAL team, but Lemke had been confident when he deployed the Rangers, and it wasn't as if they had many choices. Most of the military was either in Europe or aligning with ROT.

"How many men does Wood have?" she asked.

"According to our intel, there are two dozen ROT soldiers located at SZT Nineteen, an even match for our Rangers," Lemke said. "With the element of surprise on our side, our odds are even better. By the time Wood knows what hit him, it will be too late."

Churchill and his men passed under strings of light bulbs hanging over the road. Sandbags formed walls around storefronts with boarded-up windows. Spaces that had once been luxury clothing stores, fresh-juice bars, and sushi joints were now retrofitted to cater to basic survival. It looked more like a street in the Wild West than in upscale Los Angeles.

A message came in over the open frequency from Captain Ingves on the bridge. "Got a sitrep on those destroyers General Nixon is sending," he reported. "They're about two hours out."

"Excellent," Ringgold said. She took a moment to look at all the faces in the flag bridge. Lemke, Soprano, Nelson, and four sailors she hardly knew sat around the table. Captain Konkoly and his crew were waiting under the surface in the USS *Florida*, with orders to fire on anything not authorized to approach.

If all went to plan, the men and women of this ragtag fleet were going to be part of the beginning of a new America—a nation focused on rebuilding and peace, not caught up in a civil war.

On-screen, the three Army Rangers continued down the street, blending with filthy civilians. Most of them wore tattered clothing, and more than a few appeared gaunt and malnourished. The hidden camera revealed a bleak picture: Vendors and customers bartered over goods that months ago would have been considered garbage. Children, some of them no older than Horn's girls, were wandering the streets without anyone to look after them.

Food and power were in limited supply at most of the SZTs. Rations were already running out, and with the government in shambles, people were fending for themselves. Ringgold had heard all about the violence, riots, and rapes being reported at SZTs. Things were getting worse with ROT in control, but doing nothing to help the people in the territories.

"Do we know why Wood took the risk to travel here?" Ringgold asked.

"Intercepted radio transmissions said something about meeting with Coyote in the basement of the embassy, but we're not sure who or what that's a code word for," Nelson replied.

Several police officers patrolled the street on the monitor, but there was no sign of the ROT soldiers in their black fatigues and armor. Ringgold hovered behind her seat, too nervous to sit down.

"Churchill and his team are moving in toward the embassy," Lemke said. "The other teams are en route to the tarmac to block off escape routes. We also have several snipers in position."

"How many people live at SZT Nineteen?" Ringgold asked.

Soprano thumbed through the folder in front of him and scanned a page. "Looks like just shy of two thousand," he reported.

It didn't sound like a lot, but Ringgold had been surprised to learn it only took a healthy breeding population of 250 adults to keep the species going. They were far above that number in this SZT alone, but humanity was still dangerously close to extinction. At the end of the city street, concrete panels walled off the SZT from the city. On the other side were lawlessness, death, and monsters.

"Here we go," Lemke said, pointing at the screen. He scooted his chair closer to the table, but Ringgold remained standing. "Can we get audio?"

"Still working on it," Nelson said. He typed on his laptop, trying to secure a connection.

Churchill and his two men had moved into another street and were approaching the embassy building—a brick structure that used to be a police station, surrounded by two barbed wire fences.

At the first checkpoint stood two older men in army fatigues and baseball caps. About ten feet behind them was a second checkpoint of sandbags, set at the base of the stone steps leading into the fortress. An American flag hung from the awning set over the steps, and in its shadow stood three ROT soldiers next to their own flag, all dressed in black fatigues, with automatic rifles cradled across their sculpted armor.

"Trouble," Soprano said.

"They can handle it," Lemke said.

Ringgold appreciated the confidence, but the bead of sweat dripping down the admiral's weathered forehead told her he was nervous.

Churchill had stopped at the first barrier to talk to the guards there. Everyone inside the flag bridge went silent. It was quiet enough that Ringgold could hear Soprano's labored breathing. He was sweating heavily too.

Another message was relayed over the comm frequency. It was Ingves again, and there was tension in his normally calm voice.

"I just got a message from Captain Davis, and I have bad news," he said, pausing.

One of the ROT soldiers outside the embassy was moving down the stairs, distracting Ringgold for a moment. She gripped the back of her chair, her eyes flitting from the approaching ROT soldier on-screen to the captain's transmission.

"The PEOC was a loss," Ingves continued. "The air-filtration system failed, infecting everyone inside with the hemorrhage virus. However, Senior Chief Blade and

Captain Davis were able to recover an audio message from Wood about the attack. We should have everything we need to send it out to the other SZTs now. This will clear your name, President Ringgold."

Her heart ached at the news of Vice President Johnson's death, but she couldn't help but feel relief about the intel SEAL Team Four had uncovered. She would mourn those she'd lost once Wood had been defeated.

"Blade and Davis are downloading more data now, and then they're going to head back here," Ingves said.

"Any word on Captain Beckham?" Ringgold asked.

"We left him at the chopper, but he wasn't showing any signs of infection aside from a headache," Ingves replied.

"That's two pieces of good news," she said and finally sat in her chair to watch the video feed. "Soprano, see if you can get a message to Kate. I want her to know that Captain Beckham is okay."

"Yes, ma'am," Soprano replied.

Pushing away thoughts of Vice President Johnson and everything else, she focused on Churchill and his men. They were being directed through the first gate, but the ROT soldier on the stairs raised a hand as they approached the next checkpoint.

Not being able to hear the conversation was beyond frustrating, but the USS *Abraham Lincoln* was almost half a world away. Even if she had been able to hear it, she was powerless to do anything to help anyway.

The ROT soldier still had a hand up, and his lips were moving. He stepped closer and pulled off his sunglasses, as if he was trying to get a better look at Churchill and his men.

"What's happening?" Ringgold asked.

Before anyone could answer her, the ROT soldier's

mouth opened as though he was screaming an order, and he dropped his sunglasses. An instant later, he raised his rifle.

The Army Ranger on Churchill's right, a veritable Viking who rivaled Horn in size, had already flipped open a trench coat. He pulled out two submachine guns and pointed them up the stairs while Churchill raised a sawed-off shotgun at the lead ROT soldier.

Churchill fired. The blast hit the man in the chest, tearing into his rib cage.

Ringgold laced her fingers together tightly as the battle broke out in front of the embassy building. She couldn't see what happened to the first two guards at the barricade, but no one tried to stop Churchill as he bolted toward the second checkpoint, leaped over the concrete blocks, and then loped up the stairs.

The three Army Rangers moved into a tiled lobby with vaulted ceilings. One of them fired on the soldier stationed at the front desk, and he slumped over the surface, blood gushing out of his neck.

"Ha! Got it," Nelson said.

The speakers on the wall-mounted monitor inside the flag bridge suddenly crackled with audio. The boom of a shotgun sounded as Churchill fired at another ROT guard who had run into the open space.

The first blast missed, splintering the wooden desk the soldier took refuge behind. But the Ranger with the submachine guns put three holes into him from a different angle.

Blood pooled across the tile floor, and empty shell casings clanked in the warm fluid from the automatic gunfire.

"On me, Shepherd!" Churchill shouted. "Perry, you hold security here."

The three men pushed through the lobby, yelling and gesturing for the civilians inside the open space to get on the ground. Churchill and the larger Ranger, who must have been the one he called Shepherd, moved into a hallway and then down a stairwell.

Ingves relayed another message over the comm channel. "We just got a message from Lieutenant General Frank Curtis. He's aboard one of those Seahawks, and he claims to know where the *Zumwalt* is. They should be landing in a few minutes."

A grinning Soprano clapped Nelson on the back, and Ringgold closed her eyes for a moment to let the news sink in. She wasn't smiling yet, but the tide did appear to be turning in their favor.

The mission to the PEOC at the White House had revealed the intel they needed to bring down Wood, and now they had the location of his stealth ship, as well as his location. Maybe they could win this war after all. All they had to do now was catch the weasel.

Churchill had his side arm out now. He moved around a corner with the pistol directed down the landing. Two muzzle flashes lit up the dim passage, and a soldier in black hit the ground at the bottom of the stairs.

Bullets lanced into the wall next to Churchill. The camera rattled, bobbing up and down as he moved for cover. He tripped and fell on the stairs, sliding to the bottom while firing his pistol at targets Ringgold couldn't see.

Shepherd squeezed past on the left and took a knee at the bottom of the stairs near the dead ROT soldier.

"Two contacts!" Churchill shouted.

"Stay down!" Shepherd yelled back.

That's when Ringgold saw Churchill had been hit.

He was lying on the stairs, trying to flatten his body to avoid the bullets punching into the wall. The camera was angled to show only part of the hallway.

"Get to cover!" Churchill yelled at Shepherd.

The camera jolted again, going topsy-turvy and then focusing back on the hallway. Churchill had fallen down the stairs and was on his back, providing a view of Shepherd, who was still firing from a kneeling position.

More gunfire streaked down the passage. At the other end, two ROT soldiers hid behind a corner, taking potshots at Churchill and Shepherd.

"They have to get out of there," Ringgold said.

Shepherd went to change his magazine and was hit with several rounds in the arm and chest. He slumped against the wall. He raised a pistol and fired off a few more shots before his body gave out.

Churchill was crawling, using his elbows to drag himself away. The two ROT soldiers at the other end of the hall emerged from around the corner with their rifles shouldered.

"Drop your weapons!" one of them shouted. The other man fired, and a red streak lanced into Churchill's chest. Blood bloomed around the camera, blocking the view.

This wasn't the first time she'd seen men die on her watch, and Ringgold knew it wouldn't be the last. She hoped none of the others noticed as she reached up to swipe the tears from her cheeks.

"Jesus Christ," Nelson said.

"Where are the other Rangers?" Soprano asked. "What about Perry?"

Ingves shook his head. "Perry was KIA, but we have another team moving in."

Lemke pounded the table. "Do *not* let Wood escape."

The hatch opened, and an officer walked inside the

flag bridge. Every eye flitted toward the young man who said, "Sir, Lieutenant General Frank Curtis just landed on the deck."

"Bring him up here," Lemke said, frustration in his voice.

"Yes, sir," the officer said, hastily retreating into the other room.

They could still win this, Ringgold reminded herself. The other Ranger teams were closing in around the embassy, and there were snipers set up to prevent Wood from escaping. While she waited for a report, there was another knock on the hatch, and this time it opened to reveal a tall man in an army uniform with a chestful of medals.

"Lieutenant General Frank Curtis, I presume?" Ringgold said.

The man nodded, did a quick scan of the room, and said without preamble, "I'm here on behalf of General Nixon. We know the location of the USS *Zumwalt* and are prepared to take you there."

"We're in the process of tracking Wood down right now," Lemke said. "Have a seat if you'd like to watch us catch the piece of shit."

Curtis grabbed the chair next to Ringgold. She looked back at the screen. The feed was still blurred from the blood gushing from Churchill's wounds. There was movement and voices in the hallway, but she couldn't tell if they were friendly or hostile.

Another message crackled over the comms. "Admiral Lemke, this is Captain Konkoly—we just had a radar hit on a submarine."

Lemke slowly stood and narrowed his brows at Ringgold.

"Submarine?" he said.

The hatch banged opened, and the same officer who

had interrupted them before said, "Sir, we've got torpedoes incoming!"

"How the hell did this happen?" Lemke roared.

An answer surged over the comms: It was Konkoly again, and there was a flat note to his voice that scared Ringgold far more than Lemke's yelling. "We've been betrayed."

The Klaxon on the USS *Abraham Lincoln* went off as an explosion echoed through the ship.

"Are we hit?" Nelson shouted.

"That wasn't us," Ingves replied. "Oh God, the *Florida*. Sir, the..."

"Captain," Lemke said. "Captain Konkoly, do you copy, over?"

There was no answer, and for a moment everyone in the room remained still, all eyes flitting to Curtis. The lieutenant general stood stiffly and said, "Listen very carefully if you want to live."

"What is this?" Lemke said, his features twisted with confusion and anger.

Curtis cut a glance at Ringgold. She couldn't read his expression; he looked almost rueful. "Wood and Nixon have made a deal, and unfortunately that deal is to deliver Madam President to the USS *Zumwalt*," he said.

"You son of a bitch," Nelson said.

"We won't let you take her," Lemke said.

Curtis swallowed, his Adam's apple bobbing. "Nixon was afraid of that, which is why our submarine just sank the *Florida*. It was your last out. Our weapons are now targeting this ship, as well as every other ship in your fleet. I'm sorry, but it's over. You have nowhere to run, Ms. Ringgold. Please come quietly, and no one else will be hurt."

Lemke reached for his side arm, but Ringgold put a hand on his shoulder.

"It's over," she said, hardly believing the words. She drew herself up to her full height and met Curtis's gaze. The officer looked away first.

"The bloodshed ends now," she said. "I have to go with them."

21

Andrew Wood had never wanted to be president. As a kid, he had dreamed of being an astronaut, of finding new worlds and bending them to his vision.

Now, as an adult, he looked at fourteen-year-old Madeline Nixon and wondered what she wanted to be when she got older. He almost laughed at the absurdity of the idea. The girl wasn't going to grow up to be anything if her father betrayed him.

She glanced up from the shadows of her prison cell, a ten-by-six concrete block that had once been used as the drunk tank in the old Los Angeles police station. Now it housed General Nixon's only daughter.

Madeline sat cross-legged, clearly rattled by the gunfire in the halls outside but still pretending to be tough. She glared murder at him. This time, he did laugh.

"Scary," he said.

"Fuck you," she spat.

He shook his head. The language these kids used today. Wood rapped on the metal door leading into the station once, then twice. Kufman opened it, holding his SCAR-H at the ready. The former Delta operator said he preferred the gas-operated battle rifle that fired 7.62-millimeter rounds over the SCAR-L due to the caliber. Judging by his determined gaze, Kufman was itching to use it.

"Sir, I need to get up there and bury these fuckers," he said.

"Settle down, Kufman." Wood kept his voice low to make sure the girl couldn't hear them. "Do you have a sitrep?"

"The hostiles in the embassy have been neutralized. We've got three birds en route with reinforcements, but we think there are other hostiles in the SZT. Snipers, maybe two additional teams."

"Who the fuck are these guys, and how did they find out I was here?"

"Ringgold's people would be my guess, but we won't know until we catch one and interrogate 'em." Kufman spat on the ground. "We managed to take down a guy in the next hallway who's still breathing, but we don't know for how long. He's shot up pretty bad."

Next hallway? Damn, they got close, Wood thought.

Out loud, he said, "I'll come meet the breathing fucker in a few minutes, when I'm done with this brat."

As soon as Wood stepped back into the room, Madeline spat at his feet. "My dad is going to come get me," she snarled, showing the braces on her teeth.

"You're the daughter of a general, indeed."

She pushed herself to her feet, testing his patience further by pulling on the chains binding her right leg to the wall.

"And you're the son of a psycho bitch. I heard your brother was—"

Wood backhanded Madeline before she could finish her sentence. The smack reverberated in the room. She cupped her face with a hand, letting out a gasp and moving away from Wood.

"You're right about my mom, but no one talks about my brother. Got it?"

Madeline glared back, but didn't reply.

"Got it?"

"Sure," she replied.

That was good. Wood really didn't like hurting kids. That was a red line that he normally didn't cross unless absolutely necessary. At least, he tried not to hurt them *personally*. The kids who had been hit by the hemorrhage virus when he'd dropped it on the SZTs were inevitable casualties.

He shook away the thoughts and took a moment to size up the feisty girl. She was in her teens, with blemished skin, dark brown eyes, and braces: not much different from him at that age. He even had the acne scars to prove it, and straight teeth from four years of braces.

"What are you going to do with me?" Madeline asked, pulling her hand away from her cheek.

"That depends a lot on your dad."

She shook her head and, to his surprise, smirked.

"My dad is going to wring your neck and throw you into jail for the rest of your life."

"You really don't learn, do you?" he said. She was a teenager, but damn, she was really testing his patience. "Your dad is going to be lucky if he survives Europe. Stupid fuck should never have gone over there. *If* he makes it back from the war, I might have a spot for him in my army, especially after what he did for me, but..."

Madeline narrowed her thick eyebrows. "What he did?"

"Well, what you did too," Wood said slyly.

"What are you talking about?"

He turned back to the door and knocked twice. Kufman opened the hatch and looked in.

"How's it coming out there?" Wood asked.

"Still searching the territory," Kufman replied. "Found a sniper. What do you want me to do with 'em?"

Wood thought back to the mayor of SZT 15 and said, "Skin him and hang him from the top of those hippie farms."

"It's not a him," Kufman said.

Wood could see a slight hesitation in the soldier's eyes. "Do you have a point you'd like to make?" Wood asked.

"No, sir."

Wood slammed the door again and kicked the dog food bowl at Madeline's bare feet. The soup, or whatever was in it, sloshed over the sides.

"What are you talking about?" she asked again, pulling at her restraints.

Wood smiled again. She was starting to remind him of the creatures he would capture as a kid, right before he would torture them or toss them against the barn—frantic and terrified. Kind of like her dad. It had taken only a single message to General Nixon to get him to betray President Ringgold. Thinking of that short conversation reminded him of how weak the general was.

Wood needed a man with the balls of a horse, not a pony.

"Yeah…" Wood said, squinting. "I really don't think I'm going to keep your dad around, but I'll have to see about you. We did make a deal."

"Deal?"

Wood shrugged and told her the truth. "I told your dad I was going to feed you to a Variant unless he gave up Jan Ringgold and her allies." He paused to watch her reaction and then added, "I still might if you don't start acting like a lady."

A gunshot rang out down the hall, distracting him. He unholstered his favorite gun—a 1911A1 with an ivory grip. It had been a gift from his brother, Zach, back in 1979, just seven years before the military switched to Beretta M9s as the standard-issue pistol. After checking the magazine, he palmed it back in and tapped twice on the door.

"What are you doing?" Madeline said.

"Going to finish these fuckers off. Be good while I'm gone, and I'll think twice about giving you to the Variants outside the walls as a snack." He winked at Madeline and left.

Kufman had his SCAR directed down the hallway. "Two men got past the defenses," he said. "Better stay inside, sir."

"Fuck that. If you guys can't handle this shit, I will." Wood pulled back the slide to chamber a .45 round. Then he directed Kufman to take point down the hallway.

The bank of overhead lights cast a white glow across the tile floor and concrete walls. Whoever these guys were, they hadn't been able to shut off the power, which told him they either were amateurs or didn't have much firepower.

Wood was going to have fun killing them.

He approached one of his soldiers, standing guard at the end of the hallway. The dark-skinned man kept his gaze on his gun's sights and said, "Hostiles in the lobby upstairs, sir. Please stay behind—"

Wood walked around the corner, completely ignoring the soldier. Kufman hustled to keep up. There were two crumpled ROT soldiers in the hallway. At the other end were two more bodies, both dressed in civilian clothing. A pair of Wood's soldiers stood there with their rifles angled up the stairs.

"Which one of these fuckers is still breathing?" Wood asked.

Kufman pointed at the man at the bottom of the stairs who was lying on his back. A second, larger man with red hair was slumped against the wall, his freckled face caved in from multiple gunshots.

Wood couldn't hold back a chuckle. The guy looked like one of the shattered bullfrogs he had tossed against the barn in his backyard as a kid!

The other man, a middle-aged guy with a five o'clock shadow and a sharp nose, was still breathing a few feet away. The rattle in his chest told Wood he had a punctured lung, or perhaps two. He wasn't going to last long.

Wood bent down and said, "Who the fuck are you?"

A pair of brown eyes roved toward Wood. Then they moved back to the ceiling. The man was probably doing what most men did before they died—thinking of their family, or all the things they would miss out on now, or perhaps trying to focus on something other than the pain. Not giving up his name and unit was honorable, but Wood wasn't going to let him off that easy.

He pulled out a blade sheathed on his belt and used the tip to open the man's shirt beneath a trench coat, plucking off buttons and exposing a flak jacket soaked with blood. A small camera was mounted on a cord that snaked down the armor.

"Well, what is this?" Wood asked. He pulled out the camera and wiped the warm blood off on the man's pant leg.

"President…" the dying soldier wheezed. "President…"

Kufman crouched down and snapped his fingers in front of the man's face. He was wheezing harder now, struggling for each breath, lungs crackling and blood bubbling out of his mouth.

President…" the man said again.

Wood rolled his eyes. "Come on, brother, I know you've got a few words left in you besides my title."

The soldier glanced at him again, and Wood saw an anger in his gaze that must have prompted enough adrenaline to help him speak. In that moment of clarity, the dying soldier said, "Jan Ringgold is the true *president*, you piece of shit." He hacked up blood and spat it onto Wood's face.

Wood remained froze in place, the blood dripping down his chin and his body on fire with the rage swirling inside of him.

Kufman handed Wood a handkerchief, but Wood pushed it away.

"You better start talking," Kufman said.

The injured soldier looked away and focused on Kufman. In that split second, Wood jammed the tip of his blade into the man's left ear. A complicated rattling sound emerged from the man's bloody lips, and his eyes bulged wider as Wood pushed his blade deeper.

"Jan Ringgold is not the president!" Wood screamed, thrusting the blade as far in as he could. He left the knife inside the man's skull and directed the camera toward his face. "I'm in charge! Me! You get that?"

After exhaling, Wood finally wiped the blood off his face, took in another deep breath, and then smiled politely at the camera, hoping that General Nixon's men hadn't captured Ringgold yet so she could hear this.

"Jan, I presume you're watching this," he said, narrowing his gaze at the tiny lens. "Your time is up. I'm coming for you and everyone you care about."

Beckham sat in the troop hold of the Seahawk, eyeing Crew Chief Ronaldo and the Beretta M9 still angled at him.

"You really think I'm infected?" Beckham said.

Ronaldo didn't shrug or nod. He simply said, "I'm following orders."

"Orders." Beckham snorted and looked back at the dark woods at the edge of the field. He was really getting sick of orders. For his entire life, he'd been following them, and watching bad men carry out the orders of even worse men.

Beckham reached down with his hand and attempted to untie the bonds on his boot and blade.

"Don't do that," Ronaldo said.

Beckham looked up but continued struggling with the tie. "There still might be infected out there, and I'm sick of waiting for Davis and Blade to get back. Now, you can either sit there and look dumb when trouble shows up, or you can—"

The *whoosh* of an incoming helicopter cut Beckham off.

"Are we expecting company?" Ronaldo said to the pilots who were still sitting in the cockpit.

"Negative," Pressfield said.

Omstead shook his head.

"Untie me, right fucking now, and give me a gun," Beckham said to Ronaldo.

The crew chief looked at the pilots, who both gave reluctant nods.

"Hurry," Beckham said.

Using a knife, Ronaldo cut the tie around Beckham's boot and blade. As soon as he was free, Beckham ducked out of the troop hold to look at the sky.

The surrounding area was so quiet it wasn't hard to track the choppers. Judging by the noise of the rotors, they were MH-6 Little Birds—the same helicopters ROT used.

"Someone contact Davis and Blade and let them know we got company," Beckham said.

"They said radio silence," Ronaldo replied.

"This is a fucking emergency," Beckham said. He grabbed an M9 from Ronaldo and staggered out into the grass to search the dark skies while Ronaldo relayed a transmission over the comms.

In the glow of the moonlight Beckham glimpsed the outline of three Little Birds heading in from the north and moving in the direction of the Greenbrier.

"They're finishing up downloads," Ronaldo said with one finger pressed to his earpiece. "Bravo team has been compromised. Watson isn't answering on the comms."

"Goddamnit," Beckham said. "Tell them to haul ass back here. You two, get ready to fly."

Ronaldo sent the second message and reached for his M4. Beckham eyed the M240 door gun, wishing Big Horn was here to carry it. He would have turned the ROT soldiers into meat in no time. Hell, Beckham would have been able to use the gun three months ago, but in his condition, he could hardly fire a rifle.

"Ronaldo, grab the M240 and follow me," Beckham said. "That's an order," he added before Ronaldo could protest.

Beckham grabbed Ronaldo's M4 and set off into the woods while the pilots fired up the chopper. Trip sticks and weeds filled the path ahead. He moved through the forest as quickly as he could manage. His blade was still damaged, so he put more weight on his boot. He nearly fell when he scanned the skyline for the Little Birds. They were already closing in on the Greenbrier.

"Come on!" he shouted back at Ronaldo.

Swollen, fatigued, and covered in blood, Beckham wasn't anywhere near fighting shape, but once again, he had no choice. At least he wasn't facing monsters. He would rather battle ROT soldiers over a Variant any day.

Even with the full moon guiding him, he couldn't see much and tripped on a root that sent him sprawling to the ground.

Ronaldo reached down to help, but Beckham shook off the crew chief's free hand. He pushed at the dirt with his stump, but slipped.

Gunfire cracked in the distance.

"Davis is reporting contacts," Ronaldo said.

Beckham grabbed his hand and let the crew chief help him upright. This time Ronaldo took point with his night-vision goggles.

Another flurry of cracks sounded.

At least six rifles, maybe more.

Ronaldo led Beckham out of the forest onto a manicured lawn divided by stone walls. Rays of moonlight illuminated ornamental brick piers and planters stuffed full of flowers.

The gunfire seemed to be coming from the other side of a hill.

"That way," Beckham, said, pointing.

Ronaldo guided them around the maze of piers. He hurdled the stone wall and began the ascent up the hill with the M240 cradled. Beckham quickly fell behind and struggled to keep up. When he got to the wall, he carefully climbed over.

The hill was even harder to climb. At the top, he dropped to his knees, panting and taking in the view of the grounds beyond.

The three ROT Little Birds were parked on the lawn between the parking lots outside the front of the building, and three fire teams consisting of four men each were slowly advancing on the left, center, and right wings. Gunfire crisscrossed the gardens and shattered the windows at the front entrance of the building, where Blade and Davis appeared to be holed up.

"Melnick's been hit," Ronaldo said.

Beckham cursed and propped up the M4 on his stump. He couldn't see much through the scope, but he did a quick scan to form a plan of action before the lead started flying.

"You take the assholes to the left, I'll take the ones on

the right. And conserve your ammo, man. Sustained rate of fire," Beckham said. "Every round counts."

"Got it, Captain." Ronaldo finished setting up the bipod of the M240 and then lowered his helmet, whispering, "Goddamnit."

"What?"

In a pause amid the gunfire, Beckham heard, "Melnick is KIA."

Beckham swallowed hard, the senseless death of the SEAL building the rage inside of him. He put the scope back to his eye with renewed focus. Somewhere out there Kate was waiting for him. He was going to make it to her, one bullet at a time.

With a squeeze of the trigger, Beckham started the madness. The first rounds from his M4 lanced into the dirt behind one of the black silhouettes on the lawn. The bark of the M240 followed, rounds whizzing downrange at the unsuspecting ROT soldiers.

Beckham was born and bred a soldier—it was in his DNA, much as an Olympian was born to compete in a specific discipline. He didn't like killing and didn't take pleasure in doing so, but it was his duty to protect his country—a duty he took very seriously.

But killing the ROT soldiers was different than killing Variants and terrorists. He felt satisfaction in taking the lives of men who had sworn allegiance to Wood. Deep down, under muscle, grit, and blood, Beckham knew how dangerous it was to feel anything but disgust and necessity in killing.

This was war—war should never be pleasurable.

Ronaldo killed one of them with his first shots and mowed down the pilots standing outside the Little Birds, but Beckham, who could hardly see in the darkness and with his bum eye, missed all three of his targets as soon as the ROT soldiers began to move.

They bolted for cover in the parking lot to the right of the gardens. A lucky shot took one of them down with a hit to the leg, but he was pulled to safety behind a car.

Then came the return fire.

Bullets whizzed past Beckham and cut into the ground. He flattened his body against the grass, cursing and frustrated. He was already down to half of his magazine, and Ronaldo had only given him three back at the bird.

"I got two of 'em!" Ronaldo shouted.

Beckham waited a beat and then aimed for a soldier hiding behind the bumper of a minivan. The bullets shattered glass, punched through metal, and deflated a tire, but didn't hit their target.

You're shooting like a kid with a BB gun.

Two ROT soldiers popped out and unloaded on his position. He ducked his head down, listening to rounds whiz overhead. Return fire clipped the earth around him, and one bullet hit the ground to the right side of his face, stinging his bruised cheek with dirt.

Ronaldo reported another friendly casualty; this time it was Dixon. The SEAL had been hit in the knee, one of the most painful places to take a round. Beckham thought he could hear the man screaming, but the high-pitched noise seemed too animalistic to be human.

He peeked over the hill again to see shadows moving from the right wing of the building and into the parking lot where his targets were all camped out behind vehicles.

Bravo team, he realized. The former SEALs were no longer gun-wielding warriors. Infected with the hemorrhage virus, they bounded across the parking lot, screeching as they tore into the ROT soldiers there.

Beckham quickly turned his fire on the ROT soldiers who were in the gardens. Two of them were dead or too injured to move amid the flowers, but he spotted two more muzzle flashes near trees.

A round zoomed past to his left, but this time Beckham didn't push his head down. He lined up the sights where he'd seen the muzzle flash and pulled the trigger several times.

There was no return flash.

Gotcha.

Beckham had finally killed another one of the bastards. He ducked back down to change his magazine.

"How many targets you got left?" Beckham shouted.

The bark of the machine gun suddenly stopped, but Ronaldo didn't respond to the question. Beckham jammed the new magazine into his M4 and turned for a look at Ronaldo.

The crew chief was facedown in the grass.

"Ronaldo, come on, man!" Beckham shouted. He moved over and used his stump to push at the crew chief's limp body. His head rolled toward Beckham, a hole where his face had been. Blood spewed from the gaping wound.

"Fuck," Beckham said. He quickly pulled off Ronaldo's headset and then his night-vision goggles. After putting both on, Beckham grabbed the M240 and readjusted the bipod.

"All right, you old son of a bitch, Blade and Davis are counting on you now," Beckham muttered.

He pressed the butt of the gun against his shoulder and used the optics to do a quick scan of the battlefield. On the left, two ROT soldiers appeared to still be in action. In the center of the gardens, another two were firing at the pillars. On the right, the infected members of Bravo team had torn the ROT soldiers in the parking lot to pieces. They were now bolting toward the central gardens, their shadows bending and distorting in the light like living scarecrows.

Beckham pushed the black bead of the comm link to his mouth and focused the M240's barrel on the ROT soldiers to the left.

"Blackbeard One, this is Ghost One. Do you copy? Over," Beckham said, hoping he'd gotten Davis's call sign right.

"Roger, Ghost One, what the hell are you doing out here?"

"Just listen," Beckham barked. "When I tell you to run, run as though your life depends on it, because it fucking does!"

He wasn't sure how much ammo was left in the M240, but every round was going to have to count. The butt kicked against his shoulder as he squeezed the trigger, unleashing a burst of rounds that lanced toward the ROT soldiers in the left parking lot. He let up on the trigger, then fired again at the side of a sedan. The rounds tore apple-sized holes into the metal. Several rounds whistled back at him, but these ROT soldiers were amateurs and didn't even come close.

Raising the gun's barrel slightly, Beckham squeezed the trigger, taking off the top of a helmet and skull. In the green hue of the night-vision optics, the other ROT soldier scrambled for cover. Beckham clipped the man in the shoulder and finished him off with three more hits to the back.

The adrenaline was flowing now, and Beckham transitioned into the killing machine that had earned him the role of team lead of Delta Force Team Ghost. The pain of his injuries, the fear of losing Kate and his family, and the bloodlust were all buried beneath the instincts of his training and experience.

He was a methodical killer again.

The goddamn Grim Reaper. That's what I've become.

A muzzle flash came from under one of the Little Birds, where an injured pilot had taken refuge. Beckham moved his barrel toward the chopper and held down the trigger. The windows shattered, and ripped through the metal. The small bird exploded into the air and fell back to the ground, pinning the man underneath, where he burned alive.

"Run!" Beckham yelled into the mini-mic.

Several figures bolted out of the front entrance of the building. Blade had Dixon over his shoulder, and Davis was firing her M4.

Beckham centered the barrel on the two men in the middle of the gardens. They were firing at the surviving infected SEALs now galloping across the ground like wild animals.

He fired a volley of rounds at the ROT soldiers. The deadly spray severed a leg and an arm off the man standing in the flower gardens. He crashed to the ground, blood geysering out of him like water from an ornamental fountain.

Two infected SEALs of Bravo team barreled into the final ROT soldier. Beckham saved his ammo and watched Blade and Davis move through the parking lot.

"Scorpion One, Scorpion Two, this is Ghost One. Get that bird in the air and meet us out front of the Greenbrier," Beckham said over the comms.

The fight on the grounds wasn't over. The final ROT soldier had killed one of the infected former SEALs, but the other infected was still alive. It had slashed at the ROT soldier's throat and ripped off one of his arms.

Closing his blurry eye, Beckham held in a breath and pulled the trigger. The gun clicked, dry. He pushed it away and grabbed his M4. By the time he zoomed in, the infected SEAL was gone.

"Davis, Blade, we got a rogue infected out here," Beckham reported.

He searched the gardens, the parking lot, the flaming Little Birds, and the lawns, but there was no sign of the beast. In the distance came the thump of the Seahawk's rotors.

Davis and the two uninfected SEALs were working their way up the hill when Beckham finally sighted the beast. It was Watson, Bravo team's former leader and the largest man on SEAL Team Four. All 270 pounds of muscle were moving toward their location on all fours.

"Three o'clock!" Beckham shouted. He fired at the creature, but it leaped into a row of hedges, tearing through the foliage. The rounds punched through branches and slammed into the dirt. He eased up on the trigger and waited for the beast to reappear.

Rotor wash hit his back, and the mind-rattling thump sounded just overhead. The pilots lowered to the bottom of the hill, and as soon as they set down, Blade and Davis helped Dixon into the troop hold. Beckham climbed in after them and yelled, "Go, go, go!"

He collapsed on the floor, M4 still in hand. Blade kicked the bottom of a seat and screamed a curse. Then he bent down next to Dixon. The only surviving member of SEAL Team Four besides Blade was clutching his kneecap and groaning in pain.

Davis hovered over them, her hands shaking and chest heaving.

Beckham sat up, trying to catch his own breath.

"There was no one left," Davis said between gasps. She took a seat and put her hands on her helmet, fighting for air. After a few minutes, she pulled a thumb drive from her vest. "But we got the intel that will end this."

Blade, who was working on Dixon, looked up. "I hope so, because I lost a lot of good fucking men today!"

Beckham wiped the blood and sweat from his forehead. They had lost four SEALs and the crew chief, but it was worth it if they could break Wood's grip on the SZTs.

"Nothing will bring back your men, but know this—they died for something worthwhile," Beckham said.

Blade flared his nostrils and focused on Dixon. "This is going to hurt, Papa Smurf," he said as he tightened a dressing around Dixon's knee.

"Contact the USS *Abraham Lincoln* and tell them we've got the goods," Davis told Pressfield over the comms. She joined Beckham at the open door as they flew over the gardens surrounding the Greenbrier.

"Watson is still down there," Beckham said.

Blade looked up from Dixon. "You saw him?"

"Yeah," Davis replied. "He's one of those things now."

22

Fitz didn't have time to bury Stevenson before the convoy left the village of Hardanges. His corpse was in the back of a Humvee somewhere at the rear of the convoy traveling down the deserted highway.

The Twenty-Fourth MEU had rolled out minutes after saving Team Ghost from the ambush. The EUF in Paris had fallen, and the war was moving full steam ahead. Burying the dead would have to wait.

Fitz gripped Stevenson's dog tags in his sweaty palm. Stevenson hadn't been the most likable guy, and he sure as hell hadn't been the most polite, but he'd been one of the team.

After a quick prayer for his comrade, Fitz slipped the dog tags into his vest pocket. He bit the inside of his bottom lip to fight off the no-sleep hangover. He'd gotten a few minutes here and there but hadn't slept more than two or three hours in the past two days. Add to that his injuries, his lack of nutrition, and the loss of Stevenson, and Fitz was about to crash.

He felt as though he was in the middle of a race that wouldn't end.

The radio blared from the front of the vehicle, where Bradley sat shotgun, listening to intermittent transmissions about the battles raging across France and Europe.

"I'm sorry about your man," he said in between messages. "We lost a few on our way here, and a tank."

Fitz dipped his helmet. He could feel the one-eyed glare of the colonel, but Fitz was focused on the new pair of prosthetics they'd given him. The blades looked as if they had been pulled from a junkyard, a far cry from his old black carbon-fiber blades. These were rusted and chipped.

"We got sixty-seven marines in fighting shape with the addition of Team Ghost," Bradley said. "Right, Domino?"

Domino, who sat next to Fitz, looked down at an old-school yellow notepad. He flipped a page and reported, "We've got two Humvees, two LAV-25s, two M1A1s, five MATVs, and sixty-*eight* marines in fighting shape."

Fitz felt his face warm. He didn't want Bradley or Domino seeing him despair, but the numbers were startling—just a fraction of the marines who had landed in Normandy were still alive.

Bradley drowned his sorrows with a drink from a flask and listened to the new report crackling over the radio. It wasn't good: A battalion that was part of the Seventy-Fifth Ranger Regiment was taking heavy casualties to the north from camouflaged Variants. The Second Cavalry Regiment was also reporting heavy losses. Another column of tanks had been hit by an acid attack from fully grown juveniles.

"Despite what you're hearing, the fuckers are on the run," Bradley said. "We're pushing them to the borders of Paris. Those bombs we dropped worked. The resistance we're finding out here is pretty light. The meat of the army is in the capital."

"Good news, sir," Fitz said. There were a dozen questions in his mind, but he let the officer speak.

"Good news for now," Bradley said. He took another drink and dragged a sleeve across his lips. "But Paris is going to be crawling with the fuckers. The EUF forces that managed to evacuate the HQ have formed a perimeter on the west side of the city. That's where we're headed—the front lines."

Domino looked up from his notepad. "The Eleventh MEU should be at the first rendezvous point, sir."

"How long till we get there?" Bradley asked.

Domino looked out his window at one of the M1A1s chugging alongside of the Humvee.

"At this pace? Three hours, maybe a bit less," Domino said. "Then it's just another hour to Paris."

The colonel twisted in the passenger's seat and centered his gaze on Fitz's new prosthetics.

"Those going to work out for you?"

Fitz nodded. It didn't matter what he thought, since these were the best blades he was going to get.

"Good, 'cause we got another mission for you," Bradley said.

Fitz knew he'd been called to the command Humvee for a reason, but he was still reeling from Stevenson's death and too tired to guess what kind of a mission they had in store for Team Ghost this time.

"EUF Command believes there is a high-value target in Paris that's controlling the army there."

"Like an Alpha?" Fitz asked.

Bradley scratched at what was left of his left eyebrow. "This ain't no Alpha. Scientists now believe the insect-like Variants are taking orders from Queens in different cities that all have their own nests. Word is, if we kill the bitch in Paris, the army turns on itself. Cut off the head of the snake..." He paused and shrugged. "Something like that."

"Is that a fact or a theory, sir?" Fitz asked. He didn't mean to be disrespectful, but the comment slipped out.

Bradley arched the brow he was itching. "That sarcasm I hear, son?"

"No, sir—sorry, sir. I'm asking because it sounds as if most of the Variants are seeking refuge in the city, and we already know there are a ton of them there, which means we're going to be vastly outnumbered if we go to try and locate this HVT."

The Colonel stopped Fitz with a raised hand. "If it were up to me I would hit Paris with all the MOABs and bunker busters we got left. Problem is, we don't have many, and the EUF wants to save what's left of Paris. There are still civilians there, believe it or not."

Fitz dipped his helmet in acknowledgment.

"The main battle for Paris will start miles away from the city limits, but the most important battle will likely occur inside the city. Team Ghost is one of many teams we're dropping in to terminate the Queen," Domino said.

"We'll find and destroy the HVT, sir," Fitz said as the convoy began to move again.

"I know." Bradley heaved out what might have been a sigh as he turned to the front of the truck. "We'll have a bird pick you up once we've reached the front. Right now, Command isn't authorizing any flights due to the concentration of Reavers in this area."

"Sir, I have a...concern." Fitz paused to consider his words. He knew how strained the military was, but they couldn't take Alecia with them.

"Speak, Master Sergeant," Bradley said, agitation rising in his voice.

"Sir, a civilian snuck into our vehicle back at the FOB

in Normandy—a teenage girl. I was hoping we could get her airlifted out of here to safety. She's a real fighter, and she's been through a lot."

Bradley wagged his head and cursed. "I'll see what I can do. I mean, that's what we're here for, right? Saving the locals."

"Sir, yes, sir."

Bradley motioned for the driver to stop the vehicle.

Fitz knew the drill. He scooted off the seat, opened the door, and jumped out into the dirt with his rusty new blades. He jogged back to the MATV, climbed inside, and did his best to remain calm.

Tanaka glanced over from the wheel, and Rico, Dohi, and Alecia looked to the front. Apollo glanced up from the cup of water Rico had poured for him. Even the dog was trying to get a read on Fitz.

"Well?" Rico asked.

"Everyone grab some sleep when you can," Fitz said. "We're all going to need it."

Kate stood with Orlov and Bruno outside the clean room, listening to the report from the EUF in Paris. Horn was there too, with his rifle cradled. Orlov and Bruno didn't seem to have a problem with the gun now. Horn and his team had saved their lives, and the lab.

"I can't make out any of this shit," Horn growled.

The message playing on nearly all frequencies was in Spanish. They had missed the one in English, and Kate understood only a few words of Spanish.

"They are saying Phase Two of Operation Reach is currently under way," Bruno translated. "All EUF forces and allies are being instructed to locate and terminate the Queens throughout Europe."

"So they do exist," Orlov said. He muttered something in Russian and ran a hand through the crest of his thin, greasy hair. "The beasts defy science."

"So did the Variants," Kate replied. "That's why I never focused on a cure. I didn't think it was possible."

Horn shifted uneasily. "Not as if you really had a choice. Colonel Gibson pretty much ordered you to make the bioweapons."

Orlov snorted. "Your military caused *all* of this," he said.

Horn didn't argue or apologize. He merely watched the scientist.

"Now the assholes in America have tried to start it over again," Orlov continued. "You should all—"

"Listen, bub, I get where you're coming from, but me and my boys saved your ass earlier, so don't direct that vitriol at me and Kate. We're Americans too, and we're here to save your buns."

Kate held back a smile. She had never heard Horn use a word like "vitriol" before. The big man liked to play up his simple Texan ways, but deep down he was razor sharp.

"I know you've been cooped up in this rattrap for a while, but if you didn't know, we sent a shit-ton of troops to help in Europe," Horn continued.

Orlov rolled his eyes. "Big macho American, just like the others. Well, your boys and ladies aren't doing a very good job of taking back Europe, now are they?"

Horn took a step forward, and so did Orlov. The Russian scientist's eyes came up to Horn's chin.

"Stop," Bruno said. "Both of you. This isn't helpful."

"We understand how you feel," Kate said, trying to make peace. "But President Ringgold is a good woman and she will make up for the sins of Colonel Gibson,

Colonel Wood, and the other men who created monsters that doomed billions of lives."

"We just have to give her a chance," Horn said.

Kate nodded. "That's why this cure is so important."

"Yes, so let's finish it," Bruno said. "We should be seeing the first results from the nanoparticles now."

That seemed to calm Orlov down a bit. He looked over his shoulder at the storage area inside the clean room where they kept the caged rats.

"Let's go check on them," Kate suggested to Orlov and Bruno before glancing up at Horn. "Why don't you go try and get ahold of the USS *Abraham Lincoln* and give them a sitrep. See if they've heard anything about Reed yet too."

Horn curled his lip at Orlov, but the Russian scientist backed down this time.

"Now, Big Horn," Kate said.

He cursed two syllables under his breath and retreated back to the upper decks.

"That was beautiful, just beautiful," Bruno said sarcastically. "They're here to help us, you know."

Orlov shrugged a shoulder as he walked away. Bruno offered a warm smile to Kate. They hardly knew each other, and Kate was still skeptical of Bruno, but the Italian scientist seemed as though her heart was in the right place. In the end, they wanted the same thing—a cure.

Kate walked over to the wall of the clean room to look at the rats, while the other doctors got suited up. The infected rodents were idle inside their cages, sedated to keep them from breaking any bones or cannibalizing themselves.

She bent down to look at the dried blood in their fur. Under the influence of the hemorrhage virus, the creatures had all undergone significant physiological changes: hair loss, elongated nails, and rashes speckling the hairless patches on their hides.

Orlov took a sample of blood from the first sedated specimen, and Bruno did the same with the second. They both moved back to their stations, where they prepped their samples.

Kate sat at her computer, where the information would feed out. In a few moments, she would know if the nanoparticles were working on the VX-99 chemical particles in the rats.

At first glance, they didn't seem to be doing much. The creatures were still clearly infected with the virus, although it was hard to gauge any improvements due to their sedation.

The sight of the bloody rats transported her back to the early days of the outbreak, when the rhesus monkeys were all infected with the hemorrhage virus. Ellis and Kate hadn't sedated the beasts and were forced to kill them all with gas when they broke into a frenzy inside their cages.

She shut off her mind and prepared for the results on the computer screen. While she was waiting, Horn returned down the ladder.

"Kate, I need to talk to you," he said.

She could tell by the urgency in his voice that something was wrong. Her mind snapped back on, jumping from scenario to scenario.

"This is remarkable," said Orlov over the wall-mounted speaker.

"Doctor Lovato, are you seeing this?" Bruno asked.

Kate was already walking over to Horn.

"No one is answering on the encrypted line," he said. "My girls, Kate. What if something happened to my daughters?"

"What do you mean, not answering? Is it possible the fleet has gone radio silent?"

Horn shook his head. "No way. That's what the encrypted line is for. Something must have happened."

Kate felt nauseous. Her mind scrolled through the terrible things that could have happened to the fleet. But the only scenario that seemed plausible was an attack from ROT. If Wood had somehow located Ringgold, it was possible he would use his weapon of choice—the hemorrhage virus.

"I'll be upstairs in a few minutes," she said. "Stay calm. We'll figure this out."

Horn nodded and ran back up the ladder.

"What's that all about?" Bruno asked as Kate walked back to her computer.

"Our contact on the USS *Abraham Lincoln* isn't answering," Kate said, her heart pounding. She took a seat at her computer and clicked on the monitor, finally seeing what the other doctors were calling remarkable.

On the screen were the nanoparticles that Orlov and Bruno had designed. Normally the tiny particles and VX-99 were invisible, even under a microscope at this magnification, but as they snowballed together, they formed jagged lumps that were near the size of red blood cells. It appeared that the nanoparticles were actually attaching to the VX-99 chemicals and attracting the phagocytes. They continued bumping into the snowballed VX-99 particles and devouring them like Pac-Man.

It was working.

The cure was actually working!

Kate could hardly believe her eyes, but the implications were enough to make her choke out a sob. If this was a cure, then perhaps the billions of people she had killed with VX9H9 could have been saved—perhaps her brother, Javier, could have been saved.

She wiped away a tear. There was no time to consider the past. There was only the future. Beckham and her friends were still out there, and if Wood had hit the fleet with the hemorrhage virus, there was something Kate could do this time.

"Get the cocktail into a syringe and make as many as you can," Kate said to the other doctors.

"Hold on," Bruno said. "We don't know if it works on a human yet."

Orlov folded his arms across his chest. "Only one way to find out."

Sergeant Piero Angaran was dead.

He'd opened his eyes to find himself trapped. His vision was still blurred, but he could see flames raging in pots set in the corners of a stone prison cell, the light flickering over the silhouettes of figures crucified and impaled on metal spikes.

It certainly looked the way he'd pictured hell. But the pain was even worse than he imagined. His entire body seemed to be on fire, every centimeter of his flesh burning. Sweat prickled out of his pores and soaked what was left of his uniform.

Demons danced around the cell, their feet slapping the ground and their grunts taunting him. The moans of damned souls came from all directions. It took Piero a few minutes to realize his voice was among them. He hardly recognized the guttural sounds coming from his throat.

He tried to move, but his skin was stuck to something,

a pole, or perhaps a cross. The itching and burning across his flesh made it feel as if he was inside an oven. Every time he tried to move, the pain would intensify. The mental anguish was just as bad. The longer he was aware of his condition, the worse it grew. He felt as if he was in quicksand, but instead of sand, it was fire ants that were biting and crawling across his skin.

"No," he cried.

He realized he would never see his family again, for they would be in heaven. He would never see his friends, and never see Ringo.

At least the mouse had survived.

He blinked and tried to focus on the demons on the stone floor. The fires seemed to be moving with them. Piero managed to wipe his right eye on his shoulder. His vision cleared enough to see rays of white light streaming in through a window somewhere at the top of the tomb's walls.

There were other figures hanging from the wall on his right. He recognized the woman from the other night and the human shape next to her that must have been her daughter.

How is that possible? Piero wondered, his mind a confused mess.

His brain couldn't comprehend what his eyes were seeing. This was supposed to be hell. He was supposed to be dead. Were these tortured souls next to him just part of his imagination? Was he hallucinating?

He blinked until his vision was as clear as a photograph. The pain seemed to fade away, and in that moment, he realized he wasn't dead after all. Piero Angaran had been cursed with an even worse fate.

With renewed sight, he realized that the moans and grunts weren't coming from the other humans hanging on the wall. His ears were picking up the noise the monsters made when they were breeding.

He rolled his head to the left to see that the fires weren't fires either. The red was the Queen's flesh. She moved into focus, and he saw her chitinous upper body and egg-shaped skull crested with small spikes. A pair of almond-shaped eyes were set above a bulbous, warty nose that dripped a green sludge over swollen, wormy lips. Like a macabre god, she was creating monsters right in front of him, breeding with Wormers, Beetles, Pinchers, and Reavers.

She hovered over a male Reaver half her size, spread her wings out like a dragon, and then straddled the male beast that squawked in their otherworldly language. The Queen's fleshy wings folded around their monstrous bodies, covering the act of procreation with a curtain of wrinkled, red skin.

"No. This isn't real. This is *worse* than hell," Piero mumbled.

The metal spikes and crosses in the room were plastered with a host of humans and animals. Resting on the floor were dozens of baby monsters, all of them waiting for their first taste of flesh.

Piero wasn't dead after all. He just wished he was.

"Kill me," he grumbled. "Get it over with…"

He moved again, resulting in a flash of pain. The glue, or whatever the hell it was holding him to the wall, had marinated in the wounds inflicted by the Reaver that had dropped him here. He couldn't see the gashes, but he knew his body was covered in them.

He sobbed again and watched the massive Queen finish mating. She stood a full height of nine feet and stretched her wings in both directions, revealing an unarmored section of flesh just above her reproduction organs.

A draft of air that smelled like rotting lemons hit Piero's nostrils.

The beast folded the leathery wings behind her back and lumbered over to the next creature to continue building her evil army.

Piero squirmed again, pain flashing across his flesh. A squeaking sound followed. He glanced up to see a pink nose and a small pair of black eyes looking down at him.

Ringo...

The mouse leaped off the body to his right and perched on Piero's shoulder.

No. Get out of here, little buddy.

The furry creature trembled with fear, but it wasn't deterred. It bent down and began clawing at the glue holding Piero's hand and arm to the wall.

Ringo was trying to free him.

But even if his tiny friend could get him off the wall, there was nowhere to run or hide. The tomb was filled with monsters. He fought to pull his head away from the stone, but the hair on the back of his skull stuck to the glue. Finally, a patch ripped out, and he managed to lower his head to search for anything that might be useful.

An empty pistol holster and knifeless sheath were attached to his duty belt, but below that he could hardly see anything in the weak glow of light.

The pain was starting to make him light-headed, and he closed his eyes for a moment while Ringo continued gnawing and scratching at the glue around his right hand. He moved his index finger, and then his entire hand.

When he opened his eyes again, he noticed something his brain had ignored. The pain vanished for a moment while he took in the sight.

No … No, it can't be.

Ringo could scratch and chew all day long, but even if the mouse managed to free Piero, he wasn't going anywhere. Ribbons of flesh hung from his knees like spaghetti. His legs were gone, fed to the baby monsters sleeping all around him.

He gagged at the acid stench, knowing now it was the glue keeping him alive. It wasn't the first time he'd seen the monsters preserve their meals with the chemical substance.

"Get out of here, Ringo," Piero stuttered. "Go on, get…"

The mouse looked up at him, tilting its head.

"You can't save me, little buddy. Save yourself." Piero whimpered in pain and despair. It was all too much, even for a soldier. *You* were *a soldier. Now you're a dead man.*

He couldn't fight anymore—his fight had ended.

Across the room the Queen had moved on to another beast. Ringo went back to chewing at the glue around Piero's hand. He tried to swat the mouse away with a finger and in the process broke his hand free. It brushed against the radio in his MOLLE pack.

Ringo crawled up his arm and began working on the glue binding it to the wall.

"Get out of here," Piero whispered. His vision faded, and Ringo blurred into triplets.

Your fight isn't over yet, Piero thought. *You still have one more mission. You have to kill her.* He looked back down at his vest. He didn't have a weapon to shoot or stab the beast, but he did have something even better.

Piero wiggled his hand and wrist until he could reach the radio. Plucking it slowly from the pouch, he then carefully turned it on. It was already set to the correct channel. All he had to do was bring it to his mouth.

"Crow's Nest, this is Sergeant Angaran. If anyone is listening to this, you have to blow up the Vatican. The Queen is here, under the building. You have to destroy it," he whispered. "Destroy everything."

Static crackled out of the speakers, and Ringo stopped chewing on his arm. He skittered up to Piero's shoulder and squeaked as if to tell Piero to stop the noise.

There was no response over the radio channel, but the Reavers prowling the room replied with hisses. One of them got to all fours, folded its wings, and tilted its head in his direction.

Piero repeated his message again, adding, "The Queen won't escape this time. Bomb the Vatican. Bomb the Vatican!"

Ringo squeaked louder as two of the Reavers skittered over. When they were a few feet away, the Queen let out a clicking sound, stopping the beasts midstride. She flapped her wings and spread them out, holding them in place.

Both of the smaller Reavers retreated into the shadows.

"I love you, little buddy, but you have to go," Piero whispered. "Go and find a new home and new friends."

Ringo squeaked again and nuzzled up against Piero's neck. A tear streamed down Piero's cheeks.

"Go," he whispered. "Go home."

The mouse licked the salty tear from Piero's cheek and then took off across the wall, using the other bodies to climb. He watched his friend vanish into a hole in the ceiling while he relayed one more message over the radio.

"Bomb the Vatican and end the nightmare in Rome."

The Queen slowly crossed the room, walking until she was just inches from his face. A spiked tongue flicked through the black hole between her swollen lips.

The speakers crackled on the radio, forcing the beast to rear her head back.

"Sergeant Angaran, do you copy?"

Piero tried to bring the radio to his lips, but the Queen let out a screech and slapped the radio from Piero's hand, her talons scoring deep lacerations in his flesh. Blood pumped from his veins and coated the floor.

There was the crackle of static, and then another message. "Sergeant, if you can hear this, we just launched a bird from an aircraft carrier. You have fifteen minutes to get the hell out of there."

The Queen stepped away from Piero and walked over to the radio. Using a clawed foot, she crushed the device, screeched again, and went back to breeding.

Piero closed his eyes as the blood pumped out of his veins. Not even the glue would save him from bleeding out now. He pictured his family as vividly as in the photograph he kept in his locker on base. They were all gone now, and he would be joining them soon, hopefully in heaven rather than hell.

He drifted in and out of consciousness, recalling better times and taking solace in the fact Ringo was safe and free.

The roar of a fighter jet snapped him alert.

The Queen stood just ten feet away, hunched over several of her creations sleeping on the floor. The baby monsters stirred awake, opening jaws already lined with jagged teeth.

Piero rolled his head to look at the woman and her daughter on the wall. They were both unconscious, oblivious to the nightmare awakening in front of them.

The Queen tilted her head toward the ceiling as the scream of the fighter jet neared.

It was all about to end for everyone—and in one fiery blast, it did. The flames blew out the windows and enveloped the room, incinerating the baby monsters and their mother before swallowing Piero and the two human women in a torrent of fire.

23

Davis spotted a small cluster of lights in the distance. Months ago, the entire horizon would have dazzled with city lights, but the safe-zone territory set up in Charlotte, North Carolina, was only five city blocks, and only two of them appeared to be lit up.

"There it is," she said.

"Good thing, because we needed a drink a hundred miles back," reported Colonel Pressfield.

Davis was honestly surprised the Seahawk was still in the air. Even with the reserve tanks, they were down to fumes. After leaving the Greenbrier, they had put down in a field to plan their next move. Problem was, they couldn't get ahold of anyone on the USS *Abraham Lincoln*.

Beckham, Blade, and Davis all knew something had happened to the fleet. The three of them had decided to go to SZT 68 in Charlotte to rally support. It was the closest SZT still loyal to Ringgold. Mayor Marie Gallo had been one of Ringgold's first allies, but it was only a matter of time before she too folded and aligned with ROT, or was found with a bullet in her head.

Davis waddled over to Dixon, who was lying on the floor of the chopper. Blade was at his side, checking his vitals.

"How is he?" Davis asked.

"Morphine's working, but we need to get him to a doctor," Blade announced.

Beckham sat stoically across the troop hold, lost in thought, like a monk meditating. She had a feeling he was thinking about Kate and his unborn son. That's what she would be thinking about if she were in his shoes, but her family was dead, and her final mission in life was to kill Wood.

"Once we land, we'll take this intel straight to the mayor while the pilots refuel again. Then we're headed back to the fleet to plan our next move with President Ringgold," Davis said.

"That's your plan?" Beckham asked. "What if Mayor Gallo has already flipped? What if ROT is there waiting for us? They know we were at the PEOC."

"Yeah, but they don't know if we got any data from the PEOC. Every ROT soldier back there is dead," Blade said. "As far as Wood knows, those fuckers were all infected."

Beckham shook his head wearily. "We really don't have any good options."

"Not really, but this is the only thing that makes sense." Davis held up the thumb drive from the PEOC. "This is our best shot at taking down ROT. It's our *only* shot."

Blade nodded. "She's right."

"Yeah, but you guys are forgetting something," Beckham said. "The moment Wood hears this message going out, he's going to start hitting SZTs, starting with SZT Sixty-Eight. All the message does is clear Ringgold's name. Wood still has WMDs and an army working for him. We have to kill him. It's the only way."

"And how do we do that if we don't even know where he is?" Blade asked.

Beckham lowered his head for a moment as if he was considering something. He finally glanced up with sad, brown eyes. "Wood's main goal is simple: He wants revenge. He wants the people who killed his brother, and when he finds out I'm still alive, he's going to come after me. We need to use that to our advantage."

"We're cleared to land," Pressfield announced before anyone could respond. "I told 'em we have a medical transport in need of assistance."

Blade stood and walked to open the troop hold door. Davis and Beckham joined the SEAL to look at the tarmac set inside the barrier of the SZT's eastern concrete wall. Figures were already moving across the helicopter landing pad in the moonlight.

It would be morning soon, and Davis wanted to be back in the air before the sun came up. She had considered taking Dixon back to the fleet, but without knowing more, and in his condition, they couldn't risk it.

"I have a pretty shitty feeling about this," Blade said.

"This isn't the end," Davis replied. "Just follow my lead."

She eyed the group from a distance, glimpsing Mayor Gallo standing among the soldiers below. The woman stood out in her white coat among the drab clothing the soldiers around her wore.

"On second thought, you guys stay here," Davis ordered. She liked the idea of dealing with the woman one-on-one.

As soon as the pilots set down, she jumped out and, keeping low, jogged over to the mayor and her staff.

Quick and steady, Rachel.

"I'm Captain Rachel Davis, with the United States Navy," she said. "I'd like to speak to Mayor Gallo."

Gallo made her way to the front of the group. She was at least twenty years older than Davis, with shoulder-length gray hair and white-rimmed glasses that matched her coat. A tall soldier with a long, braided beard stood to her right, glaring at Davis suspiciously.

"Why are you here, Captain?" Gallo asked.

"We have an injured Navy SEAL on the bird," Davis said.

Gallo nodded at a man to her right, and several soldiers took off for the chopper to grab Dixon.

"And the other reason you're here?" Gallo asked.

"We need your help, Mayor. We have intel to prove ROT attacked those SZTs, not President Ringgold."

Gallo exchanged a glance with the rough-looking soldier with a long beard.

"I guess you haven't heard the news then?" Gallo asked.

Davis didn't reply, giving the mayor a chance to speak first.

"From what we've been told, President Jan Ringgold has been betrayed by General Nixon. The fleet that was protecting her was attacked and is now being relocated. Ringgold herself is on her way to the USS *Zumwalt* for execution."

Davis felt her guts roll. They were too late. Everything they had done had been for nothing.

"I tried to hold out," Gallo said with a frown. She shook her head. "I'm sorry, Captain. I believed in President Ringgold and her mission to restore the United States with the safe-zone territories. I, like many of the other mayors, didn't believe she would attack them, but I'm afraid I can't hold out any longer. If I don't align with Wood now, we'll lose everything. We can't afford to get caught up in a civil war."

"It's not too late," a voice said.

Davis turned to see Beckham's bruised face in the moonlight. He limped up to her side and held out his hand.

"Mayor, I'm Captain Reed Beckham, and I need to borrow a radio. It's not too late to stop Wood. I've got an idea for how to end all of this."

Andrew Wood was getting sick of prison cells. Presidents weren't supposed to visit prisoners, they were supposed to spend their time in the Oval Office meeting foreign leaders, or on the golf course talking about legislation.

So far it seemed as though all he'd done was interrogate and kill the people who opposed him. The killing didn't bother him, but he was ready for some R&R.

First, though, he was going to meet the woman who had given him a headache for several weeks now.

Kufman led Wood through the brig aboard the USS *Zumwalt* and stopped outside a hatch where two ROT soldiers stood guard. They saluted as Wood approached.

Wood felt a chill of excitement as he grabbed the handle of his knife and ran a finger across the side of the twelve-inch saw-toothed blade.

Kufman opened the hatch, and Wood instructed him to stay put.

"Yes, sir," he replied, eyeing the knife, then nodding.

The hatch clicked shut behind Wood, sealing him inside the small, dark room. Ringgold was sitting on a bunk with her hands cuffed and her head down like a child.

"What should I do with you?" Wood said. He stroked his jaw and studied the former leader of the free world, or what was left of it. She was a nice-looking older woman, with sharp bones, full lips, and kind brown eyes. Wood really didn't want to hate her, but he couldn't forgive her for what she'd done.

"You made a pretty epic error at Plum Island that has set in motion a chain of events that have killed a lot of people," Wood said. He scratched his face with the tip of the knife's blade and crossed over to stand in front of her.

She finally met his gaze.

"Just get it over with. You outsmarted me, I'll give you that, but there's no reason to drag this out any longer. I surrendered. You are the president of the United States of America, a country that, at one point, you swore to defend. If you have any decency you will stop destroying this wonderful country and finish what I started—rebuilding our home."

Wood chuckled. "You think I'm destroying the country? I'm cleaning up your mess. Those deaths are on your conscience, not mine. Those people died for a purpose."

Ringgold arched a brow in disbelief. "You really believe that?" She shook her head. "If so, then your mind is more diseased than the monsters you created."

"I didn't create them," Wood said, quickly losing his patience.

Ringgold focused on the knife in his hand. "Just finish me off. I can't stand being in your presence another moment."

Wood ran his fingers along the saw-toothed blade while he considered where he would plunge it into her flesh first.

A knock on the hatch interrupted his thoughts. He wagged a finger at Ringgold and said, "Your execution has been delayed, but don't worry. You will meet your maker soon enough."

Kufman opened the hatch and looked into the cell. "Sir, we have a problem."

"I'm busy. Can't this wait?"

"Afraid not, sir."

"Go ahead then. She can hear whatever it is."

Kufman wasn't one to hesitate, but he paused long and hard before continuing. "The message you sent her," he said, jerking his chin toward Ringgold. "When she was in the PEOC, or was supposed to be."

"What about it?" Wood said.

"It's playing on the radio waves, sir."

"Which channel? Isolate it and kill whoever the fuck is playing it."

"It's playing on almost all of the channels, sir, but I can try to figure out where it was played first."

Wood balled his hands into fists and looked back at Ringgold. Had she tricked him? Was this part of her plan?

"There's something else, sir," Kufman said. He held up a satellite phone. "There's someone who wants to talk to you from SZT Sixty-Eight. We got the call from the mayor's office."

"Who is it?"

"Some lady, but she wouldn't give me her name, sir," Kufman said. "I'm guessing it's Mayor Gallo."

Wood snatched the phone from his bodyguard's hands and brought it to his face.

"Who the fuck is this?"

There was a short pause. "Captain Rachel Davis."

Wood laughed. "That's fucking hilarious. Captain Rachel Davis is dead."

"You're wrong. I'm very much alive. I'm the one who blew up my ship."

Wood's smile faded. The voice did sound oddly familiar. His eyes flitted from Kufman to Ringgold.

"I have a proposal," Davis said.

"You're in no position to be making proposals," Wood snapped, white hot with anger. "Now you listen to me, Cap. I have an arsenal of hemorrhage-virus missiles. I've got an army, and I've got Ringgold's 'fleet.' You have no bargaining chips."

"Wrong. The SZTs know the truth now. You won't be in power long. They will rise up to face you in massive numbers."

"Hah! Now that's funny. The moment one of them does that, I'll paint their SZT with the hemorrhage virus. So what else have you got?"

"Hold on a second," Davis said.

There was a flurry of static, and then a deep voice. "Hello, Andrew."

"And who the hell is this?"

"Captain Reed Beckham."

Wood laughed again, nervously. Was it possible? Two ghosts back from the dead? "Now I *know* this is all bullshit," Wood replied. "I dropped you in the middle of SZT Fifteen. I saw you die."

"Did you?"

"Yes, I . . ." Wood's words trailed off again. He looked at Ringgold again, narrowing his eyes.

"I helped kill your piece of shit brother, and now I'm going to kill you," Beckham said.

Wood gripped the blade of his knife so hard that his knuckles popped. Beckham was smarter than Wood had given the Delta Force operator credit for. He'd done something that Wood didn't anticipate—he'd survived the impossible.

But his luck had run out.

"You don't know when to quit, do you, Beckham? If that's really you, then Davis was right—she does have something I want. So I'll tell you what: You want to kill me? I'll even send a bird to pick you up. No one else has to die, besides Jan, your friend Joe Fitzpatrick, your dumb dog, and you."

"You'll fight me one-on-one?" Beckham asked.

"Sure," Wood said, recalling how bad Beckham had looked the last time he saw him. He would easily win a one-on-one fight against the broken-down soldier. And although part of him wanted to torture the piece of shit and make his pain last, killing Beckham in hand-to-hand combat would remind every ROT soldier why Wood was in charge.

"I'll be waiting for you at SZT Sixty-Eight," Beckham said.

"I'll have a bird there in a few hours, and then we get to meet again." Wood smiled as another idea struck him. "Oh, and Beckham, bring your little friend Rachel with you. I've got plans for her too."

"It burns!" shouted Dr. Orlov. He squirmed violently against the restraints holding him to the gurney inside the medical ward aboard the *Thalassa*.

Horn looked through the porthole window. "This shit doesn't seem to be working," he said.

Bruno bit her nails. "I can't watch this. He's all I..."

Her words trailed off, and Kate noticed a tear welling in Bruno's eye. She had been a rock since Kate arrived on the ship, and seeing her cry rattled Kate more than watching Dr. Orlov.

Orlov shook the table, pulling Kate from her thoughts. Horn gripped his pistol, but Bruno clicked her tongue.

"You will not shoot him," she hissed.

"Okay, lady, but damn, he's really messed up."

Kate looked at her watch. "It could still take some time to work," she said. "We infected him with the hemorrhage virus thirty minutes ago, and Resurrection shortly after."

Bruno wiped the tear from her eye. "Something's wrong. The nanoparticles must not be—"

Orlov strained against his bonds, blue veins bulging

across his skull. He raised his head to look at the port-hole. His red eyes gushed bloody tears.

"I won't... No, I won't," he said, shaking his head. "I won't kill them. I can't, I can't..." Orlov mumbled.

Kate recognized the symptoms: hallucinations, erratic behavior, bloodshot eyes, bulging veins, and bleeding from multiple orifices.

Next came the snapping joints.

Orlov squirmed in the restraints again, his legs and arms clicking. He twisted his body to the left, snapping his shoulder out of a socket so he could pull the arm out of the restraints.

"Shit," Horn said. "We can't let him get out of those."

Bruno put a hand over Horn's as he reached for his gun.

"Give it a few more minutes," Kate said.

Horn moved his hand away from the pistol's grip and snorted his disapproval. "Whatever you say. I'm just—"

Orlov's screaming cut Horn short. They all looked back into the room as the Russian doctor shook violently on the table. His red eyes rolled up into his head, and bubbles frothed out of his mouth.

"He's choking," Bruno said, stepping toward the door.

This time Horn was the one to put a hand on hers.

Kate watched in horror as Orlov jerked, in the clutches of a seizure.

It was all over in a few seconds, his body suddenly still on the table. A foot kicked, and his fingers moved slightly. He let out a long groan and then drew in a deep breath.

"What's happening?" Horn asked.

Kate shook her head. "I'm... I'm not sure."

"I have to get in there," Bruno said. She tried to move to the door, but Horn blocked her way.

"No, goddamnit!" he snapped. "I get that you have

feelings for him, but he made his choice, and I can't let you put your life or Kate's life in jeopardy."

Kate continued to watch while Horn and Bruno argued.

Something was happening to Orlov's skin. The blue veins were less pronounced now, and his muscles had all relaxed.

He let out a groan and squirmed on the table.

Kate moved to the side of Horn for a better view. The Russian scientist was still bleeding from his eyes and ears, showing the Ebola infection, but the effects of VX-99 seemed to be going away.

"I think it's working," Kate said.

Bruno and Horn both stepped up to the glass to watch. She cupped her hand over her heart.

"The Ebola infection will take a while to go away, but the effects of VX-99 look as though they've stopped," Kate said. "The cure is *really* working."

"I'll be damned," Horn said. "It's like our boy Boris Yeltsin's back from the dead."

"Not the dead—more like back from the paths of insanity," Kate added.

Bruno bent her head, praying rapidly in Italian.

Orlov lay on the table, completely still save for his chest rising up and down. The blue veins slowly faded, and his pale flesh took on a salmon-pink color.

"It does work after all," Kate said, feeling the ghost of a smile. The shock of seeing a cure in action brought with it a flood of conflicting emotions, but there was no time to think of any of them.

She reached out and touched Bruno's arm. "He's going to be okay. But we have a job to do now. We have to go and make as many doses as possible."

24

Fitz couldn't see the battle, but he could hear the thump of artillery fire and mortar rounds raining down on the buildings where the Variants were seeking refuge. The crack of automatic gunfire a few streets away had woken him from a quick nap.

"We're here," Tanaka said, turning the wheel of the MATV. "This is the rear of the front lines."

Fitz rubbed his eyes groggily. He knew a few marines who could sleep through gunfire, but not a man or woman who didn't flinch during a serious artillery bombardment. That sound would wake him up in the middle of the night, shaking like a damn dog.

He checked his watch.

1900.

The sun was going down on the horizon, the Paris skyline swallowing the orange globe. Fingers of smoke rose away from destroyed buildings.

Rico, normally the historian of the group, didn't seem to be impressed by the sight of the city. She hadn't said much since the attack that left Stevenson dead. The melancholy drive toward Paris had passed in silence, broken only by the occasional crack of gunfire.

But the quiet wasn't a bad thing.

According to EUF Command, the Variants were on the retreat and preparing to take their final stand in Paris. Team Ghost and every other squad was surrounding the city.

Fitz took a slug of water and used a handful to splash on his flushed face, still trying to wake up. Tanaka followed the convoy into a narrow street of apartment buildings, where most of the cars had been pushed onto the sidewalks. The alleyway had seen battle months before, high-caliber rounds and rocket-propelled grenades leaving behind gaping scars in the brick and stone exteriors.

A girl and a man, presumably her father, huddled in the shadows on the second floor of a building where the wall to their living room had once been. The exterior looked like a mouth with most of the teeth knocked out. The child raised a hand at the convoy as Tanaka passed by and smiled warmly.

"See why we're not bombing the city?" Rico said. "There are still survivors here."

"I'm surprised anyone survived, to be honest, but it shows how resilient our species is. Take that kid, for example," Dohi said. "She's got a freaking grin on her filthy face."

Rico, still chomping on the same piece of gum, nodded and replied, "Who was it who said humans are like cockroaches?"

It was the most the team had spoken since losing Stevenson. Morale was shit, and Fitz didn't know how to fix it. He was lost in his own thoughts about home and about the mission moving forward.

A pair of F-16s screamed overhead, the first Fitz had seen for hours. Missiles streaked away from them and hit a skyscraper in the distance. Both jets peeled off in different directions.

Fitz couldn't see their targets but imagined they had hit a Reaver nest, or another HVT. From the street level, he couldn't see much. The sky appeared void of choppers and other aircraft, but he did see several Reavers that looked like bats flapping around the larger buildings in the distance.

The airborne threat made flying a helicopter almost impossible in the light, and the mission to find the Queen had been delayed until dark.

"Looks as though we're not going to be able to count on much air support," Rico said, echoing his thoughts.

"Command is low on everything: fuel, artillery, bombs, missiles, and aircraft," Dohi said. "We're going to be on our own once we get into the city."

Fitz knew what Stevenson would have said.

We're always on our own.

But Fitz couldn't let morale slip anymore. He had to own this situation—he had to do what Beckham had taught him to do.

You have to lead.

"Okay, Ghost—take a good look at those civilians, and take a good look at the men and women in front of us and behind us. A lot of lives are likely counting on us. If we kill this Queen we can save a lot of people," Fitz said.

"Oorah," Rico said. Apollo stood on the back seat, wagging his tail.

Dohi stopped sharpening his combat knife. "We're with you, Master Sergeant."

"You know I've got your back," Tanaka said. He pulled the MATV over at the next intersection and parked in a row of other vehicles. An entire platoon of infantry was marching down the street behind a pair of M1A1s that were heading east into the city.

"All right, we're leaving the MATV here for now," Fitz said. "Everyone out and follow me."

They left the MATV on the street and hurried toward the FOB set up in one of the only structurally sound buildings left in the neighborhood, a four-story stone structure with a tile roof.

Major Domino met them outside and waved at Fitz.

"Got new orders for you," Domino said. "We need you to help on the front lines before we send you into the city. Air support is still not being authorized at this time."

"Roger that, sir," Fitz said. He turned to Alecia and motioned for the girl to come forward. She gripped Rico's hand.

"You have to stay here," Fitz said.

"I want to fight," Alecia said. "I've proven I can."

Apollo sat on his haunches next to her. Fitz didn't have time to argue. He walked over and bent down in front of her on his creaky new blades.

"I'm sorry, Alecia, but you can't come with us," Fitz said. He didn't know how to tell her that Team Ghost was going to a place that kids should never see, because she had already seen the worst of man and the worst of Mother Nature.

An explosion sounded in the distance, the work of an M1A1 tank shell blowing off the top of a building close enough to give the street a shiver.

"I've got a mission for you, kid," Domino said.

Alecia looked up at the major.

"Most of your friends, the Ombres, were evacuated a few days ago, but a few who are old enough stayed with the Twenty-Fourth MEU. They're all on medical duty now, helping our wounded. It's a dangerous job that will send you out into the streets, but it's important, and hell, you might even get to shoot at some Variants," Domino said. He pointed at a tent set up across the plaza, where Fitz saw several of the Ombres who hadn't been evacuated. They were all in their teens, the younger kids having been shipped off to somewhere safe.

Alecia followed his finger and then looked back to Fitz.

"Master Sergeant Fitzie, I wanted to avenge *Maman* and Michel," she said.

Fitz almost chuckled but kept a straight face. He glanced at Rico, who was smiling. She had clearly rubbed off on the girl.

"I know, and you already have," Fitz said, his gaze flitting back to Alecia. "Thank you for fighting with us, k—" He stopped himself. "It was an honor fighting with you. We wouldn't be back here if it weren't for your actions."

Alecia nodded proudly and scanned the members of Team Ghost in turn, stopping on Rico last. Rico bent down to give Alecia a hug and whispered something in her ear. Alecia nodded again and smiled. Then she walked over to Apollo, patted the dog on the head, and said, "Good boy."

After a wave good-bye, Alecia followed Domino across the plaza to the front of the FOB, where she was reunited with some of her friends.

Fitz jerked his chin at his team, relieved that he wasn't going to have to worry about Alecia any longer. She was a fighter, but he wasn't sure that mattered on this final mission for Team Ghost.

They returned to the MATV and followed the platoon of marines marching toward the front lines. The men were all running toward the sound of gunfire and the occasional mortar round that thumped overhead.

Command was setting up a perimeter now that the sun was going down. No one would be going past this block until morning, when the Variants were less active—no one except Team Ghost and a few other teams.

Explosions and shouting filled the city, and they weren't even at the center of the action. In another two blocks, Fitz had a feeling things were going to be nuts. He saw movement on the rooftops overhead, where snipers were setting up shop. Gun barrels pointed out of the windows that had already been cleared, and at the end of the street, several soldiers wearing flamethrowers stood behind concrete barriers, spraying fire.

An adult Variant scrambled into the street, wrinkled flesh alight, looking like a burning raisin. It bounded over the barrier and landed behind the men with their flamethrowers. It reared up, prepared to attack, before its head exploded from a sniper round.

The burning corpse smoldered behind the trio of soldiers still toasting targets around the corner.

"Holy shit," Rico said.

The Variants seemed to be testing the front lines on the edge of the city. Monsters skittered across the exteriors of the buildings in the distance, under a sky the color of pomegranates.

Fitz hadn't seen many of the old creatures in Europe, but Command had warned that Paris was still full of them. In some ways, the original Variants terrified him more than their mutated offspring. The Variants, especially the Alphas, seemed way smarter, and resembled humans more, which made them even more horrifying to Fitz.

Soldiers in the windows and on rooftops suddenly opened fire on a target Fitz couldn't see. Tanaka parked the MATV on the side of the street and waited for orders.

"Combat intervals once we get out there," Fitz said. "Dohi, I want you on point."

Marines ran past their parked vehicle and filed into

buildings or took refuge behind vehicles or concrete barriers. Fitz grabbed the door when a Reaver came out of nowhere and nosedived at the flamethrower unit fifty meters away. The creature was riddled with bullets before it came close and fell lifelessly to the street behind the men.

A pair of juveniles bounded out of the smoke with fire coating their armored plates. Rounds lanced into their armor from above, and they rolled up like hedgehogs in front of the barriers.

"Tanaka, on the M240!" Fitz ordered. He wasn't sure where the juveniles had come from, but it was obvious the men with flamethrowers had been caught by surprise. They started to retreat and had made it a few feet when the street behind their position cracked and gave way to a sinkhole. One of the men vanished into the opening, letting out a burst from his flamethrower that coated the other two men with fire.

Their screams were overshadowed by a massive explosion that boomed across the street. Fitz ducked behind the MATV with Rico, Dohi, and Apollo.

The bark of the M240 sounded above, and as soon as the shrapnel and hunks of the soldiers finished raining down, Fitz flashed signals to his team. Rico and Dohi ran to a flanking position, and Fitz looked for a target with his MK11, Apollo staying behind the MATV.

Wormer tentacles on fire wriggled back and forth like a burning squid's. One of the juveniles was blown in half, and the other was dragging its burning body across the street while bullets pecked at its armor.

Fitz lined up a shot and fired a 7.62-millimeter round into its left eye. He roved the gun's barrel for another target as an RPG streaked away from the building to his right and impacted the rooftop of a building a block away.

"Hold the line!" someone shouted.

The comms came alive with chatter that made it difficult to hear. Fitz pulled the earpiece out and heard tracks crunching over debris.

An M1A1 rolled into the street behind him, smashing a car into a storefront. The tank commander put up a pair of binoculars while the drivers backed up and then turned back onto the road. He put the binos away and then ducked back into the hatch, a hint at what was coming.

"Fire in the hole!" Fitz shouted. He caught a glimpse of the target lumbering through the tidal wave of smoke and shadows where the team of flamethrowers had been moments earlier.

Two Black Beetles stampeded around the corner, letting out a guttural hiss that sounded like a tornado siren.

"Everyone down!" Fitz yelled.

The bark of the M240 went silent, Tanaka ducking back into the MATV as a shell whooped overhead. The second shell quickly followed. The blasts were apocalyptically loud, like an MOAB going off. The MATV that protected him vibrated from the shock wave and then shrapnel pinging the armor. Apollo hunched down behind Fitz.

Stunned, Fitz patted himself down and then patted Apollo down for injuries, feeling for anything wet. Finding nothing, he crawled to look around the bumper, fear rushing into him when he saw the smoke rising up into the sky in the distance.

A voice called out across the street, and he looked over to see Rico and Dohi hiding behind a vehicle.

"Fitzie, you okay?" she shouted.

The tank rumbled by, the tracks so close to Fitz that he could feel a draft of hot air hitting his flushed cheeks.

He raised his hand at Rico after it passed his position.

An eerie calm settled over the street as marines and

other soldiers slowly rose from their positions to check the damage at the end of the road. The Variant attack was over—a test, it seemed.

Fitz pushed himself up, still rattled by the last blast from the tank. He drew in a breath of smoke and dust that made him cough. It was just a distant echo, and when he yelled for Team Ghost, he couldn't hear himself.

The team gathered around him as the tank continued down the street.

A carpet of darkness flooded the streets. The lampposts remained dark, the grid down. Fitz forced down some water, closed his eyes, and counted to ten to collect his thoughts. When he opened them again, Team Ghost and the other soldiers on the street were all gathered, some of them pointing at pillars of smoke rising toward the first glistening stars of the night.

Fitz blinked several times until his vision cleared and he saw the pillars weren't smoke at all: They were Reavers, hundreds of the waspy creatures flapping into the night sky.

Several hushed voices broke out around Fitz. He scrutinized the soldiers standing in the street. Most of them looked like teenagers or retirees. All of them were looking at Team Ghost.

"Fitz, Bradley is on the comms, asking to speak to you," Rico said.

Fitz pushed his earpiece back in. "Ghost One here," he said.

"Ghost One, as you can see, the sky isn't the friendliest of places right now. You're authorized to take your MATV into the city instead. I'll send you coordinates in a few minutes. We think we might know where the Queen is."

"Roger that, sir."

Fitz directed his team back into their vehicle.

The platoon sergeant and lieutenant in command of the men on the street started barking orders. The men filed back to their positions, forming a barrier for the night to come, while Team Ghost drove away from the front lines and into enemy territory.

"Reed—is it really you?"

The scratchy voice on the other end of the line sure didn't sound like Kate at first. He clutched the satellite phone to his ear, his heart full.

"Kate, baby, I...I can't believe it's you. How are you? How is..."

"I'm fine, and Javier Riley is okay too. We miss you! We need you to come home!" There was a trace of something that sounded a bit like anger in her voice, but Beckham didn't blame her for that. He'd broken a number of promises to Kate over the past seven months, and he was about to do it again.

"Listen, Kate, we don't have much time. There's something I have to do—something I have to do for everyone."

"What are you talking about, Reed?"

"You have to trust me, Kate. You trust me, right?"

There wasn't even a second of hesitation in her response. "I trust you, but whatever it is, there's someone else who can do it. You don't have to be a soldier anymore, Reed. You need to come home to us."

"And you didn't have to help find the cure for the hemorrhage virus...I heard what you did, Kate. I'm proud of you, and I understand why you risked leaving the fleet. But you have to remember—we don't have a home right now, and we won't, unless I embark on this one final mission."

"Final missions," she said with a huff. "It's always one final mission."

Beckham could hear Horn saying something in the background. He could picture his best friend there by Kate's side, and the image filled his heart even further.

"I'm sorry, Kate, but this time it really is one final mission. Tell Big Horn I love him and thank him for protecting you. I'm going to finish this, Kate. I'm going to make sure Wood can't hurt anyone else. If I don't make it back, you know how much I love you, and Javier Riley. Tell Horn and his girls the same thing."

"You tell him," Kate said.

Beckham looked at the skyline. The chopper wasn't in sight yet, but it would be here soon.

"Boss?" asked a voice.

"Big Horn, brother! It's been a beat," Beckham said.

"I thought you were dead, man. I mean, I had hope, but damn! You've had me and your lady scared as hell."

Beckham wiped a tear from his eye. "You take care of her and your girls, Big Horn."

"That sounds like some final shit to me, boss. You better not be doin' nothing stupid."

Swallowing, Beckham took a moment to reconsider his plan. It was a plan, but not a great one, and nothing he could share with Horn, for fear Horn would be the one to do something stupid.

"I've got to finish this, Big Horn. I love you, brother. Tell Tasha and Jenny the same."

"Boss, tell me where you're at. Tell me what you're going to do."

"Put Kate back on the line," Beckham stammered.

"No! Let me help you, brother!" Horn choked.

"You've done enough, man. I have to do this on my own. Now put Kate on, Big Horn—that's an order."

There was a pause, and then: "I love you, brother. Come home to us."

Beckham wiped another tear away and waited for

Kate's voice. Hearing it reminded him why he had to go through with his plan.

"I know there's no talking you out of this," she said, "so I'm just going to tell you I love you."

Holding in a breath, Beckham nodded at the words. "I'll do everything I can to make it back to you. I love you and our son more than you will ever know."

"I'm not going to say good-bye," she said, her voice breaking. "I'm not going to say it because you're coming home soon."

The line clicked off, and Beckham walked back to Captain Davis and the others. He handed the phone to Mayor Gallo. Her bodyguard, who had introduced himself as Jack Wall, and Senior Chief Blade both nodded at Beckham.

"I'm not sure I like this plan," Gallo said. "It requires a lot of stars aligning to be successful."

"It'll work," Beckham said. He readjusted the new prosthetic hand they had constructed for him. Gallo's doctors had also patched up his injuries and given him a warm shower and a new prosthetic leg. He wasn't exactly a new man, but he would be able to fight, assuming Wood lived up to his end of the bargain. After what he had said about the man's deceased brother, Beckham was betting on it.

"Okay, let's go over this one more time," Davis said. "Beckham and I will head to the *Zumwalt* with the transmitter. As soon as we reach the ship, Lemke will blow up the submarine that attacked them, kill Nixon's men, and take back the fleet. They will then send their fighter jets to take out the hemorrhage-virus missiles on the *Zumwalt* while Beckham keeps Wood busy."

Beckham nodded. "And back at home, Wall and Senior Chief Blade will help lead the uprising at the SZTs, starting with this one."

The senior chief massaged his thin mustache. "Wall's already got the ball moving on that. We've got rebel units ready to move on ROT as soon as we give the word."

"Don't worry," Wall grumbled. "You can count on my friends and allies. We've been fighting Variants for seven months and we can handle a few ROT terrorists."

"You're certain that ROT isn't aware of our plans?" Gallo asked. "We're taking a big risk helping you."

"If they were, we'd all be dead already," Davis said.

"Trust me, Mayor," Wall said. "I was a lawyer in my past life. I know all about deceit."

The joke prompted a laugh from everyone but Wall, who raised a brow.

"You were a lawyer?" Davis asked, giving him a once-over.

Gallo laughed. "It's true."

"I'm also a marine," Wall said.

Gallo pushed her white-rimmed glasses into her gray hair and massaged the top of her nose. Then she shrugged and said, "Okay then. Ringgold better promote me for this shit."

Davis chuckled, and Beckham cracked a half smile. The hot shower, tea, and Advil had helped the physical pain, and the jokes helped ease his mind, but he couldn't stop thinking about Kate and Javier Riley, wondering if he would ever meet his boy. The fear also drove him to move forward with their plan.

It was all for his family: Kate and Javier Riley, Tasha, Jenny, Big Horn, Fitz, Apollo, and all the other survivors, from Bo and Donna to Jake and Timothy. They were all worth dying for.

Wall raised a paw toward the horizon. "There's your ride," he said.

A black dot emerged over the rising sun.

Beckham ran a hand over his short-cropped hair and

turned to say good-bye to Mayor Gallo, Senior Chief Blade, and finally Wall.

"Good luck, Captain," Wall said. "From what I know about you, Wood won't stand a chance, but what happens after you kill him?"

"Let me worry about that," Beckham said.

Blade reached out and gave Beckham a fist bump, and Gallo shook Beckham's hand. She followed Blade and Wall off the tarmac, leaving Beckham standing there with Davis. They were both weaponless and dressed in civilian clothing that covered their transmitters.

The ROT chopper, a Seahawk by the looks of it, was already lowering over the husks of destroyed buildings in the distance.

"You're sure you're up for this?" Beckham asked.

Davis nodded firmly.

She wanted revenge, and so did Beckham, which made their mission even more dangerous. They both needed to be smart about this if they were to have any hope of killing Wood. It was all a gamble, and Beckham was breaking his rule by leaving himself very few outs. Gallo was right: In order for their plan to work, a lot of stars needed to align.

He raised his new prosthetic hand to his eyes as the chopper landed on the tarmac. A tall man opened the door and jumped out. It was still dark, but his athletic build and rough face looked familiar to Beckham.

Inside the troop hold were several other ROT soldiers. They remained inside, their weapons angled at Beckham and Davis.

The soldier crossed the tarmac and stopped a few feet away, focusing ruthless dark eyes that Beckham remembered all too well.

"Hello, Beckham," said Kufman.

Beckham could feel Davis looking at him, but he kept

his focus on the former Delta operator. He was the last man Beckham had expected to see get out of the bird, but then again, it made sense.

"Been a while, Kufman. I see you're still a snake."

Kufman clenched his jaw. The man was stone cold, just the way Beckham remembered him.

"I'm exactly where I should be," Kufman said. "And you...well, you're looking pretty rough. You always were a pussy."

Beckham shrugged. "I'd rather be a paraplegic than betray the country I swore to defend."

Kufman came within inches of Beckham's face. He could smell the rotten breath streaming through the gaps in Kufman's teeth.

"My country threw me under the bus after the Mog," he said, voice gruff and filled with anger. "Now I'm collecting what's due to me."

Beckham recalled the top secret mission in Mogadishu, Somalia, that had earned Kufman a one-way ticket home and a dishonorable discharge. Horn had nearly torn Kufman's head off that day.

"You killed kids," Beckham said, narrowing his brow. "Babies."

"I also killed their terrorist parents. That grenade saved American lives."

"There is a line we were ordered never to cross, and you crossed it. You and Wood deserve each other, as far as I'm concerned, and I'm going to kill you after I kill him."

Kufman licked his lips. "We'll see about that." He gestured toward the chopper. "Let's go."

Beckham and Davis walked in front of Kufman to the bird, where they were stopped. After a pat down, they were directed into the troop hold. Beckham's heart was still pounding. They hadn't discovered the transmitters.

He took a seat next to Davis, across from the ROT soldiers. They all wore scarves or bandannas to cover their features.

I'd be doing the same thing, Beckham thought. *Filthy fucking traitors.*

A few minutes later, the Seahawk was pulling into the bright morning sun. The rays spread over the landscape of their troubled country for yet another day. Beckham had a feeling this one was going to be one that went down in American history as a turning point.

Kufman kept his gaze focused on Beckham but didn't say another word for most of the flight.

"What did you do to piss this guy off?" Davis asked.

"His real beef is with Big Horn," Beckham replied. "Wish Horn was here to kick his ass."

"Shut the fuck up," Kufman said. "I'll find Horn as soon as I'm done with you. He's as dumb as an ox. It's only a matter of time."

Beckham rested his head back on the bulkhead and closed his eyes, his mind racing for hours as they flew south over ruined cities and farm fields overgrown with weeds.

It wasn't long before he saw the ocean and the *Zumwalt*. The stealth ship glided through the teal waves in the distance. Kufman opened the door and gestured for Beckham and Davis to stand.

They stepped up to the edge of the troop hold, the glistening water passing below. Kufman stood behind both of them, and for a moment Beckham wondered if he was going to kick them out. But the disgraced Delta operator simply stood there with his arms folded across his chest.

The pilots descended toward the small tarmac on the stern of the ship, where three Little Birds were already parked. Beckham saw the two MGM-140 Army

Tactical Missile System delivery vehicles fully loaded with hemorrhage-virus missiles on the bow of the ship as they lowered.

Kufman instructed Beckham and Davis to raise their hands as soon as the wheels touched down. They did as ordered, allowing another ROT soldier to put flak jackets over them.

"You afraid someone's going to shoot us before we get to Wood, or what?" Davis asked.

Beckham raised his arms above his head, the action sending sharp pains up his back. He almost didn't feel the blade that struck him below his shoulder blade, but he heard the crunch. Kufman buried the tip deep in Beckham's flesh. He let out a gasp and blinked at the white-hot pain.

In his blurred vision appeared three men. One of them was waving from the deck as he crossed over to the bird. Vision going in and out, Beckham saw it was Wood. He twirled a machete in one hand and continued waving with the other.

President Ringgold was on her knees behind Wood, head bowed.

"Sorry, Reed," said Kufman, his gruff voice spitting in Beckham's ear. "But you had to have known Wood wasn't going to fight you fairly after you had his brother shot like a dog."

25

The MATV rumbled down Rue de Sèvres, an abandoned street, in the flame-scorched night. Thirty minutes after leaving the front lines, Team Ghost had managed to drive over four miles into Paris without being spotted.

Look-at-me fire continued to thump from the front lines, sending a steady volley of artillery into the city. The distant explosions flashed like a brilliant fireworks display, attracting thousands of Reavers. So far, the distraction seemed to be working.

The winged creatures flapped over rooftops and soared toward the glow of the blasts, while Tanaka drove the MATV deeper into enemy territory. The Delta Force Team Ghost logo on the hood was visible through a thin layer of smoke and fog that had settled over Paris.

All around them were places Rico had told Fitz she'd always wanted to see: the Eiffel Tower, Notre-Dame, the Louvre.

Their short conversations about history and landmarks were the only good memories he'd made in Europe so far, and looking back at the woman, he realized again how much he appreciated her company.

She sat in the back seat, staring at the historic

landmarks with a face that was part smile, part frown—like a kid who had opened a birthday present but didn't understand the contents.

That about summed up Fitz's feelings about the war in Europe. The excitement and buildup across the Atlantic had been met with loss after loss. This mission was Team Ghost's last chance for a win.

He gripped his MK11, the one thing he trusted besides his team and friends back home. The rifle had gotten him through multiple tough spots since he swore to defend the United States of America over a decade earlier.

All it takes is all you got, he thought as he scanned the skies. The Reavers were moving in V formations toward the front lines.

Reports hissed into his earpiece.

The initial attacks were just tests—the Variant army version of recon and suicide units. Now they were hitting the EUF positions with all of their forces.

"Wolf One, this is Wolf Two. We're being hit hard by packs of juveniles," reported a sergeant. "Requesting track support."

"Roger that, Wolf Two—sending you a mechanized unit. Hold the line at all costs until they get there," replied the platoon lieutenant. "Wolf Three, sitrep."

"Got some Wormer tunnels in sight," replied another sergeant. "They're headed right for us."

The lieutenant raised his voice in reply. "Wolf Three, do *not* let them flank us."

Fitz pushed the black bead to his lips and switched to the channel with the Twenty-Fourth MEU. "Lion One, you've got Reavers incoming."

"Roger that, Ghost One. We can handle 'em. You just focus on the HVT. Over."

The sky continued to fill with the flying monsters.

They lifted off from the rooftops of ancient buildings they had turned into rent-a-castles like gargoyles set in motion.

Rico popped between the driver's seat and passenger's seat, pointing. For the first time in days, she wasn't chewing gum. Instead of chomping, she let out a gasp.

"There's the Eiffel Tower," Rico said.

Fitz flipped his night-vision goggles into position to take a look. The beasts were pulling away in droves.

"Unreal—there have to be hundreds of them up there," Fitz said.

"More like thousands," Tanaka said.

Dohi looked up from his map and scanned the skyline, then went back to studying.

"How far are we from the coordinates?" Fitz asked.

"We still have to cross the Seine," Dohi replied. He flitted a small flashlight across the map. "Then it's a straight shot to Notre-Dame, where those paratroopers last radioed in from."

"Watch out!" Rico screamed.

Fitz twisted back to the front, bracing himself with a hand against the dashboard. Tanaka didn't have enough time to swerve and avoid a Variant juvenile hunched over a dead soldier in the middle of the road. The beast looked up just as the cowcatcher fastened to the front of the truck slammed into its armored plating. A screeching followed—the combination of skidding tires and the monster's high-pitched shriek.

The MATV eased to a stop a hundred feet away from the beast. It somersaulted over the pavement and hit a wall.

"Where the hell did that thing come from?" Tanaka whispered.

"Everyone okay?" Fitz asked.

Four nods and a tail wag from Apollo confirmed they were.

Fitz opened the door and stepped out into the chilly night. The monster, a full-grown juvenile, was already pushing itself up on all fours. Scabby, chitinous armor covered a body three times the size of a human's. Two almond-shaped eyes homed in on Fitz.

"Fitzie, what are you doing? Get back inside," Rico whispered, a bit too loudly.

The beast took a step toward Fitz before he buried a 7.62-millimeter round deep inside its skull. The hulking monster hit the ground with a thud, kicking up a cloud of dust that joined the knee-high smog.

Fitz lowered his rifle and scanned the area for any hostiles. Despite the distant thump of explosions, the city was silent—there was no sign of other creatures.

"Come on," Rico said.

Fitz quietly closed the door and ordered Tanaka to keep driving. They passed the dead EUF soldier, who lay on his back, and Fitz noticed that the man's skull had been scalped like one of General Custer's men at Little Bighorn.

He forced himself to look away. Soldiers were dying back at the front lines—soldiers Team Ghost still had a chance to save.

The Seine was just ahead. Stone walls covered in vines, and vegetation formed a barrier along the river. The explosions increased in the distance. Tanks had joined the din of the battle, and Fitz could even make out the crack of automatic rifles. The Variants were throwing everything they had at the EUF.

But where were all the other creatures? The roads were mostly empty save for the single juvenile. There wasn't another mutated Variant on the ground. Surely they weren't all attacking the front lines...

"No more stopping until we get to the coordinates," Fitz said quietly.

Tanaka gripped the steering wheel tighter and nodded. His iPod earbuds hung around his neck, and Fitz could make out the faint tune of rap music blaring from the device.

He focused back on the road. The bridge crossing the Seine had taken a direct hit from a missile.

Tanaka maneuvered around the twisted rebar and hunks of concrete littering the street. Once they were clear, he sped off the bridge. The diesel engine chugged as they retraced their route.

Tanaka followed a road back to the Seine, where they crossed another bridge and turned onto Boulevard du Palais.

Fitz balled his hand into a fist at the sight of an elephant graveyard of military vehicles scattered across the street. Scorched pieces of metal that looked like tusks extended from a truck blown to pieces by friendly fire.

At the front of the line, an EUF Humvee sat idle, with all the doors wide open. Wormer holes peppered the ground. It wasn't hard to guess what had happened here.

"That was the EUF HQ before it fell a few days ago," Dohi said.

"It's called Sainte-Chapelle," Rico said. "Residence of the kings of France until around the fourteenth century. It was built sometime in the mid-1200s."

The Gothic chapel, normally a gorgeous relic, was now abandoned in the war against the Variants. Reflections in the cracked stained-glass windows flickered in the flame-scorched night.

The column had been driving away from the medieval chapel, a final attempt to escape before being overrun. Barbed wire fences and concrete walls formed a tight perimeter around the structure, but those barriers hadn't protected the EUF soldiers trying to hold the nearly eight-hundred-year-old chapel and surrounding grounds. From the looks of it, they had put up a hell of a fight.

"Keep moving," Fitz said.

Tanaka steered around the vehicles, taking to the shoulder and navigating around the tunnel openings. He cut across the lawn and pulled onto another road called Quai du Marché Neuf.

Fitz turned the radio up to listen to the chatter about the battle raging on the front lines.

The Twenty-Fourth and Eleventh MEUs were holding their ground, but the Second Calvary Regiment and all of the current three battalions from the Seventy-Fifth Ranger Regiment were suffering major casualties from Wormers that had flanked their positions. On top of that, the ragtag EUF units were being torn apart by poor communication and lack of leadership in commanding the troops on the ground.

A frantic voice surged over the channel. "They're gone! I need help. It—it burns!"

The EUF operator who replied told the young man to get off the open channel, but he continued to shout. "My entire platoon was wiped out by an acid attack. I'm the only one left. I'm the—"

Fitz turned the volume back down. "We have to hurry," he said. The comms were a mess, adding to the confusion of separated units and commanders with little to no experience thrown into battle.

"The cathedral isn't far. Just another couple blocks," Dohi said.

Tanaka pushed the vehicle to its max speed and raced down the road. In another minute they were within eyesight of the spire and the flying buttresses on the east side of the Cathédrale Notre-Dame de Paris. While Rico was admiring the architecture, the Second Cavalry Regiment had started the retreat from several locations. It wasn't a surprise when Bradley's voice boomed in Fitz's earpiece.

"Ghost One, we're getting our asses kicked. Where are you?"

"We're closing in on the cathedral, Lion One. Heading in on foot now."

Fitz pointed to the side of the road. "Park us out of sight, Tanaka. We'll head in on the western side for a better look."

Team Ghost piled out of the vehicle as soon as it came to a stop. Rico hurried over and met Fitz in front of the hood with Dohi and Tanaka.

Aside from the distant barrage of artillery fire, the street was eerily quiet. They scanned the rooftops and architecture of the apartment buildings towering over the street. Nothing stirred on the iron balconies or behind the French doors.

Fitz gave his orders with hand signals: Dohi on point with Apollo, Tanaka on rear guard, Rico with Fitz. Eyes high and low. He finished by putting his fist on the Team Ghost logo.

All it takes is all you got, Marine.

Then he pulled up his smiling-joker bandanna and directed the team to move out. Each of the team members tapped the Ghost logo before taking off. Apollo went to work, his nose sniffing the ground, checking for a scent.

It didn't take long for him to pick one up. Apollo trotted ahead, moving in a snaky path while the rest of the team jogged after him into a narrow alleyway. Fitz checked the storefronts: an espresso and patisserie shop, a bar, a shoe repair shop. They were passing through a neighborhood that had been here for hundreds of years.

A squawking stopped the team, and everyone moved for cover. Fitz and Rico took up position under a red

awning and behind a bench. Tanaka and Dohi moved to
the right side of the street, but Apollo remained standing
in the center of the alley.

Fitz let out a low whistle. The dog's ears perked, but
he stood his ground.

"Apollo, get over here, boy," Fitz said.

The dog suddenly took off running, and Fitz barreled after him. Something really important must have
caught his attention, because Fitz had never seen Apollo
do anything like this.

The other members of Ghost fell into position
behind Fitz. They moved into the next street with
weapons raised, sweeping over the layer of smog on the
cobblestone.

The skinniest Variant Fitz had ever seen bolted away
from Apollo on all fours, moving more like a chimpan-
zee than a monster. Fitz raised his sniper rifle and centered it on the creature's bony body. Pale flesh covered by
cobwebs of blue veins seemed to stick to a bony, naked
body.

Holding in a breath, he waited for a shot, then
squeezed the trigger. The suppressed barrel fired a
round into the monster's neck, nearly severing its head.
Apollo continued running, right past the dead Variant.

What the hell, boy?!

Fitz waved his team onward and followed the dog's
tail through the knee-high level of smog. Apollo finally
stopped outside an apartment building.

Dohi was the first to get there. He looked around the
next corner, then walked back to Apollo, who was sitting on his haunches. Fitz arrived a moment later with
Tanaka and Rico.

"Looks as if Apollo found those paratroopers," Dohi
said.

Three men, or what was left of them, were sprawled

on the ground. Fitz crouched down next to Dohi, who was checking their corpses.

"Two-Face," he said quietly. "Two-Face did this."

Fitz would have expected the bodies to be picked clean, but instead, they were covered in lacerations and mutilated beyond recognition. It was difficult to even decipher their gender.

Rico had a hand cupped over her lips.

"Why didn't those things eat 'em?" Tanaka asked.

Dohi pointed at another body hanging from a balcony above, the uniform and flesh skinned completely off the body. He looked over at Fitz and whispered, "Whatever did this is a different type of monster—an evil beast that's not interested in food. This is just a game to Two-Face."

"I've got a really shitty feeling," Tanaka said.

Rico glanced over at Fitz, her hand still covering her mouth. There was terror in her gaze.

"Police their ammo," Fitz said, pointing to the guns scattered on the street. "We might need it."

After they gathered the extra magazines and a few weapons, they moved toward the apartment building overlooking the cathedral. Fitz wanted a look at their target before continuing any further, especially after seeing the dead paratroopers.

Dohi was right. Whatever killed these men was evil—more evil than even the Alphas back in the United States.

Tanaka took point and kicked open the door of the four-story building. They moved up a winding staircase with yellow-white wallpaper covered in mold. Fitz pulled his joker bandanna up higher over his nose to keep out the smell, not that it would help much.

At the top floor, Dohi slipped into a hallway and found an open door on the west side. Tanaka remained in the passage, holding security with Rico and Apollo, while Fitz and Dohi moved into a dusty room. Furnished with crystal chandeliers, antique tables, and white couches, the place looked like something Fitz had seen on HGTV.

Fitz made his way over to a pair of shattered French doors that opened onto an iron balcony. Across the street was the western façade of Notre-Dame. With Dohi's help, he carried a desk in front of the window, where Fitz then set up his MK11 and bipod.

Taking a seat, Fitz magnified his view of one of the most famous churches in the world. The western façade towered over a stone courtyard. He flitted the scope along part of a flying buttress on the other side of the building, and then focused on the stained glass of the rose window. The intricate design was breathtaking, and the window was surrounded by some of the most detailed stonework he'd ever seen.

He continued to scan the structure, noting gargoyles and other statues on its face. Next, he took in the three front entrances on the western side and the decorative tympanum cresting each of the double doors.

The second floor had more doors with tympanums on each side of the rose window. Above that were two towers. The eastern spire protruded over them, reaching toward the moon.

Fitz saw the first beast in the glow. The Reaver was hanging on to the spire, watching over the city with reptilian eyes. Two more of the beasts were perched at the very top of the right tower, where they remained frozen like the gargoyle statues.

"Contacts," he said.

Dohi brought up a pair of binoculars.

A message hissed in Fitz's earpiece. "Ghost One, Lion One, sitrep."

"In position, Lion One. Just need a single shot and the Queen is mine," Fitz replied. "Unless you want to call in air support."

Another Reaver walked across the arched flying buttress on the eastern side. There were several more on the cathedral roof behind the towers.

"Do you have a confirmed sighting?" Bradley asked.

"Negative, sir, but she's got to be here. The cathedral is surrounded by Reavers."

"So are a shit-ton of other structures in Paris," Bradley said. "Until you have a sighting, Command will not authorize any air support. We can't waste the fuel or the bombs."

"Roger. Stand by," Fitz said. He looked over at Dohi, who was still looking through his binoculars.

"They have to be protecting the Queen."

Fitz agreed with a nod. "Yeah, but the question is, how do we get inside to kill her?"

Dohi lowered the binoculars.

"Leave that up to me and Tanaka. You stay here with Apollo and Rico. I'll draw Two-Face out."

Davis stared at the MGM-140 Army Tactical Missile System delivery vehicles on the deck. They were angled west, toward Florida. She wasn't sure how far out they were from the mainland, but she had a feeling they were within range of an SZT.

"Ah, Rachel Davis, I presume," said Wood. He walked away from President Ringgold, twirling his machete through the air like a kid with a play sword. Two soldiers in black armor, with their features covered by black masks, followed him toward Beckham and Davis.

Two more soldiers had weapons angled at their backs.

They were completely surrounded, which wasn't really a surprise. Two naval destroyers, the USS *Gridley* and the USS *Mustin* patrolled the waters to the east. The bastards aboard made Davis sick. Did they not know how many sailors ROT had killed?

She gritted her teeth and focused. All she had to do was delay the inevitable and wait for her friends.

"This is going to be *a lot* of fun," Wood said. He stopped about ten feet from Davis, his hazel eyes flitting to Beckham. "Look at you—the dog that won't die."

"I should have known Kufman was part of your team," Beckham said, his words slurred. He stood next to Davis, trying his best to keep his balance. Blood from the knife Kufman had jabbed in his back trickled down the new shirt Mayor Gallo had given Beckham at SZT 68.

But Beckham wasn't complaining. She'd never heard him complain, even once, since meeting him, and they had both known the risks of coming here. Fortunately, Wood seemed to have no idea a storm was barreling toward the *Zumwalt*—a storm of men and women loyal to the Constitution of the United States of America.

She looked toward the leader of their nation. Ringgold was on her knees, tear-swollen eyes looking toward the sky. Three men guarded her, and at least a dozen more were standing at the edges of the deck. None of them seemed to be paying attention to the skyline.

"No 'Hello, how's it going'?" Wood asked. He looked over his shoulder at Ringgold. "Your friends came to rescue you, and they don't even have the courtesy to say hi. That says a lot, Ms. Ringgold. *A lot*."

"Let's get this over with," Beckham said. He staggered forward. "I'm here to end this. One way or another."

Wood shrugged and dragged the machete's tip against the ground, the blade screeching over metal as he walked closer to Beckham and Davis.

"I'll get to you, Beckham, but first I'm going to deal with your friend Captain Davis here." Wood twirled the blade again and pointed it at her throat.

"Someone give this woman a weapon," Wood said.

The man with a gun to her back stepped around and proferred a knife half the size of the machete. Davis gripped the handle. It wasn't fair, but she wasn't protesting. This was the opportunity she'd been waiting for.

"You said you were fighting me," Beckham stuttered.

Wood wagged a finger. "You'll get your turn, shithead—but first I want to introduce you to Ryan Meyer."

A skinny ROT soldier stepped away from Ringgold and walked toward them. He pulled his mask down, revealing a chiseled jaw, a sharp nose, and green eyes that were directed at Davis and seemed to be smoldering with rage. She studied his flushed features for a moment, trying to remember if she'd met him, but he didn't look familiar. Was he some navy dropout, or perhaps a sailor who had served under her command?

"Ryan had a brother named Matt—a brother whom Captain Davis killed during the attack on the USS *GW*," Wood said. "I'm a man of my word, and I told Ryan he would get a chance to avenge his brother."

Wood gestured with his machete toward Davis. "So have at it, Ryan!"

Davis readied the knife and stepped back as Meyer came charging with his own blade. Still partially in shock, she hardly had enough time to jump back from his first slash. Using her elbow, she parried the attack with a smack to his chin.

Quick and steady, Rachel!

She wasn't a knife fighter, but she had been trained in self-defense and knew enough to hold her own. Beckham, on the other hand, was too injured to fight. He reached for a knife that Wood dangled in front of him like a handler taunting a dog with a treat.

"Come on, boy," Wood said, pulling the grip back every time Beckham got close. He swiped at the blade with his prosthetic hand, coming close before Wood yanked it back. He let out a laugh as Beckham stumbled.

Davis focused on Meyer, who stood and wiped blood from his lip. "I'm going to gut you, cun—"

Before he could say the one word she hated more than any other, she silenced him with a jab to the face. Her bare knuckles cracked his nose. Wood, still taunting Beckham to her left, let out a bellowing laugh.

"Meyer, you've got to—" he started to say.

This time Beckham silenced Wood with a left hook to his face. Wood fell to the ground, and Beckham jumped on top of the leader of ROT.

Meyer used the opportunity to barrel into Davis. He speared her in the stomach with his skull, knocking the air from her lungs and taking her to the ground in a tangled mess.

"Die, you bitch!" he yelled, thrusting the knife at her throat as she gasped for air. She caught his wrist with both hands and pushed upward. Then she wrapped her legs around his, trapping him.

"I'm not"—Davis began to say as she prepared to make her move—"a bitch!" she gasped. Using her boots, she twisted Meyer's left ankle until he let out his own scream of pain. She rolled him onto his back and got her arm into position. Wrestling with the boys in high school had served her well. Her opponent was in a choke hold a few seconds later, his back to her chest, her right arm around his throat, and her other arm pinning his left arm.

Meyer tried to butt her with the back of his skull, but she moved to the side and squeezed his neck until he dropped the knife. It clanked on the ground next to her. She continued to tighten her arm around his windpipe as he flailed for the blade.

While she choked Meyer, Beckham beat Wood's face with his prosthetic and his left hand. The ROT soldiers had circled around, but Kufman held a hand out to keep them back. They cheered on their leader and Meyer, calling Beckham and Davis every name in the book.

Wood was shielding his face with one arm and reaching for his machete with the other. His fingers grasped the blade, cutting into his flesh as he pulled the weapon across the deck.

"Beckham, watch out!" Davis yelled when Wood grabbed the handle.

He brought up his prosthetic hand just as Wood swung the machete. The blade stuck into the plastic arm like an axe in a tree. Wood used his other hand to hit Beckham in the jaw. The impact cracked and echoed, but Beckham hardly even flinched. He head-butted Wood a moment later, the crack ten times louder than Wood's punch had been.

Beckham pushed himself off and yanked the machete out of his prosthetic hand.

"Finish him off!" Davis shouted.

Wood scrambled to his feet, the gash on his forehead dripping blood. He reached up and palmed the wound. His wide, crazed eyes roved from Davis to Beckham.

"I'm going to enjoy sending you in pieces to your bitch girlfriend, Kate Lovato," Wood snarled.

Beckham let out a scream and swung the machete at Wood, who jumped back. Beckham stumbled forward on his prosthetic leg but remained standing.

Wood grabbed a knife that Kufman handed him. He sliced at Beckham's left arm, the blade ripping through his shirt. Beckham landed a punch that knocked Wood on his ass.

Davis smiled at that. She focused on finishing off Meyer, who was still kicking and squirming in her grip.

"Quick and steady," she whispered as she twisted her arm. A snap sounded, and his body went limp in her grip.

Beckham suddenly shouted in pain as Davis pushed Meyer's heavy body off her. She had stood and was preparing to help Beckham when something hot sliced through her vest and into her gut. Her features clenched as a red-hot wave raced through her body. She squinted through the pain at Wood's blurry face.

A few feet away, Beckham was on his knees, gripping his arm, blood sliding through his fingers. Kufman towered above him from behind, holding a glistening knife in his hands that he suddenly jabbed into Beckham's upper back.

"No," she choked.

Wood snapped his fingers at Davis to get her attention and tilted his head as she blinked at him.

"You stuck?" he said. "You look as if you're stuck. Let me help you."

Wood pulled a long blade from her gut and stepped back as Davis crashed to her knees. The pain flashed across her midsection. She reached down and cupped the wound, still staring at Beckham, who was bleeding out on the deck in front of her.

"Coward," she managed to choke. "You're a fucking coward."

Wood replied, but Davis couldn't make out the words. She focused on the skyline, searching desperately for the help that was supposed to come.

"Stop," Beckham mumbled. He could feel his blood gushing from his body. Fast, too fast. His time on earth was limited. The last life in his bank was gone, used up like Lieutenant Jim Flathman's. He would be joining the lieutenant in hell soon.

Davis crashed to her stomach a few feet away. Her sharp jaw smashed against the deck, her eyes locked on his. Blood flowed from her guts.

Wood stood between them, looking back and forth and back and forth again with a wide grin. He stomped the deck. "That's what I'm talking about!"

The other ROT soldiers, including Kufman, stood with the same emotionless gazes. These men were used to seeing atrocities, and taking part in them.

Wood put on a pair of gloves and then reached out. Kufman handed him something Beckham couldn't see. Then Wood walked over and bent down in front of Davis. She managed to spit at his boots. It was her final action, her eyes rolling up into her skull as Wood stuck her with what looked like a syringe. He moved over to Beckham next, whistling a tune.

Crouching down, he held the syringe out for Beckham to see. Then he jabbed it into Beckham's arm and pushed the rest of the liquid into his flesh.

"A few months ago, I heard a quotation—something about how in order to kill a monster you have to create one," Wood said. He glanced back at Ringgold. "So I'm leaving that up to you now, Beckham. I've infected you with the hemorrhage virus, and now I'm going to throw you and Captain Davis into a prison cell with Ringgold and let you kill the traitor yourselves."

He grinned a toothless smile, his swollen lips covering his mouth. "Oh," he said, before rising to his feet. "Your bitch girlfriend probably told you that the hemorrhage virus helps speed up healing in the infected, so you and Captain Davis might well survive those injuries long enough to kill Ms. Ringgold. We'll have to see. Should be fun to watch—and watch I will."

Wood tossed the spent needle into the ocean and then put a finger on his chin as if he was in deep thought. He glanced back at Ringgold. Tears streaked down her cheeks.

"You know what?" Wood said. "I think I might just make this more interesting...I might just give her a knife. It will be a great experiment to see if she has what it takes to kill, since she seemed to be so good at ordering other people to kill my brother."

Beckham closed his eyes for a second, thinking of Kate, Javier Riley, Horn, and everyone else. He had failed them—he'd failed them all.

"I ordered your brother shot, not President Ringgold," he said, opening his eyes.

Wood scratched at his jaw and shrugged. "She was in charge. It's her fault."

Two ROT soldiers grabbed Beckham by the arms and dragged his body across the deck after a nod from Wood. Beckham tried to squirm, but he'd used up all of his energy.

"Oh, and your friend Fitzpatrick and your dog, Apollo," Wood called out. "I just found out they're in Paris. They're both in for a nice surprise very soon."

26

"Ghost One, we just got word the HVT in Paris will be a red Reaver. Repeat, the HVT is a red Reaver," Bradley said over the comms channel. "Some soldier in Rome called the Italian Stallion and his pet mouse apparently confirmed the sighing of a Queen in Rome."

Fitz frowned—there were more than one Queen after all. He wasn't sure if they were all the same species, but what did it matter? The abominations all had to die.

He paused for a moment to think of the solo soldier and his pet mouse. The duo sounded like one hell of a team. He looked down at Apollo. They were a hell of a team too.

"I hope you can perform a miracle with that MK11, because we need you to turn water into wine! We're hanging on by a thread out here!" Bradley said.

Fitz bit his lip at the news. The EUF was losing the battle on the front lines, and it wasn't even midnight yet. EUF fighter jets and several F-16s rushed over the city, dropping their payloads before screaming away, a final act of desperation of a military running on fumes. The distant thuds added orange blooms to the scorched skyline.

"They're destroying everything," Rico said. She watched

the explosions to the south with her face against the window.

Fitz raised a finger to silence her, but Rico kept talking. "You know there are almost eight thousand pipes in Notre-Dame's organ?" Her eyes widened. "It's, like, one of the most famous cathedrals in the entire world, and Dohi is about—"

"About to light it up," Fitz said. "If you knew what was inside, you wouldn't be complaining. Don't forget those paratroopers back on the street."

Rico sulked behind him, flinching at the thumps in the distance. The desk Fitz had positioned in front of the open French doors vibrated from the explosions. He pushed the scope of his MK11 back to his night-vision goggles and shifted the butt of the gun until it was in the sweet spot of his shoulder.

The vantage was perfect, providing a view of the western façade of the cathedral. Even better were the drapes on the windows that helped disguise their location. So far, the Reavers hadn't spotted them.

If the Paris Queen was inside the cathedral, he would have the perfect shot. All they had to do was get her into view.

One shot. Just one.

The chambered round was ready to fly.

Apollo sat on his haunches behind Fitz, watching the hallway with Rico. She leveled her shotgun into the inky darkness. He trusted them both to have his back, but if the Variants found their location they were—

Don't think that way. All it takes is one shot, Marine.

"All it takes," Fitz whispered, "is *all* you got."

Reports of the battle raging on the front lines filled his earpiece. He could picture the battle in his mind: Wormers tearing into the streets, mutated beasts emerging through the tunnels, and Reavers swooping in to pluck soldiers from their rooftop positions. Several thousand human soldiers against tens of thousands of monsters was hardly a fair fight, even with armored units, and automatic weapons, and bombs.

Maybe Stevenson was right—maybe they should have just blown the cities to pieces from the beginning. The battle for Paris was turning into Operation Liberty all over again, and Fitz had the ability to end it all.

He said a short prayer for Stevenson and the soldiers on the front lines.

Screeching tires pulled his attention to the road south and west of his position. He moved his gun's barrel and spotted the Team Ghost logo on their MATV.

"I sure hope they know what they're doing," Rico whispered.

The Reavers on the cathedral took to the air, screeching in their otherworldly language. The long bony beasts plumed away from surrounding buildings, bringing their numbers to two dozen.

Tanaka drove the MATV over the curb and onto the terrace on the western side of the cathedral, passing planters stuffed with flowers and weeds.

"What the hell are you doing?" Fitz whispered. He glanced over his shoulder. "Watch our six, Apollo. Rico, you get over here. We may need your M4 in this fight."

She walked over to the open French doors and exchanged her shotgun for the M4 resting against the wall.

The hatch on top of the MATV popped open, and Dohi emerged as the MATV barreled toward the western façade of the building. The M240 roared to life, its *GAGAGAGA* reverberating over the distant artillery fire.

The sound of the big gun was music to Fitz's ears.

Rounds peppered the stones of the façade and shattered what was left of the stained-glassed windows.

Dozens of Reavers took off from the other end of the cathedral, rising away from the spire. Fitz did a second count of at least thirty of the beasts before pressing his NVGs against the scope of his MK11.

"You got this, Fitz," Rico said.

He lined up his first shot and pulled the trigger. The round streaked into a spikey back, severing the creature's spine. Paralyzed, the Reaver fluttered back to the ground and landed on an abandoned vehicle, smashing through the windshield and setting off a car alarm.

Shots two and three of the twenty-round box magazine blew gaping holes in the wing of another creature to the southwest. The Reaver fought for altitude, but Fitz stopped its ascent with round four to the head.

"Thatta boy, Fitzie," Rico said. She raised her rifle, but Fitz shook his head. "Not yet. We don't want to draw their attention unless we have to."

A Reaver flapping toward the MATV twisted in their direction. It hovered nearby, flapping its wings, and shrieked a message. All at once, six of the thirty monsters changed direction, flying right for Fitz and Rico.

Fitz aimed for the beast that had made their position. Was this the HVT? Was this the beast that could end the battle for Paris?

Shots five and six blew gaping holes in the monster's torso, guts and blood gushing out as the Reaver crashed to the ground. Crumpled and gasping for air, it finally died with shot seven to the forehead.

Fitz scanned the skyline, looking for any sign of a change in the Reavers' behavior, but the abominations continued to attack the MATV and sail toward the apartment.

"Open fire," Fitz ordered.

Rico pushed her M4 through the open window and pulled the trigger. Spent casings from 5.56-millimeter rounds rained down on the floor, mixing with the discharged 7.62-millimeter casings already there.

Tanaka had parked the MATV in front of the cathedral, and Dohi lobbed several grenades through the shattered rose window before ducking back into the turret. The explosions blew the front doors on the right side off the building from the hinges, flames and splintered wood belching out.

Rico fired with calculated precision, keeping away the beasts soaring toward the apartment. They fanned out to avoid her wrath, and Fitz used the opportunity to scan the beasts swooping toward the MATV, looking for one that might be the HVT.

But all of the creatures looked the same—long bony bodies, leathery flesh, frayed wings, and tails whipping from their tailbones. They were moving fast too, so fast he was forced to lead them with his barrel. He maimed another Reaver and pushed the scope away to look at the MATV when it started moving again. Tanaka was gunning the engine toward the western façade.

"What the hell are they doing?" Rico asked.

Fitz licked his dry lips and pushed his mini-mic up to his mouth, but it was too late to stop Tanaka. The determined soldier rammed the middle doors of the building. The cowcatcher and armored front of the vehicle shattered the stone walls and double wooden doors.

Tanaka quickly reversed the truck, and Dohi popped out of the turret. Another three grenades sailed through the air and rolled into the building.

"Crazy sons of bitches," Rico said.

Flames burst from the entrance, and the chime of bells rose over the roar of gunfire and cries of monsters. The ringing filled the cathedral with a peaceful song that set the Reavers screeching and frenzied. Smoke funneled out of the destroyed front entrance and out of the shattered stained-glass windows.

Another blast rocked the inside of the cathedral, the carillon ringing again like a dinner bell. Fitz looked through the MK11's sights and fired on a Reaver soaring in their direction, wings spread out like an angel's.

Three more of the beasts trailed the first Reaver. Between Rico and Fitz, they cut the creatures out of the sky. Dohi kept the other beasts at bay with the M240. The rapid fire tore through leathery hides and wings. He was almost as good on the gun as Big Horn. Damn—Fitz would give anything to have Horn and Captain Beckham with him now.

"Changing," Rico said.

"Ghost One, Ghost One, this is Lion Two, do you copy? Over," hissed a voice in Fitz's earpiece. This time it was Major Domino. Fitz was afraid to ask what had happened to Bradley.

"Copy that, Lion Two. Ghost One here, and I'm a little busy," Fitz said between trigger pulls.

"Ghost One, Command is preparing to pull back. We're losing men and women by the second."

"I just need a bit more time, Lion Two," Fitz said. "Just give me…"

A flash of motion in his peripheral vision gave him a warning to duck down. The Reaver slammed into the side of the building, wings and arms gripping the exterior while talons groped for him inside.

Fitz bent down over his desk just in time to avoid razor-sharp claws, so close he could feel the *whoosh* of air as they passed.

Rico raised her shotgun over Fitz's helmet and pointed the barrel at the monster's leathery midsection. Everything seemed to freeze in that second. This was the closest

Fitz had ever been to one of the creatures. He could see its hair growing in a patch between barreled chest muscles and two black nipples. Worst of all, Fitz could smell its rancid sweat.

The beast squawked as Rico fired a blast into its rib cage. Hot blood coated Fitz, snapping him out of battle time. The boom of the gun rang in his ear, and he cupped it with his hand.

Rico pulled the smoking shotgun back and pointed outside. Her mouth moved, and he could tell she was screaming, but he couldn't hear a word.

He wiped blood off his face, grabbed his MK11, and angled it at the sky. Rico smacked his right arm and pointed at the western façade of the building.

A tidal wave of Variants flowed out of the smoking entrance, funneling out onto the stone terrace, where Dohi was still firing at the Reavers in the sky.

Fitz magnified his view of the bony, emaciated monsters. Wrinkled flesh, covered in burns, and shrapnel wounds flickered across his sights. The beasts were almost all hunched over, running just like chimps.

"Christ almighty," Fitz said.

He realized he could hear again when Bradley's voice came over the radio: "Ghost One, Lion One. We're falling back, repeat, we're falling back."

Fitz was too distracted to reply. Below, the MATV reversed while Dohi directed the now rapid fire of the M240 at the army of Variants. The attack cut the sinewy beasts down with ease, but the redirected fire also gave the Reavers a chance to attack.

"Rico, keep them off the MATV," Fitz said. He switched back to the channel with Bradley. "Copy your last, Lion One. Still no sign of the HVT here. We've got hundreds of contacts, repeat, hundreds of contacts."

Rounds fourteen and fifteen of Fitz's magazine took

down another Reaver on a trajectory for Dohi. Three more of the beasts nosedived through the air. Fitz killed one of them before the others slammed into the side of the vehicle, the crunch of metal echoing over the suppressed rounds coming from the apartment.

The creatures crashed into the side of the MATV. The injured beasts flopped and flapped their shattered bones and frayed wings on the pavement. Fitz used the opportunity to kill them both with rounds sixteen and seventeen.

As he brought the gun back up, he saw the attack had just been a test. Seven more of the creatures were nosediving toward the vehicle.

"Watch out, Dohi," Fitz said over the comms.

Dohi ducked back inside the vehicle and Tanaka swerved, but it was too late. Five of the six Reavers slammed into the vehicle's side, tipping it to the left.

For a moment, it looked as though the MATV was going to fall back to all four tires.

"Three o'clock!" Rico shouted.

Fitz brought the MK11 up and followed the two Reavers coming in for another pass. He fired round eighteen and lined up round nineteen. The shot ripped through the first Reaver's upper wing, but it was an inch off, allowing the beast to slam the passenger's door of the MATV, sending it crashing down on its left side.

"No," Fitz choked. He quickly pushed the scope down. The army of Variants surged toward the vehicle. The tires squealed as Tanaka pushed down on the gas pedal, but the two-ton truck wasn't going anywhere.

Apollo barked behind them, and Fitz twisted just as a Variant rushed into the room. The dog took it down by its throat, ripping away a ribbon of flesh.

"Rico, our six!" Fitz shouted.

Two more gaunt figures bolted into the room. Rico

brought up her shotgun, blasting the first one back through the open doorway. Apollo took the second one down by the neck.

Fitz focused his attention back on the MATV.

The hatch popped open and Dohi climbed out. Tanaka was already on his feet outside, firing bursts with his M4 from right to left and back again at the horde of a hundred Variants barreling toward them.

"Fall back!" Fitz ordered over the comms.

Dohi fired a grenade from his M203 attachment that blew five of the monsters to pieces. They fanned away from the kill zone, tumbling over one another and leaping in the air to be the first to the kill.

Fitz raised his rifle to the Reavers in the sky—hoping one was the HVT. He could end all of this with a single shot, saving Team Ghost and the men and women on the front lines.

Another boom from Rico's shotgun echoed through the apartment. Apollo's growl and the high-pitched shriek of a monster followed. The sounds filled the small apartment, but Fitz kept focused and frosty—knowing everyone was counting on him.

So this is what Beckham said about the burden of leadership and deciding who lives and who dies.

Fitz killed another Reaver before his magazine went dry. He didn't have a second to waste. Everything was falling to shit around him, and his duty as a sniper was to deliver death with a single bullet. At other times during his service, he had waited hours or even days for the shot, but now he had only seconds, and there were only three beasts left that could be the Queen.

He palmed another mag in the gun, pushed the butt back into position, and killed two more of the Reavers with rounds one and two, leaving a single beast soaring through the sky.

The *pop, pop* of an M9 echoed behind him. Rico was down to her side arm. Apollo yelped and then growled.

Don't look. Kill the Reaver.

Tanaka and Dohi retreated across the terrace, firing rapidly in all directions. Another grenade tore a dozen of the beasts apart, fertilizing a bed of weeds and flowers with blood.

Fitz trained his sights on the final Reaver. It already had two holes in its wings, but it still flapped through the sky, monitoring the battle from above. This one looked different from the rest—bigger, with a ridged spine and a black tail the length of an anaconda. Could it really be the Queen?

Deliver death with a single bullet, he thought as he pulled the trigger.

Fitz ended the abomination's life with a kill shot to the temple. It cartwheeled into the Variant army below. He stood for a better look, watching the beasts trample the monster and continue their charge across the terrace as if nothing had happened.

"Fitz!" Rico shouted.

He unholstered his M9 and brought it around to shoot another Variant that had entered the room. Rico was on the ground a few feet away, straddling and stabbing a beast in the chest while Apollo tore at its legs.

Fitz did a quick scan. Four bodies near the door. Two more in the hallway. When he turned to the window, Tanaka had drawn his swords, and Dohi was down to his M9 and hatchet.

The army of Variants flowed around the two men, surrounding them. The hunched beasts slashed and growled, but they kept a few feet distant from the soldiers.

The Reavers were all dead, and the army wasn't turning on itself as Bradley had said would happen if he killed the Queen. Maybe Command was wrong—it wouldn't be the first time.

"I don't understand," Fitz muttered. He sat back down at the table and picked up his MK11. One of the beasts bolted from the crowd below. Tanaka used both swords and sliced the monster's head clean from its neck. The body crumpled to the ground.

Another beast made a run for Dohi. Fitz dropped it with a round to the heart. The crowd of diseased flesh began closing in around the two men. It was just a matter of time now.

Rico hurried over with Apollo, both of them panting and covered in blood. She wiped her frosted tips away from her face. The dog nudged up against Fitz's rusty left blade and looked up, revealing a gash on the side of his head, his fur soaked in blood.

Fitz's heart ached at the sight.

"Oh my God," Rico said. "We have to do something."

A guttural hissing, followed by a rattling sound coming from the cathedral, distracted them both. The army clamping down around Dohi and Tanaka froze on the terrace, every head shifting toward the western façade.

Fitz reached up and put his hand on the top of Rico's barrel.

"Wait," he whispered.

The smoke swirling out of the open door gave way to two Black Beetles and several fully grown juveniles. They trotted out onto the terrace, armored plates clanking across their muscular bodies. A dozen of the beasts emerged before Fitz saw it...

"The Queen," Rico whispered.

Fitz zoomed in on the red, chitinous upper body of their HVT. The abomination had an oddly shaped skull covered in bony spikes, but he couldn't see her face.

Leathery wings were folded against her sides, and she moved on arms covered in ridged armor.

"Take the shot," Rico whispered.

Fitz swallowed and pushed the mini-mic to his lips.

"I've got eyes on the HVT," Fitz reported over the comms. "Repeat, eyes on HVT."

There was no reply over the channel, but the sporadic boom of distant explosions told Fitz the EUF was still fighting.

He focused the sights on the Reaver's skull, waiting for the kill shot.

A section of the pale army parted to allow the Black Beetles and juveniles through. Dohi and Tanaka stood their ground, swords and weapons angled at the creatures.

"Tanaka, Dohi, when I tell you to run, you run," Fitz whispered into his headset.

"Nowhere to run," Tanaka said. "There's only one way out of this."

Before Fitz could reply, Tanaka bolted for the Reaver Queen, tossing his Wakizashi short blade like a spear. It narrowly missed the monster's face and sank into the chest of a nearby Variant.

Fitz held in a breath and fired a shot that pinged off the top of the Queen's armored skull. The juveniles closed in around her like a phalanx, screeching in rage.

"Shit!" Fitz muttered.

Dohi fired his M9 and let out a war cry that distracted the juveniles while Tanaka sliced his way through several of them with his Katana, twirling, slashing, and stabbing like a samurai. He thrust the blade through a juvenile's skull, yanked it free, and then swung it in an arch that beheaded a Variant and stuck into the neck of a second beast. He pulled it out again, blood gushing out of the now nearly headless creature.

Tanaka killed another juvenile before coming face-to-face with a giant Beetle that towered over him. Tanaka jabbed the demon in the midsection twice. On the third jab, the tip of the ancient blade broke off, and the creature grabbed his wrist and snapped it like a twig.

"*No!*" Dohi shouted over the comms.

Tanaka screamed in agony as it grabbed him with its other claw and launched him through the air. He landed in a crumpled mess in front of the Queen.

Dohi buried his hatchet in a juvenile's skull before he was captured by a Beetle. The beast slammed him to the ground, leaned down with open mandibles, and screeched in his face.

"Take the shot," Rico whispered.

The juveniles were guarding the Queen so closely Fitz couldn't get a target.

Just one. Please, Lord, just give me one shot.

"*Up here!*" Rico shouted, waving her arms.

The MK11's sights flickered over the face of the Queen as she looked in his direction—and Fitz saw the humanoid features as vividly as a picture. Two-Face was one ugly son of a bitch, with fangs protruding out of bulging lips set on a face covered in warts.

All it takes is all you ever had.

Fitz pulled the trigger as the Queen let out a hissing noise. As soon as it started, the noise stopped—the 7.62-millimeter round splitting through her bulbous nose and crunching through her skull to her brain.

The Queen crashed to the ground, blood gushing out of the gaping hole in her face. The monsters all seemed to screech at once.

"HVT is down," Fitz said into the comms, not even able to hear his own voice. "I repeat, HVT is KIA."

By the time he finished relaying the message, the Variants, juveniles, and Beetles were all shrieking in their otherworldly languages. Without their Queen to control them, they tore into one another, leaving Dohi and Tanaka curled up on the ground. Only Dohi seemed to be moving at all.

Fitz stood and grabbed his M4.

"Let's go, Rico," he said.

She limped away from the windows, and he saw the gash on her left leg. It was bad—she was going to need stitches.

"I'm okay," she said, when he looked at her.

Apollo trotted over, his fur matted red in several places. The dog wagged his tail, his way of saying he was okay also.

Injured and facing daunting odds, the three hurried out of the room, all of them prepared to lay down their lives for one another.

"Dohi, Tanaka, hang on, we're coming!" Fitz shouted over the comms.

By the time they cleared the stairwell and reached the streets, the thump of artillery had given way to the thump of a helicopter.

Fitz glanced over his shoulder at an HH-60 Pave Hawk flying low over the buildings to the east. The bark of its M240 sang from the sky. He felt a rush of joy when he heard Bradley's voice over the comms.

"You son of a bitch, you did it, Ghost One. These freaks are tearing one another apart!" he shouted. "I owe you a barrel of whiskey, Fitz!"

The momentary feeling of victory didn't last. Dohi and Tanaka were injured, and injured badly. Fitz ran around the corner and spotted their fatigues in the sea of pale flesh and armor.

The Variant armies slashed into one another on the terrace, seemingly oblivious to the fact that Dohi was limping away with Tanaka over his back.

The M240 unloaded on the meat of the army.

The beasts noticed that.

Dozens of the creatures fanned out, squawking in horror. The juveniles and Beetles hissed and roared, but they too ran when the rounds lanced in their direction.

Fitz, Rico, and Apollo ran out to meet Dohi and Tanaka. They set up a perimeter on the stone steps, guarding their injured brothers.

The Pave Hawk hovered for several minutes while the soldiers in the troop hold killed any stragglers. Fitz bent down next to Tanaka and scrutinized his wounds. He sucked air, his chest rattling. A laceration had carved his face, cutting off the tip of his nose and through both lips.

Dohi was already applying bandages to stop the bleeding. He was in bad shape too, with a broken arm and a deep gash on his leg.

Fitz grabbed Tanaka's hand and gripped it in his own.

"You're going to be okay," Fitz said.

Tanaka tried to nod, but the action made him wheeze for air. He coughed up blood.

"Hang in there, brother," Dohi said.

Apollo licked Tanaka's arm, and the man looked over at the dog, his eyes wide and terrified.

Rotor wash whipped over the team as the chopper set down on the street.

"We need a medic!" Fitz shouted.

An officer Fitz had never seen before ran over, two men following him. Fitz felt Tanaka's wrist. His pulse was weak, he'd lost a lot of blood, and he was struggling for air.

The officer from the Pave Hawk stopped and looked down. One of the soldiers took a knee and opened a medical bag.

"Watch out," he said to Dohi.

Dohi moved out of the way but remained on one knee next to Tanaka.

"I'm First Lieutenant Arnold Rollins. I'm here under orders from General Nixon," the officer said. "Which one of you is Master Sergeant Fitzpatrick?"

"I am," Fitz said.

Tanaka sucked in a long gasp, his lungs wheezing. He exhaled and met Fitz's gaze for a single second. His shredded lips clamped shut and his chest deflated.

"No, no, no!" Fitz yelled. He squeezed Tanaka's hand harder and then felt for a pulse.

Dohi bowed his head, and Rico sobbed, while the medic began CPR on Tanaka.

"Master Sergeant Fitzpatrick," said Rollins.

Fitz looked up at the lieutenant, expecting condolences or perhaps a commendation for their bravery that had resulted in the death of the Queen, but instead Rollins jerked his chin at Fitz, and the other soldier stepped forward with a pair of handcuffs.

"You're under arrest for the murder of Colonel Zach Wood," Rollins said.

27

"Stay back," Beckham growled. He bared his teeth and snapped them together so hard one of them chipped.

President Ringgold took two steps backward with the blade Wood had tossed into the room clutched in hand. Captain Beckham was sprawled on the floor next to Captain Davis, struggling to stand.

Davis twitched, still unconscious but already showing symptoms of the hemorrhage virus. Tears ran freely down Ringgold's face. Her friends were transforming into monsters before her very eyes. It was just like her recurring dream about her cousin.

Except this was real. She was living a nightmare.

Andrew Wood waited outside, looking through the porthole like a curious child. He waved and grinned when she glared in his direction.

"Don't worry, Ms. Ringgold! It will all be over soon!" he shouted.

Beckham jerked on the ground, causing the wounds on his broken body to spurt blood. He reached up with his left hand, fingers dripping red.

"Kill me," he shuddered. "You have to kill me before—"

A violent spasm shook his body, and he let out a

long groan, his mouth agape like that of a fish trying to suck air.

Tears welled around Ringgold's already swollen eyes, blurring her vision. She took another step back until she was up against a bulkhead. The knife in her hand felt as light as a feather, but she couldn't bring herself to use it.

The pool of red spread toward her, the infected blood still pumping out of Davis and Beckham.

How were they still alive?

Davis's left leg jerked and then kicked. A spasm ripped through her body.

"Kill us!" Beckham shouted.

Ringgold studied the knife again, following the curve of the blade to the sharp tip. Wood handing her the blade was a test—everything was just a test to him.

Beckham fought the spasms, his body contorting. He suddenly sat up and clawed at his eyes with his left hand, painting his face with blood. When he pulled it away, Ringgold glimpsed the terror in his eyes.

Terror, and rage.

It wouldn't be long now. Even a hardened warrior couldn't stop the VX-99 from taking over his body and mind.

"If you make it out of here, tell Kate how much I love her," he said in what might be his last moment of clarity. "Tell her and Javier Riley both how much I wanted to be with them."

He scooted across the floor until his back was against the opposite bulkhead, putting as much distance as possible between himself and Ringgold. Shaking in horror, she looked back at the porthole. Wood was still there, with the same shit-eating grin.

He wasn't a man. He was a monster—more of a monster than Beckham and Davis.

She gripped the knife and considered the other way out of this. A quick slice to her wrists would end it all.

Has it really come to that? Ringgold mused. *You're the president of the United States! You will not kill yourself!*

But she had to do something to make the nightmare end. She just couldn't take it anymore. Through all of the horrors, she'd persevered over the past seven months, surviving the monsters during the outbreak at Raven Rock, surviving an attack by Lieutenant Trevor Brett and a coup by Lieutenant Colonel Marsha Kramer. But the one person she couldn't seem to beat was the bastard peering through the porthole, and she was sick of playing his games.

She knew she couldn't kill Beckham and Davis either, even if they were turning into monsters. Not after all they had done for her.

No, President Jan Ringgold would not play Wood's demented games any longer. Her eyes shot back to Davis, who was flopping on the floor like a caught fish. A deep cackle came from her mouth as Davis pushed herself up on all fours, joints snapping as she tilted her face toward Beckham and then at Ringgold. Studying. Calculating. The transformation was almost complete.

Saliva dripped from her ruby-red gums.

"No," Ringgold whispered. "Rachel, please..."

It was the first time in her life the president had begged. She clamped her jaw shut and looked back at Wood. Closing her eyes, Ringgold summoned the last of her strength. Instead of slitting her wrists or killing Davis and Beckham, she dropped the knife and flashed Wood the bird.

"You won't win, Andrew," she said. "You can't. In fact, you've already lost."

His smile faded and he turned toward Kufman, who stood outside the hatch speaking in a raised voice. There was a low humming sound, and then a vibration in the prison cell. What sounded like the engines of a fighter jet roared in the distance.

The *Zumwalt* suddenly shook violently, the ceiling groaning and the bulkheads ringing. The impact knocked Ringgold to the floor, her palms splashing in the infected blood. She quickly wiped them on her pants.

An explosion rocked the ship. Davis slammed into a corner so hard it knocked her unconscious, though that wouldn't last long. Ringgold crawled away from her friends as more blasts tore into the upper decks.

The light above blew into pieces from another impact, raining glass on them all. Ringgold shielded her face with her arm. The emergency sirens screamed over the shouts outside the hatch.

When she pulled her arm away, Beckham's eyes had closed, but his chest was still moving up and down. Wood pressed his face against the porthole, his expression wild.

This time she was the one to smile at him.

"Your time's up, Andrew," she said. "You die first."

Kate followed a three-man team through the narrow passages of the USS *Abraham Lincoln*. An hour earlier, Horn had escorted her onto the ship and then evacuated his girls and the other civilians to the *Stallion*, a US Coast Guard ship. Three of his soldiers were assigned to protect Kate and Resurrection—the cure to the hemorrhage virus inside the biohazard box she carried.

They hurried up a ladder and came upon a body covered with a white curtain. Blood had soaked through in several spots. She wasn't sure if it was one of General Nixon's men or one of theirs. The battle had left sailors and soldiers dead on both sides.

She could still hear gunshots ringing out through the passages.

"Keep moving, ma'am," the lead Ranger said. He stopped at the next junction and waved her onward. She hugged the bulkhead, clutching the biohazard box closely to her side.

They were getting closer to the upper decks—and the gunfire. It sounded louder than rifles, though, more like the big guns that were mounted on the deck or on a helicopter.

Something slammed into the aircraft carrier again. The two Rangers behind her reached over to help steady her. The vibration passed, and they made a run for the next ladder. Another body was crumpled there, freshly killed, by the looks of it. The sailor had been shot through the forehead.

The lead Ranger balled his hand and cleared the next passage before waving them onward. Sailors were moving quickly in the next compartment. The Klaxon rang out, a warning Kate had little time to heed.

"Prepare for impact!" said a voice over the comms.

Kate hunched down and one of the Rangers shielded her body with his own. The ship jolted violently, the bulkheads seeming to bend and sway as a missile tore into the side of the carrier. The explosion knocked Kate and the Rangers to the floor with such force it took the air from her lungs.

"Ma'am, are you okay?" shouted one of the men.

The next blast sounded like a clap right next to her ears. A shock wave thumped against her body. She managed to cup her stomach with her hands and hunched over to protect Javier Riley.

A light blew out above her, and the air thickened with smoke. Stunned, she remained curled up like one of the fossilized victims shielding a child at Pompeii. She remained there for several seconds, maybe even a minute. Then came the voices, and coughing.

She was coughing too, hand over her mouth, eyes burning from the smoke swirling around her. Hands grabbed her under her armpits, and she realized she could hear again. There was a ringing in her ears—or was it the Klaxon?—and a man calling out her name.

Kate patted herself down to feel for any injuries. She did two passes over her stomach. Everything seemed okay, and Javier Riley moved inside of her as if to confirm he was fine.

The boy was a fighter, just like his dad.

The lead Army Ranger limped ahead of Kate, his leg soaked in blood. She grabbed the biohazard box, checking it over to make sure it was undamaged before following the team.

They moved up two more ladders, squeezing past injured sailors they had no time to help, and worked their way through passages choked with smoke. A few minutes later, they emerged at the island, which was guarded by a heavily armed squad of marines. The men waved them inside, where Captain Ingves and Admiral Lemke were standing at the helm, looking out over the water with binoculars.

Fighter jets tore away from the deck of the aircraft carrier and pulled into the blue sky. Smoke plumed from the deck where the missiles had struck.

To the east, bubbles frothed around a circular blast zone in the water. Debris was already floating to the surface. Three Seahawk sub-hunter teams circled overhead.

"We got 'em," said an officer. "Enemy sub is confirmed destroyed."

Several officers clapped, and Chief of Staff Soprano

whistled. Ben Nelson bowed his head and seemed to be praying. Lemke balled his hand into a fist of victory, but the celebration was short lived.

"Give me a damage report," Lemke said.

"Fires on decks four, three, and one, sir," Ingves replied. "We're taking on water, but we're still functional for now."

"Close off the compartments," Lemke replied.

Kate coughed into her sleeve and approached the admiral with tears streaming from her burning eyes. She tried to blink them away and focus.

"What about the *Stallion*?" she asked. "Is the *Stallion* okay?"

"Doctor Lovato," Nelson said. "When did you get here?"

Lemke stepped away from the observation window and lowered his binos. "The *Stallion* is fine, Doctor. The submarine and Nixon's helicopters were only targeting us and one of our destroyers. They weren't interested in civilians."

Kate felt a trickle of relief knowing Tasha, Jenny, and the other kids were unharmed.

"Have you located Reed and Jan yet?" she asked.

Lemke gestured toward Nelson, inviting him to take over answering her questions, and then went back to consulting with Ingves.

"Not yet, but the raid on the *Zumwalt* is under way," Nelson said. "Rest assured, our fighters were ordered to only knock out their missile-delivery vehicles. Their secondary goal is to rescue President Ringgold, Captain Beckham, and the other prisoners."

Kate wasn't reassured. She maneuvered past a radar station and stepped right up to Lemke, invading his personal space so he couldn't ignore her. "Sir, I have a request."

"One moment, Doctor," Lemke said.

"Is that Resurrection?" Soprano asked, looking at the box she was holding.

"Yes," Kate said. "Now if you'll just listen to me..."

Soprano put a hand on her arm. "President Ringgold wanted me to tell you she was sorry for leaving things the way she did, and that she's proud of you."

Kate was sorry too, and now she wasn't sure she would ever get the opportunity to tell her friend. "Thank you," she murmured.

"You really did it, huh?" Soprano asked, looking at the box.

"Most of the work was already done," Kate replied. "All I did was—"

"Well, you did it just in the nick of time," Soprano interrupted. He tightened his tie nervously. "I've been made aware of some pretty horrible news."

"Uprisings at the SZTs are under way," Nelson announced from one of the stations. "SZT Nineteen is already back in our hands."

There was more applause. Chatter broke out from nearly every station, but Kate kept her focus on Soprano.

"What were you going to say?" Kate asked.

"We have reason to believe Wood is using the hemorrhage virus on his prisoners."

Her heart flipped. She reached out and tapped Lemke on his shoulder. The admiral finally turned to look at her as another fighter jet peeled away from the deck.

"Yes?" he said, a touch of exasperation in his voice.

"I need a ride to the *Zumwalt*." She held up the box. "This is Resurrection, the cure for the hemorrhage virus. If President Ringgold or the others have been infected, this is the only thing that will save them now."

While Lemke considered the request, Kate watched the *Stallion* cutting through the waves in the distance.

Tasha and Jenny were safe out there, but their dad was fighting for his life, and for Beckham's life. This time Kate feared Horn and Beckham weren't coming home.

Lemke paused for another moment and then nodded at Ingves. "Get Doctor Lovato on a bird."

"Fuck you!" Wood shouted at the top of his lungs. He fired his 1911A1 at an F-18 Super Hornet coming in for another run.

"Sir, get down!" Kufman said. He pushed Ringgold onto the helicopter deck of the *Zumwalt*, but Wood continued shooting .45 rounds at the hundred-million-dollar aircraft. The pilot opened up with a M61A1/A2 Vulcan 20-millimeter cannon in response. The Gatling gun sprayed the bow of the stealth ship, tearing through the two ROT soldiers firing a pair of M2 Brownings at it. Both men fell screaming into the ocean.

"*Fuck you!*" Wood yelled again, firing off three more shots as the jet pulled away. Why wasn't anybody else fighting back? He was surrounded by cowards and disloyal cretins. "Shoot the fucking plane, you imbeciles!"

"Let's go, sir!" Kufman grabbed Wood by the arm and pulled him toward the Little Birds waiting on the stern. One of them lay in a pile of smoking ruins. The scene on the deck was chaos: ROT soldiers ran for cover. One man dragged his broken body across the ground, his back leg lying severed ten feet behind him.

The two MGM-140 Army Tactical Missile Systems that had been positioned on the top of the ship were gone, scraps of twisted metal the only sign they'd ever been there. He could no longer rain down the hemorrhage virus on his enemies.

But the fight wasn't over yet. Far from it.

Wood still had two destroyers, the USS *Gridley* and the USS *Mustin*. The Arleigh Burke–class guided-missile destroyers fired RIM-66 surface-to-air missiles into the sky at the squadron of Super Hornets that had come out of nowhere.

One of the Super Hornets exploded. The MK38 MOD 2 25-millimeter autocannons on the *Gridley* and *Mustin* continued firing into the sky, and multiple Brownings unleashed a barrage of .50-caliber fire at the fighter jets.

Wood watched in shock. How could this have happened? Had Nixon betrayed him? If so, his daughter was going to be Variant chow as soon as Wood got out of here.

"We have to get to one of the Little Birds!" Kufman insisted.

Wood holstered his pistol and grabbed Ringgold by her shirt. He pulled her toward him and then wrapped his hand around her throat. They'd brought her up here because Wood needed her as a hostage, but now he didn't care. He'd tear the bitch's head off with his bare hands.

"Sir, we have contacts barreling down on us from the south. Looks like Seahawks!" Kufman shouted. "Leave her and let's go!"

Wood turned to see a trio of Seahawks coming in hot, their troop holds full of soldiers. The door guns barked to life, spraying the rounds at the destroyers and the *Zumwalt*.

Ringgold coughed in his grip, her eyes bulging. He dropped her to wave at the ROT soldiers still emerging from the hatches of the smoking ship.

"Put those rifles to work, you shitheads!" he shouted.

Several missiles streaked away from a pair of Super Hornets. One of them slammed into the water, sending a geyser into the air, but the second slammed into the bow of the *Gridley*. Return fire from a Browning peppered the fighter jet's wings, sending it in a nosedive into the ocean. The pilot ejected a few seconds before impact.

Another jet roared overhead, launching AGM-84 Harpoon missiles into the USS *Mustin* before one of Wood's loyal men scored a volley of .50-caliber rounds to the cockpit. The fighter exploded in midair over the ship. Cannon fire and missiles continued to streak over the ocean from every direction.

It was all-out battle for the fate of the nation, and perhaps the world.

Wood shielded his face from the heat, and when he finally pulled his arm away he saw the *Gridley* was also fucked. The destroyer had taken two Harpoon missiles to the guts, nearly blowing her in half.

Kufman opened the door to the Little Bird and gestured for Wood to board. Three ROT soldiers followed them with their rifles raised.

The three Seahawks were already lowering toward the deck, but they were holding their fire, likely under orders to watch for friendlies. Maybe bringing Ringgold along had been a good idea after all.

Wood didn't offer the assholes the same courtesy. He grabbed Kufman's SCAR-H and fired at the troop holds where men were fast-roping from the bellies. The troops hit the ground and took off for cover while ROT soldiers fired from all directions.

Motion in the sky caught Wood's attention, and he brought the SCAR up to fire on the pilot who had ejected earlier. He held down the trigger, pumping four rounds into the man trapped in his harness.

"Hah!" Wood shouted. "That's what you get, you piece of—"

A round whizzed past his head, his heart slamming

against his chest at the near miss. He ducked down and took up position behind the Little Bird.

Kufman pushed Ringgold into the helicopter and climbed in after her.

"Let's go!" he said, holding out a hand to Wood. "They won't shoot with her inside!"

Wood looked around the side of the helicopter and squeezed off several rounds, hitting one of the Army Rangers in the neck. Blood geysered from the wound, and the man dropped to the deck. Two of his comrades dragged him to safety, but it was too late.

"That's right, motherfucker!" Wood yelled.

Kufman grabbed him by the back of his shirt and put him in an arm guard before pulling him toward the chopper.

"No!" Wood shouted. "We have to stay and—"

A high-pitched shriek cut him off. Kufman loosened his grip, and they both turned toward the hatch across the deck. A bloody figure was bounding across the tarmac on all fours. It took him a second to recognize her short-cropped hair, sharp jaw, and sharper green eyes, now bloodshot.

"No," Wood mumbled. "It can't be."

Rachel Davis, the captain of the *GW*, was still alive. And she had all but transformed into a monster. When they had dragged Ringgold out of the room, Beckham and Davis were both sprawled on the floor, neither of them moving. He had thought they were dead, the blood loss overtaking the virus's ability to heal their broken bodies.

I should have pumped them full of lead when I had the chance.

"Kill her!" Wood ordered. He backed away, his boot hitting the corpse of one of his fallen soldiers. He looked over his shoulder at a team of approaching Army Rangers, their MK-16s pointed in his direction. A man even bigger than Kufman led the group, fully decked out in black armor and wearing a skull bandanna over his mouth.

He pointed at Wood and shouted, "Drop your weapon!"

Wood responded by firing off a shot that whizzed past the man's arm and another that cut through the armor over his right thigh.

He lined up a head shot.

Click. The magazine went dry on the next trigger pull.

The injured soldier stumbled but held his ground, gripping his thigh, and screamed, "Don't shoot the president!"

Wood took a step backward as the team charged. He felt a pair of hands grab him and looked over at Kufman, who flung Wood into the chopper like a rag doll.

He quickly managed to right himself, his eyes instantly flitting up to find the president, ready to kill her right here and now, but the woman was gone.

"No," Wood said, scrambling across the two seats for a better look. He caught a glimpse of her being whisked away to safety by the team of Army Rangers across the deck.

"Get back here, you coward!" he shouted, scooting back out of the chopper.

Kufman was still firing at the Rangers, who had all taken up position behind another Little Bird. Bullets punched through the metal and shattered the windshield.

"It's over, Wood!" someone shouted. "Put down your weapons!"

"Parker fucking Horn," Kufman grumbled. He changed his magazine and looked at Wood.

"He's right, sir. It's over." He holstered his pistol, drew his knife, and stepped out into view. "You're done, Wood, but I've still got one last thing to do."

The big man with the skull bandanna mirrored him, blood cascading down his leg where Wood had shot him. Wood didn't recognize the soldier, but Kufman sure seemed to know this man—knew him so well he was apparently willing to throw Wood under a train for a chance to fight him.

"Just you and me now, Big Horn! Just as it should have been all those years ago!" Kufman yelled.

Horn waved his men back, pulled his skull bandanna down, and grinned wide enough to show his crooked teeth. "All right, you son of a bitch. Let's dance."

28

Fitz sat in the troop hold of the Pave Hawk, looking down at Tanaka's corpse. Dohi and Rico sat across from him. Apollo was on the floor, resting his head on his paws. Every eye in the belly of the bird was on Fitz.

He shook his head, ordering his friends to stand down. His war was over in Europe, and he was being taken back to the States to stand trial for the murder of Colonel Zach Wood. There was no need for more bloodshed, not if he could stop it.

"You can't do this," Rico said. "Master Sergeant Fitzpatrick just helped *save* Paris."

Rollins didn't reply.

Dohi pointed at Tanaka's body. "We just lost our brother helping save Paris, and you show up to arrest him?" He shook his head. "You piece of shit. You disgust me."

That got the officer's attention. "My orders were to bring Fitzpatrick in, but keep that up and I'll courtmartial both of you."

Dohi, weaponless, clenched his fists and looked at Fitz.

"No," Fitz said to both Dohi and Rico. "There's nothing you two can do."

Apollo growled, sensing the tension.

"It's okay, boy," Fitz said.

"Listen, I don't like this any more than you, but I've got orders from General Nixon," Rollins said. "Wood has his daughter, and he's in control of the safe-zone territories. There's no fighting this. I'm sorry."

The apology sounded sincere, and Fitz appreciated it, but he was more worried about Beckham, Horn, Kate, and his other friends than himself. If Wood was in control of the United States, then none of them were safe.

"The dog's got to go in too," Rollins said, looking ruefully at Apollo. "Wood wants them both."

"Fuck that," Rico said, standing. "If anyone touches the dog or Fitz, I'll kill them myself."

Rollins sighed heavily. "That sounds like a threat. Is that a threat, Sergeant? Because a threat will get you court-martialed."

She looked at Fitz, and then at the three men standing across the troop hold. Apollo stood too, his tail dropped between his legs.

"Take a seat, lady," one of the men said.

Rico glared at the soldier. "Lady? Hah! That's funny."

"Stand down," Fitz said. He shook his head again and said, "Stand down, Rico. You too, Apollo. It's not worth it. We'll have a trial. The truth will come out."

One of the pilots shouted that they were about to set down, and Fitz looked out of the open troop hold as they passed over the final city blocks on the way back to the front lines. Smoke funneled into the sky from destroyed buildings. Fires raged on rooftops, and the streets were covered in ash.

Variants galloped away, their pallid flesh seeming to glow in the moonlight. Fitz spotted armored vehicles giving chase, their weapons blazing at the retreating monsters.

The battle for Paris was almost over, and Fitz had

a feeling the battles for the other cities across Europe were nearing an end as well with the elimination of the Queens.

Two-Face, Fitz thought. The demons were dead.

The Queens had been the key all along, discovered by a half-mad soldier and his pet mouse in Rome.

In the end, the mutated armies had turned on one another, mad with hunger, tearing through their own ranks and eating one another after Fitz had helped bring down their leader in Paris.

He took solace in the fact that their mission was a success, even though it had cost so many lives: Stevenson and Tanaka. Michel, *Maman*, and the other Ombres who had made the ultimate sacrifice. All of the other marines and soldiers from the United States and the European Unified Forces.

But the soldiers weren't the only ones who had made this victory possible. Kate, Ellis, and so many other scientists had helped bring down the monsters the military had created.

Fitz could live with his punishment now that it was over. This wasn't the first time in his life he'd felt as though he deserved it. Perhaps the time had come for Fitz to pay for his sins.

The Pave Hawk lowered over the streets where the battle to hold the front lines had occurred. By the light of the moon, he saw the destruction: Bodies littered the street where Wormers had tunneled. Tanks, Humvees, and MATVs sat idle, their armor still sizzling from acid attacks.

Rico tried to get Fitz's attention, but he refused to meet her gaze. He couldn't. Through all the ups and downs of their missions, he'd realized that he had feelings for her—feelings that he would never be able to act on now that he was being sent back to the States. It was better to leave that door closed than to glimpse what might have been.

The chopper set down a moment later, the tires jolting. Rollins walked over and grabbed Fitz by the arm while his men jumped outside. Fitz glanced over his shoulder to look at Tanaka's corpse, covered by a sheet in the back of the troop hold.

"I'm sorry, brother," Fitz said.

Dohi, Rico, and Apollo followed them into the street. Nixon's soldiers fell in line alongside the group. One man took point, and another moved to rear guard, guiding them away from the chopper. Across the park, tents had been set up outside the FOB, and soldiers were running across the staging area. Vehicles raced down the road with supplies and injured soldiers. Gunshots rang out sporadically, snipers taking down any Reavers that were stupid enough to show their deformed faces.

The last thing Fitz had thought he'd be doing was returning here in handcuffs.

A group of men were crossing the park toward them. He couldn't see their faces in the dim light, but he could see one of them was limping and had his arms around two other soldiers.

"All right, let's go," Rollins said. He pulled Fitz away from Dohi and Rico, ordering them to stay put. Apollo trotted alongside Fitz, loyal to the end.

"Where are you taking him?" Rico shouted. Dohi's fists were clenched again, and his chest heaved with unspoken fury.

Three of Rollins's men stayed behind to guard them, their rifles cradled but their posture stiff.

"Keep moving," Rollins said, pulling Fitz away.

They walked toward a Humvee with doors wide open, waiting to take Apollo and Fitz to an aircraft that would fly them home.

"What the hell is going on here?" growled a familiar voice.

Fitz looked back to see Colonel Bradley limping after him, his right arm around Major Domino and his left around another marine. His leg was in a brace, and his forehead was covered with a bandage above his missing eye.

Rollins halted to face the marines.

"I'm taking this prisoner to the airfield to be flown back to the United States," said the lieutenant.

"Prisoner?" Bradley asked. His voice sounded hoarse from too much screaming.

"That's right," Rollins said. He didn't show Bradley the courtesy of a salute.

That seemed to infuriate Bradley even more. He limped forward until he was just inches from Rollins's face.

"That's right, *sir*," Bradley snarled.

"Sorry, *sir*, but I'm under strict orders to take Master Sergeant Fitzpatrick to the airfield."

Bradley reared back. "You son of a bitch. You told me you were flying out there to evacuate my men—who saved our asses, by the way—and instead you're arresting him?"

"Him and his dog...*sir*."

"Hah," Bradley said without humor. He looked at Fitz and then at Domino. The other soldiers who had accompanied Rollins had all circled around. Dohi and Rico caught up, both of them carrying weapons now.

Fitz sighed. Shit was about to get real.

He couldn't let anyone die for him.

"I have to go with them," he said.

"You're not going anywhere, son." Bradley gestured toward Domino and said, "Give me Bertha."

The major unslung the rocket launcher and handed

it to Bradley. Rollins's eyes widened at the sight of the FIM-92 Stinger.

Bradley hefted it up onto a shoulder, his entire body seeming to shake under the weight. "I'll send one of these up your ass if you try to take Fitz."

Rollins swallowed, his Adam's apple bobbing in the moonlight.

"Sir," Domino said.

"Not now," Bradley said. He glanced at the other soldiers. "Drop your weapons and step away from Master Sergeant Fitzpatrick."

Rollins shook his head. "Sir, we're under orders from General Nixon, and I've been told to court-martial anyone that tries to stop us."

"Sir," Domino entreated.

"Goddamnit, not now, Major," Bradley snapped.

"But, sir, I'm getting a transmission from Command. Apparently something is happening Stateside. Sounds as if a battle has broken out between ROT and the forces still loyal to President Ringgold."

Rico had crept around behind Rollins and raised a revolver to the back of the man's head. She thumbed the hammer back with a click.

"You're not taking my Fitzie," she growled.

Fitz closed his eyes at the words. All this time Rico had felt the same way about him. Why did they both wait until now to show it?

When Fitz opened his eyes again, Rollins had his hands up. He slowly turned with both arms in the air.

"How about we wait to see who wins this battle back at home," Dohi suggested. "Then, if Nixon still wants Fitz, we'll fight you for 'em."

It was one of the longest speeches Fitz had ever heard Dohi deliver. Fitz looked at Apollo. The dog, tail wagging, pushed his muzzle up and licked his cuffed hands.

"Works for me," Bradley said, lowering the missile launcher. He winked at Fitz. "You did good, son. When this is all over, no one from Team Ghost will be going to prison. You'll be getting medals. I guaran-fucking-tee it."

Davis couldn't control her body. The hallucinations, the burning, the itching—it was slowly taking her over. But one final thought rose above the pain.

Kill Andrew Wood. Kill Andrew Wood.

She repeated the mantra, blocking out the other voices telling her to kill everything in sight. It was the only thing keeping her humanity intact. Images of Blake and Ollie emerged in her distant memories, but she pushed those away too—she would be joining her husband and nephew soon enough.

The hemorrhage virus and the VX-99 nanoparticles were racing through her bloodstream. They were turning her into a beast, but they were also keeping her alive. The infection seemed to be speeding up her healing at a propulsive rate. She wasn't sure how it worked, but she was going to use this second chance to finish what she had started.

Distant explosions and automatic gunfire sounded from all directions, distracting her amplified senses. She searched for her target, sniffing the air like an animal and scanning the faces. It was the sight of Master Sergeant Horn that made her pause. Somewhere in her demented mind, she remembered the ceremony months ago when President Ringgold had promoted Davis, Horn, and Beckham. Horn was her friend. He was—

Rip his throat out and pull out his entrails through his mouth, said the voice in her mind.

She bit off a chunk of flesh from her arm instead, satisfying the voice momentarily. When she looked up again, Horn and one of Wood's soldiers had barreled into each other on the deck. The ROT man managed to get on top. He punched Horn in the face, knocking his skull bandanna aside.

Horn raised his head and bit the ROT soldier's ear off.

A scream of agony sounded, and the man reached up to grip the frayed flesh. Davis focused on the spurting blood, licking her lips. Horn spat out the hunk of cartilage and then tackled the man, knocking him onto the deck.

"Kill the fucker, Kufman!" yelled a familiar voice. This was the voice she was searching for.

Her eyes roved toward the speaker, and she licked her lips at the sight of Wood. He was crouched behind the helicopter like a coward.

Ever so slowly, like a lion stalking prey, she emerged from behind a wall of crates. After a few quiet steps, she fell to all fours and galloped toward him, using her back legs to spring forward.

Wood continued watching the two men fight, his back turned and oblivious to the threat barreling toward him. The voice that came from her mouth wasn't one she recognized—it was truly more animal now than human. She screamed wordlessly as she pounced.

He turned just before she plowed into him, his eyes reflecting shock more than fear. Davis knocked Wood to his back.

"No, please," Wood shouted. "*No!*"

Davis fought to hold him down, but the bastard was stronger than he looked. Luckily, so was she. The other Army Rangers were moving into position with their guns angled at the decks behind Davis. Several of them pointed their barrels at her face.

She had to make this quick.

Rip his tongue out, said the voice in her head. It was a good suggestion, but she didn't have time to make him suffer. Blood dripped from her face onto his pock-marked skin.

"No," he choked, trying to blink away the infected blood.

She was giving him a literal taste of his own nightmare. But she wasn't going to let him turn into something like her. He was going to die at her hands—right here, right now.

The crack of knuckles on bone sounded, and Davis looked up as Horn hit Kufman in the face again, but Kufman hardly flinched. He swung a knife at Horn, who jumped back, planted his feet, and landed an uppercut to Kufman's gut. The blow lifted him off his feet an entire inch. He dropped his blade and bent over, gasping for air, and Horn used the opportunity to swing a downward punch that smashed into Kufman's temple with a loud crack.

Horn spat on the ground and walked over to the doubled-over traitor, kicking the blade away from Kufman's reach.

"Should have done this a long time ago," he grumbled.

Kufman looked up, fear in his ruthless gaze as Horn grabbed his head and twisted it with a quick snap.

As Kufman's body crumpled to the ground, Horn looked over at Davis. Momentarily distracted, she let her grip on Wood loosen enough for him to start shouting again.

"I'll kill you, you c—"

Davis pushed her fingers into Wood's eye sockets. He screamed soprano. She pushed harder and harder, his voice cracking as his eyes popped like broken egg yolks.

A bullet punched through her chest. The second bullet slammed into her back, knocking her off Wood.

"No!" Horn shouted, raising his hands. "Hold your fire!"

She rolled onto her back and looked over at Wood. He squirmed and screamed next to her, clutching at his ruined eyes. Horn ran over and hunched down, reaching out to help her, but then backed up when he saw she was infected.

"Shit, Captain. I-I'm..." Horn stuttered.

"S'okay," Davis managed to slur through her fever.

She dragged herself over to Wood. He wasn't dead yet, the bastard. She bent down, inhaling the sweet scent of his fear, and then tore his fucking throat out. Hot, salty blood filled her mouth. Wood jerked once and then fell still.

It was over.

Her last mission was complete.

Get up and kill them. Murder them all! screamed the voice in her mind.

She gritted her teeth, resisting with her final strength. Shouts rang out all around her, and sporadic gunshots popped in the distance.

Davis drifted in and out of consciousness. Not even the supersoldier serum could save her now. She wasn't going to heal from these bullet wounds. She opened her eyes one last time to look at the beautiful blue sky, limitless over the open ocean, a sight she had loved more than any during her days at sea. A cloud the shape of a mountain rolled overhead, casting a cool shadow over her fevered skin.

Her vision faded, and the voice telling her to kill finally retreated. As though from a great distance, she heard Horn shouting.

"He's infected! We have to get him back to the *Abe Lincoln*."

Davis managed to move her head far enough to see Big Horn carrying Beckham's limp body over his shoulder. Seeing the two best friends together again epitomized everything she had felt about being a sailor and soldier. She closed her eyes, deciding this was the last thing she ever wanted to see.

Epilogue

Three and a half months later . . .

Beckham snapped awake from a nightmare, sitting up in bed and blinking at the first rays of sunlight streaming in through the bedroom window. The soothing song of a bird sounded outside.

His hand instinctively went for Kate, patting the mattress on his left. When he turned, her side of the bed was empty. Twisting, he looked to the cradle across the small bedroom.

Javier Riley wasn't inside.

"Kate!" he called out. Beckham fumbled for the Beretta M9 he kept under his pillow, and his fingers gripped the cold steel.

A voice answered from the next room. "In here," Kate said.

Closing his eyes, Beckham exhaled and placed the pistol back under the pillow. He checked the clock next, hardly able to read the blurry numbers.

It was 0630, still early, but he wasn't going to fall back asleep.

He flung the sweat-soaked sheets off his body and

swung his legs over the side of the bed, where he reached for his prosthetic blade.

Kate appeared in the bedroom doorway, cradling Javier Riley in her arms as Beckham attached the blade to his leg. The child's cries filled the room as she rocked him back and forth.

"Shhh," Kate whispered. "It's okay. Everything's okay."

"I'm sorry for scaring him," Beckham said. He was going to have to work on staying calm. It wasn't going to be easy, though.

Kate looked up, her eyes filled with concern. "Are you okay, Reed?"

He bowed his head, running a hand through his cropped hair. "Yeah, I'm fine, just another nightmare."

"You should go back to sleep. Today's a big day."

Beckham shook his head and forced a smile. "I'm fine, really."

Kate hesitated in the doorway for another second before vanishing into the other room. Beckham crossed over to their closet and looked at his reflection in the mirror. A gaunt face stared back at him. Now, instead of well-developed muscles, all he saw were scars crisscrossing his skin. Every one of them was a reminder of the horrors Team Ghost had faced since Building 8. He'd lost twenty-five pounds during the war, but he was slowly gaining it back.

It's over now. It's all over.

He threw on a shirt and started toward the kitchen. He stopped to look out the window over the gardens of the Greenbrier. Snowflakes fluttered to the ground, covering everything with a layer of what looked like vanilla frosting. It had taken over a month to get the place up and running again, but President Ringgold had wanted to relocate the White House here after the final ROT flag fell.

The scent of roasted coffee pulled him to the kitchen. It was the first time he'd smelled the aroma since leaving the isolation ward over a month earlier. Coffee, like most small luxuries, was a hard thing to come by these days.

Kate studied Beckham as she filled a mug for him.

"You sure you're feeling okay?" she asked. "I mean, besides the normal aches and pains."

"Yeah. Fine," Beckham replied, his voice lacking confidence. He took a sip of coffee. The warm liquid ran down his throat and warmed his gut, prompting a flood of memories from that fateful day aboard the USS *Zumwalt*.

He took a seat at the table while Kate carried Javier Riley into the bedroom. Beckham barely noticed them leaving; he was caught in the grip of his worst memories as they replayed like a movie in his mind.

Big Horn was shouting inside the troop hold of a Seahawk. Three Army Rangers had wrestled him to the floor, pinning him there while Beckham bled out. The bird was lifting them away from the *Zumwalt* after an intense firefight.

"Boss! Boss!" Horn repeated. "Just hang on. Kate's on her way with the cure. Just hold on. Fight, brother!"

Beckham tried to do what his friend asked, but a demented voice was screaming in his mind, telling him to kill everyone. He might have listened to it if he wasn't cuffed and bound with ropes.

President Ringgold watched from one of the seats across the troop hold, her eyes so swollen from crying she looked like Rocky Balboa after his fight with Apollo Creed. Beckham knew he looked even worse: stabbed, beaten, broken, and bleeding from multiple wounds. It was amazing he was still breathing. The only thing keeping him alive was the very virus he'd fought so hard to eradicate.

Horn finally pulled free from the grip of his men. He bent down next to Beckham. Instinctively, Beckham snapped at his hand with chipped teeth, trying to bite his best friend.

Pulling his hand back, Horn flared his nostrils. "Boss, you got to fight it! For your kid's sake, hold on!"

The memory always ended there. That was the point where Beckham had lost consciousness.

"Reed, can you come here for a minute?"

Kate's voice pulled him back to reality, and he rose unsteadily from his seat, nearly spilling his mug of coffee. He limped into the bedroom, his mood lifting when he saw Kate with their son in her arms.

"Do you want to hold him?" she asked.

Beckham hesitated and examined his boy's features. He had Kate's blue eyes for now. They weren't sure if they were going to stay that way. At two weeks old, he was growing so fast, already sporting a full head of hair. The brown mop was impressive—it was the one feature that Beckham could take credit for.

"Reed, you're fine. You spent two months in isolation. The cure worked. You have no symptoms, and you're practically back to normal. You can hold your son—you won't hurt him."

When he didn't reply, Kate frowned. "Talk to me, Reed. What's bothering you this morning?"

"Nightmares, the usual." He scrubbed a hand over his jaw. "I just wish I could have done something to save Captain Davis."

"You did everything you could. I miss her too, but she would want you to move on. Please...this is supposed to be one of the happiest days of our lives."

"You're right. I'm sorry." Beckham held up his hands, shaking ever so slightly, and let Kate lay their boy in his arms. He felt so light—so fragile.

Kate smiled. "See? Nothing to it."

Beckham nodded again, more firmly this time. Kate leaned over to kiss him on the cheek.

"I'll make us breakfast."

Beckham rocked his son, looking down in awe at the life he had helped create. After so much death, holding Javier Riley was a miracle. Never before had Beckham's heart been this full. He'd made it home to his family, and in a few hours, he was going to make Dr. Kate Lovato his wife.

They ate a hearty breakfast of eggs, toast, and sausage links before Kate left to get ready. Beckham should have been getting dressed too, but instead he carefully sat down in a rocking chair overlooking the gardens with his son clutched to his chest.

"Snow," Beckham whispered. "It's your first snow, little man."

The trees and shrubs were airbrushed with the white powder, the idyllic view marred by with soldiers carrying M4s. The guards still patrolled the grounds, on high alert.

The battle with ROT may have been over and the Variants nearly extinct in the United States, but security was tight at the White House. Especially today, with visitors flying in.

Beckham felt safer at the sight of the armed soldiers. But he was also relieved to be inside, with no other mission than to raise his son to be a good man.

His war was over.

The time had come to be a father and, in a few hours, a husband.

Someone knocked on the door. Beckham placed Javier Riley in his crib and answered it. Horn stood in the hallway wearing a huge grin. He held up a bottle of Jameson.

"Heya, boss! You ready for a shot? You only got a few hours left on this earth as a free man." Horn slurred several of the words, and his breath reeked of whiskey.

"Big Horn, you're already on your way to being shit-faced. I need you sober today. You're my best man."

Horn reared his big head back and blinked. "Me?" he said, fingering his chest. "I'm not drunk. I'm *totally* sober."

Beckham reached out and snatched the bottle, which was more than a quarter of the way toward empty. He took a slug, wiped his mouth, and jerked his chin for Horn to come inside.

He hated needing help to put on his suit, but at least Horn had the decency not to crack jokes about it. Instead, they reminisced about old times, chuckling over the days when Riley had danced on the tables at their favorite strip club. The ghosts of their fallen brothers cast a shadow over Beckham's heart, one that he knew would never fully be lifted. But Kate had been right—Davis wouldn't want him to be sad today. None of his friends would.

"Feels as though they're here with us, doesn't it?" Beckham said.

Horn grunted and said with uncharacteristic sincerity, "They are here, brother." He thumped his chest over his heart. "They'll always be right here."

After Donna had arrived to pick up Javier Riley, with Bo and Horn's girls in tow, they made their way into the lobby of the resort dressed in suits and ties, with fancy dress shoes that hurt Beckham's foot. He fidgeted, trying to adjust his stride so he didn't limp.

"I hate wearing this getup," he muttered.

"Least your pants fit," Horn said. He looked even more uncomfortable. They couldn't find a suit that fit his muscular body, and his trousers were two inches too short, showing off black socks that weren't pulled up enough to hide his thin, furry legs.

"We should have just worn our uniforms," he grumbled.

Beckham chuckled as Horn struggled to pull his pants down over his chicken legs.

"Sorry, but you know what Kate said. Today, we're civilians." Beckham led his best man through the lobby and into the ballroom. The wedding was supposed to be small, but a glass chandelier illuminated a dozen tables with white linen furnishing the room. Several waiters were still setting out china and crystal glasses.

"Fancy shit," Horn said.

"Very fancy," a voice behind them drawled. Both men turned to see Master Sergeant Fitzpatrick standing in the hallway outside the room in his military uniform. Apollo sat on his haunches, tail beating the carpet.

Beckham choked out a response. "Fitz...Apollo!" He swallowed to hold back the tears and hurried over.

Fitz and Beckham met each other with their arms outstretched. He clapped the younger man's back. Apollo nudged against Beckham's leg, and he obligingly reached down to pet the German shepherd.

"I missed you, brother," Beckham said. He pulled away, letting Horn and Fitz embrace, while he crouched down in front of Apollo. The dog licked Beckham's face and growled playfully, his way of saying how much he had missed his former handler.

"Goddamn, it's good to see you guys," Beckham said.

"You're telling me," Fitz said. He wiped a tear from his eye and took in a deep breath before turning to gesture for someone to join them—a woman dressed in a neatly pressed uniform but with outlandish purple streaks in her hair.

Beckham patted Apollo on the head again and stood, blinking to focus on the blurred face.

"Sergeant Rico," he said. "Is that you?"

"Hi," she said, waving sheepishly. "Hope you don't mind if I crash the wedding."

Horn and Beckham both laughed and gave Rico a hug. She swiped her purple hair from her big eyes and grinned, her dimples deepening in her cheeks.

"It's good to be Stateside again," she said. "For a while there, I didn't think we were ever coming home."

"Some of us didn't want to come home," Fitz said. "Dohi is still over there with the Twenty-Fourth MEU, fighting with Colonel Bradley to clear out more cities."

A moment of silence passed over the group as they all remembered those who hadn't made it back and thought of those still carrying on the fight against the rogue Variants.

Beckham cracked his lips into a smile, deciding to celebrate the return of his friends instead of despairing about those he wouldn't see again.

"I'm so glad you guys could be here," he said. "We've got quite the celebration planned today."

Horn clapped his hands together. "Hell yeah, we do!"

"How long are you back for?" Beckham asked.

Fitz looked to Rico. "We have two weeks' leave before shipping back out. We're headed to Rome next. At least, that's what Colonel Bradley said. He sends his best, by the way."

Rico frowned. "It's kind of a bummer if we go to Rome. Apparently a sergeant with the Italian military ordered the EUF to bomb the Vatican and the Colosseum in an effort to kill the Queen there. The blasts destroyed a lot of the historic architecture."

Beckham racked his brains for the name. "Sergeant Piero Angaran," he said. "The guy with the pet mouse?"

"Yup, the guy is a legend." Fitz smiled at Rico. "Maybe they'll build a statue of the sergeant and his mouse where the Colosseum used to be. It will become a historic piece of architecture."

Rico chuckled. "I'd like to see that."

"I'm glad to hear things are going well over there," Beckham said.

Rico blew a bubble and nodded. "They're ten times better since Nixon was stripped of command. The EUF has taken back most of the major cities and is setting up the equivalent of their own safe-zone territories."

"Awesome," Horn said. "We're making a lot of headway here too. President Ringgold's been able to get most of the SZTs back on their feet again."

Beckham rubbed his freshly shaved chin, thinking of everything they'd accomplished since the SZTs rose up against ROT. "We're back from the brink. The Special Ops hunter-killer teams Command has put together have cleared the areas Wood hit with the hemorrhage virus. All that's left to do is hunt down the final Variants and juveniles. There are Alphas who managed to hide all this time, but we'll get them eventually."

"Sounds like a job for Team Ghost," Fitz said.

Beckham nodded. "Indeed it does, brother."

"This is all such great news." Rico's dimples widened and she clapped Beckham hard on the shoulder. "And I heard you're a dad now!"

"Yup, you guys will get to meet Javier Riley in a little..." Beckham's words trailed off when he saw the entourage moving through the lobby. He stiffened to attention at the sight of President Jan Ringgold and Vice President Dan Lemke, the former admiral of the fleet that had helped take back the United States from the ROT terrorists.

Ringgold held up a hand and waved at Beckham. He saluted—some habits were hard to break.

"Madam President," Beckham said. "Thanks for being here."

"Thank *you*," she said with a smile.

Beckham gestured for everyone to follow him into the ballroom. Tasha and Jenny arrived a few minutes later with Bo, and Donna, who was carrying Javier Riley. The girls were wearing white dresses and carrying baskets full of confetti.

"Daddy! Uncle Reed!" Tasha shouted. She ran across the room, with Jenny right behind her. Jake Temper, the former NYPD officer, and his son, Timothy, filed in after them.

Next came Chief of Staff James Soprano and National Security Advisor Ben Nelson, dressed in navy suits to match Horn's and Beckham's.

"Come say hi to Uncle Fitz," Horn said to his girls. He grabbed his daughters and scooped them up in both arms. "Oof, you're getting a bit too heavy for your old man."

Fitz smiled and reached out to shake their small hands. "Good to see you beautiful little ladies again." He looked over his shoulder. "This is my girlfriend, Jeni Rico."

"Girlfriend?" Beckham said with a raised brow. "So you guys are official?"

Fitz blushed as Rico linked her arm through his.

"I'd like to introduce you to my son, Javier Riley," Beckham said. Donna held his son up for Fitz and Rico to see. They both leaned in, smiles on their faces as they looked at the little boy.

"He's got his mom's eyes and my hair," Beckham said.

"Looks like a future member of Team Ghost," Rico said, beaming.

"Nah, he's going to be a scientist like his mom," Beckham replied.

A man from President Ringgold's staff, dressed in a tuxedo, cleared his throat behind Beckham. "Sir, we're ready, if you and Mr. Horn would like to start making your way up front."

Beckham and Horn said their good-byes and walked toward the raised platform. Ringgold joined them, carrying a leather folder. She was officiating the wedding. The room quieted down, and the doors closed as she stepped up to the podium.

Beckham breathed deeply as everyone took their seats and the wedding march began to play.

"You ready for this, boss?" Horn mumbled.

Beckham smiled. "I've never been more ready for anything in—"

The ballroom doors opened, and the most beautiful woman Beckham had ever seen stepped into the light, silencing the words on his tongue. Kate wore a lace gown, with a long veil pinned over her brown hair. Her blue eyes flitted to meet his as she walked down the aisle.

His heart slammed harder and harder with every step she took. He met her at the bottom step and held out a hand. They helped each other up the steps, Kate giving Beckham just as much support as he offered her. Together, they were an exceptional team. In a few minutes, they would make it official by entering into holy matrimony.

Beckham turned toward the crowd, looking out over their friends and family. Donna, sitting in the front row with Javier Riley on her lap, waved his pudgy hand at his parents.

Had he thought his heart was full earlier? Now it was fit to burst with joy.

"Today we gather to celebrate the marriage of Doctor Kate Lovato and Captain Reed Beckham," President Ringgold announced. "I can't think of anyone in this world who deserve happiness more than these two. I can honestly say if it weren't for them, none of us would be here today. They've been a light in our darkest hour, a rock in our fiercest storm. Thank you both for everything you've done."

A chill raced through Beckham at the sound of applause from the guests, who all rose from their seats. Apollo barked and whipped his tail against Fitz's carbon-fiber blades.

Ringgold's words were kind, but they weren't correct, and part of him protested. He was only here because of the sacrifices of so many of his friends. He blinked his eyes, his vision blurred by tears and the lingering damage of the juvenile's acid spray. He could almost see their faces among the guests—Meg and Riley, Lieutenant Colonel Jensen, Captain Davis.

Kate squeezed Beckham's hand, anchoring him to the world of the living once more, and he squeezed back. He wasn't sure what the future held for them, but he was eternally grateful for a chance to find out.

Acknowledgments

It's always hard for me to write this section for fear of leaving someone out. My books would not be worth reading if I didn't have the overwhelming support of family, friends, and readers.

Before I thank those people, I wanted to give a bit of background about how the Extinction Cycle was conceived and the journey it has been on since I began writing. The story began over three years ago at a time when the genre was saturated with zombie books. I wanted to write something unique and different, a story that explained scientifically how a virus could turn men into monsters. At this time, the Ebola virus was raging through western Africa, and several cases showed up in the continental United States for the first time.

After talking with my biomedical-engineer friend, Tony Melchiorri, an idea formed about the risk the virus posed. That idea blossomed after I started researching chemical and biological weapons dating back to the Cold War. In March of 2014, I sat down to pen the first pages of *Extinction Horizon*, the first book in what would become the Extinction Cycle. Using real science and the terrifying premise of a government-made bioweapon I set out to tell the story I always wanted to tell.

The book quickly found an audience and readers devoured the first three novels that came out in rapid succession and seemed to spark life back into the zombie craze. The audiobook, narrated by the award-winning Bronson Pinchot, climbed the charts, hitting the top spot on Audible.

After I released book four, Tony and I visited Rome, Italy, for a writing project. It was a year later that I decided to use my experiences and notes from that trip to create a new plotline in the Extinction Cycle. Books six and now seven follow Italian Sergeant Piero Angaran and his pet mouse on their journey through Rome. I've had such a great time writing their story, and I hope you all enjoy the setting in Italy.

With the launch of books four and five, more readers discovered the Extinction Cycle—over three hundred thousand to date. The German translation launched in November 2016, and Amazon's Kindle Worlds opened the story to other authors.

Even more exciting, two years after I published *Extinction Horizon*, Orbit decided to purchase and re-release the series. I hope you've enjoyed it. I want to thank everyone that helped me create the Extinction Cycle.

I couldn't have done it without the help of a small army of editors, beta readers, and the support of my family and friends. I also owe a great deal of gratitude to my initial editors Aaron Sikes and Erin Elizabeth Long as well as my good author-friend Tony Melchiorri. The trio spent countless hours on the Extinction Cycle books. Without them these stories would not be what they are. Erin also helped edit *Orbs* and *Hell Divers*. She's been with me pretty much since day one, and I appreciate her more than she knows. So thanks, Erin, Tony, and Aaron.

A special thanks goes to David Fugate, my agent, who provided valuable feedback on the early version of *Extinction Horizon* and the entire Extinction Cycle series. I'm grateful for his support and guidance.

Another special thanks goes to Blackstone Audio for their support of the audio version. Narrator Bronson Pinchot also played, and continues to play, a vital role in bringing the story to life.

They say a person is only as good as those they surround themselves with. I've been fortunate to surround myself with talented people much smarter than myself. I've also had the support from excellent publishers like Blackstone and Orbit.

Thank you to Orbit for bringing this story to mass market. It's been amazing seeing the books reach an entirely new audience outside of the digital world.

I would be remiss if I didn't also thank the people for whom I write: the readers. I've been blessed to have my work read in countries around the world by wonderful people. If you are reading this, know that I truly appreciate you for trying my stories.

To my family, friends and everyone else that has supported me on this journey, I thank you.

extras

meet the author

NICHOLAS SANSBURY SMITH is the *USA Today* bestselling author of *Hell Divers*, the Orbs trilogy, and the Extinction Cycle. He worked for Iowa Homeland Security and Emergency Management in disaster mitigation before switching careers to focus on his one true passion: writing. When he isn't writing or daydreaming about the apocalypse, he enjoys running, biking, spending time with his family, and traveling the world. He is an Ironman triathlete and lives in Iowa with his fiancée, their dogs, and a houseful of books.

If you enjoyed
EXTINCTION WAR

look out for

THE WAR DOGS TRILOGY

by

Greg Bear

The Gurus made their presence on Earth known thirteen years ago. Providing technology and scientific insights far beyond what mankind was capable of, they became indispensable advisors and promised even more gifts that we just couldn't pass up.

But they were followed by mortal enemies—the Antagonists—from sun to sun, planet to planet, and now the Gurus are stretched thin—and they need humanity's help.

Our first bill has come due.

Skyrines like Michael Venn have been volunteered to pay the price. They face insidious enemies who were already inside the solar system, establishing a beachhead on Mars.

*Venn and his comrades will be lucky to
make it out alive—let alone preserve the future
of all of mankind.*

DOWN TO EARTH

I'm trying to go home. As the poet said, if you don't know where you are, you don't know who you are. Home is where you go to get all that sorted out.

Hoofing it outside Skybase Lewis-McChord, I'm pretty sure this is Washington State, I'm pretty sure I'm walking along Pacific Highway, and this is the twenty-first century and not some fidging movie—

But then a whining roar grinds the air and a broad shadow sweeps the road, eclipsing cafés and pawnshops and loan joints—followed seconds later by an eye-stinging haze of rocket fuel. I swivel on aching feet and look up to see a double-egg-and-hawksbill burn down from the sky, leaving a rainbow trail over McChord field...

And I have to wonder.

I just flew in on one of those after eight months in the vac, four going out, three back. Seven blissful months in timeout, stuffed in a dark tube and soaked in Cosmoline.

All for three weeks in the shit. Rough, confusing weeks.

I feel dizzy. I look down, blink out the sting, and keep walking. Cosmoline still fidges with my senses.

Here on Earth, we don't say *fuck* anymore, the Gurus don't like it, so we say fidge instead. Part of the price of freedom. Out on the Red, we say fuck as much as we like. The angels edit our words so the Gurus won't have to hear.

SNKRAZ.

Joe has a funny story about *fuck*. I'll tell you later, but right now, I'm not too happy with Joe. We came back in separate ships, he did not show up at the mob center, and my Cougar is still parked outside Skyport Virginia. I could grab a shuttle into town, but Joe told me to lie low. Besides, I badly want time alone—time to stretch my legs, put down one foot after another. There's the joy of blue sky, if I can look up without keeling over, and open air without a helm—and minus the rocket smell— is a newness in the nose and a beauty in the lungs. In a couple of klicks, though, my insteps pinch and my calves knot. Earth tugs harsh after so long away. I want to heave. I straighten and look real serious, clamp my jaws, shake my head—barely manage to keep it down.

Suddenly, I don't feel the need to walk all the way to Seattle. I have my thumb and a decently goofy smile, but after half an hour and no joy, I'm making up my mind whether to try my luck at a minimall Starbucks when a little blue electric job creeps up behind me, quiet as a bad fart. Quiet is not good.

I spin and try to stop shivering as the window rolls down. The driver is in her fifties, reddish hair rooted gray. For a queasy moment, I think she might be MHAT sent from Madigan. Joe warned me, "For Christ's sake, after all that's happened, stay away from the doctors." MHAT is short for *Military Health Advisory Team*. But the driver is not from Madigan. She asks where I'm going. I say downtown Seattle. Climb in, she says. She's a colonel's secretary at Lewis, a pretty ordinary grandma, but she has these strange gray eyes that let me see all the way back to when her scorn shaped men's lives.

I ask if she can take me to Pike Place Market. She's good with that. I climb in. After a while, she tells me she had a son just like me. He became a hero on Titan, she says—but she can't really know that, because we aren't on Titan yet, are we?

I say to her, "Sorry for your loss." I don't say, *Glad it wasn't me.*

"How's the war out there?" she asks.

"Can't tell, ma'am. Just back and still groggy."

They don't let us know all we want to know, barely tell us all we *need* to know, because we might start speculating and lose focus.

She and I don't talk much after that. Fidging *Titan*. Sounds old and cold. What kind of suits would we wear? Would everything freeze solid? Mars is bad enough. We're almost used to the Red. Stay sharp on the dust and rocks. That's where our shit is at. Leave the rest to the generals and the Gurus.

All part of the deal. A really big deal.

Titan. Jesus.

Grandma in the too-quiet electric drives me north to Spring Street, then west to Pike and First, where she drops me off with a crinkle-eyed smile and a warm, sad finger-squeeze. The instant I turn and see the market, she pips from my thoughts. Nothing has changed since vac training at SBLM, when we tired of the local bars and drove north, looking for trouble but ending up right here. We liked the market. The big neon sign. The big round clock. Tourists and merchants and more tourists, and that ageless bronze pig out in front.

A little girl in a pink frock sits astride the pig, grinning and slapping its polished flank. What we fight for.

I'm in civvies but Cosmoline gives your skin a tinge that lasts for days, until you piss it out, so most everyone can tell I've been in timeout. Civilians are not supposed to ask probing questions, but they still smile like knowing sheep. *Hey, spaceman, welcome back! Tell me true, how's the vac?*

I get it.

A nice Laotian lady and her sons and daughter sell fruit and veggies and flowers. Their booth is a cascade of big and little peppers and hot and sweet peppers and yellow and green and red peppers, Walla Walla sweets and good strong brown and fresh green onions, red and gold and blue and russet potatoes, yams and sweet potatoes, pole beans green and yellow and purple and speckled, beets baby and adult, turnips open boxed in bulk and attached to sprays of crisp green leaf. Around the corner of the booth I see every kind of mushroom but the screwy kind. All that roughage dazzles. I'm accustomed to browns and pinks, dark blue, star-powdered black.

A salient of kale and cabbage stretches before me. I seriously consider kicking off and swimming up the counter, chewing through the thick leaves, inhaling the color, spouting purple and green. Instead, I buy a bunch of celery and move out of the tourist flow. Leaning against a corrugated metal door, I shift from foot to cramping foot, until finally I just hunker against the cool ribbed steel and rabbit down the celery leaves, dirt and all, down to the dense, crisp core. Love it. Good for timeout tummy.

Now that I've had my celery, I'm better. Time to move on. A mile to go before I sleep.

I doubt I'll sleep much.

Skyrines share flophouses, safe houses—refuges—around the major spaceports. My favorite is a really nice apartment in Virginia Beach. I could be heading there now, driving my Cougar across the Chesapeake Bay Bridge, top down, sucking in the warm sea breeze, but thanks to all that's happened—and thanks to Joe—I'm not. Not this time. Maybe never again.

I rise and edge through the crowds, but my knees are still shaky, I might not make it, so I flag a cab. The cabby is white and middle aged, from Texas. Most of the fellows who used to cab here, Lebanese and Ethiopians and Sikhs, the younger ones at least, are gone to war now. They do well in timeout, better than white Texans. Brown people rule the vac, some say. There's a lot of brown and black and beige out there: east and west Indians, immigrant Kenyans and Nigerians and Somalis, Mexicans, Filipinos and Malaysians, Jamaicans and Puerto Ricans, all varieties of Asian—flung out in space frames, sticks clumped up in fasces—and then they all fly loose, shoot out puff, and drop to the Red. Maybe less dangerous than driving a hack, and certainly pays better.

I'm not the least bit brown. I don't even tan. I'm a white boy from Moscow, Idaho, a blue-collar IT wizard who got tired of working in cubicles, tired of working around shitheads like myself. I enlisted in the Skyrines (that's pronounced SKY-reen), went through all the tests and boot and desert training, survived first orbital, survived first drop on the Red—came home alive and relatively sane—and now I make good money. Flight pay and combat pay—they call it engagement bonus—and Cosmoline comp.

Some say the whole deal of cellular suspension we call timeout shortens your life, along with solar flares and gamma rays. Others say no. The military docs say no but scandal painted a lot of them before my last deployment. Whole bunch at Madigan got augured for neglecting our spacemen. Their docs tend to regard spacemen, especially Skyrines, as slackers and complainers. Another reason to avoid MHAT. We make more than they do and still we complain. They hate us. Give them ground pounders any day.

"How many drops?" the Texan cabby asks.

"Too many," I say. I've been at it for six years.

He looks back at me in the mirror. The cab drives itself; he's in the seat for show. "Ever wonder why?" he asks. "Ever wonder what you're giving up to *them*? They ain't even human." Some think we shouldn't be out there at all; maybe he's one of them.

"Ever wonder?" he asks.

"All the time," I say.

He looks miffed and faces forward.

The cab takes me into Belltown and lets me out on a semicircular drive, in the shadow of the high-rise called Sky Tower One. I pay in cash. The cabby rewards me with a sour look, even though I give him a decent tip. He, too, pips from my mind as soon as I get out. Bastard.

The tower's elevator has a glass wall to show off the view before you arrive. The curved hall on my floor is lined with alcoves, quiet and deserted this time of day. I key in the number code, the door clicks open, and the apartment greets me with a cheery pluck of ascending chords. Extreme retro, traditional Seattle, none of it Guru tech; it's from before I was born.

Lie low. Don't attract attention.

Christ. No way am I used to being a spook.

The place is just as I remember it—nice and cool, walls gray, carpet and furniture gray and cloudy-day blue, stainless steel fixtures with touches of wood and white enamel. The couch and chairs and tables are mid-century modern. Last year's Christmas tree is still up, the water down to scum and the branches naked, but Roomba has sucked up all the needles. Love Roomba. Also pre-Guru, it rolls out of its stair slot and checks me out, nuzzling my toes like a happy gray trilobite.

I finish my tour—checking every room twice, ingrained caution, nobody home—then pull an Eames chair up in front of the broad floor-to-ceiling window and flop back to stare out over the Sound. The big sky still makes me dizzy, so I try to focus lower down, on the green and white ferries coming and going, and then on the nearly continuous lines of tankers and big cargo ships. Good to know Hanjin and Maersk are still packing blue and orange and brown steel containers along with Hogmaw or Haugley or what the hell. Each container is about a seventh the size of your standard space frame. No doubt filled with clever goods made using Guru secrets, juicing our economy like a snuck of meth.

And for that, too—for *them*—we fight.

If you enjoyed
EXTINCTION WAR

look out for

OUTER EARTH

by

Rob Boffard

In space, every second counts.

Outer Earth *is a massive space station that orbits three hundred miles above the Earth, holding the last of humanity. It's broken, rusted, and falling apart. The world below is dead, wrecked by climate change and nuclear war. Now we have to live with the consequences: a new home that's dirty, overcrowded, and inescapable.*

The population has reached one million. Double what the station was designed to hold. Food is short, crime is rampant, and the ecosystem is nearing its breaking point.

What's more, there's a madman hiding on the station who is about to unleash chaos. And when he does, there'll be nowhere left to run.

1

RILEY

My name is Riley Hale, and when I run, the world disappears.

Feet pounding. Heart thudding. Steel plates thundering under my feet as I run, high up on Level 6, keeping a good momentum as I move through the darkened corridors. I focus on the next step, on the in-out, push-pull of my breathing. Stride, land, cushion, spring, repeat. The station is a tight warren of crawl-spaces and vents around me, every surface metal etched with ancient graffiti.

"She's over there!"

The shout comes from behind me, down the other end of the corridor. The skittering footsteps that follow it echo off the walls. I thought I'd lost these idiots back at the sector border – now I have to outrun them all over again. I got lost in the rhythm of running – always dangerous when someone's trying to jack your cargo. I refuse to waste a breath on cursing, but one of my exhales turns into a growl of frustration.

The Lieren might not be as fast as I am, but they obviously don't give up.

I go from a jog to a sprint, my pack juddering on my spine as I pump my arms even harder. A tiny bead of sweat touches my eye, sizzling and stinging. I ignore it. No tracer in my crew has ever failed to deliver their cargo, and I am not going to be the first.

I round the corner – and nearly slam into a crush of

people. There are five of them, sauntering down the corridor, talking among themselves. But I'm already reacting, pushing off with my right foot, springing in the direction of the wall. I bring my other foot up to meet it, flattening it against the metal and tucking my left knee up to my chest. The momentum keeps me going forwards even as I'm pushing off, exhaling with a whoop as I squeeze through the space between the people and the wall. My right foot comes down, and I'm instantly in motion again. Full momentum. A perfect tic-tac.

The Lieren are close behind, colliding with the group, bowling them over in a mess of confused shouts. But I've got the edge now. Their cries fade into the distance.

There's not a lot you can move between sectors without paying off the gangs. Not unless you know where and how to cross. Tracers do. And that's why we exist. If you need to get something to someone, or if you've got a little package you don't want any gangs knowing about, you come find us. We'll get it there – for a price, of course – and if you come to my crew, the Devil Dancers, we'll get it there *fast*.

The corridor exit looms, and then I'm out, into the gallery. After the corridors, the giant lights illuminating the massive open area are blinding. Corridor becomes catwalk, bordered with rusted metal railings, and the sound of my footfalls fades away, whirling off into the open space.

I catch a glimpse of the diagram on the far wall, still legible a hundred years after it was painted. A scale picture of the station. The Core at the centre, a giant sphere which houses the main fusion reactor. Shooting out from it on either side, two spokes, connected to an enormous ring, the main body. And under it, faded to almost nothing after over a century: Outer Earth Orbit Preservation Module, Founded AD 2234.

Ahead of me, more people emerge from the far entrance to the catwalk. A group of teenage girls, packed tight, talking loudly among themselves. I count ten, fifteen – *no*. They haven't seen me. I'm heading full tilt towards them.

Without breaking stride, I grab the right-hand railing of the catwalk and launch myself up and over, into space.

For a second, there's no noise but the air rushing past me. The sound of the girls' conversation vanishes, like someone turned down a volume knob. I can see all the way down to the bottom of the gallery, a hundred feet below, picking out details snatched from the gaps in the web of criss-crossing catwalks.

The floor is a mess of broken benches and circular flowerbeds with nothing in them. There are two young girls, skipping back and forth over a line they've drawn on the floor. One is wearing a faded smock. I can just make out the word Astro on the back as it twirls around her. A light above them is flickering off-on-off, and their shadows flit in and out on the wall behind them, dancing off metal plates. My own shadow is spread out before me, split by the catwalks; a black shape broken on rusted railings. On one of the catwalks lower down, two men are arguing, pushing each other. One man throws a punch, his target dodging back as the group around them scream dull threats.

I jumped off the catwalk without checking my landing zone. I don't even want to think what Amira would do if she found out. Explode, probably. Because if there's someone under me and I hit them from above, it's not just a broken ankle I'm looking at.

Time seems frozen. I flick my eyes towards the Level 5 catwalk rushing towards me.

It's empty. Not a person in sight, not even further

along. I pull my legs up, lift my arms and brace for the landing.

Contact. The noise returns, a bang that snaps my head back even as I'm rolling forwards. On instinct, I twist sideways, so the impact can travel across, rather than up, my spine. My right hand hits the ground, the sharp edges of the steel bevelling scraping my palm, and I push upwards, arching my back so my pack can fit into the roll.

Then I'm up and running, heading for the dark catwalk exit on the far side. I can hear the Lieren reach the catwalk above. They've spotted me, but I can tell by their angry howls that it's too late. There's no way they're making that jump. To get to where I am, they'll have to fight their way through the stairwells on the far side. By then, I'll be long gone.

"Never try to outrun a Devil Dancer, boys," I mutter between breaths.